# THE LOVE LETTER

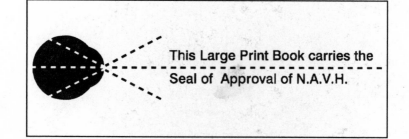

This Large Print Book carries the
Seal of Approval of N.A.V.H.

# THE LOVE LETTER

## RACHEL HAUCK

**THORNDIKE PRESS**
A part of Gale, a Cengage Company

Farmington Hills, Mich • San Francisco • New York • Waterville, Maine
Meriden, Conn • Mason, Ohio • Chicago

Copyright © 2018 by Rachel Hauck.
Scripture used is taken from the King James Version of the Bible. Public domain.
Thorndike Press, a part of Gale, a Cengage Company.

Thorndike Press® Large Print Christian Romance.
The text of this Large Print edition is unabridged.
Other aspects of the book may vary from the original edition.
Set in 16 pt. Plantin.

LIBRARY OF CONGRESS CIP DATA ON FILE.
CATALOGUING IN PUBLICATION FOR THIS BOOK
IS AVAILABLE FROM THE LIBRARY OF CONGRESS.

ISBN-13: 978-1-4328-5143-9 (hardcover)

Published in 2018 by arrangement with Thomas Nelson, Inc, a division of HarperCollins Christian Publishing, Inc.

Printed in the United States of America
1 2 3 4 5 6 7 22 21 20 19 18

*For Tony*

# PROLOGUE

## HAMILTON

*Hannah's Cowpens*
*South Carolina Colony*
*January 17, 1781*

He must finish. He must. Stumbling, he fell to the damp earth of the maple swamp with the *click-slap* of musket fire ringing through the cold dew, his breath billowing.

The smoke of guns and cannons dulled the first light, and the stinging scent of gunpowder poisoned the fragrance of winter.

He clung to the nearest tree, his back to the battle, dagger in hand. Blood from a saber slash stained his buckskin sleeve and pooled in his left hand.

The battle persisted not thirty paces hence but he collapsed, weary, as if fighting for days.

*Finish, man, finish.*

Hamilton's conflict had begun with Lieutenant Twimball long before today. And with the breath in his lungs, it would end with Twimball. Here. Now.

For what that man had done. For the deeds done by all who donned the king's redcoat.

Spots swelled and burst before his eyes, and his head seemed to float above his body. Clinging to his rifle with his good arm, Hamilton tried to stand, his damaged left wing wrapped around the tree. But his legs . . . his legs refused to obey.

Another volley of bullets drew his attention toward the battlefield. The British were charging as his brothers-in-arms retreated.

Trying once again to stand, he collapsed against the tree, a sliver of stationery fluttering past the corner of his eye. His letter! He dropped the dagger, then patted his left pocket, his finger protruding though a slice made by the edge of a sword.

The wind shuttled the solitary page over the cold, muddy terrain.

He must . . . retrieve it. Hamilton stretched, barely grasping the edge of the page with the tips of his fingers, then losing his hold as he toppled forward to the earth.

The fight waged above and around him.

The shouts and cries of warring men clung to the bare January limbs as Hamilton Lightfoot faded away, dreaming of love, dreaming of her.

# 1

## CHLOE

*Present-Day Hollywood*
*August*

You see, love stories never worked for her. She never got the guy. In life or on-screen. Instead, she died. In nearly every major role she landed.

Last year, *Variety* dubbed her "the queen of the death scene." What a stellar endorsement.

But today she determined to do something different. Stop waiting for change and go for what she wanted.

Driving her '64 red Mustang across Bel Air, the convertible top down, to the great Hollywood director Jeremiah Gonda's home, Chloe had high hopes.

Easing up to a red light, she powered up the radio.

"What you want, baby, I got it . . ."

The wind caught the loose ends of her ponytail as a black BMW pulled alongside. The driver, with his cut and chiseled profile, stared ahead, then glanced toward her with a flirting, cap-toothed smile. When their eyes met, his grin faded and he faced forward.

Chloe snarled and boosted the music.

"R-E-S-P-E-C-T."

The light flashed green, and he shot off the line. Poser. Like she'd want that fake-toothed pretty boy. Please. She'd eaten them for lunch when she was a teenager. (Not really, but that sounded good, didn't it?)

No, today was not about her past, the scandal (oh shudder), or her resumé of death and dying, but about what she wanted to accomplish. For the first time in her twenty-year career, she was asking for a part, not waiting to be called for an audition.

Yeah, you bet she'd called in a family favor. Why be the daughter of Hollywood legends — Academy Award–winning director and actress — if she didn't call in a few favors?

Her sordid career had her dying all over stage and screen. Not in slasher flicks or horror shows but on soap operas, coming-

of-age films, Broadway, and one Shakespeare in the Park.

She'd turned down at least three roles due
to the dying nature of the character she was
offered. Because at twenty-nine, she began
to wonder if she'd cursed herself.

Dying so many times, had she made some
unspoken agreement with death? She died a
hundred and fifty times her year on Broadway. A hundred and fifty!

Could such a role produce an unseen effect on her life? On her soul?

Because after Broadway came the scandal.
The death of her reputation. Chloe turned
the music up louder, forcing the ugly ordeal
to the back of her mind.

Pulling up to the Gondas' gate, she
pressed the speaker button.

"Chloe Daschle to see Mr. Gonda."

"What? I can't hear you."

Chloe lowered the radio volume. "Chloe
Daschle to see Mr. Gonda."

With a click, the ornate iron gate swung
open and Chloe eased up the stone driveway, following the curve to park in the
shadow by the front door.

Jeremiah and Laura Gonda, another dy-
namic duo, were like her parents, an award-
winning director married to an Oscar-
winning actress.

They were one of Hollywood's anomalies. Happily, faithfully married for twenty years and raising seven kids practically made them a sideshow.

Chloe's parents, also happily together for thirty-five years, had never married.

Stepping out of the car, Chloe released her ponytail, fingered the knots from her hair, and reached for her bag. At the door, she rang the bell, then stood back, waiting, the thump of her heartbeat drowning her thoughts.

*Hey, Jeremiah, I'd like to read for Esther.*

*Surprise! Listen, I got hold of this script,* Bound by Love. *Have you cast Esther yet?*

*Please, please, please let me read for this part.*

She'd heard of Jeremiah's latest film from a friend of hers, Smitty Barone, an actor-slash-Realtor in town who popped into her life every now and then. She couldn't even remember where she first met him. Acting class?

The breeze kicked up, and Chloe glanced toward the trees lining the gated grounds. Bel Air hosted a legend of stars in its day. Mary Pickford, Ingrid Bergman, George Reeves, Jerry Lewis, Johnny Carson. Even the Beatles during their '65 tour.

In years to come, her parents would

become part of Hollywood's storied past. But she, Chloe Daschle, didn't ache for immortality. She wanted to work, do something meaningful with her craft, impact hearts for good.

And if she was so blessed, break the mysterious curse of death she'd somehow enacted in her life and find personal happiness and true love. Was that too much to ask? To believe in?

The door of the angular, glass Frank Lloyd Wright–home swung open. Jeremiah stood on the other side with his newest daughter, eight-month-old Eva.

"Chloe, come in, come in." He stepped aside, smiling. The grand marble foyer featured a *Gone with the Wind* staircase, a high, wood-beam ceiling, and a nine-foot chandelier. "Thanks for coming to the house. Laura's reshooting some scenes this week, so I'm on deck all day."

"I'd rather come here than your office." She wrapped Eva's little hand around her finger. "You're so beautiful."

"And she knows it too. Ezra?" Jer called to his oldest. "Come take your sister." A gangly, cute blond teenager came around the corner, stuffing a piece of sandwich meat in his mouth, and reached for the baby.

"The nanny has the middle kids at gym-

15

nastics and dance." Jer motioned for Chloe to follow him. "So we'll have some quiet." He entered his office, the western wall of glass framing a spectacular view of the valley. "Can I get you something to drink?"

"Um —" Chloe hesitated, her leather bag swinging from her elbow. This was crazy. If he wanted her to audition for the part he'd have called. But he hadn't. No, instead, he called the likes of Ginger Winters and Sabrina Fox.

Even if he miraculously wanted to cast her, the studio would balk. She was, to her regret, typecast. The girl who dies. He'd be crazy to —

"Chloe? Something to drink?" Jer stood by the fridge built into the wall.

"Um, sorry, yes, please, Diet Coke." She entered the room, set her bag on a plush leather chair, and strolled to the window. "I'm not sure I'll ever tire of this view." Her father's office at the Daschle mansion had the same one. But from her apartment in the mansion's north wing, Chloe saw only backyard trees and the guesthouse.

"Laura and I love to come in here at night after the kids are in bed, put on some music, and just watch the lights." Jer dropped ice cubes in a crystal glass and popped open the Diet Coke before handing it to Chloe.

He retrieved a bottle of Perrier for himself, coming around to the long, deep red couch. "So you're interested in Esther?"

Chloe joined him, taking the time to sip her drink before setting it on a coaster.

"Am I too late?"

He shook his head. "You're not. She's the only one we've not cast. Did your agent send you the script?"

"No. A friend of mine, Smitty Barone." She'd run into him one Sunday. After church. Which he did not attend on a regular basis. But in the last five years, she'd grown accustomed to Smitty's strange comings and goings. "He said the screenplay was from a new writer. Said I should go for it."

"Smitty Barone?" Jeremiah sat back, arm resting on the back of the couch, his expression molded with concern. "Never heard of him. I'm not sure I like the idea of someone I don't know pitching my script around."

Chloe reached for her soda again, taking a drink to hide her nerves. "I-I hope it's okay I called."

The script had captured her from the first line. She felt Esther, as if they'd sat together on the L.P. rooftop in West Hollywood and talked through the sunset to the sunrise.

If Jeremiah would let her read, she'd give

17

Esther every ounce of her twenty years' experience.

"As a matter of fact, we just passed on Sabrina Fox for the role. She's —"

"Too beautiful." Chloe knew Sabrina. Talented, yes, but her striking looks proved to be a distraction. "She's not a colonial girl, but I am, Jer."

"We auditioned Marilyn West but passed on her too. We've been wondering where to go next." Rising from the couch, Jeremiah slipped on a pair of glasses, then retrieved a copy of the script. A prodigy of her father's, he'd risen to directorial greatness with the Oscar-winning *King Stephen I* and now the smash romance novel adaptation *Someone to Love.* One day he would be a legend.

"I get Esther Kingsley, Jer. I am Esther. A girl looking for love who doesn't believe she's worthy."

He regarded her for a long, intense moment. "That brouhaha with Haden really messed with you."

Understatement of the year. The last three years.

"Can I audition or not?" She scooted to the edge of her seat. "I'm tired of hiding. Tired of dying. I know, I know. I'm stereotyped and a risk, but if you give me a chance . . . Jeremiah, just let me read for it." Chloe dug in her bag for the script and drew it out, flipping through the pages, eyeing her notes. "I loved this story. I can't believe it's from a new writer. There's so much heart and truth in every word. It's hard to believe he didn't actually live in 1781, backwoods South Carolina."

"Jesse Gates? Yes, he's talented. Why do you think I'm making a movie of his script? He's playing the part of Flanders too."

"Who's playing Hamilton?" The hero. Esther's love interest.

"Chris Painter."

Chloe collapsed against the couch back. "Ah, I see." She kept her eyes averted. Painter was an old flame from her teen years when they both played on the TV show *High School Follies.* Chris grew up to be the current hottest actor in Tinseltown.

"Is that going to be a problem?"

Chloe found her bravado and leaned forward. "Is that a problem for you?"

"No. But I don't want any drama on the set. I don't want any romances among the cast. Clive Boston nearly cost me *King Stephen I* when he fell for one of the actresses playing a lady-in-waiting. It was chaos."

"Done. Chris is with Ginger Winters, and I'm with . . . well . . . nobody." She'd recently started a faith journey and was learning how to love God first, then others. Including herself. She'd need supernatural power to achieve the last one. "Trust me, romance is the last thing on my mind."

At least for now. In this moment. And for the duration of this film, should she get the part.

"All right. Let's see what you got, Chloe Daschle." Jeremiah flipped open his script. "Oh, hey, speaking of romance." He chuckled softly. "You going to the Steinbrenner wedding this weekend?"

"Of course. I'm a bridesmaid." Violet Steinbrenner was one of Chloe's best friends. Her father headed a major production company while her mother shuffled super talent through her boutique talent agency. "You all are going too?"

"Violet talked Laura into singing a solo." Jer grinned. "She's a frustrated Broadway star, you know." He held up the script. "So, Esther . . . She is strong, and she needs a strong actress to play her." His comment hung over Chloe in the form of a question.

Chloe stared across the room. "I have to do something different, Jeremiah. I can't be the one who dies again. I feel like I'm becoming that girl, and it's affecting every part of my life. I have to be, must be, the woman who lives." She peered at him, shaking her head. "I don't know, maybe it's time to give up acting, do something else. Write. Direct. Teach."

"I hate what this town can do to a person's soul." Sincerity gripped his confession. "Don't give up, Chloe. You're typecast, to be sure, but you're also a talented actress."

"Do you think you can sell me to the studio? I-if you like me for Esther?" She ran her fingers against the edge of the script.

She'd auditioned hundreds upon hundreds of times. She knew the routine. If the studio, in other words the money, didn't like an actor, no matter how brilliantly he or she played the part, it wasn't going to happen.

"I have some leeway here." He motioned to the script. "Let's read."

Chloe flipped to the emotional scene where Hamilton visited Esther to tell her he was going off with the South Carolina militia.

Closing her eyes, Chloe rolled back time to 1781, to an unsettled land, a rough log cabin where the scent of baking bread nearly made her stomach rumble. In the barnyard, chickens scratched and the dogs bayed. A horse peered from a stall window. Cattle wandered the winter hills.

The war for independence had moved

south and settled in the colony where classic backwater folk were farmers and hunters, traders. Hardworking, raw people carving out a life for themselves.

ESTHER: You cannot go . . . not with the militia. Father will speak to General Cornwell. You may join his troops.

HAMILTON (With heated emotion): You've heard what Huck and his men did at Hill's Ironworks . . . the raids on the Presbyterian churches. From York to Ninety Six. Can I just sit by like a coward? Must I remind you what those redcoats did to my pa?

ESTHER: I've not forgotten. But you should aim to do some forgetting — a bit of forgiving. Riding off into the battle will not bring him back. Nor will it ease your pain. I think he'd thank you kindly to live a long life and give him grandsons to carry on the Lightfoot name. Dare I ask about the pledges we've made to one another? Do I not matter? Do I not have a say?

HAMILTON: Am I going back on my word? Have I made a promise I am now breaking? If I sit aside and watch my countrymen, yes, my American countrymen die, how does that speak of me as a man, as a friend and neighbor?

ESTHER: Yes, you go back on your word when you join a fight that cannot be won. What if you find yourself at the end of a Tory musket or bayonet? How can you marry me if you're dead, rotting beneath the ground? And for what? A few tax dollars? A cup of tea? Independence from our homeland that has been so good to us?

HAMILTON: England? My homeland? Nay, Esther, the soil in which you claim I'll rot be my homeland. My heritage is here, in the upcountry. What of England? A land I've never seen. Nay, I say: what of America?

ESTHER: Your friends and neighbors fight for the Crown. You dare raise your musket against them? Against my father? Against my family? You may as well aim at me.

HAMILTON: I cannot help which side they have chosen. They fight for tyranny. But I speak for myself and my family. We fight for independence.

ESTHER (Glances about, lowers voice): Speak not of this treason in my father's house. There's no more devoted Tory in the colony. Have you forgotten he loves you like a son? If you join the militia, you will break both of our hearts!

HAMILTON (Reaches for her): Now you break mine. How will I resolve this conflict of love and war?

ESTHER (Falls into his arms weeping): Choose me, Hamilton. If you love me as you say, choose me.

Chloe lowered the pages with a glance toward Jeremiah, who stared at his script without expression.

*Falling into his arms . . . begging him to stay.*

She'd lived that scene with Haden Stuart. In fact, she felt certain Esther's last line was taken from her viral video. Had Jesse Gates seen it? Hard to say, but when the video reached twenty million views, Chloe gave up hiding out and defending herself. She stopped resisting the truth that her crushing humiliation had become a part of pop culture.

"Well . . ." Jeremiah sighed, tossed the script to the table, reached for his water, and took a long drink.

"What?" Chloe said. "I overplayed her, didn't I? Let's read it again. I can tone her down. I wasn't sure on the accent. More British or more Southern? Geez, I don't want to do a Scarlett O'Hara. That's not right." She forced a smile. "I'm so used to the drama of dying and . . . Know what?" She stuffed the script into her bag. "It's okay. I don't regret trying. Thank you for reading with me, Jer. See you at the wedding."

"Sit down." Jeremiah pointed to her chair, using his director's voice. "You're not going anywhere."

Chloe stumbled back, tripping down into the chair, a jittery flip-flop tumbling through her.

"I can't believe I didn't audition you. Wow, Chloe. You are so much better than you know. Better than I knew." His eyes glistened as he spoke.

"I-I . . . What? Really?" She smiled. "You want me for the part?" A carnival with trumpets and balloons paraded through her. "H-how will you explain me to the studio?"

"You let me worry about the studio." He offered his hand. "Welcome to *Bound by Love,* Chloe Daschle. I'll e-mail the offer to your agent. Chip Mac, right?"

"Yes, the lovely and endearing Chip Mac." She started to leave, then turned into Jeremiah with a hug. "Thank you, thank you, thank you! I won't let you down, Jer. I'm going to act my heart out. Just you wait and see."

Outside, the sky seemed bluer, the birds' song clearer. This movie was going to change her life. She felt it in her bones.

# 2

## JESSE

He never thought he'd live by the ocean. Looking out over vast amounts of water set him on edge.

But eight years from the day he arrived in California, after countless romcoms, TV movies, and failed sitcom pilots, he'd finally struck gold. Hollywood gold. Not as an actor but as a screenwriter, with a script inspired by his family lore and a one-page letter from a colonial ancestor.

A year later, after many rounds of notes and revisions from the studio head all the way down to the janitor — so it seemed — *Bound by Love* got the coveted green light. Filming started in late fall under none other than Jeremiah Gonda, one of the best directors in La-La Land.

Jesse faced the Pacific's salty breeze as it blew over the third-floor deck of the Santa

Monica beach house he was renting. A sweet deal brokered by his friend Smitty Barone.

Jesse was blessed. Given more talent than one guy could handle. But he'd also shouldered his share of sorrow.

Yet to sell his first screenplay within a year of writing it? Gold. Pure movie magic.

Of course, he had none of the gold in his pocket. Yet. The luxury beach house was magic too. The owner of the house had wanted to rent it for cheap while he was away for a year on business.

Inhaling the fragrance of the salty beach, Jesse willed the cobweb of his memories to break away. In good times it was best to forget the bad. His recent good fortune was almost enough to make him believe he'd paid the price for the past. That Loxley, while never forgotten, was behind him. And, if such a thing were possible, had forgiven him.

"Here're your keys." Smitty popped him on the shoulder. Hailing from the Bronx, he was short and lean with dark eyes and a quick smile. An Italian Jew by his own description. Jesse had met him in acting class — or was it on his first paid gig? He couldn't remember. His first year in LA, he was still very raw and broken, wounded, and nursing a dark soul.

He tucked the keys into his pocket. "Where's the lease? I'm ready to sign."

"Right this way." Smitty motioned inside to the glass-and-chrome coffee table.

The house had three levels with a bedroom, bathroom, and living area on each floor. The kitchen and a sunroom were on level one. A media room on level two. An office and den on level three. And every wall was pure ocean-viewing glass.

"Now look, Archer Doyle is an exacting man, so take care of the place." Smitty took a seat on the chocolate-colored suede sofa and handed Jesse a gold-plated pen. "I told him you were trustworthy, and all he said was don't ruin his quartz countertops. Ha!"

"I wouldn't even know where the kitchen was if I hadn't passed it on the way in. His countertops are safe." Jesse scanned the lease for legal details. "When did you say he'd be back?"

"A year at least. Maybe more. He's starting some venture in Asia." Smitty waved his hand over the lease. "All standard, trust me. I'd never do you dirty." His smile was wide. "So, my man, my man. A screenplay with Gonda Films and Premier Studios? Lucky dog, lucky dog. Hey! You think there's a part for me?"

Smitty was a caricature, a Bronx stereotype. And Jesse loved him. He'd proven to be a good friend.

"You know writers have no say in that, but have your agent call casting." Jesse signed the lease, then passed the paper and pen to Smitty. "I'll put in a good word for you."

"You're the best, my friend. The very best." Smitty sank back into the curved, leather sofa. "So, the MIT grad makes good in Hollywood." He snorted. "What say we write a geek screenplay together? Computer nerd hooks up with nerd-nerd." He pointed to himself, sporting a wide grin. "They throw a big party to meet chicks —"

"A geek-and-chicks film? Talk about cliché. Forget it. Come on, help me unload." Jesse jogged down to his car to haul in the first of four boxes and a suitcase from the back of his truck. He traveled light.

Since arriving in LA, he'd rented small, furnished places. Kept his wardrobe to the bare necessities. Acquired nothing he couldn't move in his ten-year-old Dodge RAM.

After handing Smitty a box, Jesse collected his laptop, which served as his TV, then lugged his suitcase over the tailgate.

Another two trips and they'd emptied the

truck, stacked one box in the bathroom, and put the rest in the third-story living space just off the master bedroom. The room was long and bright. Jesse's few belongings made little impact on the space.

"I'm outta here." Smitty smacked him on the back. "Keep your ear out for a part for me, buddy."

"Thanks for everything, Smitty."

"What are pals for?" The man regarded him for a long moment, his brown eyes clear, intense, almost radiating.

Jesse shifted from one foot to the next. "E-exactly."

At times, Smitty seemed to see beyond the here and now into something the five senses could not see, hear, taste, or touch. But then in a flash, he was back to himself — quick, kind, and lovable.

"Catch you later, friend." The distant slap of the front door closing as Smitty left echoed through Jesse, and the familiar friend of loneliness pulled up a chair.

*No . . . no . . . Old friend, I don't need you wrapping your tentacles around me.*

Jesse shook off the sensation and reached for the first box. He missed home. His parents, his brother, his grandmothers, aunts and uncles, his friends. But going home made him remember. Everyone tiptoed around him — even after eight years — trying to discern his mental and emotional state without directly asking.

Pushing back the box flaps, Jesse retrieved a lamp and the old iron Mom had given him, which he used on occasion.

Next he pulled out a recent package from Aunt Pat. The chance to rent on the beach came up so suddenly he hadn't had time to open it.

He felt the loneliness ease away as he settled onto the sofa and peeled off the packing tape of an old shoe box.

Aunt Pat was the family historian. She drove around the country collecting genealogies and artifacts, old diaries and cookbooks, paintings, furniture, whatever she could to piece together about the Gates-Williams-Fuller-Lightfoot family tree.

This box contained a small, framed pencil sketch of Grandpa Hamilton Lightfoot, the inspiration for Jesse's screenplay.

Found this among my brother John's things. God rest his soul. I thought of you when I saw Grandpa Hamilton's face. You look like him. Also, enclosed in the envelope is the original letter. Since you wrote a screenplay based on Hamilton's life, I thought you deserved to have it. Be mindful of it, take care not to handle it too much. If you need to read it again, use the copy I sent you. I'm in awe every time I read this, knowing I'm hearing from an ancestor who lived two hundred and fifty years ago! Remember we have a long, distinguished family heritage. Proud of you, nephew. Love, Aunt Pat

Carefully, Jesse removed the letter from the envelope, barely pinching the edges, squinting at the long, loopy script. The distinct handwriting confirmed the letter had been written by Hamilton Lightfoot.

Aunt Pat verified it with records showing Hamilton's pension request for time served in the Revolutionary War.

The letter was of thick, linen stock with Grandpa's name embossed across the top — Hamilton George Lightfoot. The paper had yellowed with time and the edges were frayed, but the writing was clear.

June 12, 1802

My Dear Esther,

I heard of your Husband's recent passing. How my Heart is with you in your Grief. You are in my Prayers. May the Lord's Peace sustain you.

My Lydia died in childbirth, and I've been raising John Hamilton Lightfoot with Aunt Mary's help. She dotes on the boy, spoiling him terribly. Though I dare say I rather indulge him too. He's Named for my Pa and is the image of his Mother.

But as time passes, I find myself thinking of you, missing you. I Pray I am not out of line for my Declarations.

I am Honored to have fought in the War. But wrestle with Regret on how the Conflict tore us apart. What would our Lives have been had I not gone to Cowpens? 'Tis of no matter now. We made our Choices.

I Trust you and the children are well.

Esther, I must confess, my Affection for you seems to have reclaimed my heart after these many years. I wonder, my Love, if you may feel the same? Would you, at last, consider marrying me?

There the letter ended. Unsigned. Unsent. And Jesse's screenplay began.

*Did I tell your story, Hamilton?*

Jesse didn't have much to go on. Only the letter and Aunt Pat's history of the family — which did not include Esther.

But his soul rattled with a deeper question. Had he told his own story?

Jesse flipped the original letter over, harboring a slight hope that words had magically appeared on the back, revealing more. But the page was empty. It was that emptiness, along with the echoing hollow in Jesse's chest, that had inspired him to write the script.

The deck lights flipped on automatically, catching Jesse's eye. Staring toward the deck, he tried once again to see his great-great-great-great-great-great-grandfather penning this letter to a woman he never married. Did he not love Lydia? Or did her death, and Esther's husband's, merely unlock a buried love?

What of his own love story? His mistakes? What would Hamilton have done differently? Would he have not fought at Cowpens?

What would Jesse change if given the chance? Never made his confession to Loxley? Walked with her out of the house? Down to the beach?

Beyond the deck, the sun set along the edge of the Pacific, washing the windows with a romantic glow.

Jesse tucked the letter away, grabbed his phone, and made his way down to the road, crossing over to the warm sand, aiming for the shoreline.

He'd not touched his feet to sand in eight years. But if the past was in the past, anything he held against himself could be dropped at the water's edge. He would let the waves baptize him and wash his guilt away.

But instead of going the distance, he dug his feet into the shifting sand, a dark sensation in his gut. And he knew. He'd never be free from the past.

No Hollywood success, no California gold, no posh place by the ocean could erase the truth. Just like Grandpa Hamilton, Jesse had to live with what he'd lost.

# 3

## ESTHER

*Ninety Six, South Carolina*
*June 1780*

She'd crossed her last ocean. Surely Father would not ask her to sail the Atlantic again. If he did, she'd refuse him. She was of age now, having turned twenty-two this past birthday.

She'd done his bidding as well as Mother's, and now she would choose for herself.

Upon Father's request, she had traveled to London for her grand society debut and to be presented at court. Taking her place in society aided Father's position with his employer, Lord Whatham, the Duke of Brogman.

Mother, of course, lived for society, so to have her daughter presented at court raised her esteem before the royals and aristocrats alike. Though heaven forbid anyone should inquire of Lady Olivia Longfellow why she lived four thousand miles from her husband and daughter.

Now back home on the safe and beautiful high ground of South Carolina and Slathersby Hill, Esther had no plans to ever leave again.

This was her domain. Her place. She'd grown up here. Acted as Father's hostess for parties, visiting dignitaries, high-ranking British officers, and even Lord Whatham, on the rare occasion of his visit.

Esther peered out her bedroom window toward the road cutting through the green hills and wondered if he'd come to see her today. She'd written three months ago of her return.

He'd not bothered to write her back. He wasn't much for penning a line, her Hamilton Lightfoot.

But she must see him soon, or her heart would most assuredly burst.

"Miss Esther? Might I come in?"

She turned to the door. "Please."

Sassy crept in, a smile on her beautiful, caramel face. "Your father is waiting breakfast for you." She crossed the room. "Shall I open your window? This room is hotter than all blazes." The free woman, who was more a member of the family than a servant, shoved the draperies wide open and raised the pane. The sweet scent of summer breezed into the room.

"Did Isaac bring in my boxes? I've correspondence from Lord Whatham for Father."

"He did. Kitch has unpacked the tea already. I feels all is well in the world with the tea cupboards brimming again. Sir Michael is sipping a cup now."

"I'm not sure he'd have let me in the house if I'd not brought a crate of Bohea. I paid a fine tax in Charles Town."

"Well worth the sterling pounds." Sassy moved around to her truck, raising the lid. "I see you brought home some pretty new dresses."

"They're too hot for South Carolina, but Mother insisted." In the mirror she brushed her hair and tied it up with a ribbon. "H-has anyone come calling for me?"

Sassy turned from the armoire. "If 'n you mean Mr. Hamilton, no. He came around weekly when you was first gone. Didn't even knock on the door, just sat on the front steps staring toward the road. Poor boy was lovesick. But two years is a long time to keep up such pining."

"Mr. Hamilton? Why would he have come

calling? I was referring to Jessica Warren or Isobel Knight." Esther picked up the books she'd acquired for the library. A new edition of the English dictionary and volume one of *The Rise and Fall of the Roman Empire.* "Hamilton Lightfoot." She feigned a laugh. "Mercy, I'd forgotten all about him."

"I'm *sure* you did." Sassy's wide, brown eyes reflected her hidden smile. "Which I say is just fine since he's more than likely forgotten about you."

Esther refused to display any emotion over Sassy's pointed comment.

"He must be married by now." She tucked the heavy books under her arm, her heart thumping. He'd last written seven, no eight months ago. Plenty of time to fall for a local girl. Perhaps that's why he ended what little correspondence existed between them.

A man like Hamilton Lightfoot needed a wife. And what up-country girl did not set her cap for him? More than handsome with his dark hair and crystal-blue eyes, he was kind and well spoken, a defender of the downtrodden and weak. Strong and strapping, a bit of a brooder, he concealed some darkness in his own soul.

"Married? Mr. Hamilton? Not to my recollection." Sassy lifted a red, silk gown from the trunk. "Well now, ain't this a pretty thing?"

Esther watched as Sassy held the party frock against her lean frame. Catching Esther's gaze, Sassy quickly moved toward the armoire, her head lowered.

"Bet you were the belle of every ball in this here dress."

"The red is beautiful against your skin, Sassy. You can have it."

Sassy paused, the gown gathered in her hands. "Come again, miss?" She slowly turned.

"Please, take it for yourself. I insist." Esther smiled with a nod. "It's too tight for me. Mother claims I dined on too many chocolates while in London. We had to let out my stays, and the dresses from my first season no longer fit. 'Tis yours, Sassy. The dress will be beautiful on you."

"And where am I to wear such a fine gown? To church? The floors are dirt and the hardwood benches full of splinters. This fine silk would be pricked and pulled."

"Sit on a blanket then." Esther shifted the books from one arm to the other. "Better yet, wear it Sunday afternoon as you sit on the front porch."

Father gave the servants a whole Sabbath to rest and reflect. He'd purchased Sassy, her husband, Isaac, and their fourteen-year-old son, also named Isaac but affectionately called Kitch, from a man down Charles Town way who aimed to separate them.

Lord Whatham, a strict abolitionist, discouraged Father from owning another human being. An admonition with which Father agreed. Besides, the upcountry had little need for slaves, but Father could not bear to see Isaac, Sassy, and Kitch torn apart.

Isaac, acting as a foreman, was Father's right hand these days, helping him tend to Lord Whatham's interests — the farm, the trading post, and hunting and trapping ventures.

Besides hoping for a glimpse of Hamilton, Esther sensed a tension in the air tainting her homecoming. The war had moved to the South since she'd been away. The London papers touted tales of the wicked Whigs and the American rebels. But surely the might and power of the British army would crush the rebellion any day.

Father had written that Ninety Six remained loyal to the Crown. But on her way home she'd seen a band of buckskin-clad American militia training with the Continentals.

Once again Sassy inquired about the

dress. "Are you sure you won't be wanting this, Miss Esther?" But she'd already set the dress aside.

"Quite sure." Esther lowered her voice. "My bosoms float over the top of the lace, and Father would never stand for it."

"Perhaps, but I bet Mr. Hamilton would." Sassy's bold laugh filled the room.

"Sassy!"

"Come now, I've seen you gaze out that window for him. But never you mind, he'll be along. Go on down to breakfast. Your father is waiting. And I do thank you kindly for the gown. I've never had anything so fancy."

"For that, Sassy, I am most sorry."

"Ah, the good Lord looks after me. For tonight's dinner, I'll bake you a pie. You can count on it. I've got dried apples and cherries."

Esther descended the broad, grand staircase and entered the dining room, finding Father breakfasting with Lieutenant Twimball, a member of His Majesty's army.

Isaac greeted her with a nod, holding out her chair. "Tea and biscuits, miss?"

"Yes, thank you, Isaac." Esther set the books on the edge of the long, polished table. "I thought you'd enjoy these, Father. The latest English dictionary and *The Rise*

43

*and Fall of the Roman Empire.* They say a second volume is due for publication soon."

"My darling daughter, you know how to please your pa." Father beamed, reaching for the books, his linen napkin tucked into his waistcoat. "Lieutenant Twimball tells me you had a rough journey from England."

Twimball, a rather puckish-looking man who regarded himself with the utmost personal esteem, had met her packet in the Charles Town harbor. He was to collect and organize fresh troops from London yet insisted she wait for him to escort her home, despite the fact Isaac and Kitch attended her.

He seemed rather keen on courting her. A notion she found repugnant.

" 'Twas rough. Let me inform you now, Father. That was my last voyage for a very long while, if ever. I detest the high seas." The very thought made her shudder.

Father laughed with a glance at Twimball. "Now you see why I sent her home. She was in need of refinement. I see her mother had no more success than I."

"Why? Because I speak my mind?"

Twimball glanced between them, a glint in his dark eyes and a smirk on his thin lips. "She seems refined enough for me."

Father ignored the remark, sipping his tea.

"I trust you slept well, my dear."

"Very well, thank you. I cannot tell you how I longed for my bed while away."

"You do not like London, Miss Long-fellow?" Lieutenant Twimball asked. "Don't tell me you're a Whig."

"I am a devout Loyalist. As for London, the streets were crowded with filth of every kind. I am beyond grateful to be home on South Carolina's green hills."

Father reached for her hand. "My good daughter. I know you to be a loyal Tory, especially after being presented in court." He wagged his finger at Twimball. "We will not abide treason at Slathersby Hill."

"If you ask me, politics are the root of all evil," Esther said, her stomach rumbling as Isaac set a cup of steaming hot tea and a warm biscuit in front of her. The sugary sweetness of the golden-brown liquid and the heady scent of Sassy's biscuit and butter brought all her memories to the fore. "King George claims to be a man of prayer. Then pray to God he listens to the Almighty and ends this war."

Father leaned toward Twimball. "This is why women do not have the vote. They care not for debate and the hard lines a man must draw for his principles."

"If we had the vote, there would be no

war." Esther motioned to the bundle of letters stacked in the center of the table. "I see you've opened your package from Lord Whatham. Is he pleased with your accounts?"

"H-he's pleased, yes." Father reached for a letter, a gray hue on his countenance. "Your mother writes you were the hit of both London seasons." Father narrowed his gaze at Esther. Were she a child, she'd fear what may come next. "She tells me you booked passage home without her permission. She'd rather hoped you'd remain with her and entertain the affections of Lord Berksham."

"Lord Berksham is a fine man. But not for me. Nor is London. Besides, Slathersby is my home. Not Grosvenor Square. I've done my duty, haven't I?"

"Tell me," Twimball said. "Where does your mother reside? Not here with you?"

"My wife prefers London, her family, and friends. Her father, the Earl of Trent, has quite a good position with the king, and such honors please her more than I do." Father took up another letter, his confession void of any emotion or care. "Twimball, you were speaking of recruiting men of Ninety Six for His Majesty's army."

Esther had long since determined her

parents no longer loved each other. Which fed her desire for true love all the more. She would not be like them, marrying for money and position only to drift apart, maintaining a relationship through correspondence.

"It begins today. Every able-bodied South Carolinian should do his duty and enlist for the Crown."

Esther spread a thick layer of jam on her biscuit. "What of those who side with the Declaration? With the Continental Congress?"

"Then they are traitors and will die a traitor's death." The lieutenant hammered the table. "We must end this rebellion." The words rang hollow, with much bravado, in Esther's ears.

"If the king wants to maintain his authority," she said, more to be obstinate than right, "he should allow the colonies their own representation. Hear their complaints."

Father leaned toward her, large and brooding. "Guard your careless words, daughter, lest the lieutenant here misunderstand your mischievous tongue and report that Slathersby Hill sides with the rebels. We'll find our barns and home burned, and you will find yourself on a voyage to London whether you like it or not." He sat back with a conciliatory smile. "I've just promised the captain my support in enlisting men for the king's cause."

Twimball cut a large bite of fried ham. "You raised a spunky lass, Sir Michael. Tell me, how old were you when you arrived in South Carolina?"

"Ten. My mother did not want me underfoot."

"She seems to enjoy your company now," Father said.

"Perhaps." But she was too late. Esther preferred South Carolina, her father, and Hamilton. "Lieutenant, how do you plan to recruit for His Majesty?"

"By speaking the truth. We are the grandest army in the world. So, did your mama send you across the Atlantic alone?"

My but wasn't he nosey? "Yes. My governess was to accompany me, but she ran off with her young man the night before. So I walked onto the ship alone, bold as you please." She'd been too young and too stubborn to realize the hazards of such a voyage.

"Your first trip? Alone? Surely someone in command took charge of you."

"I told them my mother was ill from the sea and hovering in her bed." The trip had been plagued with storm after storm. The high-pitched shrill of the wind and the crash of the waves against the bow visited her dreams still. "Father, shall we host a party now that I'm home? Invite the town?"

"What a splendid idea." He reached for another letter. "Lieutenant, you can recruit from right here. Set up Slathersby as your headquarters. We'll invite the town for a feast. Every able-bodied man will be in attendance."

"Father, we are celebrating my return, not the duties of Lieutenant Twimball. Sorry, sir, but you will have to do your enlisting elsewhere."

The conversation fell silent as Father read his letter. The clock in the hall ticktocked the hour. Nine o'clock. The china cups and saucers tinged together as Isaac freshened their tea.

Father scooted away from the table. "Pardon me."

"What is it?"

"Nothing to concern you. Oh —" Father paused in the high, arched doorway leading to the parlor. "The Lightfoots. We are no longer on cordial terms. You are to stay away from Quill Farm."

"Stay away?" Esther shot to her feet, toppling her chair. "No longer on cordial terms? Whatever do you mean? They are our friends and neighbors."

"The reverend is a traitor. Not only to the Crown but to us."

"Surely not, Father. He's a godly man, a minister. Why, I've heard you amen his sermons —"

"Esther, there is no debate here." Father's boring gaze caused her to flinch. "Perhaps I've given you too much freedom in your speech, let you state your mind and opinion without reserve, but on this matter you cannot reason me from my opinion. The Lightfoots, for all intents and purposes, are our enemy. Am I clear?"

Behind her, Isaac righted her chair and Esther slowly sat. "Yes, Father." She had no recourse but agreement.

When Father was out of hearing, Lieutenant Twimball cleared his throat and set down his tea. "Major Ferguson has tried to recruit the younger Lightfoot —"

"Hamilton."

"— to our cause, but he resists. He, too, is a rebel."

Esther held her teacup close. Twimball prattled on, but she tuned out his words.

She'd never seen Father so adamant and ardent. It frightened her. How could he turn on the Lightfoots? Their sweat and toil were part of Slathersby Hill.

But Father was her world, and she would

not allow any discord with him. Especially after such a long absence. This season was to be her happy homecoming.

Upon her arrival in Charles Town twelve years ago, she was frightened and alone, more than any child deserved to be, and she clung to him with adoration and desperation. He, in turn, wrapped her in his love. She admired no one more.

Until one day she saw Hamilton Lightfoot no longer as the pesky boy from the neighboring farm with whom she caught crawdads in the creek, but as the handsome man with an awkward elegance, an abandoned smile, and vibrant eyes.

"— Miss Esther? Did you hear me?" Twimball angled forward, resting his arms on the edge of the table. "I'm glad we've this moment alone. I want to request permission of your father to call upon you."

"Call upon me?" Esther's cup rattled against the saucer. "How kind, Lieutenant. I'm flattered. But I'm just home from a busy season in London. I'm rather weary of being coquettish, batting my eyes from behind a fan. Besides, when this ghastly war has ended, you shall sail for England. My feet, however, are forever planted in South Carolina."

The lieutenant blanched, rearing back.

"You won't give me a chance? May I ask why? Certainly you have no other attachments."

"Why, Lieutenant Twimball, are you not more astute to the fairer sex?" Esther wiped her lips with her napkin and gave the solider a coy smile. "A woman never reveals her hand."

And yes, she had another attachment. There was no suitor in the drawing rooms, salons, or ballrooms of London who compared to him.

Isaac returned with a note in hand. "This came for you, Miss Esther."

"Thank you, Isaac." She pressed her pale hand against his dark one. "I'm happy to be home with you, Sassy, and Kitch."

"As we are to have you here. Slathersby Hill is not the same without you. Your father will never admit it, but he was most depressed during your absence."

"Then he never should have sent me away."

Clearing his throat, the lieutenant stood, straightened his jacket, and excused himself. "I must be on my way. I'll say good day to your father, then be off."

"Good day, Lieutenant."

Isaac cleared away the remaining dishes, and Esther was alone. Holding the note in her lap, she peeled back the folded edges and read four simple words.

*Sundown at the willow.*

Such a flutter in her chest. The hours could not pass quickly enough. So, he knew she was home. Esther moved to the window and scanned the garden down to the road, toward the fields, and through the long, morning shadows.

She must find something to occupy herself until the evening or go mad with the waiting.

## 4

**HAMILTON**

The idea of taking up arms did not motivate him. As a boy in Virginia, he'd observed what one man could do to another with musket in hand, and he cared not to participate.

Yet deep down, in the quiet when his head listened to his heart, Hamilton knew he could not escape this war. He ached to take up arms. Give him a reason, just one, to release his rage.

Now the four men sitting at his uncle's kitchen table, including the captain of the Upper Ninety Six Militia, John Irwin, attempted to do just that — give him a reason.

"Ham, we need your skills." His friend Ben Quincy propped his elbows on the dinner table, the orange hue of sunset against the window reflecting in his eyes.

"I'm not of the mind to go killing." He let

his reasoning, not his passion, do his talking.

"You're the best shot in the backcountry,"
Irwin said. "We could use you as a sharpshooter."

Beside Irwin sat William Brown, John
Brown, and Jacob Broadway, sipping coffee
and thanking Aunt Mary for a bite of dinner.

"I can pick off a squirrel with a rifle at
seventy yards, but I don't care to aim at a
man." Hamilton shoved away from the table
and walked to the open back door, the
breeze rushing inside. "I'm sorry you all
wasted your time."

"You're a Loyalist?" Jacob weighed in.
When Hamilton first arrived in the region
as a boy of ten, scared, wounded, and alone,
Jacob had been kind and fatherly to him.
Hamilton respected the man. "Want to see
yourself in a red coat?"

Uncle Laurence leaned on his cane, the
gout keeping him from the battle. "He's no
Loyalist, believe you me."

Hamilton returned to the table, restless.
The sun drifted toward the west, and unless
he rid himself of these men posthaste, he'd
leave Esther alone at their willow tree by
the creek, wondering if she'd been abandoned.

"What about you?" Irwin turned to Uncle. "You've heard what Captain Huck and his men are doing to the Presbyterian churches. Burning them. Calling them 'houses of sedition.' Can you come along with us?"

"We've heard the news of Huck, of Waxhaw and that business up in York at Hill's Ironworks, Captain." Uncle Laurence pointed to his foot. "But I couldn't go the distance. I'll do my bit here. Plus, I put in my time during the Seven Years' War. I'm for the Cause, but I'm best here in the pulpit preaching, protecting the women and children."

"I've heard your speeches, sir. You stirred my heart for my country and my God." Irwin patted Uncle on the back, then turned to Hamilton. "Militia ain't regular army. You come along for three months, and when your time is up, you return home if you don't have a taste for the fight. Every American and South Carolinian ought to give some effort to the cause of liberty."

"I have to follow my own mind."

"Do you deny your neighbors and friends when we need you most?" Ben said. "No man in the upcountry can match your skill."

"Don't need my skill. What of the Virginia regulars? Word is they're the best sharpshooters."

"We need more. Come with us on the line. You're quick and steady." Ben refused to give up. The others around the table nodded as they downed their coffee.

"You're a good Presbyterian, aren't you?" Hamilton hated it when Irwin appealed to his spiritual side. "Do you want Huck to get away with his atrocities?"

"By committing some of my own?"

"Now, hold on here, son," Uncle Laurence said. "The Lord allows for the killing that comes with war."

"Don't mean I have to be a part of it."

"That arrogant Huck would claim to be the victor if the Lord Jesus Christ Himself came down to lead our side," Ben said.

Hamilton reached for a slice of bread. "I'm sure the Lord does not need me to defend His name. He's capable of doing that on His own."

"You sit aside, Hamilton, and you will be forced to choose." This from John Brown. "And you may find yourself aiming your musket at one of us."

"We're going after Huck in the morning, joining forces up in York." Captain Irwin started for the door, the others following. "We're meeting at dawn by Thompson's farm."

"I wish you well, my friends," Hamilton said.

Though they'd gone, the kitchen echoed with their words. Uncle Laurence moved toward the parlor while Aunt Mary busied herself with washing dishes.

"Fear is an unkind master, Hamilton," she said, turning to him, wiping her hands on her apron.

"Indeed it is. But it's not the fear of fighting that has me bound." He flipped his hat from the hook by the door. "Thank you for supper, Aunt. Now, I've something to attend."

"If not fear, then what is your hesitation?" Uncle Laurence called after him, but Hamilton continued on his way.

Uncle Laurence was his father's younger brother. He and Mary had taken Hamilton in when a redcoat's bayonet and a housefire orphaned him.

Childless, Uncle Laurence and Aunt Mary loved him like a son. And he was grateful.

"Hamilton." Uncle Laurence waddled after him, leaning heavily on his stick. "What is your hesitation? Death?"

"I don't fear dying." He paused by the well for a ladle of water. "Some days I think I'd welcome it. But if I give my life on the battlefield, who will care for you and Aunt

Mary? Who will do the heavy lifting on the farm?"

And his unspoken question — what of Esther? Hamilton glanced toward the fading golden light on the horizon. He must be off.

" 'Tis all? Just your aunt and me?"

"Yes." No. There was his true trepidation. That once he'd fired the first shot, he wouldn't stop until every man in His Majesty's army had tasted his own blood.

"Then why do I sense you are still carrying a grudge? The Lord commands us to forgive."

"Every day, Uncle Laurence. Every day." He backed down the hill toward the edge of Quill Farm, toward the path to the willow tree.

"He'd want you to join, you know," Uncle Laurence called after him. "Your pa. He'd be proud. Gave his own life for the Cause, as you know."

Pa. The image of his father's sharp eyes under bushy eyebrows stirred a longing in Hamilton. "Good night, Uncle." He refused to carry on the debate. This war would just have to pass without him.

"Where are you off to now?" Uncle Laurence stepped toward him. "To see a young beauty returned from England?"

"Which beauty might that be?"

"Careful, son, she's been presented to society and in court. She will not be the young lass who ran the hills with you in the summer. Guard your heart."

Guard his heart? He'd done nothing but, since arriving in South Carolina. For once, he wanted to let go, be free, love!

War? He had no appetite for it. But love? He'd hungered for nothing else since the day Esther wrote she was sailing home.

## CHLOE

Stepping from the bridal party limo, she made her way inside the Greystone Mansion, passing through the foyer, over the classic, marble black-and-white checkerboard floor to the outside courtyard, her pink stiletto heels dangling from her fingers.

Violet and Dylan's wedding had been exquisite, overflowing with love and romance. And it made Chloe ache.

But love did not seem to ache for her.

Her teen romance with Chris Painter ended when he confessed to a magazine, "I've not met the love of my life yet, no . . . I'm only nineteen!"

She started dating actor Clark Davis two years later when he showed up at her twenty-first birthday. He perpetually cheated on her during their first and only year.

After Clark, came musician Finley Farmer, who was a great guy but still in love with his ex.

Last but not least, the hunky, egotistical actor Haden Stuart. An on-set romance that flamed into a quick and hot relationship.

Chloe entered the reception patio and descended the low, stone staircase to the outdoor reception where the golden aura of candles, sconces, and outdoor patio lamps accented dozens of white and gold tables. Overhead, a million stars gazed down from the Beverly Hills sky.

"Our table is over there." Stella, Chloe's friend and fellow bridesmaid, met her by the fountain. "Why are you carrying your shoes?"

"The heel broke."

Stella made a face. "You'd think the bride of a hundred-thousand-dollar wedding would pick better shoes."

"A hundred thousand?" Chloe aimed for the first open seat at the bridal party table. "Times five."

"Everyone's saying they'll be divorced before her father finishes paying the bill." Stella fell in step with Chloe. She was a friend from high school, a cheerleader turned teacher. Her boyfriend was Ted, an actor.

"Good grief, Stella, wait until the honeymoon is over before having them in court." Chloe dropped her clutch on her seat at the table and her shoes underneath. Though Chloe defended the blissful bride and groom, it was well-rumored among their friends that neither one of them wanted a lifetime commitment. They both believed marriage was a temporal contract that ended when one of the parties "fell out of love."

Chloe never understood how one could simply fall out of love. Was it an open window, a trap door? Love was a verb, an action word — one that must be exercised daily. Chloe once met American heiress Corina Del Rey, who said she *chose* to love well. Even when it hurt. And she ended up married to her real-life prince, Prince Stephen of Brighton Kingdom.

Was there a prince in the universe for Chloe? One she could love well her whole life? If so, would she ever meet him?

Violet and Dylan entered the reception, and the guests rose up to cheer. They looked blissful, every bit like two lovers set to go the distance.

*Oh, please do, friends, please do.*

"Chloe, you want something to drink?"

"Please." Chloe walked with Stella to the giant, blue coolers stationed around the tables and by the bar. She searched for something cold and fizzy. Bridesmaiding was thirsty business.

Stella retrieved a water and leaned into Chloe, linking their arms. "I think Ted's getting serious."

"Really?" Chloe guzzled a cold Diet Coke, inadvertently burping in her friend's ear. "I thought you found him droll and boring."

Stella shrugged. "He's grown on me. Besides, I'm ready, you know. The husband, the bills and mortgage, maybe a picket fence, a few runny-nose brats."

"Ooo, such a picture of paradise you paint," Chloe said. "You know you're allowed to wait for the right man to come along before —"

"Look, there's Ted." Stella made a big show of blowing him a kiss. He mimed catching it and putting it to his lips.

*Oh brother.* Chloe started back to the bridal party's table — her feet were killing her — but Stella grabbed her arm. "Where are you going? You promised to entertain Ted and Dylan's friend Jesse." She pointed across the dance floor, where Ted stood with another man dressed in black tie. He stood erect, a head above Ted, with a mass of dark hair and a sculpted profile. Stella fluffed her hair. "Ted never said he was so gorgeous."

"Easy, Tallulah. Didn't you just tell me you were crazy about Ted?"

"Doesn't mean I can't keep my options open." Stella sauntered off, swinging her hips, kicking her hair over her shoulder with a flick of her hand. "Come on, let's see which one he prefers."

Chloe yanked her friend back. "If you want him, go for it, but you tell Ted first."

"Tell Ted? Are you crazy? I'm talking about some innocent flirting. What's the big deal?"

"You're talking about a man's heart, Stella. If Ted's serious about you, flirting will hurt him." If Chloe knew anything besides how to die in three different entertainment mediums, it was the pain of a broken heart.

"Oh, honey, I'm not going to hurt Ted." Stella exhaled, shaking her head. "Wow, those jerks really did a number on you, didn't they? You can't even flirt without seeing pain and humiliation."

Yes, yes! They did a number on her. Pummeled her. Raked her over the coals. Left her vulnerable and exposed.

"Forget it. Let's go." Chloe set her drink on the table and charged across the dance area to where Ted and his friend waited. She would power through this evening, then go home where she was safe, albeit alone, and dream of a day when wrongs became rights and her prince would come.

After all, she lived in Hollywood. Where dreams came true, right?

"Hey, babe!" Ted dipped Stella backward for an old-fashioned kiss, drawing the attention of everyone nearby.

When the display ended, Ted shoved his friend forward. "Jesse, this is Chloe. Chloe Daschle, Jesse Gates."

He nodded, meeting her gaze. His eyes said, *Sorry.*

Chloe's answered, *Me too.*

"Daschle?" Jesse said. "Any relationship to Raymond?" He shook her hand.

"Only if being my father counts. Please don't tell me you're an actor."

"Guilty as charged. Though recently I've gone to the dark side of screenwriting. In fact, one of my scripts has been —"

*"Bound by Love?"* she said. "Don't tell me you're *that* Jesse Gates?"

"I am." He made a quizzical face.

"Y-you've read my script?"

"I-I loved it. So much I drove over to

65

Jeremiah's house to audition for Esther."

"Really?" Shock. Surprise. Disgust? "Didn't they cast Sabrina Fox in the role?"

"Turned her down. Too gorgeous."

He seemed disappointed. Of course. Sabrina was every man's dream — poised, talented, with the name and looks any new screenwriter would kill to headline his movie. "Jeremiah offered the part to me."

"Then welcome to the cast." He was good, real good, acting past his disappointment, almost sounding pleased.

"What's this? Chloe, you're in a new role?" Stella draped her arm around Jesse, looking up at him, batting her eyes. "Ted said you were an actor but . . . a screenwriter too? What a talent. And so gorgeously good-looking."

"Stell, you're drooling on his jacket." Chloe gently shoved her friend aside. "I told you about *Bound by Love.* Jeremiah's new film. Jesse wrote the screenplay."

"Please, Jesse . . . ," Stella crooned. "Tell me the heroine lives. *Variety* labeled poor Chloe here the queen of the death scene."

"Yes, she lives." He glanced between Chloe and Stella. "That's kind of the point. It's a love story."

"No, my friend, it's a miracle." Stella looped her arm through Jesse's, pressing

66

her breasts against him. "Chloe finally lands a leading, *living* role." She glanced about. "Hey, everyone, Chloe Daschle got a movie where the heroine —"

"Will you be quiet?" Chloe yanked on her arm, drawing her away from Jesse. "It's not public yet. Besides, you're making a scene. What's wrong with you?"

"I'm merely celebrating this monumental event." Stella angled toward Jesse. "Hello — gorgeous here may have just changed your life."

She was beyond the pale. Bold and brazen — all without liquor.

Ted whispered something in Jesse's ear, and they scooted away.

"Off to decorate the car," Stella said, waving to Ted, blowing a kiss. Then to Chloe, "Look at you, Miss Daschle, with a new movie and a hunky new man."

"He is *not* my man." Chloe turned back to the bridal party table where her drink warmed by the minute. She'd not yet slaked her bridesmaiding thirst. "Besides, he's an actor. I don't date actors."

"Since when?"

"Since you-know-when. Jesse's too good-looking, and I can tell he's the type that loves to talk about himself endlessly. You know, the kind that can drive his date to stab herself with a fork just to get him to shut up."

"Miss Cynical Goes to Hollywood. Come on, Chloe, it's been three years since Haden."

"Yeah, well, it's only been one since that stupid video resurfaced." With the Internet, nothing ever died. Except maybe the truth.

"I'm no therapist, Chloe, but one of these days you have to forgive yourself. What happened to your churchy-faithy thing — whatever you were into?" Stella wiggled her fingers and scrunched up her nose. "Wasn't that supposed to make you new?"

"New, yes, not perfect. And I can do without your sarcasm."

"Sarcasm? I'm just having fun, darling." She kept her eyes fixed in the direction Ted had gone with Jesse.

"Have it at someone else's expense."

From the bandstand, a loud, single note rose from every instrument and hovered over the reception. "Ladies and gentlemen." The band leader stepped up to the mike. "Please welcome your bride and groom, Mr. and Mrs. Dylan Stux."

The music exploded over the guests' applause as Violet floated on her husband's arm under a vanguard of white lights.

Dylan twirled her onto the dance floor as

the band began a classic standard, "It Had to Be You." The female singer with a Marilyn Monroe figure wore a tight, black gown.

"You know, Chloe," Stella whispered, "you will never move on if you compare every man to Chris Painter, Clark Davis, Finley Farmer, and that wretched Haden Stuart."

Chloe faced her friend. "I don't."

Okay, yes, she did. Sorta. But she was trying to put them behind her. Praying. Seeking a better way.

"First you were the 'it' couple with Chris," Stella said, holding up one finger.

"Ten years ago."

"Followed by the press and paparazzi. Idyllic teens leading idyllic teens."

On the dance floor, Violet settled her head on Dylan's shoulder, and he gently stroked her hair. Chloe felt his tenderness and yearned.

"Then there was Clark." Stella's second finger popped up. "The cheater. How many times did he cheat on you?"

"Is there a reason we're rehashing my love life?"

"After Clark came Finley." She flashed the three fingers in front of Chloe. "Great guy, but oh so in love with his ex."

"They're happily married now. I'm thrilled for them."

"Which leads us to Haden. Fourth, final, and fatal. He crushed you, that wicked soul."

"Oh, look, Ted's waving to you." Chloe shoved her friend forward. She did not need a reminder, on this lovely night, of her abysmal failures at love.

From the bandstand: "Violet and Dylan invite the bridal party to join them for this next dance."

"Come on." Stella reached for Chloe, but she withdrew.

"I can't. My groomsman is dancing with his girlfriend. Go. Ted is waiting."

Chloe retreated to the bridal party table. She needed a hit of Diet Coke to fortify her after Stella's trip down ugly love-life lane.

Across the dance floor, on the opposite side of the courtyard, Chloe saw her parents sitting together with her sister, Kate, and Kate's boyfriend, Rob.

Dad caught her eye, smiled, and waved.

He was one good man in her life. And Smitty. She barely knew him, but she was grateful he walked into her life with a word of hope.

"Can I have this dance?" Jesse appeared, bowing toward her, offering a thick, broad hand.

"S-sure." As she slipped her hand into his,

a small flutter released in her chest and she instantly liked him. "I warn you, I'm a toe stepper."

"Good thing I'm not, since you're the one without shoes." Jesse collected her in his arms and moved her gently to the music.

"The heel broke."

"Hate when that happens."

He moved with ease. Chloe peered up at him. "You're a good dancer."

"Thank you, Miss Irene's Ballroom Dance School in Boston."

"Dance lessons, wow."

"It was the only way my brother and I were allowed to play football. My mother insisted we attend dance class." Jesse moved Chloe in a modified waltz as the band played a ballad.

*You made me love you . . ."*

"Goodness. An actor, screenwriter, dancer, footballer."

His smile melted over her. "I'm a man of many talents. I won't deny it."

"Humility being one."

"Yes, but low on the list." He frowned, shaking his head. "Very low."

She laughed and relaxed against his chest, sensing the heat of his skin through his white tuxedo shirt. "Was it worth it? The dance classes to play football?"

"Initially, no. But as we got older, Dan and I were famous for our dance moves, and in high school the girls asked *us* to the dances." Jesse swung her around, so she gripped his hand tighter and stumbled over her own feet. But he didn't correct her or ease up. "Just . . . follow my lead. Don't resist. There, okay, you got it. Easy now. You're a natural."

"You're disappointed, aren't you? That I probably have the role of Esther."

"I don't know enough about you to be disappointed." He gazed down at her, sincere and honest.

"You know I am the queen of dying."

"I trust Jeremiah. If he thinks you're Esther, then you probably are."

"But you wanted Sabrina Fox for your first movie. Now you're stuck with plain ol' me."

"You know, self-deprecation doesn't work on everyone. You should try believing in yourself."

"I believe just fine. It's everyone else I'm worried about."

"Chloe, I'm happy you're in the movie if you're the best Esther. That's all I care about. I'm lucky to be in this position. I don't take it lightly."

"I only meant —" Who was she kidding?

He knew what she meant. "I fell in love with Esther and Hamilton when I read the screenplay. I'm beyond lucky to get this part. I'd love to know your inspiration behind it."

The wind blew a loose strand of her updo over her eyes, and Jesse gently swept it away. "A letter."

"What kind of letter?"

"A love letter. My grandfather's. Well, great-times-six grandfather. Long time ago." He drew her close, and on instinct she let him.

"Must have been some letter."

The band director invited everyone to dance, playing the chorus of the song once again.

*"You made me love you. . ."*

"Hello, darlings." Mom glided up in Dad's arms, stunning, regal, and elegant. "Who's your friend, Chloe?"

"Jesse Gates." She stepped out of his arms with a glance up at him. Would he assume the look, the one every man had when he met her mother, the stunning starlet? "This is my mom, Rachel Hayes. My dad, Raymond Daschle."

Jesse nodded, his arm tight around Chloe. "A pleasure to meet you both."

"Jesse Gates," Dad said. "You're the

screenwriter. Jer Gonda's directing and producing your story."

"The one you auditioned for, Chloe?" Mom said, light and lyrical, her charm so warm and easy. "How lovely. She's a dynamite actress, Jesse. You just can't tell because she dies in every major role. I blame Raymond for it, really, I do."

"Okay, Rach," Dad said, spinning her away. "See you later, Chloe. Jesse, nice to meet you." Then he whispered something to Mom, and she tossed her head back with a thin, controlled laugh. Then she whispered something intimate to Dad and he kissed her, holding her a bit closer.

There. That was what Chloe wanted. Intimacy. A place where only those two lovers existed. For all eternity, only Dad and Mom would know and feel what transpired in that moment.

But Chloe also wanted commitment. A ring and a date. Her parents never sealed their deal. Never took their love to the next level. After thirty-five years, they still "lived together."

"What's this about your dad being the culprit?" Jesse said. "Of your queen-of-dying moniker?"

Chloe danced with him, feeling his movements before he made them. "He's not really, but Mom likes to tease him. When I was nine he cast me as a child cancer victim in one of his biggest projects."

"And you got stuck somehow."

"Somehow. Yes."

The song ended, and the guests lightly applauded. Chloe backed away from Jesse as Ted, the best man, jumped onto the bandstand.

"Good evening, everyone. I'm Dylan's brother, Ted, and his best man."

Jesse reached to a passing server for two flutes of champagne and handed one to Chloe. "Can't make a toast empty-handed."

"— so I quote the great poet Christopher Marlowe: 'Come live with me and be my Love . . .' "

Chloe breathed in the bubbles from her glass, listening to Ted's voice rise and fall with each stanza. The sleeve of Jesse's tuxedo brushed her arm, and she flushed with an intoxicating warmth.

"Raise your glass to the bride and groom, Dylan and Violet."

Chloe raised her flute, but before she could take a sip, Jesse hooked his arm around hers. "To the bride and groom."

"To the bride and groom."

Chloe took a sip, then unraveled her arm

from Jesse's. "You don't need to stay with me."

"Are you trying to get rid of me?"

"No, just letting you off the hook. I know Ted and Stella thought we'd pair up tonight, but —"

"But now that I know who your father is, I think I'll stick around." He hid his grin with another taste from the crystal flute.

"Finally, an honest actor."

"Indeed, a rare breed in LA."

"As long as we're confessing, I don't date actors. They're arrogant and self-absorbed."

He made a face. "But actresses are . . . ? Sugar and spice and everything nice?"

"Okay, so we have our flaws, but nothing compared to our male counterparts."

"Duly noted, Miss Daschle."

The band started another song. Jesse remained next to her, staring ahead.

"Are you mad?"

He glanced over at her. "Why would I be mad?"

"Just checking."

He set his champagne glass on the bridal table and reached for her. "I love this song. My grandma used to play it on the piano when we were kids."

The wedding singer crooned, "I love you, for sentimental reasons."

"Just so you know," he said. "I don't date actresses."

"Really?" Chloe frowned. "Why not?"

"They're fickle, self-absorbed, insecure, and forget *ever* asking one out for pizza."

"I like pizza."

Jesse's laugh rolled over her as he drew her into him, their dialogue fading, his cheek resting against her hair. After a moment, a soft, low, Mel Tormé kind of voice sang in her ears, each note, each word sank straight into her heart.

"I love you for sentimental reasons."

Tears spotted her eyes. *Hold on to yourself, Chloe.* Jesse was just singing the song his grandma used to play.

"I'll hope you do believe me, I'll give you my heart."

His breath brushed her skin, and for a moment, she lost all sense of herself. Heaven help her, every lyric he sang felt like it was meant for her.

# 5

## ESTHER

She waited under the willow as the June sun slowly disappeared beyond the dark line of the western horizon. For the fifth night in a row, she was meeting Hamilton here.

Each meeting, while brief, allowed them to get reacquainted. Perhaps tonight they could bypass shallow exchanges for more confidential dialogue. Perhaps, if Hamilton were willing, they could speak of how they felt about one another.

So far, they'd talked of London, the seasons, being presented at court, and Esther's voyage home.

"I'm never leaving South Carolina again!"

Hamilton had rehashed details he'd penned in his brief and few letters. Quill Farms was surviving. Aunt Mary and Uncle Laurence were well, save for Uncle's gout and now, perhaps, the sugar disease. And, praise God, he was not enlisting with either army.

When she'd asked why Father and his uncle Laurence were at odds, he'd confessed he was unclear.

"Uncle is angry at your father, over what I cannot say, other than one is a Whig and the other an ardent Tory. I know your father does not care for Uncle's preaching as of late. But he has not forbid me from Slathersby Hill. Nor you from Quill Farm. Not that I have to obey him. I'm twenty-two."

"As am I, but I try never to go against Father. He must have his reasons for being cross with your uncle."

"Yet here you are."

She'd batted her eyes and leaned into him. "Yet here I am."

Would he say it? The words she longed to hear?

*"I've missed you. Don't ever leave again."*

Yet tonight he was late. Esther peered around the tree and down the road. Surely he was coming. He'd not sent word otherwise. Behind her, a few feet away, the creek flowed with the force of spring rains, fat trout flipping along the current.

Esther knelt on the bank, wishing she had brought a fishing line. Trout made a fine meal. But if she returned with a line of fish,

Father would quiz her over her afternoon wandering, and she could not lie to him. 'Twas not her gift, to fib. She tried once, and he gave her the strap.

Not that she worried about being discovered away from the house, secretly meeting Hamilton. Father remained distracted, confined to the library, poring over his books, scribbling correspondence to Lord Whatham, sending Kitch into Ninety Six to meet a postal rider.

He claimed that when the war ended, he'd look into establishing an organized postal service such as the one the wiseacre Ben Franklin developed for the rebels.

The breeze rattled the branches as the sunlight dipped lower. What was keeping Hamilton? Back at the tree, Esther leaned against the trunk, listening to the song of the evening birds.

Now home a week, she'd reclaimed her position as mistress of Slathersby Hill. She'd taken over the household accounts and would soon ride into town with Sassy to bargain with the traders.

The chickens were producing well this year, as well as the cows. They had eggs, butter, and cream to spare.

"There you are." Hamilton dropped next to her with an exhale, slapping his tricorne against his legs. "I feared you'd tired of waiting for me."

One look into his eyes reflecting the golden evening sky and she knew she'd wait forever.

"I feared you'd forgotten me."

He stroked her cheek. She cupped her hand over his, bringing it to her lips.

"Hamilton, I must ask. Did you not miss me at all? Your letters, infrequent as they were, contained nothing but a salutation, your daily chores, and a brief closing with your signature."

"What did you want to hear?" He released her hand, settling against the tree.

"How you missed me. How you feared I'd been persuaded to marry a fancy, rich English nobleman."

"How the war might keep you away?" He slipped his hand into hers. "You demand hard things from me, Esther. The secrets of my heart."

"So you did miss me?"

He grinned. "I missed you. Terribly."

She scoffed, laughing, shoving him away. "A fine paramour you make, Hamilton Lightfoot. I declare, how do you expect to win my favor with so few words? If you cannot speak them, why not write them? A love letter —"

"A love letter?" His blue gaze examined her. "For all the world to see?"

"Not all the world — only me."

"I dare say speaking my innermost thoughts is one thing, but writing them down? I'm not sure I could ever, well, how could I, the words . . ." Blushing, he peered toward the creek, tossing his hat onto the grass. "Just because I didn't write my affections in a letter doesn't mean my heart is devoid of them."

"Then I am comforted." She rested her cheek against his shoulder.

"Do I disappoint you?" He angled forward to see her face, inspiring a familiar but disruptive flutter. He'd kissed her once. On the cheek. After a town social. She had practically floated home, fell asleep smiling, and woke up the same.

"I don't think you could ever disappoint me." She raised up, gazing into his eyes. "But one day, Hamilton, won't you tell me truly how you feel?"

His kiss came quick and firm, his warm lips touching hers with a promise of more. Esther exhaled and rested her arms about his neck. She was as light as the breeze, as blazing as the sunset.

But all too soon he broke away.

"There," he said, tapping his forehead

against hers. "Now you know how I feel."

"Yes, I believe I do."

One day he would declare his love. One day.

This was where she belonged. Not in London drawing rooms vying for some nobleman's attention. She belonged in the upcountry. She belonged in Hamilton's arms.

*I love you, Hamilton Lightfoot.* She soared, catching the current and spreading the wings of her heart. Oh, may this moment never end.

"I'll write you a love letter one day," he said, lacing his fingers with hers. "I promise."

"Will you? Really?"

"Would it not please you?"

Esther sat up, turning to him. "What can I do to please you, my love?"

"Marry me. I'll figure out this angst between Uncle and your father, and we will wed." He kissed her forehead with warm, sweet lips, the gesture descending slowly down her cheek.

Esther drew a breath with each rising sensation. So this was what the poets lauded so gracefully.

"Miss Esther!"

She jerked away from Hamilton at the

sound of Kitch's boisterous call. She felt tossed about and torn, robbed of something beautiful.

"Miss Esther? You round here? Sir Michael's been looking for you." Kitch's dark face appeared around the broad trunk of the willow, leading the horse Gulliver. "I seen you sneak out here every night. How do, Mr. Hamilton?"

"Evening, Kitch." Hamilton stood, dusting leaves from his trousers. "Esther, you must go to your father. Let us not fuel his anger." He offered Esther his hand.

"You didn't tell on me, did you, Kitch?" She rose up, dusting twigs and debris from her skirt, but kept her hand in Hamilton's a moment longer.

The fourteen-year-old twisted an invisible key over his lips. "Nary a word. Nary one word."

"Why is he looking for me? His nose was in his ledgers when I left."

"Something happened in town. Big ruckus. A rider came blazing up to the house."

There'd been talk of trouble. Captain Huck's dragoons continued their reign of destruction in the colony. Actions that Father applauded. The Presbyterians, he said, must be silenced.

Hamilton stepped around Esther. "What trouble, Kitch?"

"Don't rightly know. A skirmish in town."

Hamilton swore low. "Could be Huck and his men. The local militia feared he'd head this way, the cretin." He gathered Tilly's reins. "Kitch, see Miss Esther home. Do not stop anywhere nor for anyone. Do you hear me?"

"Yes, sir."

"Hamilton, wait." She gripped his sleeve. "Take me with you. If there's trouble in town, Father might have gone to check Whatham's trading post or his furrier concern."

"Go home, Esther." He released himself, gently shoving her toward Kitch. "If there's news, I'll ride to Slathersby. Now make haste."

Just as he mounted Tilly, another rider thundered down the road, a lamp swinging from his hand.

"Hamilton! Come quickly. We've been searching for you." It was Ben Quincy.

"What is it?" Beneath him, Tilly shifted and pranced, tossing her head, whinnying to the night. "What's happened?"

"Huck and his men . . . they . . . burned the church. Hamilton, your uncle was inside."

"Ya!" Hamilton kicked Tilly into a run and disappeared down the road without a backward glance.

Ben peered down at Esther, raising his lamp high. "Get home, Esther. It ain't safe."

"Did they truly, Ben? Burn the church while Reverend Lightfoot was inside?"

"We're hoping he made it out the side door, but as I rode out, there weren't no sign of him. You best hope your pa wasn't in on aiding the dragoons, or Slathersby Hill won't last the night." Ben's words strained through his clenched jaw. "Tonight it's better to be a Whig than a Tory."

"Father wouldn't. He wouldn't." But what truth had she? None. Only the confidence that her father, while loyal, was no murderer.

"It's war, Miss Esther. Trust no one." With that, Ben was gone.

"Miss Esther?" Kitch's hand gently rested on her shoulder. "We best get home." He reached for Gulliver's reins.

"Surely they won't burn Slathersby Hill. Father is a pillar in town." Foot in stirrup, she pulled herself up and landed on Gulliver's back. Kitch hopped on behind her. "We will be safe, won't we?"

Kitch giddy-upped to the gelding and

urged him up the road, opposite town. Opposite Hamilton and the treachery of war.

# 6

## JESSE

The band finished another song. He parted from Chloe long enough to applaud. She glanced toward her table as if she might be done with him for the evening.

But he wasn't ready to let her go. He felt cold where she'd leaned against him. Maybe it was just the mystical romance of the wedding, but he wanted to stay in her presence.

On the other hand, a wedding was a lot like being on a movie set. No realities. Everything would return to normal in the morning. So why not enjoy an evening with a beautiful woman? No strings. No expectations.

The singer began a melodic, enchanting rendition of "I've Grown Accustomed to Her Face," and Jesse reached for Chloe's hand. "One more?"

Without a word, she moved with him as if

they'd danced a thousand dances. And she made him want things he'd not allowed himself to consider for a long, long time.

"You've mastered the waltz in a single evening," he said, turning her to the music. "Dancing suits you."

"Don't be fooled. It's all you."

*"I've grown accustomed to her face . . ."*

Then the trumpeter rose for a solo, and the sound wove around them as if they were the only ones on the floor.

While Chloe made him consider love for the first time in ages, he was safe with her. First, she wasn't his type. A full-figured redhead of average height. He liked his women tall. And lean. Yeah, lean. And . . . and . . . blond. Definitely blond.

Having reasoned this in his head, he relaxed, set his cheek on her hair again, and this time kept the lyrics to himself. That was embarrassing, singing, "I love you for sentimental reasons" right into her ear.

Nevertheless, he let the music have its way and held her a little closer.

When the song ended, she stepped away, and the cold creeped across his chest again.

"I didn't mean to steal you from all the other ladies tonight."

"I promised Ted I'd dance with his girl-friend's friend." He shrugged, shaking his head. "Somebody had to do it."

She laughed and shoved his arm. "Stella begged me to dance with her boyfriend's dorky friend. An ac-tor." Chloe rolled her eyes, making a face.

Jesse laughed, wrapped his arm around her, and kissed her forehead. "We're both saints, then."

The intimate gesture caused him to freeze. What was that? The laugh. The arm. The kiss. Jesse moved left one step. Should he say something? *"Just kidding"? "Oops, let me wipe that kiss away"?*

"Yeah, saints." She gazed toward the dance floor.

In moments like these he longed, with a capital *L,* for an actor's brain. The kind fueled by emotion and the moment. The kind that could let an incident go. Instead, he functioned as an engineer. All the time. Sequential. Logical. Overthinking things, as he was right now. *Stop.*

"Ladies and gentlemen . . ." Dylan hopped up on the dais, motioning for Violet to join him. "My beautiful bride and I would like your attention." The noise settled down except for the pianist playing a soft melody. "First, thank you all for being here and celebrating this great day with us. We couldn't have done it without you all.

Special thanks to our family and friends, who put up with us during this wedding Godzilla time." Violet nudged him, feigning a pout while the guests laughed. "We love all of you." His gaze drifted to Violet. "But we have agreed to share our night with someone." Violet grabbed the mike. "Where's Ted?"

"What's this?" Chloe said, elbowing Jesse. "Do you know? Tell me. What's Ted doing?"

"Got me." He surrendered his hands. "Promise. I know nothing. But as the brother of the groom and the best man, who knows what he's planned?"

"Stella, you come up too," Violet said. "We want to give you guys a special gift for being so good to us during our wedding planning." She leaned toward Dylan for a kiss.

Something popped in Jesse's chest. Something weird and foreign. He pressed his hand against the bone, trying to make it go away.

"We wanted to give you these gifts as a token of our appreciation." Dylan handed Ted and Stella two boxes wrapped in thick, white paper and gold ribbon.

"You guys . . ." Stella pressed her hand to her throat. Ted said she was a teacher, but Jesse wondered if she'd missed her calling. "You really didn't have to do this. We love you and wanted to be there for you on your big day."

"Open them." Violet urged the crowd to cheer them on. An "open, open, open" chant bounced around the tables.

"You first, babe," Ted said, tucking his box under his arm.

"I can't imagine . . ." Stella pulled at the ribbon, letting it fall to the stage, then removed the paper. She faced the guests. "What do you think it is?"

"A million dollars," someone shouted.

"Wouldn't *that* be wild." Stella giggled and tittered, removing the lid from a box. With a gasp, she retrieved a smaller box, glancing back at the bride.

"The old box-inside-the-box gag," Chloe whispered up to him. "Classic. Now all we need is a pie in someone's face, and the night will be complete."

"Ooo, cruel, Miss Daschle, very cruel."

She winced. "I'm kidding."

Jesse nudged her. "As am I. Lighten up."

Stella opened the small box and took a step back, her long fingers covering her red lips. "Ted, what did you do?"

Slowly, he bent to one knee and reached for her hands. Camera phones flashed all over the patio reception. "Stella Eva Epstein, will you marry me?"

"You're kidding me." Stella pulled him to his feet, tossing a glance at the bride and groom. "Did you know about this?" Then back to Ted. "M-marry you? Really?"

"Yeah, really."

Next to Jesse, Chloe moaned under her breath. "Unbelievable."

"What?" Jesse said. "That one guy is proposing during another guy's reception? Maybe it's a bit tacky, but they are brothers. I'd let my brother propose at my reception if he asked. I think." Not that he'd ever have a reception. Jesse voided all thoughts of marriage when Loxley died.

"Babe," Ted said, squeezing Stella's hand. "You're making me nervous. Will you?"

"Oh, I'm sorry. Yes, of course I'll marry you. Yes!" She flung herself into his arms, visibly shaking when he slipped the ring onto her finger.

The guests of Dylan and Violet's wedding applauded for Ted and Stella.

The band begin to play "Blue Suede Shoes" as the couples embraced, and the applauding guests returned to the dance floor.

"Now that you've mastered the waltz, want to learn swing?" Jesse bent to see her face. "Chloe?"

"She doesn't really love him."

Jesse leaned closer. "Come again?"

"She doesn't really love him." She stabbed her finger into his chest. "Seriously, you didn't know he was going to do this?"

"He never said a word. What do you mean she doesn't love him? Did she tell you that?"

"Not directly, but in so many words. Didn't you see how she flirted with you when you came in?" Chloe brushed past him toward her table. "Marriage . . . love . . . they're not games, something to win or lose, toss aside when you're bored and want to play something else." She reached for her shoes and handbag.

Something was eating her. But what? "Who said they were?"

"I know women who would walk on hot coals to get a man like Ted. But to Stella, he's just next on a list of things to do. I'm not kidding. She flirted with you on purpose. To see which one of us you'd choose. She wanted to keep her *options* open."

"She was joking."

"No, she wasn't." Chloe released a long breath and pressed her fingers to her forehead. "Sorry . . . this is none of my business. It's been a long day, and I'm tired and hungry." She glanced toward the back of the mansion. "I don't know when they're going to serve dinner, and well, I think I've had enough dancing and romance for one night."

"I know a great place at the beach." Jesse offered his hand, tipping his head toward the parking lot. "Do you know a girl who'd like to get a pizza?"

She chuckled, shaking her head and pointing to herself. "The one with the pie on her face."

"Why are you the one with the pie on your face?"

"Because I'm the only one —" She stopped and pinched her lips together. "Pizza sounds good."

"Right this way." Jesse reached for her hand, then drew back, stepping around a dancing couple. As they left the Greystone Mansion together, he forced himself to let go of the feeling in his chest. A small, unwelcomed yearning for love.

# 7

## CHLOE

"I'm not jealous, you know."

"Ah, she speaks." Jesse dropped a large veggie pizza between them on the bench seat as he slipped behind the wheel. Loosening his tie, he headed down Santa Monica Boulevard toward Ocean Avenue. She liked that he drove a truck. Not a status car, like that capped-tooth poser from the other day.

"Sorry, I needed to process." She'd been quiet since they'd left the reception. Time Jesse used to call in their pickup order.

"You really think she doesn't love him?" Jesse powered on the radio, tuning it to the same classic standards the reception band had played. He lowered the volume so the sounds accompanied their conversation.

"You're an old soul, aren't you?"

He laughed, the light from the dash accenting the bold lines of his face. "My mom says so, yes." He peered at her. "What makes you say it? The music?"

"That and just . . . you. My mom says I'm an old soul too. A throwback."

"A throwback? Nice." He rounded the corner off Ocean onto Highway 1.

"You really do know of a place on the beach?"

"I wouldn't lie to you. So, what'd you conclude during your musing?"

"I don't know." She shifted in her seat. "I shouldn't judge. Stella has been known to say one thing and do another. She may well love him but acts all whatever about it, covering how much she cares. I guess we'll see if she can go the distance."

"Does anyone know if they can go the distance when they start out? Did your parents?"

"No. They met on a set. It was Dad's first job as the DP and Mom's first major role. They made a pact to have an on-set romance only. When filming ended and they returned home, their relationship would be over. Instead, they fell in love. It's been thirty-five years."

"So love can work out when you least expect it."

"For some." Probably not for her. Given her abysmal track record. "What about you?

Love in the picture for old soul Jesse Gates? The guy who wrote a love story based on his grandfather's love letter."

"I think I'd rather write about it."

"Ah, the man evades the question with a safe, reveal-nothing answer."

"We're here." Jesse turned into the tight driveway of a three-story, glass-front house on the edge of the beach.

Stepping out on the passenger side, Chloe angled back to see all three stories. "Man, I really need to start writing screenplays."

"Come on, it's better from the inside." Jesse gently tapped her arm, the fragrance of warm dough, bubbling cheese, and hot tomato sauce luring her forward.

After walking through the main-floor kitchen, where Jesse grabbed plates and napkins, they traipsed up three flights of stairs, walking out of a high-ceiling, glass-walled living room onto a wood-and-iron deck.

"This is incredible. Seriously, your first screenplay had to go for top dollar."

"It's a studio project. So, yeah, I was paid well." Jesse lit the gas fireplace, even though it was August, and flipped on a string of round, white bulbs running from one deck corner to the other.

"This is beautiful." Chloe leaned against

the railing, lifting her face to the ocean. "I think the pie is melting from my face."

"I still don't know why you're the one with pie on your face." Jesse set the pizza on a glass-and-teakwood table.

"Because I was surprised by Ted's proposal, that's all. So, paid well? Good for you."

"Except the money has to last a long time. Who knows when the next job will come along. In the meantime, I'm renting this place. The owner is out of the country for a year and wanted someone to keep an eye on things. My friend Smitty hooked me up. The rent was too much, rather, too little, to pass up."

"You have a friend named Smitty?"

"Yeah, why?" Jesse dropped a slice of pizza onto one of the blue china plates he'd snagged from the kitchen and handed it to her.

Chloe sat on the upholstered two-seater. "I have a friend named Smitty."

"It's not all that uncommon of a name. Pizza! Nice and hot."

Jesse filled his own plate, then sat next to her.

"Do you sleep with the doors open?" she said. "I love the ocean, but at night it's so dark and eerie. A mysterious abyss beyond the horizon with only the cold, distant stars as its beacon."

"I don't sleep with the doors open. I try not to think about how dark and deep it is out there." Jesse jumped up, angling for the rooftop bar. "What do you want to drink?"

"Anything. Water. Diet Coke. Tea."

He returned, tossing her a bottle of water — somewhere in the night she'd lost her bridesmaiding thirst — and took up his pizza again.

For a long while, the only sounds on the deck were the whoosh and growl of the waves, the clang of distant wind chimes, and the sighs of hungry people being satisfied.

Chloe reached for a third slice of pizza. Tomorrow she'd diet. Get ready to play Esther Kingsley. How thin were women in up-country South Carolina in 1781?

"So," she said, removing a dollop of tomato sauce from her thumb. "What happened with your grandfather and this woman he loved?"

"Don't know." Jesse ate his pizza New York style. Rolled in half.

"Don't know? Then why'd you write about them?"

He swallowed, sitting back, washing his food down with a long swig of water. "You know how, oh, I don't know, someone's grandparents or great-grandparents never went to college, so the descendants work hard to be the first ones to graduate? Or the first ones to move out of poverty? There's something about the past that needs to be settled, or changed, or answered."

"Do you think your grandfather and Esther needed an answer?"

"He proposed to her in a letter that he never sent. He married his wife in the 1780s and —"

"So you do know some of the history?"

"My aunt Pat is the family historian. She's the one who gave me the letter. She was looking for answers herself. Hamilton married a woman named Lydia, but we don't know much about her. They had a son. However, the only correspondence we have is an unsent letter to a woman named Esther where he confessed he loved her and asked her to marry him."

Chloe regarded him, chewing. "Unsent?"

"As in never mailed. In fact, he didn't even sign it. He started something he never finished."

"And your aunt Pat has no answers?"

"Not yet, but I'm sure she's on the trail."

"So weird that he never sent the letter."

"Maybe he was afraid . . ."

"Of what?" Chloe washed down her last

bite of pizza and wiped her fingers with the napkin Jesse handed her.

"That the woman he loved from his youth would turn him down. Or that what he felt wasn't real, just sentiment."

"Is this about more than your grandfather, Jesse? Finishing something for him but maybe for yourself too?"

He paused, pizza suspended before his open mouth. Then, "No . . . What do you mean?"

She angled toward him, sniffing out a deeper story. She could've been a journalist if acting weren't so deep in her bones. "You heard me. I'm sitting right next to you. Is there something you wanted answered about yourself as well?"

"No." He held her gaze. "This is their story. Imagining if he'd sent the letter. Imagining an answer to his question . . . 'Do I really still love her?' "

"But was he asking that question?"

"I don't know. Maybe. There has to be a reason he never sent the letter."

Chloe scooted down into the couch cushion, propping her bare feet against the table, her bridesmaid's gown flowing over her legs to the deck boards. "Truth is, we never know the how or why of our ancestors' decisions. We only know our present reality."

"Frightening, isn't it? That something I decide today impacts future generations. Beyond my own flesh and blood. This movie, should it have any success, could change my life, thus my descendants'. Should there be any."

"Why wouldn't there be any descendants?" Chloe said. "Don't tell me you're down on love, Jesse Gates."

"I'm not down on love."

Why didn't she believe him? Chloe sat forward. "So, what's for dessert?"

"Dessert? Good question." He finished the crust on his last slice of pizza and gathered the empty box. "When I think of this movie, I picture a guy taking a girl on their first date to see *Bound by Love* because, you know, Super Hero Movie Number Twenty-Five is sold out, and they get to talking, realize they have a lot in common, fall in love . . . For dessert, I have some M&M's left over from last week." Jesse patted his belly. "But I'm trying to get into movie shape."

"He said after a fourth slice of pizza."

"Nobody's perfect."

While Jesse disappeared inside with the pizza box and plates, Chloe moved to the edge of the deck and leaned on the railing. She liked him. A lot. He was fun. Easy to be around. Old soul to old soul, uniting.

"Success." She turned to see Jesse holding up a convenience-store bag of M&M's. He looked cute, wiggling his eyebrows, the collar of his shirt open sans tie, his bare feet thumping over the deck.

"You're the best date, I mean, friend ever."

Jesse reached for her hand and filled her palm with a half dozen M&M's. Chloe popped the first small piece into her mouth and let it melt. Chocolate was good for the soul.

"I don't know anything about our ancestors," she said. "My dad has a crest on his office wall, but he can't tell you anything about it. It's Irish or Welsh, I forget. The colors are yellow and black with the name Hobart underneath."

"Who's Hobart?"

"Our ancestors, I guess. Way, way, way back."

"Funny to think in a hundred years our descendants most likely will not remember us. Unless they have their own Aunt Pat."

Chloe popped another M&M into her mouth. The sweetness of the candy, the salty breeze, and Jesse's company settled into her memories. She would always remember Violet and Dylan's wedding for this.

"Makes you wonder why people work so

hard for immortality. More people have lived on this earth than any of us remember."

"That *is* why people strive for immortality," he said. "They don't want to be among the billions forgotten."

"Not me. I just want to work, have a family, live a —" She stopped, glancing toward the lights of the pier, then back at Jesse. She almost said too much. He was easy to be around, but he didn't need to hear the intimate thoughts of her heart. If they were going to be working together, she needed to forge a professional relationship, not one that included her deepest yearnings.

"Here, I think I've had enough." She handed back the last three M&M's, slapping her hands clean. "So, what kind of acting have you done?"

"Romcoms. Commercials." Jesse tossed the candy in a nearby trash bin. "About ten failed sitcom pilots. I was on the rebirth of the *Dark Shadows* soap for the one year of its life. That paycheck kept food in the fridge and the lights on. My parents finally stopped bugging me about giving up acting and going home."

"So, they don't want a starving actor for a son?"

"They want me to do what I love, but that

doesn't mean they understand. They saw me going another way. A different field." He finished the last drop of his water and tossed the bottle away. "What about you? How was it growing up in Tinseltown as the daughter of Raymond Daschle and Rachel Hayes?"

"Great. Horrible. Especially as an actress. You'd think I'd get extra consideration, a bit of favoritism, but nope. Neither does my sister. We almost have to work harder. Prove ourselves. But then again, when I got your script and fell in love with Esther, I had the ability to call Jeremiah Gonda and ask to read for the part."

He turned to her, arm resting on the flat top of the railing. "You really think it's a good screenplay?"

"I do, Jesse. I've never called a director and asked to read for a part before."

He nodded, his happy, little-boy grin endearing himself to her all the more. Friends. Yes, she would be his friend, but nothing more. She wanted to give her all to the part, not fall in love.

Besides, on-set romances produced so much drama *behind* the camera.

"Come on, let's sit. Watch the stars." Taking her hand, Jesse led her to the sofa.

Chloe curled her legs under her, tucking the hem of her dress around her feet. With a push, Jesse reclined the chair, and a night sky of stars unfurled before them.

"Beautiful," she whispered. "And peaceful."

She lowered her hand to her side, grazing his, an electric pulse running up her arm. With a small jerk, Chloe moved her hand to her abdomen, then carefully, coyly slipped it back down to the cushion.

Jesse pillowed his head with his other hand. "What Hollywood legends walked through your family's front door when you were growing up?"

"Funny . . . no one has ever asked me that before."

"You're kidding."

"No one interviews the actress who dies. Let's see . . . Newman, Redford, Cruise, Smith, Coppola, Ford, Fonda, Sinatra, Reynolds, Reagan."

"Sinatra? Frank or Tina?"

"Frank. But I was young. Didn't really understand who he was. Dad worked with him on his last movie in the eighties. Years later, he ran into him again on a television show, and Frank sorta took Dad under his wing. They became good friends. Sometimes late at night Dad breaks out the old hi-fi and plays some of Frank's original LPs."

Now that her belly was full and the chocolate had worked its magic, she felt silly for her reaction to Ted and Stella's engagement. She said she wasn't jealous. But maybe, just maybe, she was.

"What about you? Why acting? Are your parents in the arts?"

He rolled onto his side, propping up on his elbow, peering down at her. "My parents are lawyers. My brother is techie. An entrepreneur."

"And you were supposed to be a lawyer too?"

"No, I was on the tech side of things with my brother. Science, math, physics, computers."

"A brainiac!" Chloe raised up, propping on her elbow, meeting him eye to eye. "You could be the next Bill Gates. Hey, you even have the same last name." She gasped, touching her fingers to her lips. "Maybe you're Bill Gates's son in disguise."

Jesse laughed, reaching for her hand, lowering it to the cushion but not letting go. "No relation at all. By the way, Bill Gates is still trying to figure out how to be the next Bill Gates." Ambient light from the house touched the side of his face. "I fell into acting on a break from college. It started as . . . as something to do. I never expected to be good at it. Never expected to love it more than math and computers."

"A right *and* left brainer. Look, Mom, I found a unicorn." Chloe dropped to her back again and studied the stars. "Is that what makes you so confident? Being smart? My dad likes confident actors, by the way. In case you ever work with him."

"Thanks for the tip." He sat back, stretching out, raising his arms over his head. "Tell me why it bothered you so much about Stella and Ted."

"Can we not talk about it? I feel silly now."

"I like me some silly now and then."

She swatted at him and sat up, locking her arms about her raised legs. The frills of the cream-colored dress stuck to her warm skin. The cap sleeve slipped from her shoulder, and Jesse reached to put it into place.

"I'm not sure I should tell you."

"You don't have to tell me, Chloe. I'm just curious."

"I said I wasn't jealous, but I am. Not of Ted. Not of Stella. But of what they have, or think they have. Something I can't seem to find for the life of me."

"Love? You can't find love?" Jesse said. "Sounds like a long, lonely life. Better to have loved and lost than to never have loved at all."

"Oh, I've loved and lost. Believe me." She

109

peered at him. "You don't know?"

"Know what?"

"My romantic history? Though, it's anything but romantic."

"Should I?"

"Are you messing with me, Gates? Everyone in the country, Europe, and a small corner of Asia know." She stood, pacing, the ocean air swirling over the deck. "How long have you been in LA?"

"Eight years."

"Then you know. You *have* to. In fact, I think one line of your script is from . . . you know . . . the . . . thing." She hated talking about that video. Wouldn't it be lovely if one person, this one gorgeous, sweet man, did not know?

"If I did, I've forgotten."

She could not deny the innocence and truth in his blue eyes.

"Let's just say I've not had the best luck choosing men. Add my track record to being labeled the queen of the death scene and . . ." She dropped back to the sofa. "I feel cursed at times."

"Cursed?" Jesse slid next to her. "Curses have to have a cause, an agreement. Don't agree with it, Chloe." He touched her chin, turning her face to him. "As for love, you are far too kind and sweet to be alone. Yes,

110

love can be painful, I won't deny it." There was a weight on his confession. "But it has to be worth trying again."

"Are you preaching to me or yourself?"

He grinned, releasing her. "We're not talking about me."

"But we are, aren't we?"

"Maybe. A little."

"If I'm too kind and sweet to be alone, then *you* are too kind and considerate, and yes" — she flicked her hand toward his face — "gorgeous, to be alone. How is it you're not caught already?"

"It's not a matter of being caught. It's a matter of wanting to be caught."

"You're lucky. You're a man. You can choose. Women, even today, have to wait to be chosen. I don't think anyone will want me."

"Ah, Chloe, there are plenty of men who'd disagree with you. Men seek but never find. But trust me, there's a good man out there somewhere, waiting for you."

"If you say so." She got up, returned to the railing, needing the wind to cool her heart. Her skirt fluttered in the breeze and she almost felt free of her fear.

Jesse joined her, saying nothing, yet listening.

"Here's what bothers me," Chloe began,

low, almost to herself. "Marriage is supposed to be this holy and sacred union. At least how I see it. How it was taught to me in parochial school. What I feel in my heart, you know? Yet it's turned into a billion-dollar industry. Everyone wants the big, flashy wedding with all the hoopla, where the bride is princess for a day. But then when the day-to-day settles in and it's work and the newness fades, people just walk away."

"Pretty cynical."

"Sorry, but it's what I've seen."

"So what is it about marriage as an institution that intrigues you?" Jesse angled to see her face. "What do you want, Chloe? True love? Happily ever after?"

"Yes, I do. There. I said it." She slapped her hand on the railing. "I want the fairy tale and the romance, but I also want the day-in-and-day-out. I want to celebrate ten, twenty, fifty years with the man I vowed to love until death parts us. Marriage is the one place where no one can go but you and your spouse. One man. One woman. In a union that has baffled humanity since the beginning. It's a treasure, something to be guarded with every part of your being. You don't let a friend or coworker or, God forbid, a lover into that union. What is it the preacher says? 'What God has joined together, let no one separate.' That's amazing! Joined by God!" Her voice rose with each declaration. Jesse appeared amused and intrigued. "The union is personal, intimate. A place of protection, of service, of bearing one another's burdens." A rush of tears collected in her eyes. "In marriage, you're part of a whole, if that makes sense, and that's what I want. Where the relationship is more than a commitment, it's a covenant. My parents are committed, no one doubts that — but where's their covenant? The ceremony and celebration. That's what I want. It goes beyond love to the very core of being human." She paced back to the chaise and sat, elbows on her knees. "I sound crazy, I know."

She was drained. Poured out. Jesse remained at the deck rail, facing the ocean.

"You might have guessed I've never confessed any of this out loud before. Please don't tell me I'll see my words on the front of a tabloid next week."

Still nothing from him. What was he thinking? Did her confession kill him? Was it too much? Did he shrivel up and die?

She'd have to report a homicide.

*You see, Officer, I simply gave him my thoughts on marriage. Well, he asked! I know*

*. . . his chest just . . . imploded. Who knew?*

When the silence ticked on too long, she peeked over at him. His eyes were on her.

"I thought I killed you there for a second." A lock of her hair dropped from her updo and curled over her eye.

"You didn't kill me." Jesse walked over and sat beside her, then slipped his arm around her waist, pulling her to him. "I was thinking how cool it would be to crawl inside your head and see what you see."

"You'd be terrified, trust me." She shivered, unable to keep her attention fixed on his face. But a warmth emanated from him, and she ached to press her head against his chest.

"Where did you get this vision of marriage?"

She tapped her heart. "Right here."

"Then I hope it happens for you," he said. "Not that this has anything to do with love and marriage, but you're very beautiful, Chloe. Even more, you're sweet and thoughtful, passionate. A lover's lover."

"A lover's lover?"

"Yeah, the kind every hungry heart is searching for." Jesse leaned into her, his gaze roaming her face. She ached for his kiss. But he pulled away. "I-I should get you home."

She stood and started inside, but Jesse caught her by her arm.

When she turned, he met her with a kiss. Soft and sweet, with the slightest measure of affection. Then he inhaled and gripped her against him, and Chloe lost herself in the sensation of his lips searching hers without greed or want. Just . . .

*Love. Yes, hello love. That's precisely how it felt.*

# 8

## HAMILTON

"We can't find him, Hamilton. He may still be inside."

He charged though the church door down the main aisle, the steaming smoke burning his nose and eyes. Ashes twisted up from the floor, and the heat seeped through the soles of his boots.

"Uncle Laurence! Uncle!" He ripped his shirt from his back, wrapping the tail about his face. "Uncle!"

Overhead, the roof continued to burn and the church moaned under the burden, the wooden beams cracking with the heat and showering Hamilton with glowing embers.

"Hamilton, get out of here." Mr. Holliman of the general store clapped a firm, broad hand on his shoulder. "She's going to collapse."

"But Uncle Laurence . . ." Smoke burned

his eyes as the flames roared, mocking his desperation. A beam over the pulpit split and dropped with a resounding crash. "They said he was in the sanctuary."

When he arrived, Aunt Mary was waiting outside among their friends, weeping, calling to her husband.

"Yes . . . but the flames are too much, Hamilton. Do you want your aunt to bury both of her men? It would break her heart."

"She'll thank me not to leave her husband to burn in the rubble." Hamilton pulled free, squinting, fighting to breathe.

The sanctuary was simple. Long and narrow with no side rooms. Uncle Laurence should not be difficult to find.

Cowering as another beam cracked and swung down from the roof, Hamilton pressed forward. *Uncle, where are you?*

"Hamilton! Come out this minute."

One final scan and he resigned himself to retreat, then saw a foot protruding from the left side of the altar.

"He's here, he's here." Hamilton rounded a burning pew and reached down for his uncle's leg. Pressing his shirt against his face, he tried to inhale enough to drag the large man down the side aisle without another breath, but he filled his lungs with smoke.

"Help me!"

Mr. Holliman met him with a kerchief around his face, his store clerk following. As the first beam exploded and the front corner of the church collapsed, Hamilton, Mr. Holliman, and his clerk dragged Uncle Laurence from the church.

Hamilton dropped his shirt to the ground and gasped for air. Soot tainted his skin. His trousers smoldered where tiny embers had burned through the broadcloth.

The townspeople watched, aghast, huddled together, the glow of the fire against their faces.

At his feet lay Uncle Laurence's still, charred body.

"Here . . ." A woman with cool hands handed Hamilton a ladle of water and a damp cloth. "Put the towel over your eyes."

He dropped to the dirt, pouring the water over his face, gripping the cloth in his fist, then raising up, hammering his chest with a roar of grief.

Aunt Mary collapsed in the dust, wailing over her husband.

"Laurence, no, Laurence . . . no, no, no."

Uncle's hands and forearms were burnt black, his face contorted with red skin and seething blisters.

One of the trappers, Burt Newton, tossed

a horse blanket over him as Hamilton slipped his arm around Aunt Mary.

Behind him, a voice boomed, "Is this what you want, Ninety Six? To let the king's men run roughshod over us? Reverend Lightfoot was a man of God. Look what Huck and his dragoons have done."

Hamilton locked onto the one speaking. Captain Irwin. Walking among the stunned, the angry, the weeping, and the trembling.

"We are neighbors and friends. We've aided one another during the sowing and reaping. We've lent bread and money to the poor and sick. Now we are at the mercy of men who show no mercy. We are no longer their brethren." Captain Irwin moved among them. "Who's with us? Who will join the cause of independence? For freedom?" He pointed to the building opposite the town square. "If you are brave enough, and I hope you are, meet me in the tavern."

The captain clapped his hand on Hamilton's shoulder. "Join us. Avenge your uncle's death."

Some of the women knelt by Aunt Mary, grieving with her. Slowly Hamilton stood, his shirt dangling from his hand.

Spitting on the ground, he faced the townspeople. "Captain Irwin is right. This is our town, our land, our colony, and we don't need to be oppressed by a greedy king four thousand miles away."

Esther burst through the crowd, her hair flowing wild over her shoulders, her cheeks red and glowing. Kitch trailed along with her, panic in his eyes. But Hamilton paid her no mind. Any passion, any softness he felt in her presence had died with his uncle.

"If not King George, then it'll be the Continental Congress," a voice called from the crowd. "God save the king!"

The crowd stirred.

"Long live the Declaration!"

Ben Quincy and John Brown stepped forward, their hands resting on the pistols lodged in their belts.

Behind them, the church beams began to crumble. The crowd cried out, backing away.

"For now" — Hamilton turned a slow circle — "can any man lend me his wagon? I must get Aunt Mary and my uncle home."

"Take mine." Jacob Broadway, a saint and a deacon in Uncle's congregation, took Aunt Mary by the arm. "Frank, Burt, help Hamilton with the body."

As they loaded the wagon, the church collapsed. Hamilton's gaze fell on Esther. She took a step toward him, but an arm cinched around her waist. Sir Michael. She struggled, but he whispered in her ear and she submitted, turned, and walked away with her father. Just before disappearing into the throng and the shadows, she turned and raised her hand in condolence to Hamilton.

Of course she must go with her father. He was a Loyalist. The land agent of a powerful and wealthy aristocrat.

"Hamilton, we're ready to go," Jacob said.

He climbed on to the buckboard, his hands, his feet, his heart dull and numb. Across his viewing plane, a line of trappers, hunters, and farmers traipsed toward the tavern.

Aunt Mary clung to him, weak and moaning. "Oh, Hamilton . . . oh, Hamilton."

He slapped the reins, and the wagon jerked forward. As he passed the tavern, Captain John Irwin stood on the side of the road, hat over his heart, his dark eyes pleading with Hamilton to join the fight.

### ESTHER

Was it possible every able-bodied citizen of the upcountry had traveled to Ninety Six to bid Laurence Lightfoot good-bye?

Walking among the mourners toward the cemetery under a dark, heavy sky, passing the church rubble, she knew their world had forever changed.

A sharp cut of wind tugged at the reticule swinging from her gloved hands. Lightning slithered down from a blue-black cloud. Esther tugged her hat over her brow, shrouding her face from the impending rain and obscuring her tears.

Ninety Six seemed empty, lost, without Reverend Lightfoot. He was a good man deserving mercy, not death. She loathed the colony's politics and the hatred it spawned. Men fighting men, brother against brother. For what? Money? Power? Taxes and tea?

Didn't they all want the same? A home, a family, food in their cupboards, and a better life for their children?

Since the church burning, anxiety had settled over Slathersby Hill. For three days and three nights, Father, Isaac, and Kitch sat in watch with a loaded Brown Bess for errant patriots seeking revenge by setting a Loyalist home ablaze.

Lieutenant Twimball had paid a call, offering additional security. Father welcomed him into the library with a slap on the back and a glass of port.

His presence put Esther ill at ease. Despite his uniform, musket, and attentiveness, she saw the devil in his eyes.

But what burdened her heart was her

friendship with Hamilton. She feared its end. How could he trust her when Father welcomed those responsible for his uncle's death?

Her toe caught a rock in the street, and she stumbled forward. Pippa Farthing steadied her, but in truth there wasn't an inch to move. An inch to breathe. So great was the crowd.

At the head of the line, six men carried Reverend Lightfoot to his earthly rest. Behind the coffin, Hamilton, dressed in black, escorted his aunt. How frail she'd grown in the three days since the reverend's death. Every few minutes her sorrowful wail bled into the stormy atmosphere and sent chills through Esther.

Surely the truth was as Reverend Lightfoot preached. "We are not as those without hope. For we believe Jesus died and rose again."

A song rose from among the mourners. "When I survey the wondrous cross . . ." Esther's tears spilled over as she joined the verse.

*What trouble this conflict has wrought.*

The pallbearers stopped at a deep, black hole. Thunder rumbled, and Esther flinched when an angry cloud appeared to drop down to the earth.

Reverend Potts, a blustery man from down Charles Town way, stepped forward, a worn Bible in his hand.

"We are gathered for a sad occasion. Our hearts are filled with sorrow. Our friend, a devoted husband, uncle, and man of the cloth, has met an untimely and cruel death."

Around her, the crowd rustled. Someone shouted, "Here, here."

"What can we do, my friends, in this dark hour?" As if moved by his words, the thunder responded. The mourners oohed and aahed, clustering closer. The reverend cleared his throat and continued. "Forgive, my friends. Pray to God to love your neighbor —"

"Boo! 'Tis folly, I say." Another male voice resounded from deep within the crowd. "If ye want to avenge this innocent man's blood, then join with the Ninety Six Militia and fight our foe. Be ye a coward or be ye brave?"

"Listen to the reverend." Richard Sloan, farmer and father of Esther's friend Maggie, addressed the crowd. "He knows of what he speaks."

"Hush yerself, Sloan. You know *not* of what you speak. Lousy Loyalist."

"My good men." Reverend Potts raised his thick, black book. "Do as you see fit before your Maker, but Loyalist or rebel, you must forgive. We are nothing without it."

Nay, the crowd was restless, stirred up, unwilling to yield to sentiments of forbearance and love. The men began to argue and divide. Tory from Whig.

Esther huddled close to Mrs. Farthing, who, more lost in grief than revenge, whispered prayers for Mrs. Lightfoot.

"We must forgive, yes, but there is no law against resisting our oppressors." This came from John or Jacob Brown. Esther could not tell. "The reverend stood for the cause, for a new nation. America. Why back down now with his blood crying out from the ground?"

"God save the king!"

The men stirred, the rumbling louder, the division deeper. Mr. Farthing collected his wife. "Come, make haste." With their heads down, they escaped down the wide avenue.

Esther stood alone, exposed, the townspeople responding to the reverend with both rebellion and submission.

She moved toward Hamilton, longing to offer her sympathies. Father had not let her out of his sight since the burning. He even thwarted her attempt to send a letter to Quill Farm through Kitch.

She hesitated when Captain Irwin reached

Hamilton first. "Won't you join us? For your uncle's sake?"

Hamilton shook his head, his shoulders slouched under sadness and despair. Esther clutched her reticule to her chest.

"Do what you must," Hamilton said. "As for me, I leave this debate for another hour. Show respect for the dead." He gave the captain his back, giving again his support to his aunt.

Captain Irwin shook his head and conversed with several other men.

Now, perhaps, she could speak with him.

A disembodied voice cried out, "I say fight!"

Captain Irwin and the men whirled around. Esther withdrew into the crowd as men flocked toward the militia leader.

Then a push from behind, and she stumbled forward. More shouting. More men gathering, muskets and pistols in hand, at the cemetery's edge, where the heady stench of charred beams still rose from the death of the church.

Patriots and Loyalists faced off. Friend against friend. Riley Hough, among the patriots, stood against his brother, Eric, who was a Loyalist.

"No, no, this can't be." She spun around, trapped between the two sides.

"Miss Esther." Mrs. Trenwith stood near the churchyard oak. "Move yourself from harm's way."

Suddenly she was on the stormy sea, hovering in the bows of the ship, crying out for Mother, who never came.

The hammering sound of horses rammed against her. Dust swirled up from the thirsty ground as British militia rode through the divided factions.

The snort of a gelding brushed her ear.

Covering her head, she wailed from her belly, "Hamilton!"

A hand yanked on her arm, tripping her sideways. When she looked up, Lieutenant Twimball stood over her.

"Does your father know you are here?" He walked her toward the oak tree. "You have placed yourself in danger. These rebels have no care for our kind."

"Our kind? Do not lump me in with your deeds. *Your* kind has no respect for them either. You killed Reverend Lightfoot."

Lieutenant Twimball bent toward her. "He was not supposed to be at the church."

Esther removed herself from his shadow. "You knew of the scheme? And let it go on?"

"I had orders from Captain Huck. Now, be a nice English girl and stand clear of this brawl." Twimball spun, firing his pistol in the air. "You are gathered unlawfully. By order of Major Ferguson, you must disband immediately."

"Have a care, man." Captain Irwin came forward. "We are burying our friend and neighbor. 'Tis not unlawful to gather for a burying. His widow grieves not twenty yards away."

"Yet I say disband." Twimball kept a steady gaze on Irwin. "Now do as you're bid."

But the captain would not be dissuaded. He paced toward the waiting, braced patriots. "Do you see what he's doing? Wielding authority he does not have. Today it is Mary Lightfoot's husband, but tomorrow it may well be you and yours." He assessed Twimball and the mounted militia. "Reverend? Doesn't Scripture remind us there is a time for war and a time for peace? Well, suffice it to say, thanks to our king and oppressor, we find this to be a time of war." His declaration gripped Esther, and she peered toward Hamilton. "Join the Ninety Six Militia," Irwin said. "Stand up to this tyranny! Take courage, men."

"Captain, are you recruiting in the town square while we observe? 'Tis all but an act of aggression." Twimball slipped his pistol into his holster and retrieved his musket from his waiting horse. "I demand you remove yourselves from the square."

Half the men remaining at the funeral gathered with the captain. The others remained behind, grumbling, hurling insults, casting a tense gaze toward the lieutenant.

They were Loyalists, scared, eager to save their own hides. It was a wonder the wolves had not detected their scent and gathered.

But what of Father? He was a Loyalist. Yet he was brave and kind, a man of honor. Decorated for his valor during the Seven Years' War.

From the tree, she had a clear view of Hamilton. He tipped his hat toward her, his slow, deliberate action a balm to her heart. She understood his intent without words.

*Thank you for being here.*

"Men of Ninety Six." Twimball mounted his horse, riding among those gathering with Captain Irwin. "If you do not join with the Crown, you will face a traitor's death. Isn't the death of your reverend enough of a warning? What more do you need?"

"Don't listen to him, men. He's using tactics of fear and intimidation." Captain Irwin showed no fear. "He's the devil in a red coat."

From the heavens, the clouds responded with a loud clap.

"Enough!" Hamilton left his aunt Mary, barging forward without care between the factions. "Let us have no more of this today. Lieutenant Twimball, with regard to your duties, can you not see your way clear to stand down? You are a stranger here and —"

"I am no stranger to the commands of my major. I cannot stand down when disgruntled enemies of the crown are gathered."

A musket boomed. Feminine screams swam through the air. Masculine commands ordered every man to battle.

Twimball raised his musket. "Fire!"

"No, stop! Stop!" Esther ran forward without pause or consideration, arms flailing, crying out from her heart. "You cannot . . . Stop! At once."

"Esther!" Hamilton. Racing toward her.

"Hamilton!"

Musket fire bandied in the air, but a near, distinct sound that reverberated in her ears caused her to swerve to see Lieutenant Twimball on his mount, musket raised . . .

Crying out, she gripped her shoulder, a fierce burn shooting down her arm and through her torso.

She could not breathe. Above her, the clouds expelled a flash of light, then a raindrop, a heavenly tear, splashed against her face.

   *Hamilton . . .*

# 9

## HAMILTON

He carried her up Slathersby's high, stone steps, drenched from the rain, Esther's blood draining down his hand and soaking his white sleeve. He kicked the door with his booted foot.

"Sir Michael!"

The door swung open, and Sassy stood on the other side. "Lord have mercy, what happened?" Inhaling a throaty gasp, she headed toward the staircase. "Come this way, Mr. Hamilton. Isaac! Bring the doctoring kit. Kitch? Boil some water!"

"Twimball shot her."

Sassy paused on the stairs. "On purpose? Sir Michael! You best come quick." She hurried toward the second floor. "Esther's done been shot. Mr. Hamilton, here, in here, set her on the bed."

For a moment Esther's eyes fluttered

open, then closed, a sorrowful moan in her chest.

"Sassy, what the devil is all the yelling and stomping?" Sir Michael barged into the room. "Lightfoot, what are you doing — Esther!" He shoved Hamilton aside and sat on the edge of his daughter's bed. "What has happened? Who did this?" He whirled to Hamilton, grabbing his coat collar with his big fists. "You? You did this?"

Hamilton inhaled but did not jerk away. "Would I be here if I did?"

"Then who? Which rebel fired upon my daughter?"

Isaac hurried into the room with the medical kit. "Dear Jesus above, help us."

Sassy took the leather pouch from him. "Out! All of you. Let me get her undressed and doctored up. Sir Michael, you know Mr. Hamilton would never hurt our Esther. Now, out!"

Sir Michael released Hamilton and stepped from the room. "I'm sending for Dr. Rocourt."

"He's tending other patients," Hamilton said, his tone low, controlled, denying his brewing ire. "Twimball and his band fired upon Uncle Laurence's funeral procession."

"Never. The British soldiers are gentlemen."

"Ask any man, Sir Michael. Men you've known for years." Hamilton started for the door with a final glance toward Esther. She seemed so weak and pale, a dark stain on her black gown. "Lieutenant Twimball shot her. I saw it with my own eyes."

"Perhaps he was aiming at you? Did you move Esther into harm's way?"

"Perhaps his bullet was meant for me, but I was trying to save her."

"Do you want her to bleed to death?" Sassy shoved them from the room and slammed the door behind them.

Hamilton descended the steps, the terror of Esther being shot mingling with his anger.

"Lightfoot! Do not walk away from me."

The British redcoats were no gentlemen. He knew firsthand what atrocities they could perpetrate, and in thirteen years, not a lick had changed.

Hamilton shoved through the front door. He'd kill Twimball with his bare hands if he ever saw the lieutenant again. The man was a criminal, make no mistake.

"Lightfoot!" Sir Michael maintained his pursuit. "I demand an explanation."

Hamilton's foot slipped on the wet stone, the rain thick, falling fast. He caught himself on the wide, square porch post.

"An explanation? No, you demand your

will. My reason was not to your liking, so you deem me a liar. But upon my word —"

"The word of a Lightfoot is folly."

"— Lieutenant Twimball raised his musket and fired when your daughter was clearly in sight. How loyal are you now, sir?" Hamilton stepped near the man he had loved when he and Esther were younger. The man who had invited him, Uncle Laurence, and Aunt Mary to sit by the fire on winter nights, playing games and drinking cider. "You believe the king's men have the corner on honor? Then you do not know men. For every soldier of honor on your side, there are two on ours. And every man of dishonor fighting the cause? You'll find three or four wearing the king's red, or the green of a dragoon."

"You weave the tale you wish me to believe, Lightfoot. Come, man, fess up. You fired upon my daughter."

"Fire upon her? I'd rather kiss her. I want to marry her." The heat of his ardor branded his countenance. Had he not learned better to guard his words? Now Sir Michael knew the truth and bore the upper hand.

Sir Michael grinned, slow, wicked. "You love my daughter? You want to marry her?"

"Does this come as a surprise to you? I

thought you a keen observer of human nature."

"You speak correctly. I am a keen observer. Why do you think I sent her back to London? Yes, to make her debut to society and be presented in court, but also to be rid of you. She has the makings of a duchess or countess." Sir Michael toyed with his mustache. "She's destined for better stuff than the likes of you."

"Then why did you raise her in the backwoods of South Carolina for over a decade? Why did you allow her to return home? For your own company? Your own selfishness?" Hamilton turned away. "Go. Tend your daughter. If you've any softness in your heart, pray for her."

"You know your uncle and I had a falling out."

"About what, pray tell?" Hamilton paused on the path, under the maple where the rain collected in the leaves. "I'm not privy to the details."

"He's in possession of a tract of land Lord Whatham believes I acquired some time ago, but I did not."

"Did you squander your employer's capital? Is he now demanding an accounting?"

He laughed. "I could be persuaded of a union between you and Esther if you would give me that land."

"Give? Do you see pound sterlings falling from my pockets? Give, nay, but sell . . . Then you must face your employer with your own ill deeds." Hamilton propped one foot on the stone steps. "But what part of Quill Farm could you desire, sir?" If Uncle Laurence had purchased land, he did not tell Hamilton. And he felt sure the poorer Lightfoots purchased no land out from under the richer Longfellows with their Whatham resources.

"Not part, but all. The entire tract you call Quill Farm."

Hamilton laughed. A drop of rain dripped from the edge of a green leaf onto his cheek. "Have you gone mad, sir? Uncle's owned the land for nearly fifteen years."

Sir Michael bristled, his cheeks red, his eyes wide. "Your uncle stole the land out from under me when I was away. I've been trying for fifteen years to acquire it back."

"So your friendship with us was insincere?" Hamilton remained confident, steady, the rain trickling down the back of his collar.

"A man of business must maintain good relations with his neighbors." Sir Michael stepped down toward Hamilton. "I've been patient . . . for far too long. I should've called in his loan six years ago when he first fell ill and couldn't repay his debt."

"I repaid the debt." As Uncle Laurence fell ill, the daily burden of the farm fell to seventeen-year-old Hamilton. "Out of respect for you. Now I see you intended to do us harm."

"I will obtain the land, Hamilton. One way or another."

"The farm is mine and Aunt Mary's now." Hamilton backed away from the house with a tip of his hat. This exchange was over. "Your quarrel, I'm afraid, is with a dead man."

"Then you can forget your affections for my Esther," Sir Michael called after him. "And I blame you, Lightfoot, for her being shot. She'd not have been in town save for you. Keep your distance from her. I say, *keep* your distance."

Hamilton walked on, the rain cooling his rage. Sir Michael was right. He must bear the blame. He had not protected her, nor rushed her to safety when the funeral turned to fighting. He cared only for his own grief.

Now his hands were stained red. With her blood. Twimball and his men would answer to the Almighty, make no mistake, but he would not escape judgment either.

Coming to the road, he paused. To his left, Ninety Six and the tavern where Captain Irwin recruited for the cause.

To his right, Quill Farm, where Uncle Laurence and Aunt Mary had taken him in as their own child. It was a place to think and pray, if he dared. With a sigh, he glanced back at Slathersby Hill, then took the road toward home.

The house was dark and quiet. Sorrow filled the emptiness.

"Aunt Mary?"

He ran upstairs two at a time. She'd not yet returned home. Back down in the kitchen, Hamilton filled the wash basin with cold water from the well, then stripped off his shirt. With soap scooped from the tub, he scrubbed his hands, his face and neck, his arms, then his hair. He must . . . must . . . must wash away the sorrow and bloody stain of the day.

Memories from his childhood surfaced. Scenes of his pa's quarrel with an arrogant Englishman in a red coat.

Snapping a towel from the rod, he dried off and paced, echoes of his conversation with Sir Michael resounding.

Was everyone he held most dear to be killed? Wounded? Was he cursed in some manner? First Papa by a bayonet, then Mama and little sister, Betsy, by a fire. And Uncle Laurence, also by a fire. Now Esther, shot, bleeding.

He sat at the kitchen table. "Will you forever chase me, death? What must I do to escape your tendrils?"

Hearing a sound outside, he jolted to his feet to find young James Carter standing in the lean-to with wide, blue eyes.

"There's a meeting at the tavern. My pa sent me to fetch you."

"What for?"

"Don't know, sir." With that, the boy was gone, the rhythm of his pony racing down the muddy road leaving a heavy echo in the wind.

Propped against the door, Hamilton stared toward the barn. If he had any gumption, any energy, he'd saddle Tilly and get to it. But his body felt like lead, as if a chain of despair anchored him to something he could not see nor feel.

"I see they sent the Carter boy for you." Aunt Mary entered the kitchen, her face ashen, her dress soaked and clinging to her frail frame. Her silver and gold hair fell from its pins and curled about her face. Mud clung to the hem of her skirt.

"They did, but I won't go." Hamilton

helped her to her chair. "How do you fare?"

"He's gone, Hamilton." Circles of grief rimmed her eyes. She tried to smile, but there was no truth in it. "I cannot remember a time without him." She rose up, taking a meat pie from the larder. "We were as you and Esther, friends from childhood."

"You don't have to prepare a meal. You've just laid your husband to rest."

"We must eat. Going hungry will not bring him back. I did not feed the mourners. So I must feed my nephew." She pressed her hand to his cheek. "You should go to the tavern."

He recognized the shadows in her eyes. He saw the same darkness whenever he peered into the looking glass.

"I won't go with them." His confession rang familiar, but not so true. Was he merely being stubborn? Choosing passivity from a child's perspective and not a man's? Was he giving due respect to the cause? But could he . . . fight with honor?

"Do you stay away from the war because of your pa? And now your uncle? They would want you to fight. Laurence was just saying he intended to speak to you about going along with Irwin and the militia. He was, as your pa, an ardent patriot."

"How can I go? Leave you, a widow,

alone? Who will tend the chores and —"

"Excuses, my boy. I'm strong and able. I have Ox and Moses. They're too old to fight and they have their freedom, such as it is." The mulatto brothers had a home down by the creek, their manumission papers framed and hung over the fireplace. "Mrs. Reed will come and assist me. I'll not be alone."

"You sound as if you want me to go."

"Are you to sit by and watch your friends and neighbors take up arms, fight for you and me?"

"I've taken up arms before."

"You were a boy. Defending your family." Aunt Mary floured her work table and reached for the sourdough jar, her voice growing stronger, passionate. "Now you are a man, and you must defend all families. You must defend your nation. The war is no longer only in Massachusetts and Virginia. It's here, in our backyard, in our fields."

"I fear I'll only kill for revenge."

"Seek the Almighty. He will teach you about humility and honor. Even in war."

"And let God judge between me and the men slain by my bullets?" He left the kitchen and crossed to the parlor.

"Then you're going?" she said, wiping her hands on her apron. "I'll fetch you a clean shirt."

At the gun rack, Hamilton took down his pa's pistol and Uncle Laurence's Brown Bess, along with his own pistol and rifle. Collecting his pouch of powder and box of bullets, he addressed Aunt Mary one final time.

"What will you do if I get myself killed?"

"Do what we all must do every day. Trust in the Almighty."

He found Captain Irwin in the tavern owner's private room, huddled together with old and new recruits.

Ben Quincey stood when Hamilton entered. "At last."

One by one, each man stood, greeting him with applause. Captain Irwin welcomed him with a somber handshake. "Come, meet the men of the Upper Ninety Six Militia."

# 10

## JESSE

The kiss lingered. Saying good-bye to a friend never tasted so good. Breaking away, Jesse studied Chloe's expression, the emotion in her eyes and on her cheeks.

Did she feel what he felt? Something old. Something new. Already he wanted more. Not just a kiss, though he'd invite her lips to his any time, but he wanted the woman beneath the kiss.

Her thoughts, her feelings, her likes and dislikes. He wanted to know the reason for the quizzical glint in her green eyes. And the source of the smirk on her lips.

He turned toward the deck doors. "It's getting late."

She nodded, shoving a lock of hair from her face, a slight breathless heave in her breasts. "Yes, right. I feel like I've been trying to leave forever."

"I'll drive you." Jesse reached for her clutch on the glass end table.

"You don't need to drive me." She pulled her phone from the small, beaded bag. "I'll call for a car."

"Car? No, Chloe, I'll drive you."

"Dad has a service. It's not a problem. Hello, Chloe Daschle, number 413. Jesse, what's the address?"

He repeated the house number, waiting for her to hang up. A chivalrous man would drive her. He wanted to be chivalrous. Perhaps needed to be. And he must start somewhere. With someone.

"It'll be here in a few minutes." She stepped around him toward the door, and it took every ounce of Jesse's restraint not to scoop her in his arms and carry her inside.

"Thank you," she said. "For everything. For rescuing this crazy bridesmaid. For making tonight fun. For the pizza and washing the pie from my face."

"You didn't have pie on your face." He took her hand, leading her to the deck railing. "We can watch for the car from up here. Until then, we gaze at the stars. At least the ones we can see between the lights."

"My first role ever was as a star." Chloe propped her arms on the railing, leaning into the breeze. "Ironic, huh? I was the shin-

145

ing light over Bethlehem in my kindergarten play. Let me tell you, I rehearsed and rehearsed. Asked my mother about method acting, and on opening night I beamed with all my might."

"A star was born."

"A star was *not* born, but a five-year-old was bit by the acting bug. What about you, techie-turned-actor?"

"My first acting gig was in college. A friend wrote a script for a class and decided to try his hand at filming, directing. He saw his movie as the next *Napoleon Dynamite.* I played the lead — a goofy college kid trying to cheat his way through MIT. It was horrible. I was horrible."

"Were you? A goofy college kid trying to cheat his way through MIT?"

"Not exactly."

"Ah, so you had to really act."

"Yes, but I knew more about turning ones and zeros into pretty pictures on a screen than how to act. The whole thing was a cliché. A conglomeration of *Napoleon Dynamite,* Shakespeare, *Ferris Bueller,* Sir Arthur Conan Doyle, the Muppets, and I think *Smokey and the Bandit.*"

"Oh, now I have to see this movie." She tossed her head back, laughing. "Surely you have a copy."

"I burned it." Jesse slapped his hand to his chest. "Please . . . change the subject. This is giving me a panic attack."

"What's the name of it?"

He laughed. "Nothing doing."

"So it's online somewhere?"

"Probably."

She turned to him. "Tell me, Mr. Gates, can you find things . . . online . . . like, say, a video, and remove it?"

"If I could, I know for certain that movie would be vaporized."

"Then you can't."

He pointed up. "See the stars? So many, and the light shining for billions of miles."

"Yeah?"

"You can't capture the light of the stars, and sadly, you can't completely remove a video shared on the Internet." He peered at her. "Especially if you're famous."

"Famous? Who said anything about being famous? I'm asking for a friend."

"There are laws, you know, to prevent such things."

"She knows."

"But they didn't help?"

"Not entirely."

"She could sue the offending party."

Chloe shivered. "She doesn't want the publicity."

"How long has your, um, friend, been in this situation?"

She shrugged. "A few years. Her situation sort of resolved itself, but every once in a while . . . Oh, there's the car." She gripped his hands. "Thanks again for tonight, Jesse."

"More than my pleasure." He walked her down to where the car's driver waited by the passenger door. "Chloe, your shoes." Jesse opened his truck, reaching in for the pink stilettos.

"Right." Her hand brushed his as she hooked her fingers through the straps. Their eyes met. "Night."

"Night." Hands in his pockets, he watched her slip into the backseat. When she rolled down the window, he stepped to the edge of the drive.

"I had a good time."

"Me too."

As the taillights disappeared around the bend, Jesse jogged across the road to the beach, toward the song of the waves, the essence of Chloe Daschle resting on him. Maybe, just maybe, he was finally beginning to heal.

Shouting resounded from the library below. Stirring, Esther tried to push up in the bed, but the pain cutting across her shoulder forced her back to her pillows.

"Father? Sassy?"

Sassy appeared at her bedside. "You're awake. Thank the Lord. I'll get you some broth. Dr. Rocourt done been here and said to keep your arm still."

The dimly lit room was warm. Too warm. Esther's nightdress clung to her damp body, and the blankets were tucked too tightly about her legs. At the window, a slight touch of daylight crept around the edge of the drawn draperies.

Voices carried up from the library again.

". . . that's preposterous. They fired . . . us. My word . . ."

"Good people . . . Loyalists . . . the Crown . . . my daughter among them."

"Rebels . . . not to be trusted."

"Who fired . . . daughter?"

". . . I saw him . . . my own eyes."

". . . hold you responsible . . ."

Footsteps hammered across the floor. The front door slammed.

"Who is with Father?" Esther tried to push upright again. "Please, Sassy, open a window. And blow out these candles." Tiny flames flickered from nearly every corner of the room and from every surface. "Am I a loaf of bread to be baked in the oven?"

"Your father feared you'd catch a summer cold. He ordered the candles and blankets." Sassy opened the draperies and shoved up the sash.

"Who is quarreling with Father?"

"Lieutenant Twimball."

"Lieutenant Twimball." A blurry memory of him swept across Esther's conscious. Yes, the funeral. The fight. "Th-there was a skirmish in town."

"Three days ago."

Esther pressed her hand to her shoulder. "I-I was shot."

Sassy finished blowing out the candles and adjusted Esther's bedding. "Mr. Lightfoot say Lieutenant Twimball what done it. But ol' Twimball insists Lightfoot took cover behind you."

"Hamilton would do no such thing. Nor cause me any kind of harm." A thin, June breeze drove the heat from the room and the cobwebs from Esther's senses. Her shoulder and back throbbed something fierce.

"That's what I says." Sassy offered Esther a cup of water. "But no one is asking my

opinion. Twimball came to accuse Lightfoot, but your father gave him the dickens
about there being a fight in town in the first
place. At a funeral, of all things." Sassy
checked Esther's bandage. "You'll need a
changing soon."

"Has he been to see me? Hamilton?" Esther kicked at the blankets, freeing her legs,
a restlessness trapped in her bones. "Sassy,
I'm perspiring through my gown. May I
have a clean one?"

"You perspiring because you got hit with
a bullet. Don't worry, I got it out. Dr. Rocourt say I'd make a fine surgeon." Sassy
ladled more water into the cup. "Imagine
me, a colored woman, cutting on folks."

Esther sipped the water, fractured images
floating across her mind.

Reverend Lightfoot's funeral. The *click-
slap* of musket fire. The burning scent of
gunpowder. Running foolishly into the
center of it all. Hamilton calling her name.
The jolt and burn of a musket ball ripping
through her.

"I need to speak with Father." Esther
handed Sassy her cup, kicking her legs over
the side of the bed.

"Hold on there, young lady." Sassy gently
pushed her back. "You ain't going no-
wheres. You're confined to your bed until

the fever is broke. I'll send Sir Michael to see you." She plumped the pillows and spread a sheet over Esther's thin gown. "I'll bring up the broth. You need your nourishment."

When Sassy had gone, Esther scooted out of bed to go to the window but found she was too weak to stand. Purple and blue spots floated before her eyes, and she reached for the bed as she collapsed.

"Esther, what are you doing up?" Father entered with the fragrance of pipe tobacco and gently righted her against her pillows.

"I wanted to see outside." Esther closed her eyes, drawing a deep breath, the grip in her shoulder running all the way to her toes.

"My dear, you will have plenty of time to see the out-of-doors. First you must recover." Father pulled a chair forward, then sat beside her bed with his pipe anchored on the edge of his lips. "My darling, what a fright you have given me." He cupped his hand under hers. "What would I do without you?"

"I'm still here." She searched his face, absorbing the devotion she saw there. "No need to look so worried. I heard you argue with Lieutenant Twimball."

"He was careless."

"He shot me, Father."

"Did you see him? He claims Lightfoot played the coward and hid behind you."

"I heard a shot, turned, and before my eyes, Twimball aimed his musket at me. Hamilton came to my rescue." She had a faint memory of him speaking to her, lifting her from the ground.

"Don't think on it, love. Just rest. We can sort out the matter when you are well."

"But you are angry with Hamilton."

"I'm angry with all the rebel rabble."

"What has happened between us and the Lightfoots? Can we not make amends?"

"Here we are," Sassy said as she entered with a tray. "Did you tell her, Sir Michael, it were Mr. Lightfoot what done brought her home?" She settled the tray over Esther's legs. "Carried you all the way in his arms, he did. Like a real hero."

"Sassy, please, you paint too bright a picture of the young man," Father said.

Esther tried in earnest to sit up. "Yes, he carried me. I remember."

"But now you are home, safe with me." Father thumped his chest. "Father, daughter — the best of friends. Stay close to me, my girl, and my Brown Bess shall take care of anyone who tries to bring you harm." Father's eyes glistened. "I may be too old for this war, but not to be your warrior."

"Father, of course you shall always be my warrior." Esther hesitated, then said, "But please, if Hamilton comes, may I see him? He did rescue me."

Father drew back and lit his pipe, drawing deep, loud puffs. " 'Tis not a conversation for this hour. You must eat and rest. You lost a great deal of blood, and we must see to your recovery." He kissed her forehead. "I've work to attend."

"Father?" He turned at the door. "What has happened? You spend hours upon hours in the library bent over your ledgers, writing letters. Has something gone amiss?"

"Just the business of owning property and business ventures. Do not concern yourself at all —"

"You appear tired. Look in the glass. The crease between your eyes has deepened. You need a holiday, Father. A rest. It will do you good. Perhaps a week in Charles Town —"

"What will do me good is to work and see you on your feet again. Now, eat and I'll come in to say good night."

Esther finished her broth as Sassy entered to change her bandage. "If Hamilton comes, let him in, Sassy."

"Don't know about letting him in." She pulled a slip of folded stationery from her pocket. "But I can certainly pass this along."

# 11

## CHLOE

Dressed in a sundress and flip-flops, her hair in a loose braid, Chloe descended the stairs from her bedroom into her apartment's small kitchen. She poured a glass of tomato juice and wandered to the bay window overlooking the back lawn.

She'd lost her mind. Two weeks after the wedding she still chided herself for revealing so much to Jesse.

First of all, she didn't know him. Second of all, she didn't know him! Had she not learned her lesson? How many men must betray her trust for her to realize love and all its happiness may never be bound for her?

She'd tried and failed. Wasn't the definition of crazy — madness — to keep doing the same thing over and over?

She was halfway home from his beach

house when she realized he hadn't asked for her number. She considered it a break in her cycle of infatuation, crushes, love, and heartbreak.

They hit it off. They kissed. End of story. Besides, considering her romantic track record — publicly documented, thanks to her parents' fame and her stupidity — a romance with a fellow cast member would be in bad form.

Such liaisons rarely ended well, and someone usually got hurt. Usually Chloe.

Guests would be arriving soon. Every Saturday, the Daschles held a brunch — 10:00 a.m. to noonish. Open door. Come as you can.

Since she could remember, Saturdays were fun, filled with surprises. Everyone from legendary actors to the lowest crew member, writers, singers, studio heads, stylists, photographers, neighbors, senators, athletes, and grocery store clerks had walked through the Daschles' front door.

Kate met Rob, a British actor, at one of these brunches. He was in LA with Clive Boston on a promotional junket. Clive walked in with him, and Kate was a goner.

Love. Would it one day walk through the front door for her? She didn't mean to be so focused on it. After all, twenty-nine wasn't ancient, but ever since she could remember, she had a sense of destiny concerning the matter of love and marriage. Her own efforts to fulfill her desires had been disastrous.

On the edge of her windowed view, Chloe watched the gardener walk the perimeter of the pool, netting a scattering of leaves from the water's surface.

From under the lanai, the maid hurried toward the guesthouse gripping a stack of linens.

Mr. Crumbly must be returning. Dad's old friend from high school, a missionary, lived in the guesthouse when he was stateside.

Second only to Smitty, who introduced her to faith, Mr. Crumbly had the greatest impact on Chloe's spiritual journey.

"Tell you what, just open your Bible," he once challenged her. "Read and pray. You'll find treasure. Trust me. Your heart will change."

Humble and simple, he made her see God was accessible. Even eager to engage her. She was just so human in her efforts. Weak. Shamed. Guilty. How could God love her?

A squawk came over the intercom, an old tool that Mom insisted on using.

"Chloe, Kate and Rob are here. Aren't

you coming to brunch?"

She downed her tomato juice and hit the talk button. "On my way." It was 10:01, and Mom was worried she wouldn't be there. Like, when had she ever missed? Only if she was on set somewhere.

Despite the fact her parents never married with the hoopla and the vows, they were intense about family.

As she left her apartment and crossed the small patch of yard separating her from the main residence, she saw Dad in the guest-house driveway talking to a short, lean man with a mop of black hair.

Chloe paused and leaned for a closer look, squinting through the midmorning California sun. Smitty?

"Hey, there you are." Chloe's sister, Kate, met her by the lanai furniture. "Rob and I wondered if you wanted to go to dinner later. We have —"

"Maybe. Who is Dad talking to?"

"Don't know. Listen, Rob has a friend visiting from —"

"Oh no you don't." Chloe brushed past her sister, sniffing out their cook Glenda's crusted French toast.

"No I don't what? We just want an even number at dinner."

"Ha!" Chloe greeted her father's assistant,

Becky, with a light kiss on the cheek. "Do you think I'm stupid, Kate? It's a fix-up, and don't you dare deny it."

"Okay, fine, but he's a nice guy. Gorgeous." Kate collected a plate and started down the buffet line behind Chloe. "About as gorgeous as that man you were with at the wedding. Who was that? Rob, Glenda made her French toast."

"He's the screenwriter of *Bound by Love.*"

"The new movie you're doing? So it's a done deal? Rob, Chloe's going to play a character who lives."

Rob piled French toast onto his plate. "Well done, love."

"I haven't signed the contract yet, but Chip is working on it." Chloe snatched a thick slice of hickory-smoked bacon. Glenda purchased it from a farmer near Bakersfield. "Kate, do you think I'm cursed?"

"Are you crazy? No. I don't believe in curses."

"But you can't deny something goes wrong with nearly all of my films. My character dies and if not, then the film dies."

"You've just had a string of . . . interesting luck."

"Cursed." Chloe soaked her French toast — and what the heck, her bacon — in syrup. She didn't believe she was cursed.

Not really. She only felt like it at times. Didn't her faith challenge her to believe otherwise?

"Chloe." Dad cut in the buffet line, kissing her cheek. "Are you excited about your new venture?"

"Who were you talking to outside? Is Mr. Crumbly returning?"

"Raymond!"

Chloe peeked toward the door to see Claude Durance walking across the dining room, around the long, loaded table, arms wide.

"Claude!" Dad laughed and slipped around Chloe to embrace his old friend. "Why didn't you call, say you were coming? What brings you to town?"

"Movie magic, of course."

Chloe grinned. Like boys those two were, talking about movies.

"Your dad loves when Claude comes to town," Mom said, nothing but an egg and fruit on her plate. "We won't see either of them the rest of the day. So, you're in Jer's movie. So proud of you, darling."

"Fingers crossed. Once I sign the deal I'll feel better, but Mom, I think it has a real chance."

"And your character lives! At last, justice." Mom hated Chloe's track record nearly as much as she did.

"What did you make of Stella and Ted's engagement?" Mom rolled her eyes, walking with Chloe to the lanai where her friend Nicolette Carson waited with a tall glass of juice. "Her mother was shocked. She didn't think Stella was all that into Ted. Hello, Nicky, we've missed you around here."

"I-I think it's great." Chloe sat beside her mom, glancing to where Dad had talked with the man who looked like Smitty.

"Mom," Kate said, dropping down next to Chloe. "Tell Chloe to go out to dinner tonight with Rob and me. His friend is here from England and —"

"You've got to be kidding me," Chloe said, cutting her French toast and mopping up a bunch of syrup. She'd regret this later but for now, yum. "You're telling Mom on me?"

"Chloe, why don't you go?" Mom delicately ate her scoop of eggs. "You should . . . It's been —"

"Mom . . . please . . . I know how long it's been. But I don't want to be set up, okay?"

"You're the only girl I know who wants *true* love, then thumbs her nose at any chance."

"Thumbs her nose? How am I thumbing my nose? Haven't you seen me crash and burn in every one of my relationships?" Chloe stabbed at her French toast, her fork punishing Mom's china plate. "And just how does someone thumb their nose anyway?"

"Okay, fine, then don't go," Kate said. "You know this sacred thing you have about 'true love,' whatever that means, doesn't have to apply to every human on the planet. You could go just to have fun."

"I could, but it applies whenever and however I want. And just because you never believed in true love and still found Rob doesn't make you an expert on —"

"All right, girls," Mom said with her gentle rebuke. "Nicky didn't come here to see you argue."

"Go on, this is inspiring me." Nicolette twisted the cap from her bottled water. "My next film is about sisters. So, Chloe, you have a rule about true love?"

"*Rule* is a strong word. I just believe . . . that there is someone, *one* someone, for me."

"Really?" Nicolette sat forward with a sly grin. "How's that working for you?"

"Exactly!" Kate flipped her hand toward Chloe, nose in the air. "It's not working. Never has. But still, she holds out hope. She's made a disaster of her love life trying to find 'the one.' " Big sister stuffed a bite of French toast into her mouth. "I'd die if I had to go through what she —"

"Kate." This time Mom used her Mother voice, and Kate shushed instantly.

"Chloe, take heart. I've been there, done that. Even worse." Nicolette arched her brow. "Be glad you didn't go down my dark road." The megastar had endured a sex-tape scandal right after she broke into film. "You'll live. And, darling" — she pressed her hand on Chloe's — "you will find true love because, well, I can see in your eyes you want it. Trust karma or fate, but —"

"God?"

"Yes, if you wish. Are you religious?"

So the conversation went, bantering over religion, movies, love, and dogs. Yes, Nicolette had temporarily given up romance after a nasty breakup with a screenwriter named Holt Armstrong.

"I bought a dog instead. Cutest thing ever."

"There you go, Chloe, get a dog." Kate, for one final dig.

Chloe mopped up the last of the syrup with her bacon and headed to the kitchen. Was she foolish to still hope for true love? The one? She'd seen examples of it in her life, but perhaps they really were the anomalies. Could love merely be "the luck of the draw"?

She set her dish in the sink and stared out the window toward the guesthouse. As much as she tried to dislodge the longing in her heart, it remained.

Since her childhood, she'd known she was destined for a special love. A voice whispered to her heart, *Wait.*

Yet in her youth she ignored it. Dismissed it. And the evidence of her folly lived in her soul and on the Internet.

Now she'd changed her ways. She determined to wait. Listen. Trust. And not surrender so easily to the charm and kisses of a geek turned actor named Jesse Gates.

## HAMILTON

A week had passed since he had delivered a note to Slathersby Hill. He'd found Kitch in the field and pleaded with him to carry it to Esther.

*How do you fair? I pray all is well and you are healing. Send word by Kitch if you can. Hamilton*

Perhaps her silence proved his scheme had not succeeded. Did she believe he'd shot her? Had Sir Michael convinced her of a lie?

At his desk, the candle flickered low as his quill hovered over a pristine sheet of paper. A spot of dark ink dropped to the corner of the page. But he refused to start over. Let him write what he must, then copy it with his neatest hand.

Despite the hours of his youth spent in the fields, Ma, then Aunt Mary, insisted he study. Nightly by the fire he'd work his figures, read of biology and science, and practice his penmanship.

*My dearest Esther,*

Hamilton rested his forehead in his hand, staring at the page, a thousand words racing through his mind. Then, at once, there were none at all.

She wanted a love letter. A request he had every desire to fulfill, but how? With what words? He raised the desk's top and removed the book of Shakespeare sonnets, then flipped through the pages.

Such eloquence he did not possess. The letter he sent to Slathersby via Kitch was succinct, saying no more and no less than required.

In truth, he dared not write more. What if Kitch chose to read it? Or hand it to Sir Michael instead of Esther?

*My dearest Esther,*

Hamilton replaced the quill and shoved

away from the desk. Gazing out the window toward the night sky, the stars on glorious display, he must figure a way to see her, to speak rather than write, tell her of his plans, reassure her of his affections. After all, her father now knew of his intentions

Confessing his love with his lips did not concern him. But to write of such things with pen and paper, well, he felt rather silly. Vulnerable.

Rumors raced about Ninety Six that he'd shot Esther. A notion only the wicked Loyalists believed. Yet she lay wounded in her father's house because she had tried to save him.

In his quiet moments, Hamilton did not blame Sir Michael for his father's anger. But if he would only listen . . .

A light knock against his door startled him.

"Still awake, I see." Aunt Mary peeked inside, dressed for bed, her long braid falling over her shoulder.

"Taking care of a few details." Hamilton stood beside his desk, obscuring his letter.

"You leave in the morning?"

"At first light."

Her eyes welled up, and her weak smile left him cold and ashamed. Could he really go to war while his aunt needed him?

"Aunt Mary, perhaps I should delay —"

"Don't worry, my boy, I'm made of hearty stock. Mrs. Reed will come every day, and Ox and Moses are nearby. If I whistle, they will hear me."

"I'll only be gone three months, then home in time for the harvest."

"Three months." She leaned against the plastered wall. Uncle Laurence spent the better part of twenty years fixing up their home, honoring his promise to build her a "palace" if she left Virginia for the wilderness of South Carolina. "Is that enough time to excise your vengeance?"

"Vengeance?" He reclined against the side of the desk with a sigh. "Nay, I fight for the Cause. Captain Irwin brought me round to his way of thinking."

"Then your pa and uncle will be proud."

"Esther will not."

"Hamilton, can I give you some advice? Do not be distracted by things you cannot change. She is a lady of noble breeding."

"She was raised not two miles from here."

"I'm surprised she returned from her society debut in London."

"Perhaps she loves me."

Aunt Mary crossed the room to embrace him. "Guard your heart. 'Tis all I ask." She retrieved a folded document from her robe pocket. "This fell from Laurence's Bible when I opened it this evening for my reading."

Hamilton reached for it. A copy of the Declaration.

*When in the Course of human events . . .*

"I shall treasure it." Hamilton tucked the document inside his haversack. On the floor by the door, he'd readied his canteen and cartridge box along with his rifle and musket, bedroll, and paper and pencil to send word home when the opportunity presented itself.

To write to Esther, should words fail him this evening.

"I am proud of you." Aunt Mary brushed her hands over his shoulders, then stepped back, wiping her eyes. "Though, dare I remind you, you are all I have left in this world. No children of my own. No parents. No husband." Her tears glistened in the candlelight. "I love you more than if I'd given you life."

"You have been good to me, Aunt Mary. Became my mother when I had none." He kissed her cheek. "I will return to you, I promise."

"I will cover you in my prayers. This conflict has robbed us both. But it is just a course in the vastness of human events. It will end, and peace will come. Fight in a time of war as the man you want to be in a time of peace."

Hamilton nodded, tucking away her words of wisdom. "I will fight with honor. You've my pledge."

She turned for the door, then paused. "Oh, I found the blade given to your great-grandfather during Queen Anne's War. Laurence had hidden it away in his trunk. I believe he put it there ages ago, hiding it from your pa."

Hamilton laughed. "On that score, you can be sure."

"I put it on the kitchen table for you."

When she'd gone, Hamilton returned to his letter, but his inspiration had dissipated.

Blowing out his candle, he stretched on his bed, contemplating the days ahead. Could he fight with honor? Not seeking to avenge his pa or uncle or even Esther?

An edge of moonlight fell over his writing table and his empty letter. Restless, he slipped down the stairs in his stocking feet and out the front door, the night outside similar to the night within.

In time the sun would rise, bringing the dawn. But would he ever be in the light? Did true light even exist?

Uncle Laurence would say yes. In the

form of the Savior, but —

Hamilton tensed at the sound of an approaching rider. As it drew nearer, he moved into the shadows of the porch, his back pressed against the side of the house, and wished for the dagger lying on the kitchen table.

At the gate, a large gelding walked through a slip of moonlight, the rider slumping forward.

"Who goes there?" Hamilton squinted, his blood pulsing. "Declare yourself. Friend or foe?"

The rider tumbled from the tall, bay steed onto the ground.

He leaped over the steps, racing to the wounded, and inhaled a familiar perfume mingling with the dew of the dust.

"Esther!" He collected her in his arms and carried her inside, lowering her to Aunt Mary's settee.

He lit a lamp, then spread a wool coverlet over her shivering frame. Perspiration beaded along her forehead under the free wisps of her burnished hair.

"Hamilton," she said, raising her hand to his blouse. "I have to tell you —"

"Shh, rest. Let me draw you a cup of water." In the kitchen he fumbled in the dark for a clean cup, then drew water from the bucket by the stove. "Here, love, drink." He raised her head and tipped the cup to her lips.

Eyes closed, her breath shallow, Esther drank until satisfied. Then she collapsed against the settee. Hamilton cushioned her head with a pillow and brushed the strands of loose hair from her face. Her skin blazed with fever.

"I must get you home." She was so pale, so delicate. Blood stained the edge of her shawl, and when he eased it back, he saw her gown was also stained. "Your wound has broken open." He glanced at the stairs. Should he wake Aunt Mary?

But a firm fist gripped his blouse collar. "I must . . . tell you . . . something."

"Esther, what is so important that you risked your health coming here? In the night? I must return you to your father's care."

"Father, Twimball, they say you pistol-shot me, but I know . . ." Her grip tightened. "You did not."

" 'Twas Twimball. Taking aim at me. I was trying to save you."

"Father refuses to believe it. He's scared, Hamilton. Something in his letters from Lord Whatham. But you must forgive him. He . . . he . . . tries to be brave, but he is an ordinary man."

"He has my forgiveness, but his anger toward us is unfounded. He claims Uncle Laurence stole Quill Farm from him while he was away. Fifteen years ago."

"You must have misunderstood. Father would never . . . but he so wants to please Lord Whatham." Her words barely rose above a whisper. "Increase his holdings . . ."

"To be sure, but at our expense?" Hamilton clasped her hand in his. "I forgive him whatever obligation he has to his employer but not that he sides with the Tories over the Lightfoots. Now, I must carry you home."

"Come to Slathersby Hill tomorrow. I will beg him to —"

"I cannot." Hamilton sat back on his heels, releasing her hand. "I leave with the Upper Ninety Six in the morning."

Esther opened her eyes and struggled to sit up. "You joined the militia?"

"I could sit by no longer."

"Then I must . . . tell you . . ." She pushed into a sitting position.

"Whatever it is, Esther, it can keep until I return in three months' time."

"I . . . love . . . you." The lamplight flickered against her slight smile, illuminating her eyes. Despite her weakness and pain, they were blue and clear. "I could not wait any longer to tell you. And to say I do not believe you fired upon me."

On his knees, he cupped her face in his hands. "You love me? Are you sure? I'm nothing like the men you met at court or during the London season."

"I steal away from my father, ride into the night, tearing open my wound, and you question me?"

He rested his forehead to hers. "My girl, my brave girl."

"You are not like the men . . . of London . . . and they . . . are not like you."

He brushed his hand over her hair. "Yet I am a coward compared to you."

"No, no, you are so brave. How proud I am of you."

"I avoided your father, not wanting to anger him. Sent a line to you through Kitch rather than deliver it myself. Yet you make a great effort to assure me of your love and loyalty."

She slipped her strong hand about his neck. "Then will you have the courage to speak to me of your heart?"

Hamilton brushed his thumb over her cheeks, gently wrapping her in his arms, at last touching his lips to hers.

He meant for the kiss to last only a moment, but when she pressed her good hand against his neck, he kissed her as a man in love. Hungry. Eager. Willing.

Above them, a door opened and closed. "Hamilton?"

He broke away, rising to his feet, peering toward the stairs. "Aunt Mary, are you awake?"

"I heard voices."

He crossed over to the staircase. "Esther Longfellow rode over. I'm afraid she's aggravated her wound. Can you help us?"

"Mercy. Esther?" Aunt Mary descended the stairs with vigor. "Let me get my doctoring kit." The candle in her hand cast a long, thin shadow over the front room as she passed through. "What possessed ye to come out in the middle of the night, my girl?"

She shivered, unable to answer.

Hamilton slipped his hand into hers. "To assure me she knew I was not the one aiming a pistol at her."

"I love you," she whispered again, reaching for his hand.

Hamilton bent toward her ear about to confess the same when Aunt Mary shoved him aside. "Hamilton, light the rest of the candles. My eyes aren't what they used to be. I've clean bandages, but we should get you home. Sassy's doctoring is far superior to mine."

Hamilton waited in the kitchen while Aunt Mary tended Esther's shoulder. She loved him. How simple. How beautiful. All the while he sought to be eloquent — nay, bombastic — but she riveted his heart with a plain and direct, "I love you."

He was loved. He loved in return. Oh, what a man could accomplish when empowered by such knowledge.

He'd forgive Sir Michael. Lord above, he might even forgive Twimball and every other redcoat.

Aunt Mary returned to the kitchen with a basin of bloody water. "But be gentle. Her wound is still so tender. I couldn't tell, but it might be infected."

"I'll hitch up the cart to drive her home."

Aunt Mary caught his arm. "Mind yourself. Sir Michael isn't of a mind to show forbearance and goodwill toward us. If he sees you —"

"Did you know about the farm? That Uncle bought the land while Sir Michael was away?"

"Laurence never intended to undermine Sir Michael."

"Yet he knew Sir Michael intended to acquire the land for Lord Whatham."

Aunt Mary nodded. "I received a small inheritance from my great aunt. How could we pass on the opportunity to own our own farm? To not be at the mercy of Sir Michael or the church congregants? We thought he'd forgiven us, but lately he came, demanding we sell to him. Threatening even. Then he had complaints against us because we are Presbyterians and Whigs. However" — she shoved Hamilton toward the door — "it is late and you must get Esther home, but please be careful. Do not let Sir Michael catch you."

"I can't very well leave her on the veranda, propped against the wall. Shall I knock and run? I will not be so cowardly. Perhaps when this war is over, we will be at peace with the Longfellows again."

"That will be my constant prayer. Now, go on, hitch up the cart."

Hamilton drove the cart around, and by the light of fireflies, he and Aunt Mary situated Esther on the seat and tied Gulliver to the tailgate. Sitting next to her, he gathered the reins and chirruped to Tilly.

"I'm afraid," Esther whispered, leaning against him, "this war will somehow take you from me."

"Nothing will take me from you." He kissed the top of her head. *I love you.*

At Slathersby Hill, once again Hamilton carried Esther up the large, stone steps and kicked against the front door.

"Sir Michael."

"Mr. Hamilton." Sassy ran up behind him, clutching her shawl. "I saw you from my cabin, coming up the road. Sir Michael sent Kitch on an errand and I sat up, watching — Esther. Mercy." Sassy inserted a key and unlocked the front door. "What was she doing?"

"She rode to Quill Farm." He carried Esther up the stairs without waiting for permission and settled her in her bed. "Her wound reopened, but Aunt Mary repaired her best she could. She said you should do your own doctoring. She fears infection."

"Am I home?" Esther said, her voice a thin trail through the room.

"Yes, and Sassy's going to look after you." The negro woman pushed Hamilton through the bedroom door into the hallway. "What was she doing out? And do not lie to me."

"She wanted to tell me something."

"Tell you something? At this hour?" Sassy waited, her breath steaming.

"That, that . . ." He could not confess their deepest intimacies. He'd yet to confess out loud his own love for her. He didn't want Sassy privy to their affection. "That she knew I did not shoot her."

"What's this?" The broad, dark shadow of Sir Michael filled the narrow doorway of the room across the hall, candlelight glinting off the end of his musket. "First you aim your pistol at my daughter, now you lure her from her bed in the night? Do you care not for her reputation? Her place in our society? What have you done —"

"She came to Quill. I found her in the yard having fallen off her horse. Would you rather I leave her there?"

"For what purpose did she ride to you?" Sir Michael butted Hamilton's chest with his musket.

"To say she knew I was not the one who shot her." Hamilton nodded to the older gentleman and started down the stairs. "She was worried I believed the rumors."

"I warn you . . ." Sir Michael settled the musket against his arm, his countenance dark and hard. "Leave her be, Lightfoot."

Hamilton would not debate with the man. "I've joined the Upper Ninety Six. I'll be gone in the morning."

"Then you, sir, are an enemy in my house." Sir Michael shifted the musket as if he intended to take aim. "I'll give you to the count of ten to leave my premises. One, two . . ."

Hamilton slammed the front door closed before the old man reached the count of four.

# 12

## JESSE

He woke to a boisterous knock on his door. Squinting through the August light falling through the windows as it rose over the beach, he fumbled for his phone.

Seven a.m. Sunday morning. The knock sounded again.

"Go away, I'm sleeping." With a moan, he rolled over and buried his head under the pillow.

But the hammering, knocking, and muffled yelling persisted.

"All right, all right." Tumbling out of bed, Jesse headed downstairs, the elixir of sleep trailing him.

When he opened the door, Smitty burst inside. "I brought coffee." He raised a convenience-store cup and offered it to Jesse, then, after tossing a paper bag on the counter, charged straight for the living

180

room, pacing as if restless and caged.

"A little early, don't you think, Smitty?" Jesse popped the lid from the coffee, letting the steam and scent escape.

"No rest for the weary." He pointed to the bag. "I brought a donut too."

Jesse peeked inside. An apple fritter. His favorite. "What's going on? Is this about the movie? I told you, screenwriters have no say in —"

"The movie?" He stopped pacing. "No, no, nothing about the movie, though do bring up my name, old pal." Back to pacing, Smitty appeared bothered, ruffled, unkempt. Rare was the time the man left his place without his hair slicked back and cologne liberally applied. But this morning, his coif twisted every which way and his shirt tail swung over the top of his belt. "Though after the news I'm about to lay on you . . ." He shook his head. "I didn't see it coming. I didn't."

"Smitty, sit down, you're making me dizzy." Jesse snatched the donut bag and sat on the S-shaped chair.

His friend sat for half a second, then popped back up. "There's no easy way to say this, Jess, so I'm just going to . . . You have to get out. I'm sorry, but you do." He stopped pacing, hands on his waist. Jesse stared at him, teeth buried in the fritter. "I knew this would happen. I knew it, I knew it, I knew it. But did ol' Smitty listen to his gut? No."

Jesse chewed the crispy dough, swallowing with a hot taste of coffee. "What are you talking about? Get out of where?"

"Here!" Smitty swung his arms wide. "Archer is coming back. Monday. Tomorrow night. I need time to air this place out. I can't leave it smelling like you and Hugo Boss."

"Archer Doyle is coming home? Here?"

"Am I stuttering? Yes. Tomorrow."

"You told me he was in Asia for a *year,* Smitty. I signed a lease." Jesse stood, slamming down his coffee on the living room table as he stood.

"Ooo, not there. Coaster!" Smitty dived for the coffee, rubbing the polished, wood surface with his palm. "Can't leave a ring." He glanced around for a place to set the cup. "See, bud, you don't have a lease."

"See, bud, I do," Jesse said, the fritter still in his hand. "I sat right there and signed it with your gold pen."

"No, no, you didn't." Smitty sighed, shaking his fists at the ceiling. "Me and my bright ideas. Look, champ, it was a fake lease. I made the whole thing up."

"What?" Jesse dropped the fritter to the table. Smitty yelped and snatched it up, blowing at the sugar crumbs, balancing the pastry on top of the coffee cup.

"I'm going to have to bring in a cleaning crew . . . on a Sunday. Where am I going to find a crew on a Sunday?" He crossed to the kitchen and set the coffee and fritter in the sink. "Oh, I'm dead. Dead, I tell you. My license! I'm going to lose my license. I'm a horrible actor and an even worse Realtor. How can I be worse at real estate than acting?" He returned to the room and dropped onto the leather chaise, head in his hands.

"Smitty, what is going on?" Jesse folded his arms across his bare chest with the will to remain calm and get to the bottom of this. Wouldn't be the first time Smitty freaked out over nothing.

"I'm a heel, a bum, the worst kind of friend."

"Agreed. Now, what is this about moving out?"

"Look, Jess, when Archer told me he was going to Asia, I told him I'd keep an eye on the place. He said sure thing and gave me a key. That's when I got the bright idea to lease it to someone . . ." He flopped against the back of the couch, arm over his eyes.

"Someone worthy. You needed a new place, something fitting of your recent success, and it hit me, 'Why not rent out Archer's place? Earn a few bucks on the side?' "

"You used me? And Archer?"

"Not on purpose."

"*Yes* on purpose." Now Jesse paced, the glorious sunrise beyond the glass windows mocking the situation. "Where am I supposed to go? I put a deposit down on this place."

"Money? No problem. I'll give it back to you. Well, half. I had to pay the electric and water bills. And spend a few dollars on new clothes. And headshots. Man, those things are expe—"

"Smitty! You swindled me? I thought we were friends."

"No, now, I didn't swindle you. I found you a place to live, didn't I? Though I might have swindled Archer."

"You swindled both of us. Where am I supposed to go by tomorrow?"

"Well, today. Remember, I have to air this place out."

"I want all of my money back."

"Of course, of course. Do you take payments?"

Unbelievable.

Smitty leaned toward him. "You're not going to report me, are you? To the Realtors Association?"

"Find me a place to live today, and I'll think about it."

"You're a saint. And believe it or not, I've found you a place. I think. Again, Jesse, I'm sorry . . . What's this? A stain?" He dropped to the hardwood floor, pressing his fingers into a small, white spot. "Did you do this? Was it already here? Archer will kill me."

"Smitty." Jesse exhaled, clapping his friend on the shoulder. "Take a breath. It was already there."

"This is giving me a heart attack." He clapped his hand over his heart as he walked toward the sliding glass door, the one leading to the lower deck and the beach, and jerked it open. "Crime never pays. It never pays." He shook his fists in the air. "You'd think I'd have learned."

"Learned? Do you have a former life in crime?"

But Smitty paced and panicked. "I'm a lowlife, a bum, the worst sort of friend."

"Smitty, stop and tell me about this other place. And do not tell me some acquaintance of yours is out of town. By the way, I do take payments. Also, you should confess to Archer." Jesse popped his friend on the back. "Look, I can't move today. I'm meeting with Jeremiah Gonda to go over the script one more time. Don't know when I'll be done. So tomorrow is the best I can do. *If* I decide to trust you."

"Gonda? What do you know, this new place is in Bel Air. Sure you don't have time today?"

"No, and even if I did, you should sweat this a little."

"You're a pal. Trust me, this new place is legit. Like I said, crime doesn't pay." He slapped his hand to his forehead. "I can't go to prison. I look horrible in stripes."

"I think they wear solid colors these days. Orange."

"Orange, even worse. With my complexion I'll look like Halloween candy. And to those hungry inmates . . ."

Despite all irritation, Jesse laughed. He should be ticked, but Smitty was such a character. "Meet me here this evening," he said, drawing Smitty back into the house. "We'll pack up and move me out. But this is your last chance. If this doesn't work, I'm getting a new Realtor. And maybe a new friend."

He was going to miss this place. The view. The sound of the ocean. The memory of Chloe. It'd been a long time since he'd paired a memory of the ocean with a beautiful woman, the feel of her skin and the taste of her lips.

"So, what's up with the girl? The one from the wedding?" Smitty dropped down onto the S chair and peeked into the donut bag, his panic fading.

"Chloe? When did I tell you about Chloe?"

Smitty's cheeks reddened as he retrieved a second apple fritter. "L-last week."

"Did I see you last week?"

"No. Maybe I heard it from someone."

"Who?"

"Ted?"

"You heard it from Ted Stux? Of Ted and Stella fame? I didn't know you knew him."

Smitty exhaled, smiling, devouring his fritter. "Yeah, we go way back. Well, not *way* back, just back."

"He told you about Chloe?" Jesse perched on the edge of the wooden table.

"Said you two hit it off."

"We did, yes."

"No kidding. That's more romance than I've heard from you since we met."

"I've dated."

"A flirt on set or at a party is not dating. Not a path to love."

Jesse stood. "Path to love? Who said anything about the *L* word? She's great, in fact. She's playing Esther in the movie, but

187

we're not a thing." No, certainly, they were not a thing. "I haven't talked to her since the wedding. Which is good. We're . . . we're both in the movie, and it's best if we . . . Besides, I don't think —"

"You can forgive yourself?"

Jesse peered down at Smitty. "W-what . . . do you mean?" He'd never discussed his past with Loxley. Not with anyone in LA.

He fled here to forget. To immerse himself in the world of pretend. Why bring it up?

"Look, man, I know something's been eating at you since we met, and I figure it had to do with a woman so, if I'm right, forgive yourself. It's been at least eight years."

"You don't know anything about it, Smitty."

"Maybe I don't, but confession is good for the soul." He glanced at his watch, stood with a jerk, and made his way to the door. "I'll text you the address of the place. I'll meet you here to help you" — he glanced around — "pack." Smitty paused in the kitchen. "If you don't tell me, then tell someone."

When he'd gone, Jesse made his way to the third-floor deck, drank his coffee, and enjoyed the view one last time.

How had Smitty surmised anything about him? About forgiveness? Beyond the whole,

"Oh, by the way, you're not a legal tenant here," it was as if Smitty had crawled into his head and took notes. Ted telling him about Chloe? The intuition about a girl in his past? If he'd said her name, Jesse would've pummeled him and demanded to know where he got the information.

His brother? His mother? Those two were talkers. But Smitty had no reason to be in contact with them.

The sunrise draped a golden path across the ocean's surface. So brilliant, so wide, as if Jesse could walk to the edge of the horizon. Seagulls hovered on the breeze, calling to one another, and in this quiet moment, the man of science ached to be a man of faith.

Forgiveness felt like a cure. Almost too good to be true. But how? He'd spent eight years trying to put it all behind him. Yet Smitty saw . . . detected.

He'd love to confess his sins and seek forgiveness if it'd bring healing. If his confessor would not despise him by the time he was through. But how could a person not? Jesse despised himself.

Beholding the heavenly splendor over Santa Monica, Jesse *knew* a divine Creator existed. There were too many unanswered questions regarding the universe for Someone not to have put it all in motion.

But did that Creator see him? Know him? Care about him? If so, where was He that day on the beach?

From his bedroom his phone rang. Leaving his contemplation on the deck, Jesse went in to answer.

It was his brother.

"Hey, Dan, what's up?" Jesse crashed against the pillows and headboard, shoving aside the small, ridiculous hope it was Smitty calling back to say, "Never mind."

Or deep down, a small hope that Chloe had acquired his number and called.

The conversation with Dan was typical. *How are you? I'm fine. When does the movie release? Don't know, haven't even started filming yet.*

"Listen," Dan said. "I wonder if you could make it home this fall? Dad's talking Octoberfest. I wanted to get it on your calendar. And, oh man, you should see Gran's new pool. It'll be too late to swim, of course, but Dad went nuts when she contracted it. She spent at least forty grand. Remember that pool we saw in the Bahamas?"

"I didn't go to the Bahamas."

"You didn't? Yeah, sure you . . . Oh, right." Dan lowered his voice. "Sorry. Anyway, Octoberfest. What do you say? I know Mom is missing you."

"She was just out here."

"Last summer, bro."

Had it been that long?

"And you have to see our new office. Dia-mondBros is right in the center of down-town Boston. I have a harbor view."

"Just like you always dreamed."

"*We* always dreamed. I miss you, Jess. DiamondBros isn't the same without you."

Diamond brothers. Their nickname for themselves growing up, playing sports, chas-ing girls. Diamonds were tough yet classic. Just like the Gates boys.

Then Jesse discovered he was not as tough as he believed. His superior intellect and knowledge of numbers were nothing against the powerful matters of the heart.

"Miss me? Dan, I've never really *been* there."

"But you were . . . are supposed to be."

"Don't start."

"Okay, okay, but I want you to know I've saved a corner office for you. Paul pitched a fit about it, but you and me, *we're* the diamond brothers."

"Then you should know I finally have real success out here. Don't save an office for me. Please. Give it to Paul."

"He has his own corner office. Look,

forget all that, just come home. We'd love to see you. Octoberfest. Second weekend in October. Also . . ." Dan hesitated. "Did Mom tell you about, um, Melanie and me?"

"Melanie Trainer?" Loxley's best friend.

"We ran into each other at a party. Six months ago. She's working on the design team at Hartman Electronics. We talked shop and —"

"One thing led to another."

"Something like that. Jess, I just bought a ring." Excitement was evident in his brother's tempered tone.

"Really?" Jess walked to the window and pressed his forehead against the pane. His brother was moving on. Melanie was moving on. If they'd even stalled at all. A twisting ache vibrated through him. "That's, um, great, Dan. I'm happy for you."

"I wanted to tell you in person. But it felt right to tell you now . . . that's really why I called. Are you okay? I know we've not talked about, you know, everything in a while and —"

"Dan, I'm good. It's been eight years." Jesse shoved his hand through his hair, eyes closed, and warded off any spiking images. Logically, he understood time healed all wounds, but what could remove the scars? The memories? He chuckled quietly. "You don't deserve her."

"There's my little brother. And you're right, but I'm not letting her go. Listen, if you don't come home, Mom will think it's because of, well, everything, and order me to break it off with Mel." Dan's laugh was shallow and hollow.

"Then I'll try to come home. If not this fall, then after the movie wraps. In the spring. Tell Mom to call me if she has any doubts. I'm fine."

"Hey, Jess, I miss you, but I'm really proud of you. Getting a movie made of your script, that's something. But you've always been outstanding. Just know I still have the office space for you."

"After eight years, I don't think I'm headed back to engineering."

"Don't pop my bubble. I'm happy today. Let me have my fantasy. Oh, hey, we should coordinate calendars. I don't want to plan my wedding the weekend of the movie premier."

"So you think she's going to say yes?" Jesse turned from the ocean view, pressing his back against the sun-warmed window.

"Fingers crossed. I'll let you know in a few days."

"Send me a pic."

"What about you? Met anyone?"

"Naw, keeping it simple. Focused on work."

"Jesse, you can't —"

"Bro, leave it."

A few more pleasantries, and the brothers hung up. Jesse returned to the deck, phone in hand, and watched the waves wash over the sun's golden path, now narrow and thin, fading in the rising light of day.

# 13

## CHLOE

Sunday evening Chloe sat in her living room going over lines with her costar, Chris Painter, who checked his watch for the tenth time in as many minutes, the pages of *Bound by Love* open in his lap.

"Go already." She smacked his leg with her script.

"What? I was just checking the time." But he slipped his script into his shoulder bag and tossed back the last of his water. "What do you think about this character, Hamilton Lightfoot?"

"I love him. He's honorable and courageous. Cares about his family. Certainly cares about Esther." Chloe collected their empty water bottles and Diet Coke cans. "Do you have a date or something?"

"Ginger is waiting for me." Chris grinned just as a message pinged on his watch.

"We're going to dinner with her folks, but I told her going over the script with you was priority."

"Her folks? Wow, sounds serious."

Chris texted his answer, scribing on the phone's small face. "Well, relatively. I don't know . . . but her parents were coming into town and I figured, what's the harm? And I agree, Hamilton is a great character. Can't believe a new screenwriter pulled it off."

"What do you like about him?"

"Him who? Jesse? Why? You got the hots for him?"

"No, Hamilton. And no one says 'got the hots' anymore. Keep up, Painter."

"My bad." The superstar laughed. After their breakup, Chloe never imagined a day she'd sit with him in her living room, going over a script, talking casually about his relationship with another woman. But she was, and it felt good. Healing. "Hamilton makes me think."

"About?"

"Love, I guess. Is there the perfect person for each one of us?"

"A soul mate?"

"I know you believed in that once upon a time." Chris bore his blue gaze into Chloe's. "Do you still?"

"Can't help myself."

"After everything that happened?"

"I can't help it. It's like a part of my DNA. I was born to believe there is one right person for me."

"Is it going to be weird, us working together?"

"Not at all." She tossed the bottles and cans in the recycle bin. "We've been friends far longer than we were lovers."

He came around to where Chloe stood and spoke as Hamilton. "I only ask for the kindness of your mercy, and to remember me in your prayers. You are the reason I am willing to fight, to lay down my life." A slight blush touched his cheeks as he became Hamilton Lightfoot in the light of her kitchen. "I'm not sure I've ever known this kind of passion. You might be right, Chloe, it only happens in the movies."

"I pray I'm wrong."

He slipped his arm around her, and she walked him to the door.

"Say hi to Ginger for me."

"Will do." Chris paused in the doorway. "You are going to own this role, Chloe. I can feel it. You play Esther with heart." He flashed his famous smile and kissed her cheek. "Later."

Chloe returned to the script, staring at dialogue, considering Esther. The woman was strong, capable, assured of love. In the midst of a hard, upcountry life with war in her backyard, she chose love. Fiercely. At least that's the way Jesse saw it.

She wondered if he'd tapped into something divine.

The sound of a door clapping drew her attention. Voices bounced up from the back side of her apartment.

"Is that all you've got?"

"I told you I travel light."

Chloe went to the window. Was Mr. Crumbly home? If so, she had a few questions for him about her pastor's message on healing this morning.

She was young in her faith, and Mr. Crumbly's wisdom helped her navigate the truths she could not always see or feel.

At the window, she peered toward the guesthouse. A silhouette passed through the long, evening shadows. Two male forms carried boxes from a car into the small house.

In a few seconds every window beamed with yellow light. Chloe dived for her phone and texted Dad.

Is someone moving into the guesthouse?

One of the men walked out to the car for a final load.

Her phone pinged an answer from Dad.

Yes.

Who? Mr. Crumbly?

He's gone for a year.

She waited. When Dad offered no more explanation, Chloe started toward the guesthouse to find out for herself. Dad was generous. He often opened up the main house for people to stay, but the guesthouse, well, it was special to Mr. Crumbly. Chloe teased Dad that he hoped the kind missionary would put a good word in to the Almighty for him.

*"Never hurts to have a connection,"* he'd say.

Voices bounced within the guesthouse as she knocked on the door, slightly ajar. After a second, Chloe pushed in.

"Hello? Anyone here?"

A familiar form came from the bedroom. Jesse.

He paused, staring at her, blue eyes wide. She exhaled and fell against the door. Then, in unison they said, "What are you doing here?"

# ESTHER

*August 1780*

"Esther." Father roused her from sleep, his Brown Bess tucked under his arm, the moon's glow spilling into her room. "Wake up."

"W-whatever is the matter?" Esther shoved aside her thin blanket and reached for her robe, the scar tissue stretching beneath her healing wound.

"Rebels are approaching the house." He offered his hand and led her quietly down the hall. "Take the back stairs to the cellar. Can you make it, love?"

"Rebels? Coming here?"

Father left her for a moment to peer out a second-floor window. "Do not make a light. And mind your movements." He took hold of her hand once more. "Isaac is on alert, and I see no light in their cabin. They may well have gone to their cellar."

Esther paused on the first step. "How do you find your loyalties so devoted after what they did to Reverend Lightfoot? After Lieutenant Twimball shot me?"

"Please, Esther, I cannot argue with you now. Hurry now, love. The rebel militia from the lowcountry has arrived, and we can be

200

most certain they are not our friends or neighbors."

Rough, masculine shouts rose from the front lawn. A chill slithered down Esther's back as the eerie glow of torchlights flickered through the windows.

Had they come to burn Loyalist homes in Ninety Six? To burn Slathersby Hill? As revenge for what happened to Reverend Lightfoot?

Holding on to the railing, she inched down the narrow stairwell as heavy footsteps sounded on the veranda. She froze, holding her breath, fearing she'd cry out.

"Check the kitchen. Gather all the food," a man said. "You, Private, check for weapons and gunpowder. A Tory home is bound to have a stockpile."

*No . . . no, we do not.* Food, yes, but Lieutenant Twimball recently acquired all Father's ammunition. He had to plead for enough reserve to fill his Brown Bess.

Father tiptoed past her, finger to his lips, motioning for her to follow. There was a cellar entrance from the parlor just to the right of the back stairs.

But in truth, it would only be a matter of time before they were discovered. Surely the soldiers would inspect the cellar. Esther tugged on her father's sleeve, motioning up.

She'd be safer returning to her room.

But he shook his head, patting Brown Bess, and continued down. One step creaked under his weight.

"Father —" He must not engage these militiamen. He was not the young, virile soldier of the past. Esther pressed her hands into the thick, plaster wall covered with a gold and red paper. She'd chosen the pattern herself at fifteen. If only she could disappear into it now.

"Father." She dug her fingers into his sleeve. "We are trapped. We must go up —"

"To where?" His hot whisper brushed her face. "They will find us." Father raised his musket and dashed down the remaining stairs and into the kitchen. "Stop or I will shoot. You are trespassing."

A chorus of musket clicks answered. Esther flattened against the wall, perspiration beading over her brow and down her neck. Should she go back up? Leave Father to defend himself? If only she had a musket. Though Father had taught her to shoot, Hamilton had schooled her further in the summers after the planting was done.

"Lower your weapon, sir. We merely want food and ammunition."

"My food and ammunition are for those in the king's army. You are trespassing. I demand you depart at once."

More footsteps, more soldiers traipsed through the house. Father! He was out-manned.

Drawing her robe closer, she tiptoed down, easing toward the kitchen. She should run for Isaac and Kitch, if they were not already alerted and on their way.

Hesitation may cost Father. Haste, however, earned her a bullet wound. Her pulse rushed, stirring her adrenaline and nerves as she inched around the kitchen door.

The click of a musket hammer ignited her courage, and she barged into the room, into the silvery, eerie light of the moon.

"Please," she said, arms around Father. "Take what you want, but let there be no killing." She scanned the dark and ghostly forms of the patriot militia, four unwelcome men in her home.

"Esther!" Father pressed her behind him just before ramming the butt of his gun into the chest of the nearest man, a boy really. He stumbled back, flailing to steady himself. "My daughter bears the scar of a rebel bullet. Haven't you done enough damage? Shown dishonor to your cause?"

"We heard it was a redcoat what shot your daughter." The soldier leading the charge towered over Father, and for a moment Esther thought her strong, forceful, proud-warrior papa would capitulate. "Lower your weapon."

"Father, let them take what they want and be away." Esther pressed her back to the wall, the wound in her shoulder pulling and throbbing.

"Take nothing," Father said, "and go."

A sound echoed from outside, and the kitchen door opened with a fresh burst of night air, followed by the smack of a fist, the moan of a man, and the thud of a body hitting the floor.

The four militiamen swung around, guns raised. There stood Lieutenant Twimball, a British soldier on either side of him, bearing arms. "So, we have rebel prisoners without firing a shot."

"We only came for food and —"

"We've prisoners without firing a shot," Twimball repeated.

At once, the militiamen, in their buckskins and moccasins and tricorn hats, charged Twimball and his men, knocking Father on his heels and into the cupboard. The kitchen became a brawl, a blasted battleground.

Esther sank to the floor, covering her ears from the crack of a wooden chair and the shatter of a china plate. "Stop! Won't you stop!"

A shot rang out, and the brawling instantly ceased. Footsteps slipped over the floorboards, followed by the click of another musket being cocked.

She could not breathe. She could not. Was there to be more fighting and now killing in her house?

"Lower your firearm, Twimball."

Esther lifted her head, the flickering flame of a lantern falling across the floor. Hamilton? His long, lean form emerged from the melee. A sharp light glinted off his rifle's steel barrel. He was well. He was home!

"Lower yours, Lightfoot," Twimball said, moving forward.

"Shoot him, Lieutenant!" Father commanded. "Shoot him and all these rebels."

A steel-like hush settled over the kitchen.

"Well," Hamilton said, setting his light on the table. "Shoot me if you have any courage."

Esther shot to her feet and moved between the men, their faces shadowed and stern. "No! There will be no killing in my house."

Twimball mocked with a throated laugh. "Once again she puts herself in harm's way."

"Then lower your weapon," Hamilton said.

"After you've lowered yours."

Hamilton lowered his gun with a side

glance at Esther. "Are you all right?" he said.

"Yes." She wanted to sound confident, but her simple answer waivered.

"The troops need food. Had I known they'd aim for Slathersby, I'd have diverted them."

"Food or intelligence," Twimball said. "Perhaps your commander wanted to spy on Sir Michael." The lieutenant angled toward Father, who remained pressed into the corner as more rebels trailed in behind Hamilton. "Unless Sir Michael has changed his mind and now sides with the rebels."

"Indeed not. This household is wholly devoted to Britain and the Crown," Father fired back. "We aid and abet no rebels."

"Still you swear allegiance to those who nearly killed your daughter." Hamilton inched across the room, parting the arguing factions, going nose to nose with Lieutenant Twimball.

"She acted a fool," Twimball declared. "Running into the fray. To save you perhaps? Are you a boy in need of a woman's aid?"

"Does your Inspector General, Major Ferguson, know about your underhanded tactics?" Hamilton asked. "Disrupting a funeral? Firing on an innocent woman? Perhaps the British must kill women and children to gain victory."

Twimball raised his chin. "Shall we take our fight outside?"

"A duel perhaps?"

"Duel? Are you mad?" Esther shoved between them, her entire body trembling. "Go your own ways. Save yourselves for the real battlefield."

Hamilton took up his lamp, and she saw in his expression what he'd never confessed. Love. And fear. "Please," she begged. "Each of you, return the way you came. Let this night pass in peace."

He bore the slightest smile on his lips, along with a glint of pride in his eyes, as he nodded toward her. "You look well. Your shoulder has healed?"

"Yes, yes, but promise me, Hamilton. You will not —"

"Yes, promise her, Hamilton," Twimball mimicked. "Surrender to her feminine wishes."

Hamilton slowly turned. "I'll see you on the battlefield."

The two men stepped toward one another, shoulders back, chins raised. Esther released an involuntary sigh.

"Please, I beg of you, just go your way. Leave my father and me in peace."

Except Hamilton, he could stay. She wanted to examine him in the light, ensure her heart he was well, with no wounds or scars — no harm from this mad war.

"Let us do as she bids." Hamilton reached for Father's Brown Bess. Raising it to his eye, he examined the frizzen in the flickering light. "If you aim to defend this house, I suggest you load your musket next time." He tossed the gun back to Father, then tapped Twimball with the barrel of his rifle. "Until then, Lieutenant."

"Where you will meet a coward's end, I assure you." Twimball knocked the rifle away, then roused his men. "We leave only on account of Sir Michael's loyalty and that of his household."

Grabbing his lamp, Hamilton disappeared into the shadows, departing with the militiamen.

"Lightfoot!" Father jumped forward, chasing him down the hall to the foyer. "Stay away from Slathersby Hill. You are not welcome here, Lightfoot! Do you hear me? You and yours are traitors."

Esther listened for his reply. 'Twas nothing more than the clap of a closing door.

When Father returned to the kitchen, Twimball and his men had also departed. Father lit a candle and aided Esther to her feet.

"He saved us, Father. You could be more

gracious."

"For all I know he sent those men here —"

"For all you know he did not." Esther looped her arm with Father's, her pulse slowing, the surge of cold anxiety ebbing.

"Confess to me at once," Father said. "What is between you and Lightfoot? He says he loves you."

"And I love him, Father. Though he be a Whig and a rebel, I cannot deny my affections."

"Then gather your heart, daughter, because you won't be wedding a Lightfoot. Not as long as I breathe."

"Why? I may do as I please. I am of age and —"

"Esther!" Father's voice boomed with a cannon's force. "Be still. You will never have my agreement or blessing."

She drew back, pulling her arm from his. "Never? But the Longfellows have been your friends for twenty years. You employed them, dined with them, worshipped with them. The sweat of Laurence Lightfoot is in the very house."

"Leave it be, Esther." Father started for the stairs. "Upon his death, Laurence and I were long since parted by politics and land."

"Land? What's this about land? Does it

have anything to do with why you hover over your ledgers?" A gentleness replaced Esther's frustration as Father paused on the second-floor landing, his shoulders drooping. "Is everything well with Lord Whatham?"

Father sighed, patting her hand, his thick palm warm and firm. "I'm suddenly quite weary. Haven't we had enough excitement for now?"

Esther kissed Father good night. "You must know, Father, you are my papa and my dearest friend. I would never do anything without your blessing." There, she assured him. Eased a bit of his angst.

"Of this I am assured, my darling." His eyes glistened as he gathered his words. "Your mother wrote to me before you returned from England. She had hoped you would stay in Grosvenor Square and take your place in society. But I rejected her proposal. How terribly I missed you while you were gone. But now I wonder if I should've left you among your peers."

"Neither she nor you could have made me stay. I planned to sail home with or without anyone's consent."

He raised his chin and gazed beyond the dark window, candlelight reflecting in the glass. "Yet you've come home to a war. And what do we offer a young woman of your breeding and station? Backwoods men, farmers, trappers, and traders? Half-breeds and traitors. In London, you'd be among your peers, perhaps court a man with a title and a Cambridge degree like your dear papa."

"While I am British, a Loyalist, I am also a South Carolinian, Father. I love the up-country. The land, the hills, the streams are my home. London is a jungle I do not know or wish to know."

And yes, South Carolina gave her Hamilton. She'd bide her time with Father, let the war move on, but she would marry Hamilton Lightfoot. What was her future without him?

"Then I have failed you. The plan was never for you to remain here."

"But here I am. You cannot make me return to London." Her brash speech contained sufficient courage, but Esther knew well her submission to Father and his wishes. "As for Mother, she must deal with her own decisions. She was the one who decided I should sail to you at ten while she remained behind."

"Her own mother was ill."

"Grandmama had nothing more than a summer cold. If Mother cared about my place in society, about a possible marriage to a peer, then she never should have sent me away." This was not her first conversation with Father about Mother's distance from them.

"I believed you'd discover her love for you while you were with her," Father said. "Never doubt her affection and devotion. But she was raised with certain comforts and privileges that one cannot find in the backwoods of an American colony."

"She loved herself more than us. How can you defend her?" Esther turned toward her room yet caught something unusual in Father's expression. A sentimental smile. A jolly glint. "Father, what is it? Something I said? Something about Mother?"

"I know I've never spoken of this with you, Esther, but I love your mother. With every ounce of my being."

"You are still married, but, Father, surely . . . You've not clapped eyes on her in seven years."

"No, and I shall do my best to remedy our distance when this war is over. The up-country demanded more of me than I originally imagined. But your mother and I, we . . . correspond."

"Correspond?"

Father nodded once, facing away. "You're

an adult now, as you so pointedly like to tell me, so I suppose you will understand. We pen love letters. Often, I receive a dozen or more from her when the post arrives."

"Love letters?" Esther stepped back, as if she'd peered into a forbidden intimacy. "Then I don't understand why —"

"Good night, Esther." Father handed her the candle, adjusted the Brown Bess in the crook of his elbow, and slipped away. "I best load this gun in case Hamilton returns."

"How can he? You forbade him."

Father paused in the moonlight. "He loves you, and I suspect he knows you love him. A man armed with knowledge is strong, driven. He will return."

"Then you are coming around to my view?"

"No, my dear, I am as against you as before. In fact, I'm starting to come around to your mother's way of thinking. Perhaps I should send you home once and for all."

"Good night, Father." Esther slammed her door and set the candle on her night table with a clatter.

Send her home. Indeed. She'd refuse to go. Why, she'd run away. With Hamilton.

Taking stationery from her desk, Esther dipped her quill in the ink bottle and wrote a brief note to the man she loved.

*Are you home for a season? May we meet at the willow?*

Allowing for the ink to dry, she tucked the missive under her pillow with plans to send Kitch on an errand tomorrow.

After blowing out the candle, she whispered her prayers, the events of the night already drifting away, slumber claiming her as the voice of her beloved called from her dreams.

# 14

## HAMILTON

*October 15, 1780*

He wore the battle of King's Mountain like a millstone, heavy and suffocating. Struggling to hold his head up, Hamilton urged Tilly toward home. Rounding the bend, the old girl moved from a trot to a gallop.

Yet he reined in the horse, patting her gently on the neck. "Easy, we'll be home soon enough."

He'd not seen Quill Farm since the night he disarmed the threat at Slathersby Hill. He'd meant to lodge with Aunt Mary for a short season, check on the dealings with the farm, meet Esther at their willow . . . but Captain Irwin urged him to stay with the Upper Ninety Six, so he moved north with them, scouting, preparing, and awaiting orders.

He'd received Esther's short note well after he'd departed, replying with his own brief letter.

*I trust you are well. I've moved on with the Upper Ninety Six. Tell your Father to keep his Musket loaded and take care, My Friend. Hamilton*

But tonight he was coming home. The light of the October dusk spread a purple haze over the burnished countryside, the last of the day's warmth beginning to fade.

Breathing in, Hamilton could almost smell Aunt Mary's baking bread and roasting chicken.

In the aftermath of King's Mountain, he was bruised, worn, and torn. His right arm had taken a saber slash, which the field surgeon mended, though he had more pressing demands with the dead and dying.

He needed a clean bandage and one of Aunt Mary's poultices. And a solid meal. Hot and hearty.

King's Mountain. A bloody brawl he longed to forget, but he feared his actions there would haunt him forever.

After the enemy's surrender, 'twas nothing but sheer brutality. By his patriot brethren, not the green-vested British dragoons who murdered and pillaged their way through the south.

No, this destruction was wrought by his countrymen. A seething revenge for the destruction done at Hill's Ironworks and the torching of churches.

And Hamilton, who had fought with honor until then, almost lost himself in his brothers' savagery.

Coming round the bend, Tilly tossed her head with a whinny. Aunt Mary's gelding, Achilles, stuck his head out the stall window and returned her call.

"Pray God there's hay for you, girl." *And forgiveness for me. And a washing. For both body and soul.*

Hamilton reined in Tilly as he passed the shortcut to the willow. Esther. How he missed her, longed to see her.

He'd tried again to write her a love letter after the Slathersby confrontation, but the words would not come. The course of putting his deepest emotions down on paper, exposing his heart for any and all to see, revealed vulnerabilities he cared not to navigate.

Besides, how could he pledge his life to her now when he'd pledged his duty to his country? Again Captain Irwin prevailed upon him to stay with the Upper Ninety Six, and Hamilton had agreed. He must finish what he started.

But for now he was going home. Tilly broke into a run, and Hamilton leaned into her motion, ducking as she ran straight into the barn and to her stall, touching her nose to Achilles'.

He found the sack of oats and scooped her a hearty dinner, grateful to find the barn stocked. Moses and Ox were skilled workers with resources even Hamilton did not have. They kept the hay loft full and the oat buckets brimming.

His stomach growled for his own dinner as he wiped her down, but first he needed a washing before he went inside Aunt Mary's clean home.

Hamilton crossed the barnyard, the chickens clucking out of his way, then dropped his rifle, dagger, and cartridge belt by the well. His haversack slipped from his shoulder.

With care, he removed his shirt, the wind skirting past with the scent of fall, stirring the red, gold, and orange foliage — a beauty he once treasured. But now it was tainted with the blood of men. Of what he'd almost done.

He recoiled at the image of a Loyalist, a man not unlike him from up York way, surrendered, on his knees, begging and pleading for his life.

*"Please . . . I have a family."*

"Hamilton!"

He swung around — Esther rode Gulliver into the barnyard, dropping out of the saddle and running to him, crushing herself into his chest. "My prayers have been answered. You're home."

Her soft, feminine touch collided with the hardness of the battle. Of bedding on the ground next to his fellow militiamen for four months, eating hardtack and rotting vegetables or fruit if it could be found.

"What are you doing here?" He shoved her away, holding her at arms' length, her embrace stirring a desire in his loins.

"Why, to see you, silly."

Hamilton drew a bucket of cold water from the deep well. "Was Kitch spying on me?"

"Spying? No. He saw you come around the bend." She bent to see his face, her voice, her expression tender and beautiful. "How are you?"

"Home from battle. How do you think I am?" He did not want her tenderness, her kindness. No, he did not deserve such pleasantries. Not after peering into the depths of his own depravity. "I see your shoulder has healed."

"Yes, very nicely. Sassy is pleased. It still

219

hurts to lift my arm." She demonstrated, trying to raise her arm over her head. "So, are you well? Your arm." She reached toward his bandage. "We heard the surrendering American Loyalists were killed. In cold blood. Is it true?"

He spun to face her, dingy and foul in her clean, sweet presence. "Have you come to try me? To accuse me?"

"Accuse you? No, why would I — Hamilton, I only wish to welcome you home."

"Does your Loyalist father know you are here? Did he not forbid you to see me?"

"I do not have to give him an account of my every action." Her voice wavered with emotion, as if she might cry. "I told him I loved you. The night you rescued us."

"I'm sure he had a hearty laugh at your foolishness." Hamilton lowered the empty bucket into the well, resisting the crack her presence wedged in his countenance. He was angry, ashamed, and if it was all the same to her, desired to remain so. He needed the edge for the next battle. And to live with himself.

"H-how long are you home? Perhaps we might meet at the willow."

"I'm home to help with the harvest." He winced as he raised the bucket, the wound on his arm struggling to heal. Besides the slash, something had happened to his right shoulder in the course of battle as well, and it ached with every move.

Setting the bucket on the edge of the stone well, he scooped a dollop of Aunt Mary's fine soap and scrubbed his face while Esther looked on. When he'd rinsed, he found he had no towel.

"Pardon me," he said, turning his back and reaching for his shirt. Once white, it was stained with the dirt and grime in which he lived. What he'd become. "I cannot meet you at the willow." Patting his face, he glanced at her over the edge of his hands.

"Not even once?"

Her eyes drifted back to his face, over his chest, and to the wound on his arm. He felt exposed. Could she see his heart beating? Feel the heat of his desires? Read the depths of his shame.

Why didn't he step up, defend the surrendering Loyalists? Instead he just . . .

"I've work to do here. And I'm still engaged with the militia."

"Your devotion does you credit." She took a step closer. "Your arm. What happened?"

He jerked away when she touched him. "What do you think happened?" To his own ears he sounded boorish and rude.

"You were struck by a sword or cutlass."

He said nothing as he drew another bucket of water and soaked his head. " 'Tis nothing," he said, gathering more soap to lather his hair. But as he raised his arms, his shoulder popped and he buckled forward with a moan.

"Hamilton, let me help you." Esther's soft hands slipped over his bare shoulders, and he turned away. She was not helping. Not at all.

"Please, kneel down." Esther took the soap in her delicate hands.

"Esther, I cannot —"

"I said kneel down. Didn't the militia teach you to obey commands?"

"From a woman, no." But he was weakened by her charms and dropped to one knee, then the other, exhaling.

At first he couldn't feel her touch, but as she ladled more water onto his hair, her hands moved deeper, scrubbing, massaging his scalp. Her gentle yet firm movements drove him to distraction.

Tears smarted in his eyes and he coughed, hiding his emotion. Round and round her hands went, washing his hair. Washing his soul. Chills prickled around his neck and down his back.

As she ladled more water over his head, Esther sang a soft melody, rinsing away the soap, the dirt and mud, the blood, until the water flowed clean.

" 'The heavy hours are almost past that part my love and me.' "

He was yielding, surrendering, his tears mounting.

She began to sing another melody, gay and spritely. " 'Go rose, my Chloe bosom grace.' I'm fond of the name Chloe. What do you think? So lovely for a girl."

He listened, resisting her softness, her feminine allure. Using her own scarf, she began to dry his hair.

When she finished, he rose to his feet, snatching up his shirt, now damp and dark. "I-I should . . ." He motioned toward the house. "Go. Aunt Mary . . ."

Esther stepped into him, her dripping scarf in her hands. "Hamilton, don't you want —"

"No. I don't want . . . I cannot . . . What I've done. What I nearly did." Gripping her arms, Hamilton searched for a way to tell her no, to admonish her to forget him, but he saw the affection in her blue eyes. Before he considered the consequences, he pressed his lips to hers.

She leaned into him, her hands moving around his chest to his back.

He dropped his shirt to the dirt and took

her to himself, drinking in her pure, clean soul. But when a soft moan escaped her lips, he returned to reality. Hamilton jerked away.

"Esther, we cannot." He shoved his hair back, stooping to collect his haversack and cartridge belt.

"We cannot what? Declare our affection?" She was soaked and soapy, with brimming eyes and wisps of hair curling about her face. Her wet scarf swung from her hand.

"You cannot come here, perfumed and lovely, singing over me. Nay, I will not abide it." He paced away, running the dirty shirt over his hair. A hint of a fall chill wrapped around his torso.

"Then when can I call on you? Or should I wait for you to call on me? Need I remind you that I —"

"Love me?" He pointed to the house. "Whatever we said to one another while you lay fading on the settee is . . . is . . . folly. We are not meant to be, Esther. You deserve a much better man. One who dances with you in the grand salons of a British peer during the London seasons."

"Grand salons? You know what I learned drinking tea with my British peers?"

He turned his back to her. He did not have to listen to her rebuke. But his feet remained planted in the damp dirt by the well.

"That there is no one who compares to you, Hamilton. Why do you think I returned home? And you cannot retract my words from that night. I won't let you push me aside. I hold hope in my heart. Your rejection is just foolish talk created by the weariness of battle." She jammed her finger to her breast. "I know you love me, and there is nothing you can say to dissuade me. So be angry, but not at me."

"I almost killed a man, Esther! In cold blood." He spread his arms and bent back, face toward heaven. "Shall I confess it? Do you hear me, Lord? I wanted revenge." He seethed toward Esther. "The honor of the battlefield was long over when the men began killing the surrendering American Loyalists. I took up my dagger and knocked a man to his knees and so help me, I had every intention of —"

"Hamilton!" Eyes wide, she retreated a step, her fingers touching her lips.

"Do I shock you? Have you seen the darkness of my heart? Now you know we must not be together. To me, that soldier was the same ill form of human flesh that killed my pa. In cold blood in the town square. What was my father's crime? Printing pamphlets without a stamp because he opposed the oppressive law."

She lowered her hand. "You never said how he was killed."

Hands on his waistband, he gazed toward the rolling hills, their serenity far, so very far away. "He was a printer. And when the king imposed the stamp tax, he printed without the stamp as a protest. A redcoat, a lieutenant not unlike Twimball, demanded to see his stamp. Pa refused, and right there, without judge and jury, the redcoat shot him."

"And you witnessed it?"

"I was a boy of seven." Blood ran down his arm where the wound had opened up. "I cried out and ran to him. The lieutenant kicked me in the ribs, then dragged me to the whipping post. Said if I was that man's son, I must be an accomplice. I was to be made an example."

"No . . ."

"My father's partner intervened. Paid the soldier money to leave me be." He peered at her, her blue eyes round with sadness. "The man killed my father for nothing. Money. The mayor tried to bring charges, but it only stirred up more dissension. Ma insisted the matter be put to rest with Pa."

"I cannot imagine, Hamilton." Esther set

aside her scarf as she reached for his shirt and began washing it in the bucket.

"They killed my pa!" He gripped his hand into a fist. "Ma, Betsy, and I were left to fend for ourselves. My mother never recovered. I was nine when the house caught fire. She and Betsy died in the blaze." He took the shirt from her, wrung out the water, and spread it over the small patch of grass surrounding the back steps. "I wonder if I shouldn't have died as well."

"You cannot mean it, Hamilton."

"King's Mountain revealed what I am capable of, and shame is my mantle."

"But you didn't use your dagger. You just said so."

"Nor did I stop those who did. I'm just as guilty."

"Then change. Repent as your uncle taught. You were born for a purpose, to do good. God has surely —"

"Become tired of me," he said. "Of my ways, my doubts, my pride and wickedness."

"He is also kind and benevolent, slow to anger, quick to forgive. Surely you've learned these truths from your uncle's sermons."

"Esther, cease with your pithy replies of kindness and forgiveness." He retrieved the dagger from his boot. He would make her understand. Drive her away. "I stood over a man with this, his arms raised in surrender." He wagged the weapon before her eyes. "I nearly drove this into his heart. How can you love such a man? Well, you must not." He hurled the dagger into the ground. "I am precisely like the redcoat who shot my pa."

"But you *did not* stab him. You let him go. That's the man I love. One of reason and compassion."

Adrenaline flowing, his heart pulsing, he crossed the barnyard toward the trees. "Go home, Esther. Go home."

"Hamilton, wait —"

But he escaped into the woods where he could no longer hear her voice. When he emerged on the other side, he followed a cattle trail toward the stream.

He splashed into the current, sinking into the silt. How could he live with himself, knowing what he was capable of?

Murder. How he'd judged Twimball, when he was no better.

Meanwhile, his aggravated wound continued to fester. Hamilton splashed the cold water over his arm, washing the cut. He'd need a clean bandage.

When he glanced up, a man dressed in brown broadcloth stood on the pebbled

228

bank. Hamilton took him for a beggar.

"Be on your way. I've nothing for you," Hamilton called.

"I've come to see you." The man raised his arm, beckoning Hamilton. "Come, follow me."

"Follow you?" Hamilton scoffed, the creek water flowing over his boots as he sank deeper. "To where? Into town? Are you a patriot or Loyalist?"

"Both."

He scoffed. "Haven't you heard, man? We're at war. You cannot be both."

"Come, Hamilton, follow me."

"You make no sense. I cannot follow you unless you tell me where." As he drew nearer, his chest burned with a strange fire. Where anger had ripped and scorched, this sensation cooled and soothed.

The man's eyes radiated a color Hamilton had never seen. "I cannot tell you where unless you follow me."

"Then we are at a stalemate."

The man's chestnut hair hung down to his shoulders. He carried no bag and no weapon.

"I heard you say you cannot be forgiven, but indeed, it's already been done."

The flame in Hamilton's torso swirled until his anger and anxiety submitted like an errant child.

"You're a preacher?"

"Hamilton, come, follow me." The man bent and wrote in the dust beside the pebbles with his finger. Overhead, the setting sun drifted behind the trees, but a blade of brilliant gold flashed through the leaves and, for a moment, blinded Hamilton. When he opened his eyes, the man was gone.

"My man, where have you gone?" Hamilton jogged to where he'd been standing, peering around. "Is this a magician's trick? You cannot have just vanished."

The sun continued its path west, sending a solo, bright ray across his face. Hamilton shaded his eyes and moved to the shore. There he found a single word scripted in the dirt.

*Forgiven.*


## ESTHER

Esther sat by Slathersby's library window, needlepoint in hand, using every last muscle to give Father the appearance of composure while she tamed her roiling, tempest sea.

Hamilton had rejected her. Off hand, as if she meant nothing to him. Well, she refused to be so easily dismissed. She was one of two in the relationship, and though a man, Hamilton did not have the one and only say.

She'd given him a week to collect himself and think about what he'd said. When he didn't send word to meet at the willow, she sent Kitch to Quill with a note of her own.

Can we meet at the willow? Sundown.

Sailing home, the very idea of seeing him gave her courage when the waves rose on the Atlantic. If he believed his actions at King's Mountain were enough to deter her, he would soon learn different.

Her eyes blurred as she worked her needle. Two hours had passed since Kitch left. What was keeping him?

At last, the boy trotted up the drive on Gulliver. Esther set her needlepoint aside and reached for her shawl. "Goodness, I'm falling asleep as I sit. I think I'll step outside for some fresh air."

" 'Tis a fine idea." Father set down his quill. "I think I'll join you."

"I'm not sure how far I'll walk. Can your knee go the distance?"

Father chuckled and patted his right knee, impaired during the Seven Years' War. "My knee is capable of whatever I command. I'm too young to be old. I'm only forty-nine."

He joined her on the veranda, and Esther found no way of escape. No valid excuse to leave him behind. Until she saw Kitch leading Gulliver into the stable.

"I feel in the mood to ride. Gulliver is in need of exercise."

"Riding?" Father patted his ribs and filled his lungs. "What a splendid idea. I've not taken a leisurely ride in quite some time." He offered Esther his arm. "Shall we? No need to change into our riding kits."

She grimaced, slipping her arm through his. There was no escaping him today. At the stable, Kitch glanced toward her as he removed Gulliver's saddle.

"Saddle up Barnabas and Gulliver, Kitch," Father said. "We're going riding."

Kitch nodded, his gaze sweeping past Esther. "Yes, sir. Right away."

"I'll help," Esther said, crossing the stone floor.

"Help? Leave the boy be, love. He doesn't need you telling him how to do his job."

"I-I don't mind, sir. Miss Esther knows a goodly bit about horses."

"Well, fine." Father retrieved a cigar from his inside coat pocket. "I'm off for a light. Don't leave without me, Esther."

When he'd gone, Kitch passed Esther a

small, tightly folded note.

"What took you so long?"

"He weren't home. I had to wait under the maple." Kitch replaced Gulliver's saddle, then treated him with a slice of dried apple.

Hands trembling, Esther unfolded the letter, turning away as Kitch saddled the horses.

Esther, as I said, I cannot meet you. The harvest consumes my time. Yours, Hamilton

She crumpled the note, whirling about, her palm pressed to her forehead. " 'Yours, Hamilton' . . . as if I'm a pesky school girl with a frivolous crush. Did he say anything to you?"

"Me?" Kitch made a face. "About what?"

"Oh, I don't know . . . that he's passionately in love with me and merely frightened of his own powerful affections."

Kitch buried his face in the horse's side but could not mute his laugh well enough.

"What's so funny?"

"I ain't all that experienced with women —"

Esther sighed. "Do tell."

"But if 'n a man wants a woman, ain't no

fear that can hold him back, Miss Esther."

"Oh really?" She set her hands about her waist and leaned toward him. "How do you know such things?"

Kitch grimaced, leading Barnabas from his stall. "Like I said, I don't have much experience but —"

"When a man loves a woman, nothing can hold him back?"

"From what I'd seed, pretty much."

Esther alighted on Gulliver's back. "The same is true of women. When she is in love, there is no force more powerful." She spurred the gelding out of the stable. Father would simply have to understand.

# 15

## JESSE

"Smitty," Jesse called over his shoulder, keeping his eyes on Chloe. "You did not tell me the guesthouse was on Daschle property."

His friend shouted from the bedroom. "You didn't ask."

Jesse scoffed. "How would I know to ask? But, oh, what am I thinking?" He thumped the heel of his hand against his forehead. "I cannot trust you." To Chloe, he said, "I didn't know this was your father's place."

"What happened to your place on the beach?"

"Turns out the owner wasn't away for a year. And Smitty, my former good friend, had no authority to lease it to me."

"Smitty?" Chloe echoed.

"Chloe, good to see you." Smitty emerged from the bedroom, arms wide.

"You know her?"

"You know him?"

"We go back all of what, three years?" Smitty nodded at Chloe.

"Something like that." Chloe was good with facial expressions. Right now she was saying, *I don't believe any of this,* without saying a word.

"Yeah, sure, we met on set. A TV movie. I invited her to church."

Jesse turned to Smitty. "You go to church?"

"Yeah, Expression58. Shawn Bolz. Great guy."

"I've known you for eight years, and never once have you mentioned church."

"Neither have you." Smitty dropped down on a plush, leather sofa and stretched his arms across the top.

"I didn't know I needed to mention church." He'd considered the institution of religion after Loxley died, window-shopped a few places in LA. But the moment he walked inside, he felt the judgment from those who were holier than thou.

"Well, now you know." Smitty stood. "I'm famished. Anyone for pizza?"

"I'm confused." Chloe stepped between them. "Smitty, were you here yesterday morning talking to my dad?"

"You saw me and didn't say hi?" He looked sincerely disappointed. "I wanted to see if Jess could move in here. I needed him O-U-T of Archer's place ASAP."

"How do you know my dad?"

"Yeah," Jesse said. "How do you know Raymond Daschle?"

"We go way back. I auditioned for him a few years ago."

"You auditioned for Raymond Daschle?"

"Didn't I tell you?"

"No, but I suppose I should've asked."

Chloe smirked, shaking her head. "Dad let you borrow Mr. Crumbly's space?"

"Yeah, sure. Why not? Crumbly was okay with it."

"No, no," Chloe said with a laugh. "You do *not* know Mr. Crumbly too." She glanced at Jesse. "He's an old friend of my father's. A missionary. He stays here when he's stateside. But he's in South America for a year."

"Are you sure?" Jesse shot an icy glare at Smitty. "He said Archer was going to be gone for a year too."

"He's gone." Smitty sat confident and cocky, his arms stretched out like he owned the place. "I double-checked it. Called Crumbly myself."

"I need a flow chart to track everyone."

Jesse sat in the nearest chair, a comfortable gold leather recliner.

"So, wait," Chloe said. "Smitty, you know Dad, Mr. Crumbly, Jesse, and me? Did you know we knew each other?" She pointed to Jesse, then to herself.

"I wondered."

"How did you wonder?"

Smitty stood, patting his gut. "How about that pizza?"

"I still can't wrap my head around this." Chloe regarded Jesse. "We both know Smitty? How have we not met before now?"

"Timing is everything, kids," Smitty said. "Now, about that pizza."

"Give us a second to digest here, Smitty," Jesse said. "I meet Chloe at a wedding reception the day she reads for a part in my screenplay. Then I end up renting from her father. Last but not least, you lie to me about Archer, and now I find out you're . . . religious?"

"Well, when you put it like that. I never claimed to be perfect." Smitty wandered into the kitchen, tugging open the fridge door. "Empty. You need to go shopping." He returned to the living room. "What you need to ask yourself, Jesse, is why you don't cross a church's threshold?"

"I'm not the church-going kind." He

glanced at Chloe. "Are you okay with me living here? If not, I can hole up in a hotel for a night or two until I find a place." He grimaced at Smitty. "Without your help. You're a horrible Realtor."

"What? I found you a great deal. Twice. Just because the first one didn't work out —"

A small knock resounded on the door. Jesse, Smitty, and Chloe called in chorus, "Come in."

*Geez.* Who's place was this anyway?

Raymond Daschle entered, smiling, wearing the aura and attitude of an . . . ordinary man. A father. "How's everything? Getting set up? I see you've met Chloe."

"Dad, this is Jesse. You met him at Violet's wedding."

"Right, of course." Raymond crossed to shake his hand. "Welcome to Daschle Grounds."

"It was nice of you to let me rent this place."

"No problem. George Crumbly is gone for a year. I like to have the house occupied. Chloe's got the apartment on the north side of the house, but Kate lives in West Hollywood. No need to have the place empty if someone wants to stay here." Raymond walked over to the box on the kitchen table.

"You've started to move in. Good."

"Well, I'm all moved in." Jesse glanced at the boxes. A total of five this time. "I travel light."

"I like it. Possessions encumber a man. Weigh him down."

"Said the man with a ten-thousand-square-foot mansion," Chloe scoffed.

Jesse laughed. She looked pretty tonight, casual in her shorts and top. Like the kind of woman a man could build a life with.

"I didn't say *me,*" Raymond said. "I like my *stuff.*"

Jesse agreed with his wisdom. Stuff encumbered a man. And he wasn't looking to add *stuff* to his life. Even if she came with hazel-green eyes and the fragrance of summer.

"I'll say good night." Raymond moved toward the door, pointing to the phone on the kitchen wall. "Pound nine gets the service staff. If they're not there, leave a message. Use the pool whenever you want. You swim?"

"I used to, in another life."

"Great exercise, swimming. There are towels in the kiosk by the lanai. Just toss them in the hamper when you're done. The maid collects them."

"Thank you, Raymond. I appreciate it."

"Like I said, I like having someone here. At night I look out my bedroom window, and seeing a light on in here comforts me." He paused in the doorway. "Sort of like, 'All is well in the world.' That's what light does, you know. Says all is well in the world."

As Raymond left, Smitty ducked out behind him. "Know what, I remembered I have to be somewhere. Chloe, see you at church. Jesse?" He saluted him from the doorway. "See you in the movies."

The door clicked closed, and he was alone with Chloe.

"This feels awkward."

"Why?" she said. "We met, had a good time —"

"Shared a kiss." An amazing kiss.

"We're adults. We can handle a kiss or two, right?" She tapped the edge of the box on the living room table, taking a small peek inside. "You really did not know this was our place?"

"Nope." Jesse surrendered his hands as if to declare his innocence.

"You must really trust him." She peeked in another box. Jesse didn't mind. He had nothing to hide. At least nothing he could carry in a box.

"I used to until he lied to me about the

place on the beach. But he assured me he found the perfect place."

Chloe peered over her shoulder at him. "Did he? Find you the perfect place?"

A twist of yearning tightened his chest. "Don't know. We shall see."

She looked in one last box, then with a sheepish wince, started for the door. "I better let you unpack."

Jesse reached for her arm. "Don't go."

"Why not?" But she didn't move. Didn't try to pull away. "I-I have dinner with my sister tonight."

"Is it important?" Didn't sound important. Sounded made up.

"N-not really."

"Then how about dinner with me?" She moved him. Made him feel things he'd not felt in a long time, if ever. "Smitty gave me a stack of restaurant flyers." He scooped them from the island and perched on the edge of a bar stool. "What's your pleasure, Miss Daschle?"

When he looked up, she glanced away.

"I-I don't know."

He shuffled through the flyers calling out pizza places, Chinese, Italian, Indian, sandwiches, and wings. Then set the pamphlets aside.

"I still think of our kiss on the deck."

"We should both forget. We're going to be in rehearsals soon. Then on set, filming. Jesse, I really need this film to go well for me. I want to give it my all. Not just for Jeremiah but for my future. I feel like this film could change everything for me."

"Agreed. I need this film to go well for me too. Its success could bring all kinds of opportunity —"

"Could? No, Jesse, it *will* bring new opportunities. With directors and producers, studio heads."

"— and I don't want to cause Jeremiah any headaches. I'm going to follow him around when I'm not in a scene."

"You'll learn so much from him."

"So we have to ignore this . . . this *thing* between us." He read her expression, waiting for her to light up in agreement. "For Jeremiah, for the film. Besides, neither of us wants to start anything."

"For Jeremiah, yes. But this *thing*? What thing?" She queried him with a glance. "I only meant to say how good it will be to have a friend on set."

"Friends? Yes, exactly." So the spark of something real was one-sided? "Being friends is a *thing,* right?"

Never mind the way she curved into him the night they danced, how she fit together against him when they kissed, like pieces of a puzzle. The glow in her eyes afterward. The fire in his heart.

*Move on, man.* Jesse held up the flyers. "You choose. I'm the new kid on the block."

She hesitated, then snatched the pamphlets. "Loved those boys. New Kids on the Block. They used to stay here when they came to LA."

"No kidding? I did a scene with Donnie Wahlberg once. It was a Boston thing."

"Look there, something we have in common. New Kids on the Block." Chloe picked a pizza place. "800 Degrees."

Jesse hopped off the stool. "Let's go. My treat."

She hesitated, as if she wanted to say something, then fell into step. "Chris and I have been rehearsing, Jesse. I love the way you wrote Esther and Hamilton and their love. But I always get the sense there's more to the story. What were you thinking or going through when you wrote it? I'd love to read the letter that inspired it all."

"Lots of things."

"Are you ever going to tell me the rest of the story?"

He studied her for a moment. She had a story she'd never told him. "Are *you* ever going to tell *me*?"

"I'm surprised you haven't searched the Internet. Just type in Chloe Daschle. It's the first hit."

"I'd rather hear it from you."

She peeked in one last box on the table by the door. The one from Aunt Pat. The original letter was inside. Along with the articles about Loxley.

"Is the letter in there?" Chloe snatched her hand away when Jesse moved the box. "Is it?"

"Yes." He closed the flap, setting the box aside. He didn't care if she knew about Grandpa Hamilton and Esther Longfellow. But he cared, for now, if she knew about Loxley. "Who's hungry for pizza?"

"People are going to want to know, Jesse, about the letter," she said. "It will be a part of the movie's promo."

"I know. And it's not the letter. You ready to go? I'm starved."

"If it's not the letter, then what?" She tugged her phone from her pocket. "And yes, I'm ready. Let me text Kate . . . and you know, if we're going to be friends, one of these days we're really going to have to be honest with each other."

"Okay, but which one of us wants to go first?"

# CHLOE

*October*

"Am I late?" The first table read of *Bound by Love* was at Jeremiah and Laura's. Filming would begin in two months on location in Chesnee, South Carolina, where part of the crew was already stationed, prepping for production.

"Chris is not here yet, so no." Laura welcomed Chloe with an embrace, then led her through the house.

The aromas from the kitchen were incredible.

Laura recounted tonight's menu. "Prime rib and duck. I told Jer this will be the fastest table read in history."

"Forget the table read, let's eat." Chloe stepped onto the lanai and was greeted by a chorus of hellos and affection. People she'd known one way or another throughout her Hollywood life rose to welcome her.

Derrick Hall, another old friend of Dad's, played her on-screen father. "My daughter," he said, wrapping her in his slender arms. "I knew the truth would come out one day. You are Rachel's and my love child."

Sir Craig Townsend, who was quintessentially British and playing General Corn-

246

well, laughed. "In your dreams, Derrick, my good man. In your dreams." The acclaimed actor had been named CBE for the queen's birthday honors in the early nineties. He was kind and gentlemanly, perfect for General Cornwell, a General Cornwallis–like character. "I'm delighted to see you cast in a living role, my dear." He kissed Chloe's cheeks.

"You and me both."

She moved on to Milka Hardaway, a rising, black actress cast as Millie, the house negro. "Excited to work with you," Chloe said.

"And I you. Plus, who can resist a Jeremiah Gonda film?"

"I know, right?"

She made her way around the table, greeting and talking. Felt like old-home week. Jesse sat at the end of the table, watching her, nodding when their glances crossed.

Since their pizza date, she hadn't seen much of him. They crossed at the pool one Saturday afternoon. He'd been in Vancouver for three weeks shooting a small part in a romcom.

"Got to work when you can get it."

"You can *enjoy* your success, Jesse," she said, across the back lawn one Saturday morning.

"I want to keep working. Never know when it's all going to end."

"Do you have a fear of things ending?"

"Don't you?"

That was the most honest moment she'd ever had with her new friend.

Jesse stood when she made her way to the table's end. "Good to see you."

"And you." She gave him a shy smile.

Jeremiah tapped his glass with a fork, drawing everyone's attention. Chloe sat in the vacant seat next to Jesse and faced her director.

"When Chris decides to grace us with his presence, we'll get started. Has everyone met Jesse? Chloe, why don't you introduce him."

"Me?" She glanced around. All eyes were on her. Waiting. "Y-you discovered him, Jer."

"Yes, but he's your neighbor."

Chloe peered at the screenwriter-slash-actor-slash-MIT-grad. What could she say? Broad shouldered and winsome, wearing jeans and a fitted, gray T-shirt with his hair clipped and styled, he looked . . . good. Amazing, to be honest.

She swallowed. "Well, he's . . ." Settled. Content. And never far from her mind. So much so, she prayed about it this morning. *Please scrub him from my thoughts.* One kiss and a pizza dinner did not warrant this sort of budding preoccupation. "Smart." The rest of the table watched and waited. "Graduated from MIT with some engineering degree."

"Jolly good." Sir Craig, helping her along.

"Wrote *Bound by Love* based on a letter his great-great-great-great-great-great-grandfather wrote."

"Good golly, how many greats is that?" Sir Craig again.

"Six," Jesse said, winking at Chloe.

"He wrote this screenplay to finish a love story his ancestors never could." He nodded at her, and the warm familiarity she felt every time she was with him passed through her.

"This is his first movie, and I'm so honored to be in it."

"Here, here," echoed around the table.

Jesse squeezed her hand under the table.

Jeremiah rose from his seat, holding up his phone. "Painter is not here, no surprise, and not answering my calls or text. Let's get going. Jesse, why don't you read Hamilton's part? Someone give Chloe the fresh pages. We've rewritten the first scene again — refined it."

"Don't you want to wait for Chris?"

"No. And if you don't start reading for

him, I'm going to rethink his role in this picture. Let's go." Jeremiah flipped open his script and read the scene setting. " 'Up-country South Carolina, Kingsley estate, 1780. Esther sitting at her desk in the library with a book and microscope.' " He peered down the long table toward Chloe and Jesse. "Action."

ESTHER: Hamilton . . . you startled me. How did you get in here?

HAMILTON: Millie. Though she assured me you'd not want to be disturbed. (Walks to the desk, picks up a book.) Isaac Newton, *Method of Fluxions.* So you enjoy a bit of casual reading?

ESTHER: You mock me, sir.

HAMILTON: Nay, rather, I hide my ignorance of such studies. What have you under your microscope?

ESTHER: A poor deceased butterfly. Peer through the lens. Such beauty and detail. The finest scientific minds cannot design such a creature.

HAMILTON (Peers briefly through the microscope): It's as beautiful as the one gazing at it. Esther, I must speak with you.

ESTHER (Moves to the chairs by the

250

fireplace): You sound so serious, Hamilton.

HAMILTON: You know of recent events, do you not? The church burnings. The attacks on women and children. I've joined the Cause. I cannot —

ESTHER: What? You promised me you would not. What of us, our plans and our future? War is not child's play. 'Tis not you and Flanders running the hills, playing with sticks and stones as guns and bullets.

HAMILTON (Takes hold of her arm): I'd trade all my possessions for this revolution to be boys at play, but 'tis not possible. It's governments with skilled, trained soldiers. It's militiamen fighting to preserve the fruit of their toil. I am the best sharpshooter in the upcountry. May God forgive my hubris. They've asked me to come along, to make myself useful, attacking the British far behind the line. It could change our advantage. I go to protect you, Esther. Can I have your assurance you will pray for me, stand by me?

ESTHER: What of your word? How you promised me you would not go? "Upon my word," you said, in this very room.

Shall I call Millie as my witness? I'm sure she listened outside.

MILLIE: No, I didn't. (She runs down the hall)

HAMILTON: A foolish promise. One I couldn't keep. I must go with my brethren. Do what my heart dictates.

ESTHER: And what of my heart? Do I not get a say in the matter? Hamilton, I'd rather spend the rest of my life assuring you that you did not choose a coward's course than mourning the life and love we never shared because you met your end with a British bullet.

HAMILTON (Bends to one knee): My darling, we will share every one of our heart's desires when this conflict is over. I will not die. I will not let you go.

ESTHER (Pulls her hands free): Do not make another promise you cannot keep. Whether we are free or under the king, my life is just a short breath in the vastness of time. No one will remember our names. You will spill your blood on the battlefield only to be forgotten when it's plowed under for corn or barely. I want to marry you, Hamilton. Are you shocked at my boldness? I want to bear your children and leave your name, our names, on human hearts. Not battlefields.

HAMILTON: Your words embolden me, Esther. I promise I'll return. You will have your dream.

ESTHER: You say what you wish to be true. But when you go to war, there are no guarantees. If you must go, go. But I cannot lend my heart, nor my support.

HAMILTON: You cannot mean it. Tell me you'll support me.

ESTHER: You must follow your heart, Hamilton, and I must follow mine. (Turns to leave the library)

HAMILTON: What of our love? Our pledge?

ESTHER: You tell me? What of our love and our pledge? (Fade)

A calm reverb hovered over the table as Chloe read the last word, feeling in her being more than what was written on the paper. She peeked at Jesse, who sat back, hiding — if possible — behind the script, his finger over his lips in deep contemplation.

Her instincts were right. This script was about more than his great-times-six-grandfather.

It was about him.

Sir Craig shot to his feet, banging his hands together. "Bravo." One by one, the cast joined the applause.

"Jesse, you're making me wonder if I should've cast you as Hamilton," Jeremiah said, glancing between them. "Well done. Chloe, you're really bringing Esther to life. All right, next scene —"

The French doors swung open, and Chris Painter entered with a crooked grin on his face and Ginger Winters on his arm.

"*Hellooo.* The gang's all here." He made his way around the table, greeting the cast, his words slurred, his balance tipsy as he tried to mimic Sir Craig's accent.

Jeremiah gripped him by the arm. "Excuse us," he said, dragging Chris off to a dark corner by the pool. Their conversation was clipped and muffled but buoyant with tension.

Two hired servers hustled around the table with dripping cold bottles of water and diet sodas.

"— show up here, drunk . . ."

"Tipsy, man. Drunk is . . . negative . . . vibe."

"— I'll have you thrown off . . ."

Chloe angled toward Jesse. "You know Hamilton so well. Such a great first read."

"Thanks, but . . . what's going on over there?" He shot a dark gaze to the corner. "We need Chris. *He* is Hamilton. The star power. Without him . . ."

"Jer and Chris have a love-hate relationship. They'll argue like a couple in a bad marriage, then have a makeup golf game the next day. Don't worry."

He sat back, his expression still pinched. "I hope you're right. Hey, you were amazing. Jeremiah cast the right woman for Esther."

"Jesse, you think you need Chris but I've been reading with him, and you . . . *you are* Hamilton." She accepted a cold water from the server. "Still, I wonder. What's the story between the lines, Jesse Gates? You're trying to tell the world, tell *someone,* something. What is it?"

"You're like a dog with a bone."

"Will she know? Whatever it is you want her to know?" Yes, she was persistent, a dog with a bone.

"Depends," Jesse said. "But in all reality, no. She will never know."

# 16

## ESTHER

*Christmas 1780*

The library was cheerful with men in red-coats wassailing one another, raising their crystal cups in cheer.

Father puffed on his pipe, wishing the men a happy Christmas.

"And in the new year, a victory for the Crown."

Esther moved among their Loyalist guests, seeing to their comforts as hostess of Slathersby Hill, yet going out of her way to avoid Twimball and his band of men.

Since the battle at King's Mountain and the death of Major Ferguson, soldiers visited Father's table night after night, talking of nothing but victory and revenge. Of defeating the rebels.

Presently, four officers billeted in their

home, taking up the spare rooms and, by Esther's estimation, the spare air.

"Esther, my good daughter, can you regale us with a song on the pianoforte?" Father said, "She's a keen pianist, gentlemen."

"Can you play 'Joy to the World'?" This from Captain Lark, a new soldier to the up-country. "I heard it last Christmas in London, and it seemed most fitting."

"Yes, 'Joy to the World.' " Father joined Esther at the piano. He was quite proud of her skill, having sent for a man from Charles Town to give her lessons when she was a child.

Esther sat at the piano, shuffling through her collection.

In the last month she'd seen a change in Father. He spent less time at his desk bent over ledgers and letters, and the blue brilliance had returned to his eyes. He talked of a British victory. Of life returning to normal.

Whatever ailed him concerning Lord Whatham over the summer and fall had healed.

As she began to play, the Englishmen gathered around the piano, raising their voices in song, joyous over the coming of the Lord.

If ever there was a time for Jesus to come,

not as a babe but as a king, now would be a fitting hour. War raged across open fields, through the small South Carolina towns. The rage pitted nation against nation and brother against brother.

*"Let earth receive her king . . ."*

When the song ended they begged for another, slapping one another on the back, goodwill spilling from their weary souls.

"Do you know that new song 'God Rest Ye Merry Gentlemen'?" a young, rosy-cheeked lieutenant asked.

"Certainly." Esther found the sheet and began the jaunty melody.

The men looped their arms about one another and swayed from side to side. The women gathered on the other side of the piano, lifting their soft voices in harmony.

*"God rest ye merry gentlemen . . ."*

They held their voices loud and long on the final word and final note. Then Isaac appeared at the door, resplendent in his livery. "The buffet is laid, Sir Michael."

"Ah, ladies and gentlemen, shall we adjourn to the dining room? Esther, my love, you have such a gift. Come and lead us."

As the party crossed from the parlor to the dining hall, footsteps thudded on the veranda and the door crashed open.

"Sir Michael!" Hamilton, in his buckskins,

his dark hair flowing about his face, filled the entryway. A fire lit his eyes.

"Hamilton," Esther whispered, starting toward him. Father held her back.

"You are trespassing, Lightfoot. Get out of my home. I'll give you the benefit of the season and not ask one of these loyal Englishmen to thrash you."

Hamilton raised a crumpled scroll. "What have you done? Robbed a widow? Stolen what was rightfully hers?"

Father turned to his guests. "Please, go on into the dining room. I'll be along. This young lad apparently has misinformation."

The guests hesitated, especially the British officers, then gradually moved on.

"You too, Esther," Father said with a gentle push against her back.

"I'd rather stay, if you don't mind." Hamilton. Were she not mindful of their guests, she'd run into his arms. At last, he was here. Angry or not.

Since rebuffing her the day he returned from King's Mountain, the day she washed his hair, he'd become all but invisible to her.

He refused her invitation to meet at the willow. Then when she rode Gulliver over to Quill Farm to call him out, he'd already marched off with the Upper Ninety Six.

"Give us back our farm, Sir Michael. Or I'll —"

"What? Burn me down? I've a room full of British officers with a battalion of men at the ready. Your threats mean nothing."

"You lied to Aunt Mary. Asking her to sign a document that would protect her and the farm. But it was all a lie. You took advantage of her grief and sorrow."

"It was merely business. While I used less-than-normal tactics on your aunt, I satisfied the expectations of my employer, Lord Whatham. To whom the land belonged in the first place."

"Then you must pay her for it. Three hundred pounds, not a cent less."

"I will not waste good capital acquiring land I now own."

"What did you do?" Hamilton headed toward Father with a snarl. "Squander Lord Whatham's money on your own pleasures? Perhaps a mistress in Charles Town?"

Esther gasped as Father flared, his face beaming. "How dare you! Get out of my house at once. Leave. Now."

"Father, please, I'm sure Hamilton didn't mean —"

"What do you know of this? Have you been consorting with him behind my back?" His eyes bulged with white ire. "Are you loyal to this heathen over me?"

"Father, no." Esther lowered her voice. By the lack of conversation in the dining room, she knew they must all be listening. "Please, I'm merely concerned for your health. But did you take Mrs. Lightfoot's land?" Father was a demanding man, to be sure, but he was also a fair man.

"I did what I had to do." Father coughed, pressing his hand to his heart, then doubled over, gasping, at last dropping to one knee.

"Sir Michael!" Hamilton knelt beside him as several men rushed from the dining room into the foyer. "Esther, call for Dr. Rocourt. Didn't I see him among your guests?"

"Take him to his library," Esther said. "Dr. Rocourt, Father is in need of you."

When Father was settled with Dr. Rocourt tending him, Esther exited with Hamilton.

"He's going to be all right, Esther."

"He has to be. He must be." She pressed her hand over her heart. "I cannot imagine a world without him."

"My apologies for interrupting your evening. But I could not contain myself once I heard."

"Is it true? Father swindled the land from your aunt?"

"Yes."

Lieutenant Twimball and several of the

261

king's men waited in the foyer. "Well, well, well, we meet again, Lightfoot."

"Indeed. I'm only sorry I did not see you at King's Mountain."

"Nor I you."

Tension mounted under the outwardly cordial exchange. Hamilton looked toward Esther.

"Lieutenant Twimball, Captain Blyth, why don't you return to our dinner. I'll be along. Please, the food is hot, and we cannot let Sassy's hard work go to waste."

"I'm sorry to have disturbed your evening, Esther." He retrieved a scroll from the sack over his shoulder. "This is the legal deed of Quill. I don't care what Aunt Mary signed —"

"Are you still here, Hamilton?" Father appeared around the stairwell, Dr. Rocourt giving chase.

"I advise you to rest, Sir Michael."

"I have guests to attend. Good evening, Hamilton." Father held open the door.

"I have the deed." He waved the scroll at Father. "You cannot possibly have a legal right to Quill. I will find out what you've done."

"That matter is signed, sealed, and delivered by none other than Cornelius Jones, a Loyalist and a friend of Lord Whatham's."

Father's chest rattled with each breath, causing Dr. Rocourt to stand by his side, admonishing him again to lie down.

Hamilton narrowed his gaze. "You're a thief, Sir Michael. Nothing but a common thief, low down and —"

"Hamilton." Esther stepped in for her father. "Why don't you say good night? 'Tis not the hour to air grievances."

He started to speak, then strode for the door, his angry footsteps driving into the hardwood.

"Happy Christmas, Hamilton."

He peered back at her with a nod, sadness in his eyes. "Happy Christmas, Esther."

# 17

## JESSE

*December*

In his guesthouse by the Daschles' pool, Jesse washed and stored away the dishes that had been in the sink for far too long, his stomach rumbling for lack of lunch with no dinner plans on the horizon.

Rehearsals for *Bound by Love,* and last-minute changes in the script inspired by the actors, had consumed him since mid-October.

He'd spent his mornings writing and his afternoons training to be a Revolutionary War soldier, going through the choreographed fight scenes. Just one fight took nearly three weeks to master, so he and the other soldiers didn't appear to be playacting.

Jeremiah insisted that the story ring true. Real.

To that end, Jesse didn't see Chloe much. They had only a few scenes together, and because Jeremiah wanted to hit the ground running once they landed in South Carolina, the director put more emphasis on the physical aspects of Jesse's role than on the emotional.

Putting away the last dish, Jesse peered across the massive lawn toward the back of the Daschles' mansion — okay, toward Chloe's front door — hoping for a glimpse.

He never made it home to Boston for Octoberfest, so he had agreed to fly home for the holidays. He left in three days.

On the table, his phone rang. Jeremiah's number flashed across the screen.

"I've got good news and bad news."

"Do I need to sit down?"

"You know there have been rumblings over at Premier Studios that Prescott White's job was on the chopping block."

Jesse's heart skipped. "Uh-oh. Does that affect us?"

"I got a call today from a friend on the inside. It's going to happen."

"Please tell me that's the bad news."

"It is. The good news is we'll be on site filming before the blade comes down, and we'll be well into the shoot by the time the new head figures out what's going on.

Besides, we're under budget, so he won't be looking at us right away. It's all about the money now."

"I trust your clout, Jeremiah, but we both know the new head can pull the plug on *any* predecessor's project." Jesse had been on the receiving end of canceled projects many times.

"I'm not worried. Nevertheless, this shoot has to go well. On time. Anyway, I just wanted you to know."

"And the rest of the cast?"

"Not a word to them. Painter gives me enough heartache as it is." The aggravation in Jeremiah's voice was palpable. "If he even *thinks* the project could be shut down, he'll jump ship. I can't afford for him to do that on this film. We need his star power. If I have to reshoot, it'll cost millions."

Jesse also heard what Jeremiah did not vocalize. *With a new screenwriter, we need all the help we can get.* He started to speak but had to clear the hitch in his voice. "W-we have you, Jer. You're plenty of star power."

"Chris is a huge draw. We already have press demanding an audience. He's never played this type of character before, one with this much heart and depth. People will want to see if he has the chops."

Jesse circled the boxy living room and paused at the window when he saw Chloe tugging a Christmas tree through a wrought iron gate toward the guesthouse, a box under her arm.

"But don't worry," Jer said.

"Worry? No, of course not."

"I'll have this film in the can before the new studio head has warmed his chair."

Jeremiah's confidence boosted Jesse's. "Okay. And, Jer, thanks for calling."

"No problem. I'm really proud of you, of this project, and I want it to go well. Hey, Laura wanted me to ask if you had Christmas plans. If not, you're welcome to join our crazy brood."

"Thanks, really. But I'm going home." Jesse watched as Chloe trekked his way, his smile blooming all the way from his shadowy soul.

"Have a good time. See you in South Carolina. Did you send your travel plans to Becky? We'll arrange to get you from the airport."

"All submitted."

"Good. Merry Christmas, Jesse."

"Merry Christmas, Jeremiah."

A light knock rattled his door. When he opened it, Chloe flowed inside, bringing with her the joy of the season and the intoxicating scent of flowers and pine.

"Ho, ho, ho and Merry Christmas." She hoisted the tree onto the table by the front window. The one facing the driveway. "I rescued this from the side of the road." She stood back, admiring her work. "What do you think? Perfect? I agree."

"Where'd you get the tree stand?" Jesse knelt down to inspect the stand's viability. It was a tradition in the Gateses' household for the tree to topple at least once during the season.

"Our gardener found it in the shed."

Jesse stood, the tree stand having passed inspection. "So, do I *need* a Christmas tree?"

"Unless you're the Grinch, yes." She set the box on the floor and knocked off the lid. "Come on, help me string lights."

"I'm leaving for Boston in three days."

"Doesn't mean you can't have a bit of Christmas light in your life." She rattled an old string of lights, shaking out the tangles. "These are Mr. Crumbly's, but since he's not here . . ." She handed the plug to Jesse. "The socket's under the sill."

He regarded her for a second, pretty sure he looked like a grinning fool, then dropped to one knee to do her bidding.

A burst of red, blue, green, and golden

light warmed the room and changed everything.

"Here." Chloe handed him the strand. "You do that side, I'll do this one."

Together they wrapped the tree in lights. Chloe softly sang "O Christmas Tree." The short wisps of her reddish-gold hair freed from her braid bounced to the tune she sang.

Jesse peered at her through the branches, finding rest in the cushion of her voice. She was a blend of confidence and timidity, savvy and innocence, casual and classy, walking in a beauty she neither flaunted nor ignored.

And in those jeans — shew! A tad sexy.

"Tuck this last bit around the top," she said, passing him the end of the strand, her fingers brushing his, making this moment a come-to-life Currier and Ives.

If he could click his heels and decimate his past and unlock his heart, he'd spend the rest of his life creating memories like this with Chloe Daschle.

But he didn't have a pair of magic shoes. A way to undo what had been done. No way to justify his right to any sort of romantic happiness.

"Perfect." Chloe admired their handiwork. Jesse stood alongside her, and heaven help him, he slipped into a moment where they were married and this was their first Christmas. The scene unfolded before him like a movie. Like a life he had yet to live. The sentiment buzzed in his chest. Sent chills down his arm.

The movie, his upcoming departure for Boston, Jeremiah's recent news were a million years away. But as quickly as it came, it faded. He was flawed Jesse again, feet firmly planted in his rented guesthouse, unworthy of the woman next to him.

"Y-you're a fan of Christmas?" he said, distracting his thoughts from a journey not worth traveling.

"Absolutely! Please don't tell me you're not. I was really starting to like you." She retrieved a few baubles from the box. "I couldn't find Mr. Crumbly's ornaments. These will do until I buy more."

"You don't have to buy more."

"And have you sitting over here with a naked Christmas tree? Please. I'd not wish it on my worst enemy."

Jesse laughed. "You're something else, Chloe Daschle."

"Am I?"

His compliment, and her tone, crossed into an intimate zone. Her gaze lingered on him.

"I think you know you are." He reached for one of the ornaments, setting it on a thin branch. But it was too big and the thing just sagged.

"I try to believe, but . . ." Chloe removed Jesse's ornament, setting it on a lower, stronger branch, where it swung happily side to side. "Maybe I'm just a legend in my own mind. But since I got . . . well . . ." She peered up at him. "Saved. I've changed."

"Yeah? Seems hard to imagine, but I guess faith helps people." He picked another ornament and the appropriate-size branch. "So, you're a real fan of Christmas? Of Jesus and His birthday?"

Chloe hesitated, fixing an antique-looking, gold ball on the edge of a branch. "I am." She peered at Jesse, her eyes glossy. "He truly saved me. Quite literally."

There was a time he'd have debated her. Just because. Even if his scientific mind understood that the universe flowed under the hand of an unseen Creator. But the tone of her voice, the emotion in her eyes, stirred him toward curiosity instead of deliberation. "You'll have to tell me the story one day."

"We're building up a lot of stories to tell each other."

When they'd arranged the six ornaments and Chloe was satisfied, she motioned toward the big house. "Mom and Dad have gone out. The lanai fireplace is glowing, the tree is lit, and Glenda made her amazing chicken and rice." She tucked her fingers into her pockets. "If you're not doing anything . . ."

"Chicken and rice? One of my favorites."

Jesse walked with her across the lawn, through the cool breeze, toward the Daschles' lanai, which had been turned into a Christmas fairyland. White lights wrapped the posts and ran the perimeter of the ceiling. A grand, tall Christmas tree ornamented the corner by the fireplace, the branches stuffed with glass balls and a flowing, gold ribbon.

Music dropped down from hidden speakers. "O Come, O Come, Emmanuel."

"Have you done your shopping?" Chloe said, opening the doors to the kitchen, the warmth of the house escaping.

"None."

"Jesse Gates, you're a Scrooge!" She took two plates from the glass cupboard.

"I'll shop once I'm in Boston."

"What? Two days before Christmas?"

He grinned with a shy laugh. "I suppose you plan your gifts for weeks."

"Months." She lifted the lid of the slow cooker. The aroma of roasting chicken and rice steamed as she filled two Christmas tableau plates, handing one to Jesse. "The cutlery is in that drawer. Can you grab me a knife and fork?" She retrieved linen napkins from another drawer. "Drinks are in the outside fridge."

He followed her. How could he not? She hooked him deeper with every encounter, and like a black hole, one day he might not be able to escape her pull.

But for now they settled on the sofa, Chloe sitting cross-legged, plate anchored on her knee, popping a Diet Coke.

Jesse leaned forward, plate on his palm. "Why all the planning?"

"Christmas is personal. The gifts should mean something." She scooped a big bite of chicken and rice. "Everything about the holiday, at least in the beginning, speaks of intimacy."

He frowned. "How so?" And why did her words disquiet him?

"Think about it? God becoming man. No, a *baby.* To save the world, yes — but also to somehow save you, me. It's personal. It's the ultimate epic story. Worthy of Mel Gibson."

Jesse nodded, though the disquiet became

discomfort. "You're lucky you found the story."

She set down her fork and reached for her drink. "Lucky is one word for it. I was so, so, so lost . . . hurting. Oh! Your gift." She jumped up.

"What? Gift? Chloe, wait —"

She left the lanai, ran across a patch of wintergreen grass, and disappeared down the mansion's breezeway.

Jesse set down his dish and reached for his tea. A gift? She bought him a gift? His mind raced. He didn't deserve a gift. Did he have anything at the guesthouse he could disguise as a gift?

Chloe returned, breathless, her cheeks rosy, and handed him a large, square box wrapped in green and gold paper.

"Open it."

"Chloe, you didn't have to do this. I didn't get you —"

"Will you be quiet? Sheesh, Jesse, the purpose of a gift is to receive, not dismiss. Besides, you did give me a gift. Your screenplay."

"Hardly. I didn't even know you when I wrote it." He tugged at the ribbon, her generosity humbling him.

"But He did." She pointed upward. "You may have written it to complete your grandfather's love story, or to answer some question in your own heart, but I think Jesus said, 'Write it for Chloe too.' " She'd cupped her hands around her mouth, whispering, as if the voice of a Savior could be heard. "Go on, open it."

She took up her plate again and sat back, smiling, eating, tucking her bare foot between the sofa cushions.

After tearing the ribbon and paper away, Jesse lifted the lid from the box. Nestled in red tissue paper was a light-wood and brushed-silver frame. The glass was empty, but the bottom held a gold plaque.

*Bound by Love* BY JESSE GATES
DEDICATED TO HIS ANCESTOR
HAMILTON LIGHTFOOT

When he looked closer, he saw lines from the script etched into the glass. Bits and pieces of the story. Bits and pieces of him.

He'd not entertained tears in years. When he looked at Chloe, he could not hide them.

"This is incredible. But why? How?"

She set down her plate and leaned toward him. "I thought you could frame the letter, you know, if you wanted. I was going to sneak into the guesthouse when you weren't there, but trespassing for a Christmas present seemed a bit much." She tapped the edge of the frame. "I had a friend make it. This is cedar, because it's timeless and fragrant. The brushed silver is for redemption. How you redeemed your grandfather's story."

"And the etching?"

"The story itself. Transparent. For all to see."

Jesse cleared his voice. He was the exact opposite of transparent. "It's too much, Chloe. Th-thank you." The intimacy of the gift drew him even more to her. "It's the coolest gift I've ever received. I feel undeserving."

"Don't we all? Isn't that what Christmas is about?" She pressed her hand to his leg. "Merry Christmas, Jesse."

"Merry Christmas, Chloe." Taking her hand, he pulled her to him.

"Merry Christmas, Jesse."

The touch of her bow lips shot love — no, not love, affection — into his heart. But she was changing him. Any more moments like this and he'd lose control. His kiss was a shallow response to the depth and pleasure her gift stirred in him.

When he broke away, she tapped her head to his. "This is getting complicated."

"Thanks to you," he said, slipping his

hand around her neck and kissing her again.

"Maybe after the movie we can —"

"Chloe, we . . ." Jesse set the frame back in the box. He was twisted. Divided. Torn. Bursting to be free, to love, yet still anchored to fear. "I don't know . . . I guess . . . I'm just . . ."

"If you tell me whatever you're fighting to hide, maybe I can help. Maybe it's not as bad as you think."

Jesse stood, pacing to the fireplace, into the glow of the Christmas lights, and back again. Okay, okay, tell her. Just . . . do it.

"In the box where you saw Hamilton's letter there was something else. Something far less pleasant."

She picked up her plate and cradled it in her lap, watching, waiting.

"I feel rather numb about it all . . . it's the past . . . but also it haunts my present and, I fear, my future."

"One of those things you can never entirely shake."

"Exactly."

"I get that, Jesse. I do." Chloe thoughtfully stirred her chicken and rice, taking a small bite, gazing toward the fireplace. "Just when I think I'm free from the past, it rises from the dead to mock me."

Returning to his seat beside her, Jesse took

up his plate, his stomach rumbling, though his appetite evaded him.

"We'd dated for a year," he said.

"Ah, it's always a love story, isn't it? Not one like the movies, but a real life one. Painful. Sad."

"How long did you date your sad love story?"

"Three years. Three stupid years," she said.

"We met in class my senior year at MIT. She was brilliant, witty, gorgeous —"

"Of course."

"— and crazy." He gave Chloe a pressed smile. "But oh, we were . . . hot and heavy."

"Oh my gosh, same here. We met on set."

"Naturally." Jesse slipped a bit of chicken into his mouth.

"He was gorgeous, talented, charming. I mean, wow. I couldn't believe he noticed me. But he was a bit loco, and I don't mean in a good way."

"My brother tried to warn me. We were going too fast."

"No one warned me, but it wouldn't have done any good," she said. "He was my *soul mate,* and anyone who declared otherwise was no friend of mine."

By the music of the season, the twist of the Southern California December breeze, and the glow of the tree, Jesse and Chloe wove their stories together. Like a well-rehearsed play. Jesse wasn't sure he'd have gotten his out otherwise. He loved the rhythm of their unusual conversation.

"Spring break came," he said. "And she invited us all to her uncle's in Melbourne Beach, Florida."

"We were coming up on our third anniversary. Surely he was going to propose."

"Loxley wanted me to propose. Even took me ring shopping a month before spring break. But I was twenty years old. Book smart, yes, but extremely immature. Suddenly, the girl I thought I loved was choking me."

"Twenty?" she said, a fork full of chicken and rice suspended in front of her mouth. "You got your bachelor's from MIT at twenty?"

"No." He sipped his tea. "My master's."

"OMG," she whispered. "Now I'm intimidated."

"Don't be . . . you've not heard the rest of my story. W-what about you? What happened next?"

"I was twenty-six, fixed on finding my true love, and Haden, at least in my mind, was *the* guy. And I was also determined to have a meaningful career." She mimed an explosion. "Boom!"

"But you do have a meaningful career, Chloe."

"You've not heard the rest of my story either. What happened next with you?"

"My brother and I had already started a tech company. DiamondBros. Most of it was on paper, design ideas, where we wanted to put our efforts. Mom helped us incorporate, and Dad introduced us to a couple of investors."

"For me, I was a twenty-year veteran in the business, but I'd gone no further than supporting characters and cinematic death. Haden was up for the part in —"

"Haden." Reality dawned. "Stuart. You dated the star of *Space Avengers*?"

"Don't judge me."

Jesse sat back, hands up. "I'm not. I love that franchise. But Haden Stuart —" He'd met the actor a few times. He was a world-class jerk.

"Tell me about it. But I was in love. And supposed to play Twist, his kick-butt side-kick and occasional girlfriend."

"Really? You would've been an amazing Twist."

"But I blew it."

Jesse frowned. "How did you —"

"You go. Last I heard, young genius Jesse

Gates was in Florida for spring break."

"Right, so, on our last night there, Loxley kept hinting . . ."

"About the ring? *The* question?"

"Yep, but I knew one thing. I didn't love her. Not like a man should love a woman he's about to marry. Again, I was just *twenty.* I wasn't ready for marriage. But Lox was a list maker and a goal setter. Grad school and engagement were next on her to-dos. But I didn't feel like being someone's check box. Even if she . . ." He shook his head, the sharpness of his dark confession disrupting his peace. "Let's just say being book smart doesn't make you heart smart."

"Oh, trust me, I know. I'm not a genius like some folks sitting on this sofa —"

"Stop."

"But I was an A student. Even in math and science."

Jesse popped Chloe a high five. "Go on. Last time in our story, our heroine was hot and heavy with Captain Steel Jones."

"Ha! Very funny. Okay, well, a girlfriend invited me to dinner at E.P. & L.P. We had a rooftop view of the city at sunset. Perfect setup for a proposal. *Haden's behind this,* I thought. *He's lured me up here for a surprise engagement party.*" She arched her brow. "I'm nothing if not a dreamer. I imagined

281

this whole scene, Kathy and I arriving to find the deck reserved for a special occasion. She'd pretend to sneak up to see what was going on, begging me to go with her. Of course, Haden would be waiting for me on one knee, holding up a big, fat diamond ring."

"I was in a movie with that scenario once. I played the best friend."

"That's probably where I got the idea. The fantasy of it all."

"I take it he wasn't waiting there with a ring."

"Oh, he was there, all right." Chloe sat back, taking a bite of her dinner, motioning for Jesse to continue.

"I found a plastic ring in a gumball machine at the local convenience store. Spent about five bucks trying to get it, but I did. It was hideous. I thought, *This is going to be so funny. Giving her a fake engagement ring.*" I figured she'd get mad, tell me to grow up, and maybe, hopefully, decide I was a tasteless cad and break up with me. Have the old 'You're so immature' argument."

Chloe set her plate on the table and took up her Diet Coke. "As my girlfriend and I walked to our table — she was going on and on about a new role she'd auditioned for — then bam! There he was. Haden."

"So he was there?"

"All golden and gorgeous. Perfect. I ran over to him just as he bent forward to kiss the woman sitting next to him. Marilyn West."

"Marilyn West? He threw you over for Marilyn? Wow . . . Way to trade a million-dollar-girl for one who's a dime a dozen. The man has no taste."

"Maybe, but that moment was a knife to my heart." Her eyes glistened.

"I'm so sorry, babe." The intimate nickname slipped from his lips without warning, without premeditation. "That had to hurt."

"Oh, the story gets worse. Your turn."

Jesse set his plate aside and slumped down against the cushions, bracing for the painful edge of his memories.

"We'd gone down to the beach for a game of football and a final dip in the waves. The music was playing, the guys were running for fake touchdowns, and the girls were strutting in their bikinis. That's when I get the wild idea to fake-propose in front of everyone. The joke would be on *me*."

"Turns out the joke *was* on me," Chloe said. "I was so shocked, I walked right up to them. 'Haden, what are you doing?' " She winced, mirroring Jesse's move to duck into the sofa cushions. " 'Is this a scene? Are you shooting up here?' I even glanced around for the cameras and crew. They were filming a romcom together, but I wasn't aware of any rooftop scenes."

"Oh, he was in *Slap Happy* with Marilyn, wasn't he? But there were no cameras there that night?'"

"Oh, there were cameras, all right." Chloe swigged from her Diet Coke. "Your turn."

"We'd finished the football game, brought out all the leftovers, built a fire in the fire pit, watched the sunset. That's when I pulled my stunt. With a glance at my brother, like, *Watch this,* I bent to one knee in front of Loxley. Dan went crazy, shaking his head. 'Jess,' he said. But I ignored him, took the ring from my pocket, and said, 'Loxley, will you marry me?' "

"When Haden saw me, he jumped up like he'd been touched with fire. 'Chloe?' he said. 'What are you doing here?' I smartly replied, 'I was going to ask you the same thing.' Marilyn turned red as the sunset and said, 'You told me you two broke up.' She started to leave, and he chased after her. That's when it went down. I lost my mind. I went berserk, whacko, cuckoo. 'You're on a date with Marilyn? You're cheating on me?' Didn't help I had dated Clark Davis, who perpetually cheated on me. So I stepped on Haden's foot and socked him in the face. I screamed. Cussed him up one side and down the other. Then Marilyn got involved. 'No wonder he's done with you.' Then, oh, it was on! A cat fight like you've never seen. So irate and hurt, I didn't see the cell phones coming out."

"So the cameras *were* there."

"About fifty of them."

"Man." Jesse shook his head, stretching his legs long. "I was *horrible* to Loxley. When I got down on one knee, she gasped, started crying, looking around at her also-gasping girlfriends, and reached for the ring. She stared at it for a moment, frowning. I'm all *Hee, hee, hee, this is so funny,* waiting for her to get it." He mocked himself, the anger in his tone real. "Then she gave me a look that could've killed. 'What's this?' I snickered, 'Your ring, m'lady.' She shot me blue daggers. 'Jesse Gates, what's going on? Are you proposing or not? Where's the ring I picked out?' Right then and there, I knew my error. Big mistake. She freaked. 'Do you seriously mean to propose to me with this cheap, hideous *bleep, bleep, bleep* ring?' And suddenly I'm not smiling anymore."

"Haden broke up the fight with Marilyn and unleashed on me. Called me all sorts of wicked names." Her tears bubbled up again. "I wish he'd struck me instead. Even now, two years later, I can still hear each nasty name and the tone of his voice."

"Lox slapped me silly and stormed off, steam coming out of her ears. I caught up to her, tried to apologize, but she was livid. 'Do you mean to marry me or not?' In light of everything, I had to be honest. 'No, well, not right now. I'm only twenty. Dan and I are starting a business.' She spit in my face and demanded to know if I loved her. 'Not like that,' I said. 'I wish I did, Lox, but I don't. I think there's someone else for me.' " He huffed. "To this day I don't know why I said that."

"You had to be honest."

"Yeah, but I never imagined there'd be someone else for me. The words just came out." He sat up to bear the burden of his past.

"I went off on Haden, striking him over and over. Four-letter words flying." She batted her hands in the air, demonstrating. "Finally he pinned my arm to my side and said, 'Chloe, it's over. You're so fixated on the stupid idea of true love you can't see we're not right. I don't love you. You're not a girlfriend, you're a leech.' "

"A leech?" He couldn't see it. Never. She

was so giving and gentle. Beautiful. The perfect remedy to any man's bachelor life. "Chloe, trust me, you are no leech."

"Be grateful you've never been my boyfriend." She laughed, but he knew it wasn't real. "But it wasn't enough for me that he told me it was over in front of fifty smart phones. Nooo. I had to start crying, wailing, pleading with him to stay with me. Work it out." Chloe pressed a throw pillow to her face. "Ack, it makes me sick to think about it."

"Loxley ran off. Down the beach. Hollering for me to leave her alone. I knew she needed to process, so I went back to the house and our stunned friends. But I was convinced if she thought about it, she'd realize she didn't love me either. Not enough for marriage. She just wanted to check off her list. Her dad was a cop, her mom a nurse, her brother a professor, her sister an international financier."

"But no human heart should ever have to hear 'I don't love you.' "

"I regret my words, trust me. But if I didn't tell her —"

"Haden's confession popped my own idyllic bubble."

"Why was it so important to you? To be married? Besides the incredible ideas you have about the institution." He still mused over her confession that night on the deck of the Santa Monica house.

"I can't really explain it." Her tears spilled freely. "I've wanted it ever since I could remember. I think I was born with the longing."

"I don't know about marriage but . . . I've never confessed this to anyone . . . I knew from a young age there was someone special for me. Sometimes I imagined I could see her." His gaze lingered on Chloe's face, and when his heart thumped, he looked away.

"I've dated four men, thinking each was 'the one.' Surely they would love me because I loved them. But all I got in return was dismissed and crushed."

"I was too much of a geek to date before Loxley."

"Geek or not, Jesse, have you looked in the mirror?"

He grinned. "I've changed since coming to Hollywood."

"You got a new face? Hair implants?"

"No, but . . . Let's just say a stylist can do wonders."

"But Loxley saw beyond the awkward, poorly styled man?"

"More like awkward, poorly styled boy, but yes." He shook his head, remembering those early days. "She was the opposite of me. Outgoing, with a wit that could flay a man in one word. When she set her sights on me . . . I surrendered."

"I cried myself to sleep that night. After Haden. I hid in my apartment for the weekend. My friend Stella — well, you know Stella — called nonstop. Came by, knocked on the door. I never answered. My sister finally came over Sunday evening. When I saw her face, I knew something horrible had happened. 'You're all over the Internet, Chloe.' I couldn't believe it." She drew her legs to her chest and curled her toes into the sofa cushion. "I'd just auditioned for Twist and an amazing role in an ensemble film. Two days later my agent called. Both producers passed. I knew, I knew . . . it was the fifty videos of me battering Haden and cursing like a wicked witch."

"Our section of the beach was private, owned by a small, beach neighborhood. We had the place to ourselves. Night came. Still no Loxley. I was worried. Wallowing in guilt. So we went looking for her. Dan and I, our friends Hugh and David, Melanie, who was Loxley's best friend, and Gena, David's girlfriend. Couldn't find her. I sat up all night, kept the fire going, walked up and down the beach every twenty minutes or so. Melanie assured me she was fine, just ticked and making sure I paid. She didn't answer her phone . . ."

"Dad tried to run interference for me," Chloe said. "But in today's world, if a producer thinks you're going to be trouble, they cut you a wide berth."

"Lifeguards found Loxley on the beach the next morning. About a half mile from the house. Drowned. Near as they could figure, she got caught in a riptide."

"Oh, Jesse." Chloe sat up, pressing her hand on his arm. "You're kidding. She . . . died? I'm so sorry."

"Worst feeling in the world is to call a girl's parents and tell them their youngest kid isn't coming home. All their hopes and dreams, their future regarding her, gone. Her talent and ability, her light, all doused." His gaze lingered on the Christmas tree. "There was an investigation, of course, and afterward I tried to hang around Boston for a year, but . . . I had to get away. Escape. I moved out here the next summer."

"Dad spent thousands of dollars trying to rid the Internet of those videos. But as you know, it's impossible. I saw five seconds of one and . . ." She pressed her hand to her middle. "I couldn't believe it was me. Every six months or so, the stupid things resurface. I make some kind of best-of or worst-of list. Then it gets shared on Facebook, thus the world, all over again."

"Her parents started the Loxley Brant scholarship foundation. When I sold *Bound by Love,* I sent them ten thousand dollars."

"Jesse, that's wonderful. See, you're moving on. Being forgiven. Forgiving yourself."

"They sent it back."

"Oh."

"It's okay. I understand. You know, renting the house in Santa Monica was my attempt to move on, put the past behind me. First time I'd been to the ocean in eight years."

"But look, you ended up here." She swung her hand toward the breadth of the lanai.

His gaze blended with hers. "Look, I ended up here."

"We're a pair, aren't we?"

"Quite."

Chloe slid over next to him, lifting his arm around her shoulders and cradling herself against his chest, resting her cheek over his heart, and together they sat in silence and simply breathed.

# 18

## HAMILTON

*Hannah's Cowpens*
*South Carolina Colony*
*January 16, 1781*

It was an eve like none other. A victory at dawn could very well turn the tide of this tense conflict.

Hamilton warmed himself by the fire, the cold settling in his bones. The men with him, Georgia militiamen, said little as they stretched their hands toward the flames, shivering, perhaps more from fear than cold.

Next to him, Ralphie Standish, no more than a youth of seventeen, stared into the darkness, breathing into his cold, cupped hands. "Do you think we'll sleep tonight?"

"We should try." But Hamilton doubted he'd catch one wink. Not the way his adrenaline ebbed and flowed.

Other than the small stand of trees where he and the others sat, Hannah's Cowpens was open ground. Perfect for cattle grazing. Perfect for battle.

The field appeared to be level, but a survey revealed the terrain sloped just beyond the maple swamp. General Morgan had built his strategy accordingly. Earlier that day he'd declared, "On this ground I will defeat the British or lay my bones."

Hamilton had cradled his rifle in his arms, the barrel resting on his shoulder. Morgan made his duty, along with the other skirmishers, most clear.

"Let the enemy get within killing distance . . . fifty yards . . . then blaze away, especially men with epaulets."

Imagining how he'd execute his duty, Hamilton felt at once both old and young. At twenty-two, his life stretched before him. Yet this may well be his last night on earth.

He reached into his haversack for his stationery and the stub of a pencil he'd brought along.

In the firelight, he began.

My dearest Esther,

But his thoughts drifted to Pa and Ma, to Betsy. To Uncle Laurence and Aunt Mary.

To the Twenty-Third Psalm.

*The Lord is my shepherd; I shall not want.*

He wished for the eloquence of the psalmist David to express his longings. But he was a warrior. A deviant. Sweetness was far from him.

After the Christmas confrontation with Sir Michael at Slathersby Hill, he wrote to Esther, asking her to meet him at the willow. This time she declined. Hamilton didn't blame her. Not when he added it all up. His contemptuous attitude toward her upon his return from King's Mountain and his rude intrusion on Christmas Day.

Sir Michael sent Aunt Mary a lease — a lease! — allowing her to rent her own farm from the Whatham holdings for ten pounds a month. Ten pounds! 'Twas free and clear before his shenanigans.

Hamilton stirred, kicking another log onto the fire. Just thinking about it made him boil. When this battle was over, he'd devote every waking moment to discovering the truth.

Wilson Howard joined the circle. "Am I the only one wondering what we're doing here facing a bunch of trained redcoats?"

Bradley Holmes, from Ninety Six, was a man of virtue and courage. He fought like the dickens at King's Mountain yet did not participate in the murder of surrendered troops. "You were at King's Mountain, Howard," Bradley said. "We defeated trained redcoats there and then some. Isn't that right, Lightfoot?"

"Do not remind me."

The voice of General Morgan brought the men to their feet. "Hello." Hamilton's letter drifted to the ground as the officer emerged from the trees.

"Be of cheer. You can do this, boys," the general said. "Just hold your heads up and fire three shots. Then you're free. When you return to your homes, the old folks will bless you, and the girls will kiss you for your gallant conduct."

Around the fire, he shook each man's hand before indicating Hamilton should follow him. When they were out of earshot, Morgan said, "Colonel Pickens tells me you fought valiantly at King's Mountain. Assures me you're a fine shot."

"Yes, sir."

The general knelt and took a map from his pocket, reading it by the distant yellow firelight.

"You're one of them. They'll listen to you. Don't let them break rank, Lightfoot. They must fire three shots. Stay among the trees, but do not retreat until the call is made."

He ran the edge of his knife along the land's contour lines. "While you reload, another man steps forward to fire. Three volleys. That's all I ask. The Continental regulars and Virginia militia will be here." He tapped the map where the lines indicated a slope. "Colonel Tarleton will expect you boys to run the moment they return fire. But we're going to outsmart him." The general clapped Hamilton on the shoulder. "I'd like nothing more than to prove that old butcher wrong." The British colonel was renowned for his savagery. "Can I count on you?"

"Indeed you can, sir." Hamilton dabbed the warm perspiration from his cold brow. The sensation was familiar, haunting. An echo of his father crying out for mercy floated through him.

Then he imagined Uncle Laurence, burned and charred. And Esther, pistol-shot and collapsing under Twimball's bullet. His senses tasted revenge.

"You're a good man, Lightfoot." The general rolled up the map and returned to the fire. "Fill your bellies, boys, then rest. Tarleton prefers a dawn attack. Remember, three shots. Then lead those blasted redcoats into our trap." He looked each one in the face. "Fight with courage. For your families. The Almighty is on our side."

Hamilton sat on the log by Ralphie.

"Your stationery." The boy handed him the stiff, folded pages.

"Thank you."

"What'd the general want?"

"For me to make sure we each fire three shots before retreating to where the Continentals wait. Can I count on you, Ralphie?" Hamilton settled his stationery on his knee.

"Yes, sir." Ralphie motioned to the letter. "Do you have a girl, Hamilton?"

He tapped the paper with his pencil. "I'm not sure."

"How is a man not sure? I know I don't have a girl, and I'm glad of it. I'd hate to wonder what she was feeling now. It's bad enough I know my ma is wearing through the floorboards with her pacing."

Hamilton roped his arm about the boy's narrow shoulders, sensing a slight shiver. "But won't she be proud when you return home a hero?"

"I want to be brave but —"

"Bravery is fighting in the midst of your fear, not in absence of it."

Ralphie grinned. "You sound like Pa."

Hamilton stood. "Come on, let's try for sleep."

Stretching out on his bedroll next to Hamilton, the boy was asleep within moments. But Hamilton lay awake, hands cupped behind his head, listening to the sounds of the night.

Creeping to the fire, he kicked another log into the smoldering embers and closed his eyes, letting his heart speak instead of his head.

Hannah's Cowpens

January 16, 1781

My dearest Esther,

My recent actions have not Demonstrated my sincerest affections. I seek to Remedy any confusion now, on this Eve of Battle. Remember me as Before. When my Deeds, if not my Words, proved my Heart.

I love you. 'Tis no other Truth.

Affectionately Yours,<br>Hamilton Lightfoot

## CHLOE

*Chesnee, South Carolina*
*January*

Long hours with the hairstylist and makeup artist transformed her into Esther Kingsley, daughter of a Loyalist upcountry man.

Jeremiah had rented a large, old estate for the Kingsley home. Coming down the stairs for her first scene, she imagined the real Esther, whatever her station in life, might have dwelled in something similar.

She wore a blue dress with a cream-colored scarf tucked around the scoop neckline and black buckle shoes. The stylist fixed Chloe's real hair — she had plenty of it — into an array of tightly coiled drop curls.

Heading into the dining room, running lines in her head for the first scene, Chloe bumped into Jesse dressed as Flanders in fringed buckskin and knee-high moccasins.

"Oh —" She lost a bit of her breath. "Hello."

Since the night on the lanai, they'd become friends. Good friends. When he departed for his Christmas holiday, she missed him. And now that he stood in front of her, she trembled.

"I wondered when I'd see you," he said, smiling, tempting her to kiss him. Just . . . kiss him!

How many times had she gazed toward the guesthouse hoping to see him? *Surprise, I came back!* She was such a sucker for the unexpected, for romantic gestures.

When he called on Christmas Eve, she lay on the floor under the family Christmas tree, her new slippers — Mom always gave the family slippers on Christmas Eve — dangling from her toes as Bing Crosby crooned in the background. They talked and talked and talked until the first hour of her California Christmas morning.

He'd framed the original Hamilton Lightfoot letter and given it to his parents that night. His mom cried and his dad choked up. They loved it. Best gift they'd ever received.

"You're welcome," Chloe had said. "I told you."

"I owe you one."

But the distance also gave her time to think, consider their relationship, and raise her guard. Which seemed to crumble at the sight of him.

But he'd made no indication he wanted anything more than friendship. After hearing Loxley's story, she didn't blame him.

After telling him her story about Haden, she *still* didn't blame him. They both sat on the edge of caution.

"Wow," he said. "You look like Esther. At least how I pictured her." He touched the edge of her curls. "Is that your hair?"

"Yeah. Michele said she'd rather style my

hair than a wig."

Jesse drew her into a hug, setting his cheek against her hair-sprayed head. "I feel like I've known you forever."

She inhaled the scent of his buckskin and the fragrance of the man beneath. "Me too."

Oh, this was not good. She was falling . . . in love. Once again, her girlish romantic notions steered her toward trouble. Leaping. Sinking at the mere sight of him. Captured by a mere smile.

With a deep breath, Chloe pushed out of his arms.

"H-how was Boston?" Why did he have to look so . . . so good? Manly. He'd grown out his hair for the part and wore it loose about his neck, looking very much like an eighteenth-century backwoods man.

"Boston was good. Cold. Snowy." His posture of leaning against the doorjamb with folded arms and squared shoulders brought to mind every hero she'd imagined as a girl.

"Did you see Loxley's parents?"

"I tried. Wanted to take the scholarship money over, but they were out of town. Maybe it's for the best."

"Give them time."

"It's been eight years. I don't think they'll ever forgive me, and I don't blame them."

Since their lanai confessions, he had brought up the incident at least two more times, revealing a part of himself she'd not seen before. Chloe's friendly affection for him grew with her admiration.

"All you can do is ask." She squeezed his arm. "I'm working on forgiving myself. Letting go. You do the same. Come on, Jesse, we're on the set of *your* movie." She threw her hands in the air. "Woo-hoo!"

"Right, right. Sorry to bring up . . ." He clapped his hands together and motioned toward the window where the crew was setting up for Hamilton to rescue Esther from a runaway horse. "Big first scene. You ready? I was so excited I couldn't sleep last night."

"Me either."

"I bet. You're being saddled to a runaway horse on opening day."

"I just have to hang on for fifteen seconds, look terrified, and the stunt double will do the rest."

"Stunt double?" He made a face. "Coward."

Chloe popped him on the arm. "I'd like to live to see this film in theaters."

"Jesse? You coming?" Jeremiah walked through the house with determined purpose. "We're setting up."

"Yes, sir." Jesse started after him with a

passing comment to Chloe. "Off to learn from the master."

"Jesse?" she called.

He paused at the door. "Yeah?"

"This scene, with Esther on the horse — it's about Loxley and the riptide, right? You'd have saved her if you'd known."

He regarded her, then shifted his gaze away and scanned the grounds. "Don't read too much into everything, Chloe."

"But it's the riptide, isn't it?"

"Yeah, it's the riptide."

He walked away with his back straight and proud, and she tipped just a little over the edge of love.

Lori Twichell, the unit manager, came into the room. "You ready?" She smiled. "The trainer and horse are here. We want a quick run-through."

"Fine, but is my *hero* here?" Chloe had been in South Carolina for a week and had yet to see Chris Painter, her esteemed co-star.

"We think he's here. Not sure, but we're setting up anyway. Especially since the trainer is here . . . You might as well rehearse. Jer can get shots of you looking terrified."

"Which won't require much acting, if any." She loved horses. From afar. Her one and only childhood foray into horseback riding ended with her face-first in a pile of . . . Well, you know. Fill in the blank.

Chloe headed out with Lori just as Jeremiah charged up the sloping lawn toward the house, phone to his ear, arms waving. The director of photography, Sandy Logan, charged up the slope next to him, along with Jer's militant assistant, Becky.

"He's not here!" Jeremiah tucked his phone into his pocket, steaming, pacing, hands on his belt, his blondish hair on end.

"Painter's not here?" Lori said.

"If he is, we can't find him," Beck said. "I've called and called. He doesn't answer." She clutched her iPad, her lifeline, to her chest.

"That arrogant son of a . . . I knew it." Jer walked to the end of the porch and back. "I told Laura over Christmas that Painter was going to be a pain in my —"

Jesse joined the huddle, standing back, arms crossed, listening.

"Jer, I have his agent on the line," Becky said.

Jeremiah exploded into the phone, his face red, his free arm waving all about. But it was a short call and he tossed the phone back to Becky, then peered at Jesse and Chloe.

"He did this to me on *Someone to Love.* If the studio didn't want him for this film, I'd fire him and cast Jesse as Hamilton. We've already lost the first shoot. Lori, reschedule the horse and trainer. On to the next scene."

"Now, wait a minute, Jeremiah." Sandy, the director of photography, followed him off the porch toward his office trailer. Lori and Becky dispersed in different directions, phones to their ears.

Jesse leaned against the porch post. "You think he'll show?"

"He'll show. He cares too much about his reputation."

"Then why is he not here?"

"Chris is spontaneous. He probably went on some New Year's adventure and got stuck. When we were doing *High School Follies,* he got this wild idea to fly to Australia for the weekend. Did he calculate the time change? Jet lag? Nope. Then he got food poisoning. Had to spend a week in a medical unit in Tahiti. We missed two weeks of filming."

Buckskin cap in his hand, Jesse sat on the steps. "When I was home at Christmas, my brother offered me a job at his company." He looked up at Chloe. "Can you believe it? On the eve of my first script being made

305

into a movie, he begs me to return to Dia-mondBros. Guess it's a good backup plan in case this flops."

She joined him on the stoop and tapped her arm against his. "First of all, this film isn't going to flop."

"We're not off to a good start."

"Second, you're a screenwriter and an ac-tor. You'll write another screenplay. Act in another movie. You may think your career is doomed on this auspicious start, but what about me? I need this film to succeed or I'll forever be the queen of dying."

"Things are going to change for you, Chloe. I can feel it. You're too good to stay under that moniker."

"Hey, at least you have a fallback plan. If I'm not acting, I've got nothing. Your brother must think you'd be an asset if he's asking you back. Isn't it good he values your ability?"

"I suppose." Sunlight moved over the window, spilling a golden light at their feet. "Man, I wanted today to start with a bang."

"Better to finish with one. Don't worry, Chris will show up. You'll be a success, win awards, and your brother will realize you're doing what you're called to do."

He looked at her. "Can you just move into my head, be my constant cheerleader?"

*Yes.* "Ha, you don't need me in your head."

"I don't know, maybe I do." He raised his hand to her cheek. "Chloe, maybe we are —"

She gently lowered his hand. "Jesse, you are making it really hard to just be friends."

But oh, how she wanted his touch this morning. His kiss.

"*You* are making it hard . . . to be just a friend." Slowly he drifted toward her, his eyes searching hers.

The front door opened and closed with a bang. Jesse jerked away, scrambling to his feet.

"Painter is on his way," Jeremiah said, nearly catching them in a kiss.

"Good news," Jesse said.

"But we're still rearranging today's shoot." Jeremiah motioned for the two of them to follow. "The light is perfect for the barnyard scene. The child actors are here, so we might as well shoot their scene. Jess, this is a long shot, so we're dressing you up as Hamilton."

"Me? You can't. People will be able to tell."

"Not when I'm done. Teach Painter to miss the first day of a shoot. You're his size and build. It'll be fine, just fine."

Chloe exchanged a glance with Jesse. *Well,*

*here we go.* The barnyard scene was the last scene. The final shot. The summation of the story. But scenes were never shot in sequence. So today the end would be the beginning.

Jeremiah stopped walking and turned to Chloe and Jesse. "I didn't interrupt anything, did I? Back there on the porch?"

"No." Jesse cleared his throat. Too loud. Too deep.

Chloe shook her head.

"Good. I don't *need* any more drama. Let's go. Chloe, remember, your on-set romances end in disaster."

*And . . . thank you for that, Jeremiah.*

"That's what I get for working with a family friend," she muttered to Jesse.

"He's in go-mode, Chloe. Don't take it to heart," Jesse said, walking off after their boss and director.

But Chloe hesitated, slow to join the procession, needing time to collect herself. Jeremiah did interrupt something. A moment she wanted and ached to retrieve. Just *one* more kiss. That's all she wanted. Because something about his lips on hers made her feel . . . loved. Wanted. Valued.

Jesse waved for her to come along. Chloe started for the barnyard, heeding Jeremiah's warning.

This was no time to fall in love.

# 19

## HAMILTON

He woke while the stars lingered on the sleepy horizon and rolled up his bed, the cold morning dew seeping into his bones. He'd barely slept, but when he did, he dreamed of the battle, wrestling with men, grappling with demons.

Captain Irwin roused the men. Hamilton reached for his rifle, tucked his pistol in his belt, and faced his dawn. Today he'd cause the death of another man. Or take a bullet himself.

Pray God he'd execute his duty with honor. Pray God his final sins were forgiven.

The scent of winter hung over him. Crisp, cold, damp. Tossing his bed beyond the trees, he picked his station and settled his rifle against the tree. Then he found Ralphie. "Do away with your bedroll, then check your weapon and choose your position."

The boy moved with quickness. Hamilton determined not to send him home for a burial but for reward.

"When can we eat?" Ralphie said.

"I've hardtack in my haversack. It's yours." Hamilton dare not eat. His belly was too full of anxiety. "But remain at the ready." He snagged the boy by the arm. "Look for the epaulets. Fire your shots. Then retreat."

"Three shots. When I see the whites of their eyes."

"Good man. And have a care, Ralphie. I do not want to carry your lifeless body home to your mama."

Hamilton crouched, leaned against the tree trunk, and scanned the horizon. He'd been steadier at King's Mountain. But then he saw what seemingly good men could do to each other, and it rattled him. His own darkness disturbed him.

If the redcoats surrendered, he'd demand Loyalist and regular troops alike be given quarter. Even that louse Twimball. He'd buck General Morgan himself if need be.

He patted his side pocket. His letter. Where was his letter? Crawling to his haversack, he searched the bag, exhaling when he pulled the tightly folded note free.

He'd tied it with a string and addressed it to Miss Esther Longfellow, Slathersby Hill.

"Ralphie," he said in a rough whisper, tucking the letter into his pocket. "I've a letter." He tapped his side. "Should anything happen —"

"Pardon me, Hamilton, but I'll not carry your lifeless body home to your aunt Mary."

"Well, then . . ." Hamilton gave the courageous boy a nod.

A dark presence emerged on the horizon. Hamilton tensed, taking aim. The patriots had surprised the British at King's Mountain. The strategy was the same for Cowpens. This was no time to flirt with fear.

The sound of drumming broke through the trees, imploring Hamilton's pulse to pound in rhythm. A dew of anticipation broke across his forehead as they advanced one uniform step at a time, and he realized the power of their might.

Man upon man marched toward them. The British regulars flanked by Light Dragoons and light infantry.

Captain Irwin crouched along the skirmishers. "First line at the ready."

The British line spread along the horizon, haloed by the rising sun.

Steady . . . Let them draw within fifty yards. Hamilton slid up against the grain of the tree, sighting down the long rifle barrel. Fifty yards. Find an epaulet. His breath collected against his hand and flowed back to him.

"Now," came the command from behind him.

Hamilton stepped around the tree, aiming and firing, the release of his rifle resounding in the crisp air. His bullet hit an officer in the shoulder. Crying out, the man toppled backward from his horse.

Hamilton retreated, then ducked behind his tree and tore at his ammunition box. He reloaded, ramming the ball and powder down the barrel, feeling as if eternity, not seconds, had passed. His hands shook. His vision blurred. Ready for his next volley, Hamilton watched as Ralphie ran past, took his shot, and returned to his station.

"I hit a captain." His voice was rushed and high-pitched.

"No time for glory. Reload."

Dragging in a steadying breath, Hamilton waited for the next group of men to fire. Upon their retreat, he'd take his second shot.

As the third line fired and turned, Lieutenant Twimball rode into the trees, his saber raised, riding toward Ralphie.

With a shout, Hamilton leaped to his feet,

exposing his position. He fired as Twimball turned his mount and rode toward him.

The bullet clipped the lieutenant's shoulder, and he fell back with a cry. Hamilton retreated, his senses on fire, every bone blazing.

Back to the tree, he reloaded his gun. Then a shadow crested over his body, and he looked up to see Twimball lowering his sword, slashing through Hamilton's left arm.

With a cry, he lurched backward, his rifle soaring through the air. "Twimball!"

"Come from your hiding, Lightfoot. If you're soldier enough." The lieutenant bolted away in retreat, riding along the right side of the field, finding cover among the trees as the next round of skirmishers took aim.

Shaking, Hamilton gripped his arm, blood oozing through his fingers, and tried to assess the magnitude of his wound. And where had his gun landed?

"He got you good." Ralphie knelt next to him, tearing the edge of his blouse and making a tourniquet for Hamilton's arm.

"Leave me be. Go to your duty. Fire your final round."

"I can't leave you —"

"To your duty, Ralphie."

The boy scrambled away. When the last volley ended, the skirmishers were done.

"Retreat!"

"Hamilton, make haste." Ralphie urged him to his feet. "They are upon us."

"My rifle." Hamilton pointed to the open spot among the trees. "Where's my rifle?"

"You've no time. Come! We've lured them in."

So he ran with the skirmishers, leaning against Ralphie, drawing the charging redcoats toward General Morgan and the waiting Continentals.

The air popped with musket fire, scenting it with gunpowder.

In the race toward the waiting troops, Hamilton swerved around a stand of trees toward the maple swamp. Once again he was confronted by Twimball on his steed, rising up and pawing the air.

With a roar, Hamilton leaped toward him, yanking him from his horse.

The lieutenant kicked and struggled, and he landed headfirst on the ground. When he hopped to his feet, Hamilton jerked his pistol from his belt and aimed. His left sleeve was soaked with blood and his right hand unsteady.

Twimball retrieved the pistol lodged in his own waistband.

"Shall you kill me as you killed my uncle?" Hamilton said, taking one slow step forward. "As you tried to kill Esther?"

The men circled one another, the sounds of clashing sabers and musket fire the music for their dance.

"Shall I listen to you? A traitor, a man of no honor? You think I didn't learn of your actions at King's Mountain?"

"My actions?" But Hamilton knew he was just as guilty of wanting to kill the surrendered as those who actually did.

Hate, the Good Book said, was the same as murder.

"Yes, yours, your kind, your militia."

" 'Tis nothing compared to the blood on your hands." Hamilton inched closer. Could he fire upon this man? Or lower his weapon and lay down his life?

"Fire if you have the courage," Twimball said, a strange light in his eyes, his words slurred and slow. The left shoulder of his red coat was deepening to a dark crimson. "Go on. End it."

Hamilton took aim, his finger pressing on the trigger, the blood in his veins roaring. Should he finish what he had started? Finish Twimball?

The light filtering through the trees shifted. And in an instant, Hamilton saw the man in a new light. Scared. Weak. Seeking honor on the battlefield that he did not have at home. The strange glint in his eyes was one of a man longing for love.

Hamilton stepped back, lowering his pistol.

"What, my man? Are you changing your tune now? On the battlefield, no less?" Twimball stumbled forward, closing in, swinging his pistol from side to side.

"I cannot fire."

Twimball seethed, raising his weapon. "Then the honor will be mine."

Hamilton raised his arms out to his side, waiting. "I'm sorry, Esther."

A gunshot rang out, and Hamilton jerked at the blast. But it was Twimball who buckled with a moan and collapsed to the ground.

Ralphie jumped from around a tree. "Run!"

He did not hesitate, chasing Ralphie toward the Continentals, his pulse pounding, his left arm limp by his side. He'd not fired upon Twimball. He'd fought with honor . . .

As he cleared the muddy maple swamp, a blinding, searing pain sliced through his leg, steel severing muscle from muscle, bone from bone. He plunged forward, falling face-first into the frozen mud. He tried to shove up, but a boot slammed down on his leg and he wailed in agony.

"If you're going to kill me, do so." Twimball's hot breath slithered into Hamilton's ear. He shoved Hamilton's face into the mud, pressing harder, deeper.

Hamilton struggled, pushing up, aching for a breath.

In the distance, the *click-slap* of musket fire and shouts reverberated in the air. He couldn't breathe . . . he couldn't . . .

Then suddenly he was free.

Someone had his hands, dragging him away from the mud and conflict. Voices bandied above his hearing. His leg . . . he could not feel his leg.

A blanket floated above him, covering him. Esther bent over him, crying. The shouting stopped. The gunfire ceased. The perfume of gunpowder faded to the scent of a peaceful snow. Then a brilliant light burst through the trees. Someone called to him, "Hamilton . . . Hamilton . . ."

Pa? Hamilton sat up, squinting. There, running toward him. Pa! With Ma at his side, her arms outstretched, her face beautiful and radiant. "Hamilton . . . Hamilton."

He was on his feet. "Pa! Ma!" Tears slipped freely on his muddy cheeks. But when his parents reached him, their arms were vapor, their embrace a wisp of wind.

"Pa! Ma! Wait! Wait!"

Hamilton twisted about, searching, desperate. But all anxiety died when his attention landed on a greater, exceedingly bolder light, one the sun's brilliance could not rival. He vibrated with a sensation he could not control or describe.

A form emerged from the rays, moving as a man, yet one who had no beginning and no end. He bent near to Hamilton and pressed a hand over his heart, bowing his head as if in prayer.

"Come, follow me."

Then Hamilton drifted away.

## ESTHER

Two weeks had passed since the news of General Morgan and the patriots' victory at Hannah's Cowpens reached Slathersby Hill.

While her relationship with Hamilton seemed rather unsteady, she could not forget the feel of his soapy hair under her hands or the strength of his chest as she pressed her head against him. Nor the force of his kiss.

Say what he will, but he loved her. He could not convince her otherwise.

Esther paced before the library windows, watching the road, hoping, praying, wondering if today she'd hear of Hamilton's well-being. Was he even alive?

Kitch ran across the yard toward the veranda and she steeled herself, calmly leaving the library just as Father entered, drawn and tense. The ease and cheer of Christmas had well passed.

"What is it?" Esther said to Father while nodding to Kitch when he appeared in the doorway. He flashed a short note and slipped it under the vase by the door.

"Lord Whatham fears defeat." Father dropped down at his desk. "He is frantic over his accounts."

"Then you must reassure him. You are his trusted agent." Esther kissed his cheek. "You must take care of yourself. Remember Dr. Rocourt's warning against stress. You do not want another incident."

"I am healthy as a horse. Now leave me be." Father hovered over his stack of letters.

He was not healthy as a horse. He was pale and weak, coughing at all hours. He went to bed late only to rise early.

During New Year's festivities, when Father was merry with wine, Esther inquired about the Christmas Day exchange with Hamilton, but he laughed, putting her off.

*"Do not worry yourself, Esther."*

She'd sided with her father that day, and as the weeks passed, she began to fear she'd alienated Hamilton beyond reconciliation.

"If you don't slow down I'm going to call for Dr. Rocourt." Esther made her way toward the vase, eyeing the edge of the note. "What are Lord Whatham's fears about the war? Surely once peace is reached, we can resume normal living. Wouldn't that be a delight? We should throw a ball, Father. Like the ones we attended in Charles Town."

"A ball?" Father glanced up from his correspondence. "What's this about a ball? As for Lord Whatham, he fears the new American government will confiscate his land. Take his holdings." He held up the letter he'd just read. "Your mother writes —"

"Another love letter to you?" Esther coyly slipped the note into her pocket.

Father frowned. "She begs me to send you home to Grosvenor Square. She misses you. Above all, she fears for your safety. She reads too much about the war."

"Does she not worry for your safety as well?"

Father turned back to his desk, his shoulders rounded with the weight of care. "She understands my duty is here, seeing to Lord Whatham's interests. Blasted rebels. And that Lightfoot. I can only hope he has met his doom."

"Father! You cannot mean it."

"Indeed, I do." He muttered, speaking to the dark wood of his desk. ". . . needed that land . . . did what I had to do . . ." His back and, at least for the moment, his heart were against Esther.

"I'll pray you find your Christian charity toward the Lightfoots. And forgive any dispute over Quill Farm. If indeed there is any at all."

Sassy entered with a tray, casting a slight glance toward Esther. "Your tea, Sir Michael."

"Thank you, Sassy." Father opened another letter. "Did you bake your fine cakes?"

"Just the way you like them."

"Esther, will you pour? Let's forget about wars and land disputes for now."

"Of course." Esther moved to the sideboard with a glance at the departing Sassy. What was in the note Kitch left? By his stealthy actions, it had to be from or about Hamilton. Sassy's expression warned her the news may not be good.

"Oh, my buckle has come undone." Esther bent down to her shoes, taking the note from her pocket. Her back to Father, she unfolded the thick paper, hands trembling.

*Wounded. Billeted at the surgeon's. Dr. Nelson. Green River Road.*

She exhaled, closing her eyes. He was alive. Wounded, but alive. Smiling, she tucked the note back into her pocket.

She poured Father's tea and joined him on the divan, nodding as he talked of spring planting, his mood a bit more lively than moments ago. She masked her emotions with an adoring smile. The man she loved lay wounded in a surgeon's home nearly a hundred miles away.

While Father talked, she devised a plan. One she would execute without delay.

# 20

## JESSE

A slick, winter mist watered the early morning. After only three weeks on set, unseasonable rains had slowed production.

But Jeremiah was a clever and experienced director who knew how to utilize his time well, rearranging the schedule to shoot the indoor scenes.

On his laptop, Jesse scrolled through the daily footage Jeremiah uploaded each night, awed and amazed to see his baby come to life.

On screen, Chloe and Chris leaned in for an Esther and Hamilton kiss, and jealousy nipped at him. Her lips were touching another's. Not his.

He fast-forwarded as Chris-slash-Hamilton embraced Chloe-slash-Esther, intensifying their intimacy. He'd watched it live a few days ago and knew they were acting, playing the part. But in this moment the kiss seemed, *felt,* real.

Jesse advanced to the end. Why was he jealous? He knew acting. Understood actors. But he'd witnessed his share of on-set romances. Indulged in one or two himself. Two people who had absolutely no intention of developing a meaningful relationship would go hot and heavy while filming, while living in an alternate reality.

He wanted Chloe to himself. During filming and after. The real Chloe. The one who bought him a gift for no reason. Who inspired him to be a better man. Who spoke of faith as if it were real and dependable. Who was just as beautiful in a pair of jeans while eating chicken and rice on the lanai as she was gliding down the red carpet for a movie premier.

Ah, what was he thinking? They were friends. Just friends. Jesse paused the daily and slapped his laptop closed. Friends who kissed, sure, but those were . . . moments. Yeah. Moments.

He didn't believe his own argument. Deny it all he wanted, but Chloe was special. Maybe the kind of girl he'd waited for, the imaginary one that he spoke of that fatal night with Loxley.

How did he have any right to happiness

and love? To success?

A knock on his hotel-room door took him from his mental path. "Yeah, coming."

Chloe stood in the hall, leaning against the wall, cute and casual in jeans, boots, and a blue coat with a matching scarf. Her reddish-gold hair fell in large waves over her shoulders.

"H-hey." Jesse tried to act casual, as if he was not just thinking of her, as if she did not stir conflicting desires. As if not reminding himself he did not deserve her. "What's up?" He retreated into his room, leaving the door ajar for her to follow.

"Let's go to the battlefield. Walk it without the cameras and crew. What do you say? Looks like there's a break in the rain." She did a jig with jazz hands, her mouth open, her expression wide. "Then maybe we could grab some breakfast at that place on Highway 11, the old vegetable stand turned restaurant. Remember the crew talking about it? Said they served a mean breakfast on Styrofoam plates . . ."

"The five hot dogs for five dollars place?"

"That's the one. You game?" Her smile made him relax, settle his pulse, and forget his internal battle. "I like to absorb the local flavor when I'm on set." She squinted at Jesse's computer, wincing. "Were you watching dailies? I hate to see myself on screen." Nevertheless, she dropped down on the two-seater sofa and raised the screen, clicking play.

Jesse joined her, watching the end of the kiss.

"W-what were you thinking and feeling here?" Stupid, really. But he had to say something. Otherwise she'd note his nervousness, the flash of heat on his face.

"I don't know . . . vulnerable, I guess. Hamilton had just told Esther he was going to war, and she feared he'd never return. Then I thought how familiar Chris was to me, and then a flash of a tabloid headline: 'Chloe Daschle *dashed* after Chris Painter declared he hadn't met his soul mate.' Then Haden popped into my head. For a split second I wanted to pull back, close down, but then . . ." She ran her fingers through the fringe of her scarf. "I thought of you."

"Me?" Her confession powered his curiosity, powered his pulse. "Your little brain-people sure were busy during that scene."

She sat back and patted his thigh, resting her hand there for a second. But just a second. "If you only knew . . . So, yeah, I thought of you, how much this meant to you, how your screenplay was giving me a chance to be the lead in a film where the girl doesn't die. So I gave the kiss all the life I had." Her gaze lingered on his face. "How'd I do?"

He nodded, thumbs up. "As if that kiss might have been with the man you love." *It made me jealous. It made me want you. It made me realize I don't deserve you.*

"Thank you." She smiled. "Not only for the compliment but for your words, your characters, the story you're telling. It fills me with hope. That love truly never fails."

"But love did fail. Failed Hamilton and Esther. Failed . . . me, you, hundreds of thousands of others. And that was just yesterday. Forget this week, this month, last year, the decades and centuries past."

"Whoa, slow down, mister. I can't be responsible for human history, but I can be responsible for me. Hopeful for me." She fiddled with her scarf again. "Us."

"Us? Friends us or —"

"I don't know . . ." She wrinkled her nose. "Us, us."

"Chloe." Jesse moved toward the closet for his coat, forming his truth. "In my heart I know I did not kill Loxley, even if my behavior was inexcusable. Yet my head tells me I have no right to love, to happiness, to even this" — he motioned to his laptop — "success. To my dreams and goals coming to fruition."

"But maybe if you tried? With me." Her face, her voice, everything about her said *sweet, vulnerable, timid.* And that she put herself out there on purpose.

"What happened to our pledge? No on-set romance." Jesse pulled on his coat. "Haven't you had your heart broken enough? I'd rather be your friend than the guy who tried to love you and failed. Another one who broke your heart."

"But what if you're the guy who tries and succeeds? What if you realize Loxley would want you happy?"

"I'm not sure I know how to be that guy, Chloe." He took his scarf from the coat's pocket. What was she saying? She loved him? She was shorting his circuits with this conversation. He needed a moment to process. "How are we going on this adventure today?"

She held up a set of keys. "I begged a car from the crew."

He touched her arm as she passed. "If I were going to try, it would be with someone like you."

"Someone *like* me?" Her eyes searched his.

"You. It would be you."

"Then where does that leave us? Are you

*never* going to try? Lacking the courage to tell a girl she may be the love of your life is the same as lacking the courage to tell her she isn't."

"Love of my life? See, we're already in hyperbole while still talking in hypotheticals." He started down the hotel hallway, then whirled to her. "By the way, are you saying you want to start something with me? Are you willing to put your heart on the line again? With an actor? And knowing my story?"

"Forget it, Jesse. Forget what I said. Let's just pretend there's no attraction between us." She pushed past him, bumping him against the wall. "Do you still want to go to the battlefield and breakfast?"

"Sure, why not?"

In some sort of steamy silence, they walked across the parking lot to the car. What just happened? Jesse side-checked Chloe as she backed out of the hotel parking lot.

But if she was falling in love with him, then color him helpless. He'd not be able to resist her. Past or no past. In fact, he might be conquered by the end of breakfast.

# CHLOE

The sun broke through the clouds as they drove north toward the historic battlefield. Chloe parked at the opening of Green River Road.

Their doors clapped shut in the cold morning air. She'd been quiet during the drive over trying to figure out what happened at the hotel. Fear overwhelming the idea of love?

But sooner or later she wanted to try again. Unlike before, she had God to seek, to give her wisdom this time.

Since their wedding escapade, Jesse had become a part of her daily thoughts — a favorite memory, a yearning, his kiss the kind that made her glad she was a woman.

Her feelings for him were growing stronger, and she'd not deny it. Yet, putting herself out there, exposing her heart, had been risky.

The idea of being in love suddenly trumped her rules about on-set romance and the idea that she just picked bad, bad men to love.

But Jesse . . . oh, he was . . .

She glanced over as he joined her on the road, zipping up his coat.

Special. There was something about

him . . .

"Where do you think Hamilton was on this field?" she said.

"He was one of the skirmishers, so over there, in the trees." Jesse pointed left, tugging on his gloves.

The wind nipping between the trees was edged with ice. Chloe walked on one side of the dirt road, Jesse on the other.

"I'm trying to picture a thousand or so militia and regular army, and it seems so foreign, another life," she said.

"It was another life. Thus, the magic of movies." Jesse slowed, taking in the ancient field. "It's nice to be here without the cameras and crew." He tipped his face toward the sun.

"History was made here, Jess. Your ancestor fought for independence. On this very ground. Do you think he realized what he was doing, what kind of nation we would become?"

She stopped among the trees where the skirmishers hid. Typically, the park stationed silhouetted cutouts of militiamen down on one knee, rifles raised. But they'd been stored for the movie.

"Can you imagine what kind of nation we'll be in two hundred years? I doubt Hamilton realized the magnitude. He was a backwoods man from the South Carolina colony. Probably wanted nothing more than a successful farm, the chance to feed and clothe his wife and children." Jesse dropped to one knee, raised an imaginary rifle, and fired.

Chloe knelt beside him. "And where would Esther be?"

"Now, that I do not know." Jesse sat on the dewy grass and rested his arms on his raised knees. "Some wives followed their husbands to the battleground, but I doubt Esther would've. A single woman traveling with a single man would have been scandalous."

"Maybe she was here?" Chloe reached through his arms to tap his heart.

"Maybe." He fumbled with his words as he stood. "I'm not sure he even knew her when he fought here."

Hands in her coat pockets, Chloe walked toward the original Battle of Cowpens monument. "Do you think you'll ever know the whole story?"

"Unless Aunt Pat uncovers it, probably not."

"Yet through the power of movie magic, two people are getting the love story they never had."

"Yep. Esther and Hamilton."

"Or Jesse and Loxley." Chloe leaned to see his face.

"What is it you want me to say, Chloe? That I exercised my guilt while writing this screenplay?"

"Did you?"

"No, I wrote a story. About something that interested me."

"You never once thought of Loxley?"

He jumped up. "Yes, I thought of her. Are you happy?"

"Are you?"

Jesse peered down at her. "Did you minor in psychology at UCLA?" He sat next to her again. "There were moments while writing I stopped to cry, to tell her I was sorry. My stupidity stole any chance she had at happiness. I partnered with that riptide to end her life." His voice rose and fell with each rush of the wind.

Chloe picked at the grass by her feet. "Now I'm sorry . . . That wasn't fair." She'd pushed. Like always. Wanting more from the men who fascinated her than they were willing to give. "Forget it. I mean it, Jesse. I shouldn't pry."

She got up and walked toward the slope where General Morgan and the Continentals had waited in ambush for the British. The elevation changed so gradually she barely noticed it. But when she looked back, the road had disappeared.

In a few moments, Jesse walked into view. "It's okay. Friends help friends come to terms with their life."

"Turn around." Chloe shielded her eyes from the sun as she surveyed the field. "The road is gone. This is like looking back at the past. You can't see it. At least you can't see it clearly."

"But you know it's there. You remember. But the view is obscured." Jesse glanced behind them. "General Morgan was a genius. That's how he defeated Cornwallis at Cowpens."

"Did you ever think your aunt sent you Hamilton's letter to remind you he moved on and loved again?"

"It's crossed my mind."

"But not your heart." Chloe wandered a few feet away, trapped between the present conversation and the story of the past. "I'm sorry Loxley died, Jesse. I don't want to minimize what you went through. But maybe, for your sake, you shouldn't maximize it either."

"I'm sorry your heartbreak over Haden Stuart got posted all over the web."

"I should've known better." She caught the faintest scent of his skin, and the fragrance watered the brittle places of her heart.

"One thing, I've learned my lesson. Next time I propose to a girl —"

"Next time?" She smiled up at him, pleased with the tenor of their conversation. "Don't look now, Jesse Gates, but I think you took one step toward moving on."

"— I'm going to have a real ring, gold —" Chloe shook her head, miming the letter P. "A platinum ring with a one-carat dia—" She held up two fingers. "Two-carat diamond . . . Two carats? Who do you think I am — Raymond Daschle?"

Chloe slipped her arm through his. "No, you are the great screenwriter, Jesse Gates."

At the vegetable stand turned restaurant, Chloe ordered scrambled eggs and bacon.

"I'll have the same," Jesse said.

At the plastic table, she leaned toward him. "My agent called. Said he's getting a lot of inquiries about me."

"See, your fortune has turned."

"This movie . . ." She exhaled. "It's a gift from God." After all the pushing and prodding this morning about their relationship, about his past, she should determine if he was a man of faith.

Jesse fiddled with the napkin roll. "I'll take

the bait, Chloe. How'd you come to faith again?"

"Smitty. I met him outside a church. After the blowup with Haden, seeing the stuff people wrote about me on social media, I was so broken. My friends only called to tell me the latest tabloid headline."

"Ex-friends now, I hope."

"Some, not all. Haden refused my calls. I lost twenty pounds that month. Slept twelve hours a day and cried the other twelve. My agent tried to leverage the publicity and star me in a reality show. *Crazy Kids of Hollywood* or something. But I'd flip burgers before going the shame-fame route. I couldn't do that to my parents. Then another dying role came along and I thought, *Ha, how fitting.*"

"The typecasting continued."

"Kate took my phone and laptop so I'd stay off social media. Eventually I started driving around LA in my Mustang, hating and loving the city at the same time. One day, I stopped for coffee in the valley, I cannot even tell you where, and saw a flyer for a church, Expression58, and it was like a moment in time." She parted the air in front of her with a slicing motion. "For one second, one brief second, the clouds, the heaviness, the depression was gone and there was light. Next Sunday, I went. Terrified. What if God didn't want me either? Where does one go if the Almighty rejects you? But I was so hungry for something real, something beyond myself, I faced my doubts. As I approached the front door, Smitty stood on the sidewalk, almost as if he expected me."

"He was at the door of an acting class I attended," Jesse said, thoughtful, reflective. "When I walked in, he said, 'Jesse, hi' as if we were old friends. I had no recollection of ever meeting him before."

"But he never invited you to church?"

"No."

"Would you have gone if he did?"

"No."

"What if I asked you?"

"Are you?"

"Maybe."

Jesse sat back as the waitress brought their breakfast. "I don't think church is for me. But I'll support you. I can't see God and me having any sort of conversation. Loxley's parents don't want to talk to me. Why would an almighty being?"

"Because He's an almighty being?"

She stared at her Styrofoam plate of flat, folded scrambled eggs, crinkly bacon, and cold toast.

"Yum." Jesse shuddered, stabbing his eggs

with a plastic fork, then reaching for the ketchup.

"Hey, be kind. This is local color and flavor."

"Let's hope the food has some flavor." Jesse winced at the packet of grape jelly, making Chloe laugh. He ripped away the foil cover and dumped a grape square onto his toast. "Never pictured Smitty, or you, as a God person."

"Just how does a God person look?"

He thought as he poured cream into his coffee. "Big hair. Think they're perfect. Holier than thou. Judgmental."

"Like you're being now?"

"Pent up, buttoned down, blue oxford with khaki pants, brow beaters."

"Any more clichés in the box, Pandora?"

"Not right now." He grinned at her over his coffee. "But I'll let you know."

The divide in their faith smarted more than she had imagined it might. Her first disappointment in this young relationship.

"When I was ten," she began, giving life to a random thought, "I auditioned for a kids' show, *Sleuths.* The part was for a fun, brainiac kid who solved her detective-father's cases. I wanted that part . . . Finally, the day came. I had five minutes to wow them. I'd picked my clothes, fixed my hair, wore a pair of prop eyeglasses. I was Debbie Dough."

"I remember that show. You tried out for Debbie?"

"Sixty seconds in, the casting director takes a phone call. The producer had to 'step out for a moment.' And I knew him. Sam Aiken. He was a friend of Dad's!" Chloe propped her elbow on the table, chin in her hand, and stared toward the door. A lean, lanky man with a Vietnam-vet cap entered.

"Morning, Duke," the waitress said. "Coffee?"

"That'll be fine."

Chloe went on. "Sam returns right in the middle of my best line and says, 'Chloe, we see you more as Lizzy. Why don't you read a few of her lines?' Lizzy. The chubby girl who ate junk in every single scene. If she wasn't eating, she wanted to eat. I was devastated."

"Hollywood is not for the fainthearted. What'd you do?"

Tears welled in her eyes. She'd never talked about that audition. "I read for the part."

"Chloe —"

"As humiliating as it was, little did I know . . ." She broke off a piece of bacon.

"Since I can remember, Hollywood has been telling me who I am, what I look like to the rest of the world, and how I should behave. When I blew up at Haden, went all bat-crazy on him, it was the first time I didn't care who I was or who was watching."

"Did you get the part of Lizzy?"

"No. Sam came to the house, talked to Dad. They wanted to offer me Lizzy. Said I was perfect for the freckled, fat-girl role."

"He said that to your dad?"

"Yes. I was listening outside the door. 'Come on, Sam,' Dad said. 'She's not that bad. Why can't she play Debbie? She drove us crazy prepping for the part.'"

Funny how she remembered the conversation twenty years later.

"Your dad stood up for you then."

"Not really. At least it didn't feel like it to my ten-year-old heart. Sam goes, 'You know, Ray, if you want Chloe to succeed in this town, get her to lay off the chips and ice cream.' Dad laughed."

"He laughed?"

"He said, 'You ever get between a girl and her ice cream?' Har, har, har, yuckity, yuck. Looking back, I know he didn't mean to diss me, but I'll never forget the way I felt."

"Have you talked to him about it?"

"I think he's forgotten about it. I should too."

"What'd he do when the videos with Haden came out?"

"He tried to defend me, but what could he say? 'She didn't mean to hit Haden'? 'She didn't mean to swear like a gutter rat'? I was an adult woman." Chloe raised her paper cup to her lips. She hadn't known it then, but God was pursuing her. Her choices had led her straight to Him. "I think I'm stronger for it, you know. What about you? What'd your parents do?"

"Mostly tried to ignore it. Not speak of it. Afraid of tipping me over the edge."

"Were you on the edge?"

"Couldn't have been *more* on the edge. I was aimless, restless, really angry. Guilty. Once in a while, Dad tried to remind me it wasn't my fault. I'd blow up at him. Then he'd suggested I get busy with work. My folks are of European breeding, you know, like Hamilton. The pull-yourself-up-by-your-bootstraps kind. So I moved to LA. The land of make-believe."

"Church saved me," Chloe said, their conversation weaving as it had the night on the lanai. "Rather, the Lord did. Can I say that and not sound like a TV evangelist? My first Sunday I wept nonstop for two hours. I thought I was losing my mind. A couple of women took me aside, and while I snotted all over one's shoulder, the other told me about a God who loved me and gave His life for me. He defended me. He covered my shame." As she spoke, Jesse sobered, tearing at his wadded-up napkin. "I knew it was true. I needed it to be true."

Jesse frowned, perplexed and curious. "Are you saying you're born again?" He air-quoted *born again.*

"Call it what you will, Jesse, but in the aftermath of Haden, I was chained to despair. Then I spent two hours on a Sunday morning with people who truly loved Jesus, and I was free. When I thought I'd like to start trusting again, I —" She should just shut up. Like now. But her lips kept moving. "I met you."

Jesse shoved his clean Styrofoam plate aside. "So we're back to this."

Their eyes met, and the conversation stalled. She loved him. But she'd said enough for one day.

The waitress cleared away their plates, providing a timely distraction.

"When do I get to read Hamilton's letter?" Chloe said, reading the bill and dropping a ten on the table.

"Never." Jesse added another five.

"Never?" She grabbed her purse and started for the door.

"Never." Jesse followed, toothpick between his lips.

"Like, ten years from now, if I visit you at Christmas and ask, 'Can I read the letter?' You'll say —"

"No."

Chloe stopped at the car. "Why not?"

"Why do you want to read it?" He walked around to the passenger door. He was *so* messing with her.

"Because it inspired this screenplay. Because you're my friend. What's the big deal? Everyone is going to ask you about it."

"Watch the movie." Jesse snapped on his seat belt.

Chloe sat behind the wheel. "You'll be the death of me, Gates." She froze, her gaze creeping toward Jesse. Death? "Jesse, I'm so sorry."

"It's okay." He pulled his phone from his pocket and checked for messages. "Just a figure of speech."

"I wasn't thinking."

"Chloe, it's okay."

As she started the car, his phone rang.

"It's Jeremiah," he said. "Hey, what's up? . . . Yeah? She's with me . . . Okay . . .

we'll be there." Ending the call, he tucked his phone away with a glance at her. "Jer wants to meet with us at Chris's place."

"Did he say why? Don't tell me Chris is walking off the set." She gunned the gas, firing onto the road. "I'm going to kill him."

Once again the car was silent, and the morning sun disappeared behind a collection of ominous clouds, obscuring the horizon.

# 21

## ESTHER

"Whoa." Esther reined in Gulliver, arriving at a small home just off Green River Road, a golden light in every window. The scent of burning wood tinged the bitter breeze.

The sign above the porch overhang announced *Surgeon Dr. Robert Nelson.*

"We're here." Esther jumped from the buckboard, offering her hand to Mrs. Lightfoot.

Upon the news of Hamilton's fate, she set aside worries of her father's health and his animosity toward the Lightfoots and started the long journey to Hannah's Cowpens.

She and Mrs. Lightfoot left at dawn, pushing brave Gulliver to his limit to make the journey in a day. Eighty miles.

Last night, after Father had gone to bed, Esther gathered food and supplies, loading them into the wagon herself. But she did not escape Isaac's notice.

*"If Father asks, tell him I'm taking Mrs. Light-foot to see Hamilton."*

*"He ain't going to be pleased."* Isaac hoisted *the baskets of bread, dried fruit, and meat into the wagon, followed by the bedding and blankets, bandages, and a few of Father's old shirts and trousers.*

*"I'd like at least a day's lead, if you can manage it."*

*"If I can manage it."*

Now Esther faced the surgeon's home. "Shall we go in?"

Mrs. Lightfoot took the first step. She'd been silent most of the trip, yet confessing every hour or so, "He's all I have, Esther. He's all I have."

Before they reached the porch, a small, weary-looking woman opened the door. Her blond hair, frayed and dull, needed a wash and a comb. Dark stains smothered the apron covering what may have once been a vibrant, blue dress. "We've no room. No food. None that can be spared. You'll have to move on."

"No, no, ma'am, we came to help." Esther made the introductions. "We've brought food, supplies, bandages, and poultices."

"What?" Her voice broke with gratitude. "Who sent you? Where are you from?"

"Down Ninety Six way," Mrs. Lightfoot said. "My nephew is here. So I've been told. Hamilton Lightfoot. A militiaman."

"He's here, yes. Please come in. My husband is with him now. You say you have food? Supplies?"

"In the wagon. Is there anyone to help unload?"

The house was small, cold, and pungent with body odors. Soldiers in soiled uniforms slept in a row along the parlor floor. Several more — militiamen — languished on the stairs, bandages around their hands or arms, sipping broth from clay bowls.

"My sons, Bobby and Simms, can unload when they've finished in the barn. We can't keep up with all the chores around here." She untied her apron and ran her hand over her hair. "Since the wounded arrived, I've not had time to wash or clean. I'm not sure I can even offer you a cup of coffee."

"Mrs. Nelson, do not trouble yourself," Mrs. Lightfoot said. "We want to be no burden."

"I brought tea and coffee, along with cider," Esther said.

"Tea?" One of the soldiers perked up.

Another echoed, "Cider?"

But Esther remained intent on her mission. Another moment of anticipation and she would burst. "Is it possible, Mrs. Nelson, to see Hamilton?"

"Of course, of course. He's upstairs, first door on the right." Mrs. Nelson seized Esther as she started forward. Emotion moved across her eyes.

"Steel yourself."

Esther swallowed. "What will I find?"

"He's weak, thin, hasn't bathed in a good while, and his injury . . . quite severe. He's in and out of consciousness. But he's alive. Only on the battlefield for thirty minutes, but that day will live with him forever."

"Mercy." Mrs. Lightfoot swooned. "I believe I need to sit down."

A Continental soldier with a bandaged head offered his spot on the settee.

Esther hesitated, then started for the steps.

"You kin to Lightfoot?" The man on the bottom step spoke. "Hamilton Lightfoot?"

"The woman on the settee is his aunt. I'm his . . . friend."

The soldier nodded. "He fought a brave battle. Had a redcoat, a lieutenant, nigh on his tail, chasing him through the maple swamp." He whistled low. "Sliced his leg. Clean to the bone."

Mrs. Lightfoot moaned and pushed up from the settee. "I require air."

"But he'll be all right," Esther asked, "will

he not? With the surgeon tending him?"

The private rose, making room on the narrow staircase for Esther to ascend. "Like the surgeon's wife said, steel yourself."

Gripping the banister, Esther climbed to the second floor, growing weaker, more afraid with each step. What would she find when she knocked on his door? Could she bear to behold what ravages Hamilton had endured?

Taking a breath, she knocked softly and entered at the beckon of a mellow bass voice. "Come in."

The room was dark and stale. On a crude, slender bedside table, a lone candle flickered against the shadows. On another table, the doctor washed his hands at a basin, dripping water as he pushed his spectacles up his nose.

"He's sleeping." The surgeon reached for a soiled towel. "But a friendly voice will do him well. Who might you be?"

"Esther Longfellow. A friend of Hamilton's."

"So, you are the Esther of his dreams." The doctor set a chair beside the narrow bed tucked under the eaves. "He's lost a lot of blood. But we're encouraged by his more frequent waking moments."

Esther sat, hands in her lap, her eyes

awash with tears. She'd been warned of his condition, but no imagining could have prepared her for her bold, broad, bright Hamilton to appear so frail, so small, his pale complexion blending with the dingy white linens.

Leaning forward, she cupped her hand under his. "Hamilton, love, 'tis I, Esther."

His hair stood on end, peppered with dried mud, and his face had not seen a razor in many days.

"What does he say?" Esther peered back at the doctor. "When he whispers my name?"

"Mostly your name. And words I can't understand." The doctor removed his glasses. In the candlelight, Esther observed his weariness, and that perhaps he was not as old as his burden made him seem. "They found him facedown by the maple swamp, his leg all but shorn off and saber slashes on his arm. I patched his arm sure enough, but his leg was far gone. I amputated as fast as possible, but he suffered a great deal." The doctor raised the candle and leaned over Hamilton's pale and broken body. "God help him. I can't contain the bleeding." The doctor gently touched Esther's shoulder. "Speak to him. Pray for him." Then he quietly slipped from the room.

"My love, what have they done to you?" Tears whispered down her cheeks. "You fought bravely, I hear. A soldier downstairs spoke well of you." She rested her hand on his chest, taking in his heartbeat through her palm and listening to each soft inhale. "I love you. Please don't leave me."

Upon her word, a chill swept through the room and the candle flame flickered. Esther shivered and tucked Hamilton's blanket under his chin.

"Your side won, dearest. Does that make you happy? To the victors the spoils!" She brushed her tears from her cheeks. "Perhaps now Washington and his men shall put an end to this revolution, and peace will come to America. To South Carolina." She squeezed his hand. "To you and me."

Her eyes drifted the length of his body. Where his left leg should have been, the blanket lay collapsed.

Esther stretched to raise the cover and gasped to see to a bloody stump where Hamilton's fine, strong leg had been.

She dropped the blanket, then whirled to the window, raising the sash, inhaling the crisp January air, quelling the bile in her throat.

"My Lord, my Lord . . ."

The hinges of the door squeaked open,

and Mrs. Nelson entered with a clean water basin. "You should close the window, dear. He's much too weak."

"Yes, of course." Esther pressed down the pane. "W-will he live? His leg, it's so . . ."

"If my husband can contain the bleeding." Mrs. Nelson exchanged the new basin for the old one. "He is an experienced physician and will do all he can, but Hamilton is at the mercy of the Almighty."

"Then I will pray." She returned to the chair by the bed, cupping her hand into his once more. "I will pray. Lord, have mercy."

The doctor's wife paused by her, hand on her shoulder. "There is a man here to see you."

Esther glanced into her sad, sober eyes. "A colored?" Had to be Isaac or Boy.

"No, an older gentleman, fragrant with pipe smoke, graying at his temples."

Father!

"Tell him I-I'll be along."

He'd learned of her absence all too soon. Yet, no matter his argument, she'd refuse to return to Slathersby Hill. She was needed here. To tend to her beloved. To care for Mrs. Lightfoot. To offer aid to Mrs. Nelson.

Steeling herself, Esther kissed Hamilton's forehead, gently running her finger over the fresh scar on his cheek. "I'll return quickly, my love."

At the top of the stairs, she paused, the fetid air in the narrow passage dampening her courage.

Entering the parlor, she did not wait for Father to speak first. "Father, I can explain."

"Come. Outside." He handed over her coat and escorted her through the door onto the cramped quarters of the porch. "You traveled alone? Without telling me?"

"You would not have let me come," Esther said, slipping on her coat, though her skin was warm under her soft, wool gown. "And I did not travel alone. Mrs. Lightfoot accompanied me."

"An old woman is no protection for one such as yourself. A beautiful girl of means and station. You tempted fate, Esther. The battle may be over, but the roads are peppered with wastrels, disenfranchised soldiers. Who knows what harm may have befallen you?"

"I'm here, aren't I? Safe? Mrs. Lightfoot needed to see him. As did I. I make no apology, Father. He's lost his leg and will need all of our love and support. Can we not set aside our animosities to find common ground in charity and neighborly love?"

Father paced through the thin light of the windows. "Lost his leg, has he? Now my resolve is all the greater. You cannot marry him. That is what you're thinking, Esther, is it not? Come on, confess."

" 'Tis what I want."

"As does he?"

"Yes," she declared in complete faith. He must love her. He spoke her name in his sleep.

"I will not allow it, Esther. This is not like you to completely disregard my wishes."

Father's opposition shook her confidence. Nevertheless, she raised her chin and straightened her tired shoulders.

"Father, why have you come?"

"To bring you home." He pointed to the carriage, where Isaac and Kitch waited.

"I am sorry to disappoint you, but —"

"You listen to me, Esther Longfellow." The growl in his voice alarmed her. He rarely, if ever, spoke to her in such a manner. "It was one matter when you loved a Lightfoot with two healthy legs, willing to subject yourself to the rigors of a farmer's wife in this wild country. But it's another matter when the man is lame, a cripple. What sort of future will he drag you toward? What chains must you wear, wedded to such a man? Do you not see, my dear? The harshness of his consequence shall be yours. You will be the one tending him, the house, and the fields, ordering about servants and laborers, minding your children, if he could even —"

"Father!"

"Nay, Esther, I did not raise you for such a position. Your mother is right. I was self-ish and foolish to keep you in the upcoun-try for so long. For allowing you to return after debuting in London."

A long, jagged bolt of lightning slashed the inky night. Then thunder. Muted. Some distance away. An icy cold saturated the wind.

"I would've come home to South Carolina with or without your permission. You know Hamilton, Father. It is not in his character to lie about. He will work. We'll manage together."

Father's warm exhale billowed in the January chill. "If he is the man you claim him to be, then he will realize you are bound for greater things than he could ever offer. He will not hold you to any informal pledge or romantic assumptions."

Hadn't he done so already? After King's Mountain. That day at the well. But she refused to let the trials of war taint their love. If he wanted to be rid of her, let him do it in peacetime.

"You surprise me, Father. I considered

you a keener judge of character. The loss of a limb does not ensure the loss of the man, nor the loss of love. He may be without his leg, but he is not without his heart and soul. And most assuredly, he is not without me."

Father roared. "You are your mother's daughter. Stubborn. Determined."

"Mother's? Those words describe you, Father."

"Do you imagine he will formally propose, seek your hand and my blessing, when he has no means to support you?"

"Give him back Quill Farm."

"You ask the impossible."

"Why impossible? Come now, Father, confess. Have you mishandled Lord Whatham's accounts? I see you despairing over your ledgers." Esther leaned into her father's expansive shadow. "So to protect your name, you steal from a widow and now a cripple?"

"Your impertinence does you no credit, Esther. You are not winning my favor."

"Your favor? What of mine, Father? Do you care to win mine?"

A light cracked through the darkness, falling across the porch boards. Mrs. Lightfoot stepped onto the porch.

"Are you discussing my nephew?"

"Mary, talk sense into her. Advise her to

return home where she belongs. Hamilton will not propose to her now. Not with his future so unsure."

"Since we now rent the farm instead of owning it?" Mrs. Lightfoot placed her hand on Esther's shoulder. "But your father is right. Though it pains me to agree with him. Now that I am apprised of Hamilton's wounds, I can say with sincerity he would not like you to see him in his present situation. He prefers his dignity over humiliation. You know it to be true. In fact, did he not put you off after King's Mountain?"

"What's this?" Father said. Esther closed her eyes. Mrs. Lightfoot just handed him the ammunition he lacked.

"Yes, he put me off, but he was battle weary. Wounded. Ashamed of something he considered but did not do against the American Loyalists."

"The murdering?"

"He didn't murder, Father. He lowered his blade."

"Well, if he was ashamed then, what must he be now?"

Mrs. Lightfoot moved to stand with Father. "Take your disappointment and go, my dear. I know Hamilton. He will not marry you now."

"I do not believe you. Has he told you

so?" Esther backed away from the consortium of Father and Mrs. Lightfoot. "I will go only if he speaks for himself."

"He's barely aware of his surroundings. He cannot speak for himself." Mrs. Lightfoot seemed well versed in her arguments. "Go, he'd not want to see what he's become in your eyes."

"But I've already seen him."

"He doesn't have to know."

"But *what* has he become in my eyes? A hero! Nothing has changed for me. Nothing at all."

"My dear, stubborn daughter, you are full of zeal and zero wisdom. Listen to Mrs. Lightfoot — she is right. Say your goodbyes and return with me to Slathersby Hill. We've a long journey ahead."

"I cannot. I will not."

"Esther, you are not wanted or needed here." Mrs. Lightfoot's tone, low and driving, echoed over a distant memory. Mother. Complaining to Grandmama.

*"She's so flighty. I cannot manage her. I'm sending her to Michael. Let him bear the burden for a while."*

Burden. Underfoot. Not wanted or needed. Esther spun between Father and Mrs. Lightfoot.

"Surely I can be of some use. To Mrs.

Nelson. To Hamilton —"

"He does not need you, dear." Mrs. Light-foot wielded her words like a sword. Sharp and cutting. "I can tend to him. You'll only be in the way, another mouth to feed."

But she'd been the one to bring food and blankets, supplies. Wasn't she a good girl? A generous girl?

"Mary's right. This is no place for you, Esther. Come home with me."

She'd lost her breath. Her strength and will. When Father touched her elbow, steering her toward the carriage, she moved without resistance. Once again, she was ten years old with no control or say over her life.

But as she arrived at the carriage and Kitch jumped to open her door, she pulled away, her senses coming around.

"Wait." Esther stepped back, freeing herself from Father. "At least let me say good-bye." Her thoughts tumbled, imagining a plan.

"What is it?" Mrs. Lightfoot hurried from the porch. "You must make haste if you are going to travel through the night."

"I want to say good-bye."

"He's asleep, Esther." Mrs. Lightfoot trailed after her, almost pleading. "He's lost a great deal of blood."

"Speaking to him will not cost him any more." Esther burst into the house and up the stairs.

In Hamilton's room, she dropped to the chair by the bed and lowered her head to his chest. "They are making me go. They say I am not wanted. Your aunt believes you will be ashamed of your condition. You'd not want me to see you, but I am not ashamed of you. I love you. This changes nothing."

Her words conformed to tears, which turned into prayers.

*Save him, O Lord. Heal him. Bring him home to me. I love him, I love him.*

Her tears abated when a large, warm hand pressed upon her head, flooding her with peace. Hamilton! But when she raised up, he slept, his arms by his sides, his expression peaceful.

A man dressed in brown broadcloth, his hair hanging around his shoulders, stood next to her. Esther jumped up, tripping over the chair, startled but not . . . not afraid.

"He will live." The man's eyes radiated light as he spoke, as if each one contained a thousand stars. "But you must follow me."

"Follow you? Sir, I do not know you."

"Go home with your father." He motioned to the door. His instruction, his movements contained no doubt. "I will stay with Hamilton."

"You mock me? If I go with Father, how can I follow you? Are you one of the militiamen? Gone and lost your mind?"

"I do not mock you. Go, do your father's bidding. There you will learn how to follow me."

"I do not understand."

He smiled. "You will, Esther, you will."

His words pressed into her, and for a moment she could not move. Backing into the wall, she slid to the floor, tears twisting down her cheeks.

"Help me understand."

She woke as from a deep sleep and sat up, still in her chair and not the floor, pressing her hand to her forehead. A dream. Surely it was all a dream. She must have drifted off while praying for Hamilton.

She glanced around to the writing desk, examining it for pen and paper. Father would be livid, waiting upon her. How long had she dozed? Far too long by her energy and refreshment.

Opening the inkwell, she dipped the quill and began her message.

My dearest Hamilton,

I've little time to pen this Letter. Father has come for me and demanded I return to Slathersby Hill, and I feel bound to Honor his Wish. Your Aunt, as well, bids me leave.

So I write this to declare my unfailing and undying Love for you. Father, and your aunt Mary, argue that you will not want to Marry me now that you are lame but I cannot, will not Believe it.

Your current predicament does not Dissuade me. I am yours more now than ever. Do not doubt my Love. Send Word of your condition as you can. You are forever in my Prayers. Forever in my Heart

Es

# 22

## JESSE

God.

Since leaving the vegetable stand turned restaurant on their way to meet Jeremiah, Chloe's testimony pestered him, took up residence in his thoughts.

He'd never considered the Big Guy an option before. As a scientist, he observed unexplained elements of the universe and conceded to the idea of a grand design. A Creator.

But a personal Savior — did he need a Savior? — seemed preposterous. In college, his roommate turned Christianese into a drinking game. Just tune into any Christian radio or TV station and take a drink every time some slick preacher said, "Praise God."

If a man wanted to get drunk fast —

Yet Chloe spoke with a passion, a truth he'd not seen or heard. In her time of need,

Chloe's desperation led her to God. Jesse's brought him to Hollywood.

"You okay?" she said, taking the turn toward Chris's place.

"Fine. Just thinking."

"About Chris?" she said.

"Yeah, about Chris." Why not? The truth felt too weird.

"He's quit. I know it."

"How do you know it?" Jesse looked over at her.

"Because this is my life. My first big break. Something is bound to go wrong."

"Where's the woman of faith I heard back at the Styrofoam-plate place?"

She tried not to smile. "She's scared."

"Doesn't God assure you everything will work out?"

"You know what's really annoying?" Chloe said. "When people who don't know God tell people who do what He's like. What He should do and say. How we should believe and behave."

Jesse surrendered, hands up. "Fine, then be scared."

"Sorry." She sighed. "I'm just nervous." Chloe slowed at the security gate, entering the code Jer had texted.

"Look, maybe it's nothing. You really think Chris would walk out? Why? Things are going well despite the rain delays. He's great as Hamilton, and you two . . . the chemistry is perfect."

"Do you ever wonder if life will just never go your way? If you don't have the 'it factor'?" Chloe drove slowly, examining the house numbers, heading toward the lake houses.

"There's no such thing as an 'it factor.'"

"How long have you been in Hollywood? There is most certainly an 'it factor.'" She turned down the long driveway of a two-story brick home with giant windows, curving down and around, the lake cutting into the grounds.

She parked next to a dark-tinted limo and cut the engine.

A limo? Was Chris on his way to the airport? Jesse's pre-Christmas call with Jeremiah surfaced. Maybe the new studio head had flown out to check on the project. Wouldn't be unheard of.

"Don't like the looks of that." Chloe pointed to the limo, popping open her door.

"Probably nothing." Sure. It was just the new studio head giving the project another green light. Jesse took hold of Chloe's arm. "Hey, wait a sec. You're right, I can't tell you about your faith or God. But the girl at the restaurant who told me how He saved her was onto something. I felt it. You almost had me believing. Chloe, be confident in what you know, what you believe. If you gave your life to God, then trust Him. What a gift to know you're not in this world alone."

"You . . . always surprise me." She angled toward him, kissing his cheek. Her eyes met his, and the kiss became more real, lips to lips and heart to heart.

Jesse slipped his hand down her back. He wanted more. He wanted her in his arms —

Chloe broke away, fingers pressed to her lips. "Jesse . . . I'm sorry."

"Please don't apologize on my account." He eased his arm around her waist.

"We can't keep saying we're friends, then go back to kissing."

She was right. But what *was* this weird allure between them?

Out of the car, Jesse escorted her up the stone steps that led to a portico. He rang the bell, exchanging one more glance with Chloe.

"Whatever happens, Chloe, I got your back. I don't know what power I can wield in there. Don't know what's about to go down, but you will finish this movie, Chris or no Chris, as Esther Kingsley, your *living* heroine. I promise."

She gave him a wry smile. "Thank you. But don't make promises you can't keep, Jess."

Chris answered the door shirtless, his jeans riding low on his hips, looking like he'd just rolled out of bed. "Hey! Come on in. We're in the back," he said as he walked off, running his hand through his long hair.

Jesse crossed the foyer and entered a large, square living space with windows facing the lake and the kitchen on the opposite side. The air was chilly and gray, the lifeless fireplace a black hole.

Chris sat, falling over the arm of a chair, his feet in the air, jamming a cigarette in his mouth. A man Jesse didn't recognize sat in the chair next to him, and a petite blonde stood in between, holding a leather attaché.

"Want to do the introductions, Jeremiah?" the man said.

Jer leaned against the kitchen island, arms crossed, his expression boney and sober. "This is Greg Zarzour, new head of Premier Studios. Greg, Jesse Gates."

Jesse shook his hand. "It's a pleasure." Time to play nice. His career was in the man's hands.

"The pleasure's all mine." Zarzour remained seated, barely shaking Jesse's hand. He wore the typical uniform of the nouveau riche — an Armani suit. His dark hair was clipped and gelled. "Please, have a seat."

But Jesse couldn't sit. He was too ramped.

"Do you know Chloe Daschle, Greg?" Jer asked.

Zarzour stood this time and moved toward Chloe. "Your dad is a hero of mine, and your mother was my first Hollywood crush."

What a creep. Who says that to a woman's daughter?

"I'm sure she'd be flattered." Chloe, a model of graciousness. "So, what's going on? Jer?" She remained standing next to Jesse.

"I like the way she cuts to the chase." Chris tapped out his cigarette into a crystal bowl. Not an ashtray. The owners probably had a no-smoking policy, but he was Chris Painter. The rules didn't apply. "Greg here wants me for another part."

"What?" Panic flared in Chloe's wide eyes. "We're in the middle of shooting."

"Chloe, sit please." Zarzour motioned to the same chair he'd indicated for Jesse, but she remained on her feet, the edge of her arm lightly brushing his.

"An action-adventure," Jeremiah said as he walked toward the window. Beyond the frame, the lake inlet curved toward the clipped lawn. "*Sea Dragon.* The lead actor is all wrong for the part." He glanced at Zarzour. "I told your predecessor not to hire Sherwood. He's a thespian. He plays the parody and farcical elements of an action-adventure too literally. You can't believe him."

"Well, we're six months late and ten million over budget, and the crew is about to mutiny. Something has to change." Zarzour took a seat in a tall, winged chair, a king holding court. "Bookman can't manage him. I need a director who can. The board fired Holloman because he couldn't fix it. They hired me because I could. My first fix is these two. Painter and Gonda. I need you in New Zealand next week."

Chloe blanched. "They want you too, Jer?"

Jeremiah's stone expression was her answer. "I told you I never abandon a project, Zarzour."

"Just turn it over to someone else. Who's your AD?"

"Sharon Lee."

"Perfect. I've no problem with her. She can take command."

"But it's my . . . I put this project . . ." He couldn't even speak plain. "Look, Painter's the heart and soul of the film." Jeremiah nodded toward Chloe. "Along with Daschle here."

Chloe leaned against Jesse, muttering, "I knew it . . . I knew it . . ."

"Find a new heart, then. We've hired a script consultant to —"

"A script consultant?" Jesse flared. "The script was perfect. Do you know how many rewrites we went through?"

"They want it cut," Jeremiah said with a near heart-stopping resolve. "Ten percent."

Zarzour reached into a leather shoulder bag and tossed a crumpled script onto the center of the table. "There are some scenes that can go. Also, what's on B-roll? Use it."

Jer picked up the script, flipped through a few pages, then tossed it to Jesse. "Just use B-roll. Sure, why not?" He shot Jesse an apologetic look. "Hey, I can use the extra scene where Chloe comes screaming out of the barn claiming a rooster was trying to kill her. How about that, Zarzour?" Jer flipped through the last pages and slapped the script down on the table. "Death by rooster. We'll turn this film into a parody, a farce."

Chris laughed. "When was this? How'd I miss it?"

"You were still celebrating New Year's," Jer said.

"I told you I was sorry, man."

"And now I have to work with you seven

thousand miles away."

"That rooster *was* trying to kill me." Chloe pecked the air with her fingers.

The silent blonde between Zarzour and Chris laughed softly.

"Be serious, Gonda. Now look, Jesse, the changes should be straightforward," Zarzour said.

He picked up the script and skipped through the pages, finding the last half filled with red lines. The cuts were deep. And costly. It was over. His first movie. Done. Failed.

Chloe leaned to see, squeezing his arm.

"We're not cutting the script." Jeremiah remained determined. "This is a serious project, Greg. We've spent too much money to —"

"Agreed, Jer. The changes we're suggesting are not major. Just little snips. You're under budget here, so I'm rerouting some of your money to make up the losses on *Sea Dragon*."

Jesse had always known Jeremiah Gonda to be calm and in command. But now he flew around the room to confront the studio head.

"You can't just hack up a war-period piece, Greg. This isn't a ninety-minute rom-com. The script went through all the proper channels, we took our notes, made our changes. Jesse worked tirelessly on this. You can take me out and hand it over to Sharon, but Painter has to finish. As is."

Zarzour remained unmoved. In his posture. In his countenance. "What do you think, Jesse? Can you make the changes?"

"Greg," Jeremiah said, his voice low and taut, the sound of a man losing a fight. "This is my project and —"

"My studio's money."

"I won't go to New Zealand if you slice and dice this film."

Zarzour sat forward, his countenance dark. "If you don't go to New Zealand, I'm closing down this shoot. What you've already spent doesn't compare to the money hole Bookman and Sherwood dug in New Zealand." He offered a fake smile, adjusted his suit coat, and reclined again. "Premier Studios and Gonda Films have enjoyed a long and prosperous relationship. Let's not have this hiccup ruin things. Right now I don't see *Bound by Love* as one of our lead films next year, but I might reconsider . . . if things go my way."

The man held all the aces and knew it. Everyone in the room knew it.

While Jeremiah didn't need the studio system, ruining a powerful relationship with

Premier would be foolish.

The tension settled over Jesse, consuming his raw spaces, the ones that echoed with his past. He glanced at a white-faced Chloe and moved into the debate.

"I'm looking at the notes," he said, flipping through the pages again. "Th-they're pretty good. Shortening a scene here and there." He glanced around with a shallow smile. "I can work on these this afternoon."

"There you go, Gonda. A team player." Zarzour beamed. Round one to Premier Studios.

"Yeah, I think we can live with most of these." He paused as he neared the end, where red lines eliminated the pivotal Christmas scene between Hamilton and Esther.

"Jess, what is it?" Jeremiah reached for the script.

"The Christmas scene," he said. "We can't cut this. It's pivotal to the love story. Where Hamilton and Esther declare their love."

"It's not a love story anymore. It's a war story." Zarzour reached toward Chris, begging a cigarette from him. "You got anything to drink around here?"

"Water. Soda." Chris tossed Zarzour his pack of cigarettes, then got up to go to the kitchen. "I'm off alcohol for a while." He launched a passing glance at Jeremiah. "Why do you think I smoke?"

"I'll take a soda. Diet." Zarzour lit the cigarette, exhaling smoke into the pristine room. "So, you can make the cuts? Good."

"But it is a love story." Jesse retrieved the script from Jeremiah. "Hamilton and Esther must be together in the end." That was the point. His grandfather's love story. Esther's. And yes, Loxley's. It meant closure for Jesse, and perhaps some mystical closure for his long-gone ancestor.

"We like the idea of Esther becoming a war hero," Zarzour said. "She goes to the battlefield to find Hamilton, and when he gets killed, she takes up his musket for him. Maybe she fires the cannon. A Molly Pitcher type. That happened during the Revolutionary War, right? Women stepped up. Then" — Zarzour moved to the edge of his seat — "we grab the viewer by the throat. Esther weeps over her dying fiancé, she fires the cannon, taking out a passel of redcoats, tears streaming down her face. The audience is enraptured, cheering. Just when victory is at hand, Esther takes a bullet right to the heart. Drops dead on the battlefield, a hero."

"No," Chloe shouted, leaping into the middle of the room. "No, no, no!"

"It's perfect! Why not?" Zarzour inhaled a long, arrogant drag from his cigarette, polluting the house with more than smoke. "Esther dies a heroine's death. A patriot. A freedom fighter. People write poems and songs about her. She's an icon in American history. It's pure movie magic."

"She cannot die, Greg." Chloe shivered. "She lives. She lives! I refuse to die. I will not die."

"Chloe, what's the big deal? If she dies, we cut an additional four minutes from the film. As you know, time is money." Zarzour narrowed his gaze at her, his true darkness peeking out. "Besides, I've seen the dailies. I've never bought that Hamilton loves her. It's the other guy . . . what's his name —"

"Flanders," Jesse said, low, burdened.

"Right, Flanders." Zarzour's cigarette ashes tumbled to the hardwood. "You can see that he's in love with her every time he's on the screen. You could have *him* pick up her lifeless body and walk off into the sunset so we know she had someone who buried her after Hamilton is gone. You play that role, don't you, Jesse? Are you in love with Chloe here? Because every time —"

"Greg!" Jeremiah said.

But Jesse was already on the move. "Flanders doesn't love her! It's Hamilton. He's the one. Did you not read the script? If anyone saves her, it should be him."

"Esther cannot die!" Chloe screeched, wild and frantic. She whirled to Jeremiah. "You promised me I'd live in this role. Jesse, you promised me —"

"Chloe, sweetheart, they aren't in charge any more." Zarzour perched the cigarette on the edge of his lips. "Jeremiah, how about you kill off Hamilton in the first battle, so I can get Chris down to New Zealand and working on his part? There's a lot of action for him to learn and rehearse."

Chris moaned and slid down in his chair. "Jeremiah, can I please have a shot of bourbon?"

"No."

Zarzour turned to his silent assistant. "E-mail Halston, tell him to get Aaron Heinley to fly out here." She started tapping notes into her phone. "He might have to make the cuts for us."

Jesse felt the wrecking ball swinging toward his dreams. *Boom.* They'd lost. From the center of the room, Chloe sank onto the edge of the coffee table, her eyes brimming with a watery sheen.

"Don't bother, Greg," Jeremiah said. "We'll do the cuts."

"Good. I knew you'd see things my way."

The studio head had all the answers, didn't he? Except what to do with the ashes falling from his cigarette. He finally tapped them into the crystal bowl Chris had used. "How long will that take, including reshoots? Two weeks? You've only been filming a month, so there shouldn't be too much more. I can stop the *Sea Dragon* bleed for two weeks."

"Two, yeah." Jeremiah dropped into the nearest chair.

"So, what am I doing?" Chris said. "Going to New Zealand?"

"As soon as possible. Jer, how about releasing him in a week? He's got a lot to learn." Zarzour turned to Jesse. "Think you can handle the changes?"

Chloe rose and drifted down a dark hall, her muffled cry bouncing against the walls.

"No, Mr. Zarzour, I can't. I won't."

"Excuse me?"

"You heard me. I can't and I won't." His confession started out weak but grew stronger with each passing moment.

Jeremiah lifted his head. Chloe reappeared from the hallway. Chris sat up, amused.

"I thought you were a team player, Gates," Zarzour demanded.

"You can't kill Esther. I wrote this screenplay to finish a story my ancestor started. I wrote it to finish my own . . . *another's* . . .

love story. If you kill Esther, you kill those women too. In this movie, the hero and heroine do not die. They live happily ever after. This story is about love, not death. And Chloe? She's an amazing actress, but for some reason, Hollywood won't let her live. She's typecast. But on this project, we're reversing that course."

He sounded way more confident than he felt.

Zarzour doused out his cigarette in the bowl, losing his jocular demeanor. "I didn't know you were in charge, Jesse. You're a screenwriter. Who got lucky. Now, make those changes or I'll find someone who will. We needed them yesterday. And if Chloe is such a great actress, she can give us an Oscar-worthy death scene." He stood and pushed back his jacket, anchoring his hands on his belt. "*Sea Dragon* is our lead film next year. It cannot fail." The man exhaled and walked toward Jesse, visibly gathering his composure. He popped Jesse on the arm. "You make these changes, and I personally promise a movie from one of your scripts. Within two years. You're an actor, too, right? We have a film coming up early next year I'd like to cast you in."

*Clever, Zarzour. Appealing to my ego.*

He glanced toward Chloe. She leaned

against the wall, staring toward the lake view, arms folded, her green eyes rimmed red.

Zarzour turned to his assistant. "You ready?" She nodded, and the two of them started for the door. "Jeremiah, Chris, I'll be in touch with *Sea Dragon* details. In fact" — he motioned to his assistant, who took more notes — "I'll have the script and production notes sent over today."

"I won't do it." Jesse tossed the script on the table, pulse pumping. Shooting himself in the foot never felt so good.

Zarzour turned, making a face, returning to where Jesse stood. "What do you mean you won't do it?"

"You want the changes, make them yourself. Hire Aaron Heinley for all I care. I'm not doing it."

"Jesse, this is your script, your movie." Jeremiah stepped toward him. "Make the changes. You can do it faster than anyone else. Keep some control. And set yourself up for the future."

"I'm not cutting the Christmas scene, nor am I killing Esther."

Zarzour scoffed. "Don't challenge me, Jesse. Make the changes or you're fired."

Fired? Suddenly none of his Hollywood aspirations mattered.

"Jesse . . ." Chloe moved toward him. "Make the changes. It's not that big of a deal."

"Yes, yes, it is." Jesse glanced at her, then at Jeremiah. "Are we really going to let him do this to our project?"

"Jesse, this is the movie business —"

"And it's about making money," Zarzour said. "You should know that by now. You're still in good standing with me, Jesse. I can guarantee your future. So make the changes."

Jesse's gaze met Chloe's. She stood between him and Zarzour, hands clasped at her waist, slowly shaking her head.

*Don't hesitate now, man.* "Then I guess I'm fired." Jesse walked around the sofa toward the door, adrenaline pounding in his head.

"Jesse! No, wait!" Chloe jostled Zarzour aside, reaching for Jesse's arm. "Don't do this. Please. You took a stand. Made your point. Don't ruin your career for me. Don't let someone else write *your* story. *Your* ancestor's story."

"If I make those changes, I'm breaking my promise to you. I can't do it, Chloe. I can't let you down."

"It's just a movie, Jesse." Tears glistened in her eyes as she stepped closer. "I'm not Loxley," she whispered.

"If it's just a movie, then how come it feels so real?"

Freeing himself from her, he headed outside and down the driveway toward the road. He'd need every mile of his walk back to the hotel to work this out.

"Jesse." Jeremiah caught him halfway to the road. "I don't like this any more than you do. What you did back there? Standing up for yourself, for Chloe . . . It took guts, and I respect you for it. But I need you to make those changes. We'll work together on it —"

Standing there, trembling, he knew the reality of his refusal. "I can't let her die. Not again. Don't you see?"

"Are we talking about Chloe?"

"Yes . . . no . . . I don't know." Poor Jeremiah, caught between Jesse's past and his future. "Either way, I'm not writing her death scene. I'm sorry, Jeremiah." With that, he flipped his collar against the stiff wind and marched down the long driveway toward the road.

# 23

## HAMILTON

He awoke in a dark room, his leg throbbing, his toes tingling. A soft fragrance reminded him of home.

"Esther?"

He'd seen her. Just a moment ago. She spoke to him, kissed his forehead and cheek.

"Hamilton, you're awake." Aunt Mary's pretty face appeared over his.

"How long have I been asleep?" He tried to sit up, but his arms failed him.

"In and out for nearly three weeks. Many times we feared losing you."

"We? Esther? Is she here? I am certain I heard her voice. She was speaking to a man."

"The surgeon?"

"Perhaps. But he seemed rather large. As if life itself could not contain him. I cannot recall. Perhaps I was dreaming."

"Of course, that's it, you had a dream."

"But was she here?"

"Sh-she escorted me here, y-yes. Then her father came for her. She departed with him the same day." Aunt Mary aided him upright, fluffed the pillows and linens, then pressed a cold cloth to his head. "You must be famished."

"A bit, yes, feeling weak. Rather out of body." He gazed about the room. "Am I not home?"

"We're at the home of Dr. Nelson off Green River Road. He saved your life."

"Saved my life?" He tipped his head back, trying to remember. "The battle . . . what became of the battle?" A blurry image of Lieutenant Twimball swung across his mind. His saber . . . the cold mud . . . the light . . . his pa and ma.

"The patriots were victorious. Colonel Tarleton and his dragoons were routed. We captured over eight hundred British regulars."

"They were not murdered?"

"No, indeed. Taken prisoner."

He nodded. "As it should be."

Aunt Mary tied back the curtain and inched up the window sash. "There. How's about a touch of fresh air? Here's a newspaper, if you like, from Charles Town with an account of Hannah's Cowpens. I saved it for you. Now, let me fetch some broth. Oh, my boy, it's good to have you among the living."

"I saw Pa and Ma," he said, eyes closed, trying to recall every detail. "In a dream. It was so lovely."

"They must have been praying for you. Did you see your uncle Laurence?"

"I did not. Yet, another man . . ." Perhaps an angel. Some heavenly being. "Like the one in my room. Extraordinary in size. There was no end to him."

Aunt Mary patted his arm. "The soul does odd things when the body had been distressed. Don't trouble yourself remembering. All things in good time. Just rest." Aunt Mary moved to the door. "I'll fetch your broth."

"Did Esther say she would return? Did she leave a letter?" In the back of his mind, he saw a gathering of redcoats in Sir Michael's foyer. Esther wore a red gown with a green ribbon in her hair. She asked him to leave. But why? Something in his hand. He was angry with her father.

"A letter? Nay, not that I found."

"My letter." He pressed against the thin mattress, struggling to sit up. "My coat? Where is my coat?"

"I told you, she left no letter."

"Nay, my letter. To her. Where are my things?"

Aunt Mary went to the wardrobe, removing his tattered and stained coat. "Nothing here, Hamilton. Perhaps you also dreamed of this letter."

He exhaled, falling against the pillow. "Ralphie. He must have done as I bid and carried the letter to her."

"Of course, there is your answer. Now, let me bring you sustenance. The sooner you regain your strength, the sooner we can go home and stop burdening the surgeon and his wife."

When she'd gone, Hamilton tried to read the paper, but his thoughts drifted to the battlefield, to Twimball lowering his sword.

The day beyond the window was bright — clear and hopeful. A bit of food to strengthen him and he'd be himself again, able to ride home and claim Esther.

Having done his bit for the war, he'd return home a free man. A free, American man. Free to fall in love, to marry, to raise Lightfoot children.

What he must do was reacquire Quill Farm. Blast if he'd pay ten pounds a month to rent his own land.

His letter. He must check for himself

among his coat and haversack. To be sure Ralphie indeed carried the note to its intended.

Struggling to sit upright — his legs were stiff and uncooperative — Hamilton pushed from the bed, swung his legs over the side, and planted his right foot on the cold floor, then his left, stretching against his aches and pains.

As he stood, his arms flailed as he toppled forward, desperate to catch himself before slamming down on the floor.

But he crashed with a thud.

"Blast!" He gripped the edge of the bed and sat up, a dull, aching pain seizing his left leg while his toes tingled with a fiery sensation.

Pressing up, he tried again to stand, seeing then a vacancy where his left leg used to be. No knee, no shin. No foot. Only a bloody bandaged stump.

His cry burst his lungs. "What have you done to me?" He hammered the floor with his fist. "Surgeon! Surgeon! What have you done?"

The clock on the desk ticked the time. One second. Two seconds.

"Surgeon!" Again, he hammered the floor, the pain against his knuckles a fair price to pay. "Where is my leg?" A fresh crimson stream of blood stained the bandage. "Someone! Tell me where my leg has gone. Aunt Mary!"

The door burst open and the surgeon, along with an ambulatory private who had only a bandage around his head, grabbed Hamilton under his arms.

"Where is my leg? I demand an answer. Why do my toes tingle when they are not there?"

"Let me settle you in your bed, Hamilton. On three, Private. One, two, three."

Blood stained the sheet where his leg, his *stump,* had rested. The sight, the realization swarmed him.

"I believe I'm going to be sick."

The surgeon sat him on the edge of the mattress and reached for a pail. Hamilton wretched but expelled nothing from his empty insides.

Nothing but his fear. His disgust. His poverty of being.

"Your aunt is coming with broth." The surgeon situated him against the pillows. "What were you trying to do? Didn't she tell you to remain in bed?"

"She said nothing." He caught the surgeon's hand as the man tried to install a blanket over him. "My leg. Where is my leg, you butcher?"

"You took a sword slice and it could not be saved. Your friends tried, but the damage was too great." The surgeon sat next to the bed. "Do you remember the events of the battle?"

"No . . . some . . . yes. I remember Lieutenant Twimball. His sword is responsible for the wounds on my arm and face."

"And your leg."

"He swung at me, though I did not believe he'd done much harm."

"Your brothers-in-arms say you were valiant, and when you had opportunity to fire upon him, you lowered your pistol. It was a young Ralphie Standish who shot him."

"Ralphie. And what of Twimball?"

"He's buried in the field."

Hamilton sighed, collapsing against the pillows with a surge of emotion. He had no use for Twimball. None. But now that he was gone . . .

"I wonder if at any other time we might have been friends."

"You did your duty," the surgeon said. "On that you can rest assured."

His tears slipped to the corners of his eyes. "Rest assured? 'Tis a dream. I'm not sure I will ever rest again. Let alone with any assurance. I have lost my leg. How am I to

389

work? To care for my family? My aunt is a widow. Her farm has recently been stolen from her, and I am all she has to keep her from shame and starvation. If I cannot work, I cannot eat. If I cannot eat, I starve. We all starve."

"Surely there are charities —"

"Charities? For the rest of my life? I cannot expect nor accept it." He grabbed a fistful of air. "I want to work, to farm, to marry and raise a family. But with one swipe of an Englishman's sword, 'tis gone. All of it."

"You will heal. The leg will support a prosthesis, a peg. I've seen —"

"A peg? What work can a man do with a wooden leg? The work will take twice, nay, three times as long."

"You've workers, don't you?"

"Do you mean slaves? We do not. We are abolitionists. We hire laborers, but such an expense will eat into my profits, should there be any." He fixed on what remained of his leg with loathing. "And what of Esther? How can I marry her now?"

"I saw your Esther when she arrived with your aunt. She seemed most devoted. Do not discount her loyalty."

"Hamilton, you must be famished." Aunt Mary came through the doorway, a tray in her hand, anxiety in her eyes. "Dr. Nelson, your wife prepared the concoction and poultice you wanted."

"Thank you, Mrs. Lightfoot." The surgeon reached for the cup on the tray. "Drink this. Then you must take the broth." He settled the cup in Hamilton's hand. "When I was your age, I too believed I had the world sorted out. But indeed, I did not. I never imagined myself living in the backcountry of South Carolina. I was Harvard trained and educated. The southern colonies were for despots and the poor. But life, or the good Lord, had other plans for me."

"What sort of good Lord would do this to a man?" Hamilton peered into the cup, then downed the golden-brown brew, the liquid both sweet and sour, burning as it went down. A warmth flowed through him as he took up the heady broth. "I depend on myself now. The ways of the Lord are not good. He took my pa and ma, my sister, my uncle. Now my leg, which will cost me more than I can afford." He gulped the hot broth, caring not how it burned his mouth. "I used to say, what good can come from redcoats? Now I wonder, what good can come from God?"

The surgeon patted Hamilton's good leg. Dare he say, his only leg. "You must endure this trial of faith. You're not abandoned in your hardship. All the more to look to the Almighty."

"I've had my fill of trial. Will faith give me a leg? A wife and children? The return of Quill Farm? Nay, f-f-faith is . . . for . . . f-f-fools." He struggled with his protest as sleep began to overtake him. "Wh-what was in your concoction . . . Surgeon?"

The cup slipped from his fingers, and as he drifted down, down, down and away, a voice called to him through the haze, "Come, follow me."

## MARY

She pressed her forehead against the door, tears dripping from her chin. Her boy, Hamilton, the closest she'd ever come to a son, was broken, crushed. From the outside in.

How could God be so cruel to him? Losing his parents and sister, then his uncle, and now his leg. How much must one man be required to bear? She patted her pocket, where she'd stowed Esther's letter.

What of her own pain? Barren, called to raise another woman's child, which she did with joy! Let it not go unsaid. She welcomed young Hamilton into her heart without reservation.

But now she was a widow with nothing but her small farm and lame nephew. She lived amid a war both public and private. Whatever Laurence had done to acquire the land by the creek, it stirred Sir Michael's ire and set him on a war path.

Then the man tricked her into signing a document surrendering the farm to him. What a fool she'd been.

Mary needed Hamilton, his masculine presence and wisdom. And he needed her.

So she must gather her wits and contend for what was hers. She'd not be left to live in squalor, a barren, old widow.

Pressing her fist to her lips, sensing herself yielding to selfish darkness, she fought the tug within her breast.

She carried Hamilton's tray down to the kitchen, thanking Mrs. Nelson for her good broth. Walking outside, she found the Nelson boys building a fire, tossing on clothes and bandages that could never be washed clean.

She patted her pocket as a thought flashed. No. She could not. *Mary, you are of better character.*

What she and Laurence had built from the ground up out of the wild backcountry of South Carolina was proof. But they were young and in love, full of dreams. They left

Virginia with hope in their hearts of preaching the gospel to the heathens and unsaved.

Then, at last, owning their own farm.

She slipped the letters from her pocket. Two. The one Esther had left for Hamilton. And the one she had found in his haversack, muddy, crumpled, bloodstained, and addressed to Esther.

God forgive her, but she'd read them. Hamilton's a direct confession of love. Esther's containing Mary's worst fears — his amputated leg did not dissuade her but deepened her resolve to make a life with him. She would not desert him.

Mary tapped the letters against her hand. Esther Longfellow may declare one thing, her mind full of lofty, romantic ideals, but Mary knew the truth.

The girl would break her boy's heart. Esther was her father's daughter, after all.

Mary inched toward the fire. How could Esther, a girl raised in the luxury of Slathersby Hill, live on a working farm?

Her only consolation was if Hamilton married Esther, Sir Michael might tear up his fraudulent document. Unless Sir Michael cut off all capital as a way to control her.

But Esther would grow bored and complain, stirring up Hamilton to provide for her, to enlarge their living quarters, thus putting them into debt.

She may have been raised in the upcountry, but she was a member of the British aristocracy and so accustomed to a certain standard of life.

Esther had grown up with Sassy and Isaac seeing to her every care. Even Kitch catered to her. Her girlish notions of love had blinded her into believing she could do away with such refinements and toil alongside her husband from dawn to dusk.

A husband with all of his limbs would be taxed by the fields, the woods, the wind and rain. But one leaning on a crutch would face twice the hardship.

Nay, the girl did not grasp what lay ahead for Hamilton. She would soon find herself more a farmhand and nursemaid than wife and lover.

She'd break his heart. Of this, Mary had no doubt. And inflict a pain more severe than losing a limb. One from which he may never recover.

Mary considered the letters once again. Dare she act upon her own will?

"Mrs. Lightfoot? Can I disturb you for some help?" Mrs. Nelson called from the door, retreating before Mary could answer.

"Certainly." She walked to the fire pit with

a final glance at the letters in her hand.

"Want to throw something on the fire, Mrs. Lightfoot?" This from fresh-faced Simms.

"Indeed, I do." She passed the boy one letter. "Can you toss this in for me?"

The boy nodded, taking the note without a word, and flinging it into the flames. Mary considered the second letter and returned it to her pocket.

The deed was done. As the letter burned, she'd sealed her own future.

# 24

## CHLOE

The heart of the film stopped beating when Jesse left. The flow, the rhythm, the inspiration, everything, vanished.

Zarzour's proclamation had pierced its very soul, and Jesse had left it to bleed.

In a rocking chair on the veranda of the Kingsley home, Chloe sat in costume, the blue dress she'd loved so much on the first day, waiting in the predawn light for her ride to the battlefield.

Today was her last day of shooting. And perhaps her last day in films. Ever. She wasn't simply quitting. Or prepping for some lavish, dramatic pity party. She was waking up. Understanding. Coming to a heart-wrenching revelation.

The movies did not love her. She was in the wrong business. Her lofty goals of entertaining the masses with touching, inspiring, romantic stories endured the final blow when Jeremiah handed her the revised script.

"I'm so sorry."

"I know you are. I'll give it my all."

He embraced her, kissing her forehead. "You are too good for this town."

So she read her scenes. Embraced her death. And rehearsed like a pro. She was an actor. And actors acted.

Backed into a corner, Zarzour had no choice but to allow Jeremiah to finish the film with Chris as Hamilton.

He released the canceled funds while cutting the shooting time line by three weeks. Jer and Sharon Lee worked three days straight making the script changes, dividing the scenes among themselves. Jer took the battle and outdoor scenes. Sharon, the romance and indoor shoots.

The entire set was chaos. Cast and crew nipping at one another. Confusion abounded. They were the *Titanic* sailing full steam ahead toward the iceberg.

Lori rushed past the house, a small light affixed to her forehead. Her blond and pink hair stood straight up, and when she looked at Chloe, the light cast a ghostly hue over her face, accenting her black-rimmed eyes. She wore the same clothes from yesterday.

And the day before. And the day before.

"Are you ready?" Lori flipped through her scene list. "You're in the parlor with Millie . . . Wait, no . . ." She swore. "You should be on the battlefield with Chris. The car is on its way."

"Good." Chloe moved to the porch post, watching the sunrise bleed into the dusty, blue dawn.

Winter still gripped this first March day. Was that the scent of snow she detected?

Since his exit, she'd not heard from Jesse. Well, save for one brief, curt text exchange.

*Come back, Jess. Please.*

He didn't answer until the next day. *Have a great shoot. Jer will make this work.*

In his weird way, that was his good-bye. The slamming door reverberated in her chest. He'd failed, and for reasons she didn't completely understand, the burden of Loxley chained him all over again.

She missed him. His steady presence and logical demeanor. His defense of her in front of everyone lived in her mind. In fact, the notion had packed a suitcase and moved into her mind. He'd ended his career on a matter of principle.

No one had ever done that for her. Dad, bless his heart, tried but failed when Sam told him she wouldn't get the part of

Debbie Dough. Mom, while strong, always acted as a mediator, seeing both sides of a situation. Chloe's boyfriends cared more about expressing themselves than protecting her.

Then there was the thing with Haden on the E.P.'s rooftop, where her actions were indefensible.

The car pulled up, and the driver stepped out to open her door. Sitting in the back, Esther regarded the scene beyond the window, snapping memories of the landscape, of the rising light, and of how she felt. Not just her emotions, but Esther's.

How did she feel when Hamilton married another? Was she in love with her husband who died and left her a young widow?

Why did Hamilton not send the letter proposing after they were both widowed?

Chloe was Esther in so many ways. Lasting love was just not meant to be. And in some ways, she was like Loxley. Not physically — God rest her soul — but emotionally. Dying to herself. Quitting. Giving up.

*I loved you, Jesse.*

Yet . . . deep down in the part of her soul she could not see, peace ruled. Since the day she'd cried in church for two hours and surrendered herself to the One who truly, unconditionally loved and defended her, a

400

new hope was born.

Jesus would heal her past and take care of her todays and her tomorrows. Her good Father held her future in His hands.

The car arrived at the shoot, and Chloe walked historic Green River Road toward the set. An extra dressed like Flanders walked by, prepared to die. Chloe's eyes misted.

*Please, Lord, may this not be the death of Jesse's dreams.*

War. That's how this whole project felt. As if the powers of hell determined to defeat love. Yet Love had already won. Chloe smiled.

"You look cheery for a girl who's about to die." The DP, Sandy, came alongside her, weary and wearing a dark expression.

"I just realized . . . love has already won."

"Sure doesn't look like it to me."

"Sandy, I can go out there and die, not in defeat, but victory." Chloe moved toward the field. "I can give this scene my heart and soul. Even though this is not what any of us wanted, we can end this with excellence and hold our heads up high."

"Okay, you're more tired than you look. What victory? What excellence? This film is a mess."

"I told you. Love has already won." Truth.

Revelation. The Spirit washed over her. "I don't have to be afraid."

Sandy made a face. "What love? Who? Chris?"

"No, Jes—"

"Jesse?" Sandy sparked to life, slapping her hands together. "I knew, I knew it. I told Jer you were more than friends. You tried to say you were just friends, but who were you kidding?"

"Sandy, no, not Jesse. Jesus. I was going to say Jesus loves me. His love has already won!" Speaking it out loud helped her make sense of the feelings in her chest. "He's got this, and if I never act again, He'll have something just as amazing for me to do."

"Jesus? Since when?"

"Since a crazy night on the rooftop of E.P & L.P."

"Sandy, let's get set," Jer called. The director of photography ran off with a backward wince at Chloe. Jer called action.

Chloe leaned against a tree, watching the first element of the battle unfold. Flanders ran toward a redcoat, then jerked backward to the ground, meeting his end with a movie-prop musket.

Flanders. Dead. Chloe's eyes filled again. Such a great character. Played by such a great actor. A great man.

"So, you're not in love with Jesse?" Chloe turned to see Lori leaning in. "Sorry, I overheard you talking to Sandy. Becky and I had a pool going . . ."

Chloe winced as a cannon exploded. Jeremiah ran through the smoke with one of the cameras, then whirled around to catch Hamilton's reaction to Flanders's death.

"A pool?" she said. "About me and Jesse?"

"Yeah . . . Hey, are you crying? Look, it'll work out. Jesse will calm down and you two, well, you two are so perfect for each other. And you know Jeremiah will work his magic and turn this disaster into a cinematic beauty. Zarzour is an idiot."

"Lori, I'm not in love . . ." *Well, don't lie to the girl.* "There's nothing between Jesse and me." True. "I just feel bad for him. His first film. Hacked to bits."

"We feel for both of you. Especially you, dying once again."

Chloe returned her attention to the scene. "You know, Lori, I think that's the point. I need to die and stay dead. Then, only then, can I live."

"Girl, you are tired. Talking nonsense. Are you going to quit acting? Don't. Please. Jeremiah will make it up to you. No one anticipated the Zarzour effect."

"I'm not quitting, Lori. Just waking up."

On the field, Chris charged a troop of redcoats, sword drawn. He and Ian Rainier moved through the choreographed fight. Then Chris stopped, walking over to Jeremiah, their voices heard across the vastness.

". . . not right . . ."

"If I'm fighting Ian, then what happens to . . ."

Jer's voice boomed over Lori's walkie-talkie. "We need the pages. Apparently we're just making stuff up out here."

"On my way."

When she'd gone, Chloe leaned against the tree, hand over her heart, over the mushrooming sensation. Peace. Amazing, otherworldly peace.

In the movies she may play dead, but in life she had the victory of Christ. Perhaps she should live more like a winner than a loser.

"Chloe, Chris, let's go." Jeremiah charged toward her, reading Lori's clipboard. He was in beast mode. No more evaluating. No more reshooting. No more rehearsing, discussing, or letting the actors act. Just set the scene and go.

"Chris, you're getting shot."

"Why don't we just shoot everyone?" Chris said. "Or, I know, how about the boys in red winning this one?"

Jeremiah leaned toward his star. "So help me, Painter. I'll make three months in New Zealand miserable for you if you don't shut up. I don't care what Zarzour says."

Chris backed up, hands surrendered. "Lighten up, Gonda. Just a bit of humor. Got to admit, we're killing a lot of main characters."

Jeremiah replied with an exhale, shaking his head, muttering to himself, "I know, I know, but it will work. It has to work." He motioned for Chloe and Chris to take their places, tapping Chris on the shoulder as he walked past. "Sorry, man."

"Forget it."

"Okay, Chloe," Jer said, scanning Lori's clipboard. "After he falls, run over to mourn him, then take over with his rifle."

"I'm supposed to use the cannon."

"You were until it jammed. Take up his rifle."

"It won't be loaded," Chris said. "I will have just shot the British captain. She'll have to reload."

Jeremiah swore. "Then use his dagger. Stab someone."

"Esther is going to stab someone?" Chloe paused for the stylist to touch up her makeup. "She would never —"

"Aim for his chest. Just as you're making contact, Hastings will shoot you. All right, people, let's go." Jer bent beside Sandy to view the shot. "The light is perfect. Let's get this in one take, everyone."

"Picture's up." The AD, Sharon, stepped from behind the camera. "Sound. Speed."

"Action!" Jeremiah's voice bellowed over the field.

Anxiety charged Chloe as she watched the scene. The stage felt real. She wasn't just acting, she was telling someone's story. Hers.

The volley of musket fire armed her adrenaline. Chris ran across the field toward a British soldier, firing his weapon. Then he recoiled, taking a bullet, gripping his chest and twisting down to the ground.

Tears tapped the corner of Chloe's eyes. *We can't die. Jesse . . .*

"Chloe . . ." Jeremiah waved her forward. "When you're ready."

For the umpteenth time, Chloe Daschle ran to her silver-screen death. She dropped next to the bleeding Hamilton, kissed his forehead, and whispered her love.

HAMILTON: Esther, my love, what are you doing here? Your father . . . furious.

ESTHER (Tearing the hem of her dress for a bandage): I couldn't sleep after our row. I had to see you, to tell you I'm sorry.

HAMILTON: I'm to blame. Arrogant and selfish, with no look to your cares.

ESTHER: You think one little confrontation will rid you of me? Nay, you're going to marry me one day. We'll have a dozen bothersome children. You'll regale our grandchildren with an exaggerated tale of your battlefield wound.

HAMILTON (Reaching up, pulling her down to a kiss): I love you.

ESTHER: And I you.


Esther's tears dropped to Hamilton's bloody, dirty, scarred face. Tears of sorrow. Tears of healing. Tears of hope.

"Chloe?" Jer's voice broke her reverie. "The dagger . . ."

Chris squeezed her hand. "Go get 'em. Die brilliantly."

Picking up the prop, she spotted the extra running toward her, a thin cutlass raised over his head.

She lunged toward him, aiming for his heart. To kill one's enemy, aim for what gives him life.

Charging faster, faster, her blood pumping, she launched through the air with an ear-crunching yell, sailing toward the extra with her weapon raised, exploding with all the love, angst, and pain in her heart.

"Death, you cannot have me!" Just as she was about to strike, the *click-slap* of a musket resounded.

Chloe dropped to the ground, spent, drained, empty, waiting for Jeremiah to call cut. Instead, he loomed over her with the camera as she continued to die.

The director zoomed in, smiling, giving her a thumbs-up, mouthing, "Amazing!"

On the winter field, where an ancient battle for freedom had been fought and won, Chloe Daschle found her own freedom, dying to her fears, her reputation, her resumé of death scenes, and even her desire for true love.

When Jeremiah called, "Cut," she pushed up from the ground smiling, alive, because she was finally and truly free.

"That's a wrap, everyone." Jeremiah drew Chloe into his arms as they stood among the trees, the day just beginning. "I have chills. That was incredible."

The actors and crew applauded while Margo from craft services popped bottles of champagne.

The other actors patted her on the back.

"Chloe, what an ending."

"Take that, Zarzour."

"I can't find that line in the script. Where did you come up with it?"

Just like that, Chloe's inspired improvisation breathed a bit of life back into the cast and crew.

When the champagne had been poured, Jeremiah gathered everyone together, his glass raised. "We were dealt a blow on this one, but you are all my heroes. Thank you for your hard work. And, Chloe, wow, what a way to end it."

The cast and crew applauded her again. She smiled, trembling under her costume, shaken by the emotion of the scene and the power of her declaration.

*Death, you cannot have me!* She felt healed from a disease she didn't know possessed her. As if she'd lost thirty pounds of emotional baggage.

"To Jesse Gates and *Bound by Love*," Jeremiah said.

The cast and crew chorused, "To Jesse and *Bound by Love*."

But the celebration was short-lived. A car awaited Jeremiah and Chris and the crew heading to New Zealand with them. Assistant director Sharon Lee would remain behind to oversee their exit from Chesnee.

Chloe sank to the ground, her legs unable to hold her any longer. Chris strode toward her with a cocky grin, his buckskin garb stained with fake blood. Dropping to the ground next to her, he roped his arm around her neck and pulled her in for a kiss on her forehead. "Way to kick death in the teeth. Where'd that banshee yell come from?"

She rested her arms atop her raised knees, the dark-blue wool skirt covering her legs and feet. "I don't know . . . it just came out." She peered at Chris. "Was I really okay?"

"You had me in tears." He took a small sip of his champagne, then poured out the rest. "I sorta like being alcohol-free. And yes, Chloe, you were really okay. More than okay. Best death scene I've ever seen."

Jeremiah stooped down in front of her, cupping her face in his hands. "You . . . I'm still playing that moment over and over in my head. I am so proud of you. I know dying was a huge disappointment, but wow! You best get an Oscar nod. I'll personally campaign for it."

"Me too." Chris popped Jeremiah a high five.

"Thank you." Chloe motioned to where

she'd flown through the air, shouting down death. "I'm sorry about my spontaneous —"

"Roar?" Chris said. "Don't be. You rattled my bones."

Jer grinned. "Rattled your bones? Well, that's one way of putting it." He motioned to Chris. "We should get going. I have twenty-four hours at home, and I want to see my kids and make love to my wife."

"TMI, Jer." Chris hopped up, reaching down to help Chloe. "Have you heard from Jesse?"

She shook her head. Her adrenaline had ebbed, but the calm remained. She was strong and alive.

"I texted him," Chris said with a sigh. "He never responded."

"Chris." Jeremiah walked backward to the limo waiting on Green River Road, motioning for his star to come along. "Let's go."

"See you back in LA." Chris kissed her cheek, started away, then returned. "Hey, Chloe, I just want to say . . . you know . . . if I hurt you back in the day, or made you think —"

"Chris, it's all good." Her eyes welled up and spilled over.

"I'm sorry you knew me during my jerk phase. But you're one of the best people I know." He gripped her hands in his. "It may

411

look like you've had this subpar career, and
God only knows why you kept getting cast
as the girl who dies, but you're alive, Chloe.
I see it in you in a way I don't see in any
other people in our biz."

"Chris, any day now!"

He smiled at Chloe. "Sheesh, you'd think
the man was anxious to see his wife." Chris
wiggled his eyebrows, and she laughed
softly.

"Thanks, Chris. I mean it."

He kissed her forehead. "I love you, Chloe
Daschle. Someday you'll tell me about the
light in your eyes."

For a long time she stood alone beside the
battlefield, watching the crew pack up. She
scanned the winter grounds where the real
Continental army, their forefathers, had laid
in wait for the British. Where Jesse's ancestor, Hamilton Lightfoot, was wounded and
maybe — no one knew — lost the woman
he loved.

"You think we'll ever know what happened to Hamilton Lightfoot and the mysterious Esther?" Lori handed Chloe a Diet
Coke.

"No." Chloe popped the top of the cold
can. And she may never know what happened to Jesse Gates. As light as she felt
inside, she had a sinking sensation about

412

him. "Hey, Lori, do you think unrequited love just dies? Like, goes away? Or does it try to find a home somewhere else, drifting through time until —"

"It dies. Trust me. If two lovers weren't meant to be, their love has to die. Why would there be any remaining?"

"I guess."

The unit manger made a face. "*Pffft,* but hey, don't listen to me. I can't figure out my own love life, let alone the essence of love and all its paths. Do you believe in true love?"

"Since I was born," Chloe said.

"That's a long time. You think you'll ever find it?"

Chloe nodded. "Yeah, I think I already have."

That day she met Smitty outside Expression58 and the women prayed for her. The day she went to the Cross. From there? Her possibilities were endless.

## ESTHER

*March*

The spring morning bore the bone-chilling kiss of winter. The sun, a golden globe resting in the blue sky, shed no warmth on

413

Slathersby Hill.

Worse, there was no warmth in Father, nor his library, despite the blaze in the fireplace.

Dressed in her traveling suit, Esther paced beside the window, watching as Isaac and Kitch tied her trunks to the top of the carriage, her hands pressed together, her thoughts in turmoil.

With an exhale. she whirled toward Father for one final argument.

"You cannot send me away."

A month ago, Father announced his intention to send her to England. Idle threats in her estimation. But the tide of the war had turned, and the Americans were winning.

Correspondence had been coming in large piles from Lord Whatham, and Father spent long days at his desk, muttering to himself. Words like *capital* and *accounting.* Then he'd call Isaac, and together they'd ride into town, inspecting Lord Whatham's interests there. In the evening, men knocked on the door, demanding audience with Father, disputing raised rents and increased prices.

"Father? Do you hear me? I will, I must, determine my own path."

He did not look up but dipped his quill in the ink bottle. "Since the rebels have gained more victories, I fear for your safety. Who knows what the rabble will do with an ounce of confidence. No, you must be away."

"Yet you have no qualms about sending me out upon a dangerous, winter sea? Might I add, where Continental ships sail."

"They will not fire upon a passenger packet." Father stood, settled papers in a leather case, and made his way from the library.

She chased after him. "How do you know? Did they write? Send you a promise?"

"Esther, listen to me." At the door, Father held up the case he carried. "Deliver this to Mr. Wallace Hobart the moment you're settled at Grosvenor. He's a barrister working for Lord Whatham. I've sent word of your journey to his office, and he'll be expecting you."

"Wallace Hobart? Lord Berksham's son?"

Father handed the case to Isaac, who carried it out the carriage. "Yes, poor lad, the youngest of three boys. No title or land for him to inherit. Perhaps some money. He's a clever one, I hear. Earned brilliant marks at Cambridge. Has a keen eye for finances. Lord Whatham hired him as his barrister, to oversee —"

"His accounts and investments?"

Father's cheeks paled. "Indeed." He placed his hands on her shoulders. "I will miss you, my dear, darling daughter, but I am doing what is best for you. I know I am in the right."

"I fear I must disagree with you, Father. I believe I know what is *right* for me."

In a few moments she was to ride to Charles Town with Isaac and Sassy, board a private packet, *Glorious,* and sail to London.

"I am older and wiser."

"What if I refuse to board the ship?" she said. "What if I return to Ninety Six and lodge with one of my friends?"

"Esther, I do not have the fortitude to go round with you. Please say your good-byes and climb into the carriage. Do you have all of your possessions?"

"All of my possessions?" She studied her father. The morning light falling through the open door cast a ghostly light on his sallow complexion. "Why would I need them? I've only packed enough for a few months with Mother."

"Esther, I asked you to take all of your things." Father sat in a nearby chair and appeared to fade before her eyes. "Sassy," he called with a great effort of breath, "did you not see to her packing?"

Sassy came down the hall, tugging on her gloves. "Yes, sir, Sir Michael. I packed most everything. I'll have to ship some of the gowns."

"Everything? Father?" Esther knelt beside him, cupping her hand on his arm. "I am returning to Slathersby Hill, am I not? When the war is over? Hamilton will wonder —"

"Hamilton Lightfoot is a cripple who cannot walk!" Father found his voice with enough energy to boom at her like a war cannon. "He is not for you, Esther. Please, you must come to your senses. You are not a schoolgirl running the fields with your playmate. You have obligations and a right, a right I tell you, to marry well. To be established in society. Besides, you heard Mary Lightfoot. Hamilton will not hold you to any commitments or declarations. Nor will he honor any of his." Father shoved up from the chair, escorting Esther to the veranda. "Now hurry. Climb into the carriage. You have no time to delay."

But she could not take the first step toward this new venture. She shivered, locking her hands together at her waist. Mother had once abandoned her, and now Father was leaving her as well. Sending her away. His heart felt so distant from her, a sensation she'd never experienced with him.

He held her gently and kissed her forehead. "Give my love to your mother. I'll see you soon."

As Father started back to the library, Esther turned to Sassy. "What has he said to you?" She held herself in reserve, fearing she'd simply fly apart. "Am I never returning?"

"My dear girl, I'm not sure there will be a Slathersby Hill in the future." Sassy shuffled out the door, two large cases in hand, calling to her husband. "Come, take these, my dear."

Esther charged through the foyer and burst through the library's closed door. "Father, you must tell me. What is going on?"

"You are traveling home, to be with your mother, to be safe."

"Father! Tell me!" She slammed her fist down on his desk. "I will not leave until you —"

"Esther!" He stood, toppling his chair, his ire flaring. "Will you leave me with some dignity? Can I live out my failings without you demanding an intimate account?"

"Failings? What failings?"

"If only the world were as simple as you see it." His eyes brimmed, and she pressed her cheek agent his chest.

"What is it? Tell me."

His hand settled tenderly on her back. "Keep your innocence, my dear. Guard the kindness and tenderness of your heart. Let not fear nor greed or selfish ambition take hold."

Warm tears slipped down her cheeks. "How can I leave you now? You are my father, my dearest friend. You need me. Whatever you face, we shall face it together."

"I need you to go. To carry that case to Wallace Hobart." Father held her at arm's length now, his pale cheeks flushed and his breathing labored. "Please do as I bid, Esther, and do not let the case from your sight."

She rested her forehead on his broad chest, her heart breaking, her thoughts wild, searching for a solution. "Send Isaac with the case —"

"Esther! I am sending *you.*" He touched her chin and raised her face. "You know full well I cannot send Isaac alone. Would you risk his life to make yours more at ease? To win this argument?"

"Then when am I coming home?"

"I do not know."

"Will Slathersby Hill remain? Sassy said —"

"Mercy, I'm worn to the bone." Father

squeezed her hand. "Can you not just do as I bid? That will greatly ease my burden."

Well, then, there was nothing more to say. Her pleading was of no consequence. "I will do as you bid, Father. I love you."

"And I you, Esther. And I you."

"Esther?"

She whirled at the sound of a masculine voice. A man stood at the library door. The same one she had encountered in Hamilton's room at the surgeon's. "It's time to leave. Come, follow me."

Startled, she peered at Father. Did he know this man? This intruder? But her father remained undisturbed, staring toward the window, his hand slowly slipping from Esther's.

She turned back to the mystery guest. "Who are you and what do you want?"

"For you to follow me."

His voice, his countenance, his presence purchased her deepest fears, and she knew at once he must be obeyed. Gone were the cold emotions from the war, the house, and Father. She embraced a radiating peace.

"To where, my Lord?"

But he did not answer. He merely turned and walked away. This was going to be a journey of faith.

Father said his final good-bye at the

library door. At the carriage, Esther bid Sassy a tearful good-bye, then drew Kitch into a sisterly hug. "You are the closest thing to a sibling I've ever had. Take care and stick to your learning."

He squeezed her tight. "I'll miss you, Miss Esther. Won't be the same without you."

"Off with you now, Kitch," Sassy said, wiping her cheeks. "Let Miss Esther and your pa go. They must meet the second coachman along the way."

But Esther had a detour in mind, and as Isaac aided her into the carriage, she whispered, "Quill Farm, please. I must say good-bye."

The carriage swayed from side-to-side, hitting every rut in the road as Esther imagined what she might say to Hamilton.

She'd not seen him since the day at the surgeon's. Mrs. Lightfoot had kept him away, healing, for nearly six weeks. They'd only just returned to Ninety Six.

Hamilton had not written to her, and Esther battled with the truth. He meant to put her off. He'd withdrawn his love. The war had changed him.

"Whoa." Isaac drew the horses to a halt at the front of the Lightfoots' home.

"I'll only be a moment," she said, squeezing his hand as she exited the carriage.

Her three short raps on the door were answered immediately by Mrs. Lightfoot.

"Esther."

"Good morning. I'm sorry to disturb you, but I've come to say good-bye."

"Oh?" She did not flinch or move aside to invite Esther in. She appeared weary and worn, her hair uncombed and her apron stained. "Where are you bound?"

"London. Father is sending me home. To tend to some business on his behalf."

"Hamilton is sleeping."

The peace deposited in Esther by the divine visitation began to wane. "Can you tell him I've gone away? I sail from Charles Town on the *Glorious* packet in five days."

The woman regarded her for a tense moment, then stepped aside for her to enter. "Do you care to leave a note?"

"Do you not hear me? I am leaving. For England. No, I do not want to merely leave a note." Esther pressed past the woman into the small sitting room, the highs and lows of the morning tugging her every which way. "Hamilton! Where are you?"

"Esther, hush. He's sleeping. Which he desperately needs to do."

"Upstairs? In his room?" Esther glanced at the stairwell, then darted toward the steps. "Hamilton!"

"Esther! Leave him be!" Aunt Mary ran after her, their footsteps hammering in alternating rhythm.

She knocked on the closed door, then burst inside. Dark and warm, the air was depressed with the scent of human waste in the pot and unwashed flesh.

"Hamilton," she said, trembling, unable to move forward or turn in retreat. "Are you awake?" He did not stir. "I'm leaving. Father is sending me to England. He fears the rebels. Or so he says. But I rather think he's in some trouble with Lord Whatham. I dare say Quill Farm is somehow involved." His shoulders rose gently as he breathed, but he did not turn toward her. "Hamilton!" Esther hammered the floor with her heel. "Do you not hear me? I am leaving. Going away. Who knows when I will return?"

She waited. *Please answer me.*

"You best go, Esther." Mrs. Lightfoot touched her arm.

"Will you not speak to me? After all we've meant to one another? You claim to no longer love me, but I do not believe you. Hamilton?"

One second. Two. Then three.

"You heard my aunt. Go."

423

"I will go only if you turn over and face me."

"Esther! I said go!"

She whirled out of the room and tripped down the stairs, bursting from the house into the clean, morning air. Isaac stood ready at the carriage door.

How could he treat her so? Is that all her friendship, her love, meant to him?

"Esther, wait, please." Mrs. Lightfoot ran after her. In the sharp, morning light, her weariness was evident. Her tired eyes, unkempt hair, faded dress, stained apron. "Forgive him, he is not himself." She pressed a tightly folded letter into Esther's hand. "God bless you, my dear. Truly. God bless you."

When the carriage pulled away, Esther slid from the seat to the carriage floor, weeping.

Hamilton Lightfoot did not love her. He'd tried to tell her, but she refused to believe. Now she had no cause to doubt.

Tousled by the rough road, she mourned her fading childhood, the present she could not control and the future she could not see.

Father willed her to leave Slathersby Hill. Hamilton willed her to leave him. And the Man she'd encountered in the library — Jesus, to be sure — asked more of her than any woman could bear.

To leave herself — her dreams, hopes, and desires — for Him.

Love required her complete surrender. But in turn — oh, pray to heaven, in return — love would bring her everything.

# 25

## HAMILTON

He heard the clap of the front door and the hammer of horses' hooves, the sound of a carriage disappearing down the road.

Tears stained his pillowcase. He'd barely had the strength not to turn over and beg her to stay.

But he could not, would not, ruin her life. Aunt Mary was right. He could offer her nothing. If her father was sending her away, 'twas for the best. She belonged in England with her peers.

His door creaked open.

"Hamilton?"

"Leave me be."

"Are you sure this is how you want to part? She's not far down the road. I can help you hitch Tilly —"

"I am sure." He sat up, shoving the blanket away. His leg had healed enough to practice walking with a peg, but he hated the sound of the stick against the floor. And in the yard, the blasted thing stuck in the dirt. Often after the smallest exercise, his leg ached and burned, the skin blistered and bled.

As if the war had not robbed him of his last shred of dignity, now he was a man who must be a burden.

"She came here to see you, to tell you how she feels. Do you realize what it cost her to stand here and —"

"Do you not realize what it has cost *me*? I love her." He snatched his crutch from against the wall. "I let my foolishness drive me to war, and now I have lost her."

"Lost? She was just standing here. Her perfume lingers. Go after her. Do not let foolishness, or your pride, keep you from the one you love."

"Why do you care? I'd rather thought you prefer me here with you. You said as much, did you not? 'It's best Esther is with her father. You and I will make a go of it, nephew.' Were those not your claims?" He shoved aside the curtains, allowing in the light, and raised the sash, expelling the dank presence of the room.

"Yes, those were my claims. I confess, I was scared when you were wounded. When she came to the surgeon's to see you, I feared for us all. But now I cannot help but think —"

"Aunt." He moaned, perching on the edge of his bed, one eye toward the peg. "Please, I am in no mood for hyped optimism."

"Nevertheless, you will hear me out. You went to war, Hamilton, and lost your leg. A fact we cannot change. But you still have your mind, do you not? Your wits, your heart, and heaven above, your freedom. Your life." She knelt next to his bed. "I cannot imagine your thoughts or feelings, or how it feels to have been a man so capable of doing whatever he wanted when he wanted without aid or even much thought. But you gave yourself to the cause and now —"

"My bitterness, my desire for revenge, has left me maimed. As I deserve!"

"So what are you to do? Lie around the rest of your days? Wallow in pity? To what end, Hamilton? What of your faith, your hope —"

Her voice rose with cheer and confidence — which he found annoying.

"In a Lord who took my pa and ma, little Betsy, Uncle Laurence, and my leg? Does He love me or consider me a toy to be trifled with, dangled over the tormenting fires of hell?"

"Have you no sense? Have *I* no sense? Listening to your uncle all those years, preaching of a good God, a God of love."

"Preach not to me, Aunt, but to yourself."

" 'Tis what they say of you in town. That you've left yourself. You'll never recover because of your bitterness."

"Who is saying such about me? Who?" He slapped the crutch against the floor. "I most certainly will recover, but I am also a realist. I know when I'm defeated. But I will return to the fields. I'll hunt, trap, perhaps start a venture in town. With any luck, I'll wrangle the deed to Quill away from Sir Michael. Otherwise, we'll buy a new and better place."

Aunt Mary stood, arms folded. "Well then, there's the door. What's keeping you from even the slightest chore?"

"Because!" He threw the crutch against the wall. "Without her, none of it has meaning. Because I am ashamed. I am weak. I have a stick under my thigh instead of flesh and bone. She does not want a man who must lean on her but a man on whom she can lean."

"You underestimate her. I underestimated her as well. Love works both ways, my boy. Did not your uncle lean on me in his final years?"

"He was an old man. I am young. Besides, what can I offer Esther when any number of men in the upcountry as well as the low, even as far away as London, would long to court her? Men with means, with substance, if not wealth? Men with two legs, with industries, titles, and money."

"She does not love *other* men. She loves you, Hamilton. There is only one question you must ask yourself. Do you love her? Do you want her?"

"With every fiber of my being."

"Then go after her." Aunt Marry pointed toward the door. "Tell her. Don't let her final thoughts of you be your silence. And if she rejects you, at least you will have given your love a chance."

He sat in the desk chair, rubbing the ache in his half leg. "I wonder if we are just not meant to be. Even my letter to her on the eve of battle was lost. When Ralphie came to visit, I inquired of my letter to Esther and he confirmed he had not delivered it to her. God must surely be punishing me."

He stared out the window, yearning to stand and run, to taste the wind and see the sun rise. Then he caught his reflection in the shaving mirror nailed to the opposite wall.

He looked like a mountain man with his

long beard and unkempt hair. Color had yet to return to his complexion, save for the pink scar running down his cheek and into his beard. His eyes sank into his gaunt expression. He was a sight to behold.

"If God is punishing you, then He must also punish me." With a sigh, Aunt Mary sat on the edge of the bed.

"Surely not. You are good and kind. What could you have possibly done to deserve punishment?"

"Plenty. One of which I'm most ashamed. But I was afraid . . . more afraid than I can ever remember."

He regarded her, her frame so slight, her posture so frail, her dark hair laced with gray, frayed with grief. "What do you mean?"

"Esther left you a letter when she visited the surgeon's."

When he didn't respond, Aunt Mary continued. "I burned it." Her shoulders shivered with her confession. "I feared you leaving me. Feared being alone. Feared she'd eventually tire of you, leave, and break your heart."

"I would never leave you. Esther would embrace you as her own. As for her leaving me, well, we cannot say, can we? We'll never know."

431

"Sir Michael was so dead set against your uncle. Against you. I have such regret for signing his document without discussing it with you. What a fool I am."

"You must forgive yourself, Aunt."

"He came to Dr. Nelson's and manipulated Esther away. And I aided him. He said with no hesitation he did not wish her married to you. Oh, Hamilton, I was awash with terror. What if she defied him, married you, then tired of caring for a cripple? Tired of life on the farm. Tired of chasing after the children, should there be any, on her own?"

"So you and Sir Michael chose for us."

"The decision seemed prudent, even wise at the time. But these past months have given me time to think." She smiled softly. "But, Hamilton, I still wonder. What would become of you, when after all you've endured, the love of your life forsook you? Abandoned you? Tell me? Then what, Hamilton? Then what? You can recover from a broken limb, but a broken heart? I feared for you . . . feared."

Her soft words carried a fierceness that reverberated in the small room.

"Yet now you urge me to go after her?"

"Because I am more ashamed of my meddling than my fears. I hear the sound of longing and love in her voice, and I know she is what you need, my boy. Her love will bring you back to life."

"What do you want of me?" He hobbled on one foot for his crutch and stared out the window. "Why do you torment me?"

"Hamilton, leave your stubbornness behind and go after her. Be the man you are meant to be whether you feel it or not. Rise up and let your heart, for once, have its way."

## JESSE

He'd started an e-mail an hour ago, deliberating over what he was about to write. But the time for debate was over. He knew what he needed to do. Next to his computer in the Daschles' guesthouse, his phone pinged. It was Becky, Jeremiah's assistant.

She's on her way home. You said to let you know.

Thanks.

Jesse set down his phone.

Since his dramatic departure from *Bound by Love,* he was lost. Adrift. It was as if this film became a bookend to Loxley's death, capturing every day in between. From death

433

to death.

He was restless. Anxious. Confused. Burdened by walking out on people who believed in him. Trusted him. Jeremiah assured him there was no ill will on his part. He'd have walked out on the project himself if he could have.

But the assurance of a great director couldn't change the reality — Jesse had killed his career.

His agent was livid. "You walked out on Greg Zarzour?"

"He wanted me to make crazy changes to the script. I couldn't do it, I tell you. I couldn't."

"Jess, you're the new kid in town. You make the changes until you've earned the right not to. Even then, you don't walk out. Think of your career! Think of mine. Everyone is talking about this. I can't contain it. We may need to rethink our arrangement."

Since walking off the South Carolina set, Jesse's love for show business had evaporated. His reasons for being in LA no longer made sense. Because Loxley died? How long would her death haunt him?

Closing his laptop, Jesse picked up his phone and gazed out the window toward the pool.

He'd miss this view. And Chloe. During

filming he'd started to dismantle the borders of his heart. Maybe it was time to let someone in. Someone like her.

When he left, everything clear became cloudy. Except for one thing.

"Jesse?" A soft knock sounded against the door. "Raymond Daschle here. You got a minute?"

Jesse invited him in, but the mega director motioned for Jesse to follow.

"Walk with me. I'm expecting a call from Hong Kong on the landline."

They talked college basketball through the gourmet kitchen, past the marble and crystal foyer, and into Raymond's hardwood and leather office. He motioned for Jesse to take a seat, then paused at the wet bar. "Care for a drink? Soda, water?"

"Diet Coke?" He surveyed the space. One Jesse wouldn't mind having himself one day. It spoke of success and comfort. As if great ideas could be born here.

Opposite the windows overlooking the valley was a stone-and-beam fireplace with a family crest of some kind over the mantel.

"Is that your family's?" Jesse pointed, rising to see the image closer. The design was a white-and-black crest with a golden star, a warrior's helmet, and a shield of crosses.

"Yes, it belonged to my grandfather. But I

cannot tell you more. Isn't it sad how we lose our heritage after one or two generations? But who am I talking to? A man who wrote a movie based on an old family love letter." Raymond handed him a cold bottle and a glass of ice, taking a cold cola can for himself. "So you walked off." He perched on the corner of his desk.

"I did . . . yep. I keep wondering if this is a bad dream and I'll wake up any minute." Jesse poured the caramel-colored drink over the ice in the glass, the fizzle filling his temporary silence. "How much damage have I done to my career?"

Raymond shrugged. "Can't say. Depends on Zarzour."

Jesse gulped the cool drink, the carbonation scratching his dry throat. "My agent said I shot myself in the head and the foot."

Raymond laughed. "Agents . . . love to exaggerate. But don't give up. When you finish your next script, let me have a look. You've got a friend in me, Jesse. And in Jeremiah."

Jesse regarded him for a moment. "Why are you so nice to me? You don't owe me anything."

"I pride myself on recognizing talent when I see it. But when a man walks out on a project because he refused to kill off my daughter, I fall a little bit in love." Raymond chuckled, raising his Coke can.

"She begged me to make the changes. Said it didn't matter to her but —"

"It did, and you recognized it." Raymond stared absently toward the window and the scene of LA nestled in the valley. "You saw more in her than I did. Her own father, not sticking up for her when she was a kid because I didn't think it mattered. She was cute, freckly, round. Not fat, round. She wanted to be in acting so badly we let her, but I didn't mind the rejections because I thought I was keeping her from being caught up in the business, the hype. Then I cast her as a kid with cancer and . . ." He cleared his throat. "If I had known . . ."

"How could you?"

"I have few regrets, but that is one of them. And that mess with Haden. I never liked him, but she was twenty-six, a grown woman . . . I didn't think I should interfere."

"I regret walking off the set. I feel like I let her down some. I should've made the changes." He sipped his drink, laughing low. "On my way home I came up with a great idea for the end. It would've saved time and money *and* allowed Esther-slash-Chloe to live. And I think Jeremiah and Greg would've gone for it."

"What was this keen idea?"

"Simple. After the battle scene, fade away, leaving the viewer to wonder, *Did she live?* Then show Hamilton and Esther on the farm X number of years later with their children. Like an epilogue. There is some fun B-roll of Chloe running out of the barn, declaring a rooster is trying to kill her."

Raymond arched his brow. "You're right, that is a good idea. And would've worked."

"Yeah, but I walked out. Don't have a right to say anything now. Besides, it's too late. Greg Zarzour hit me like a truck. Didn't give me time to think. He wanted Esther's dying to be an emotional manipulator. Grab the heart of the viewer. No matter it had nothing to do with the rest of the story." Jesse poured more soda into the glass of ice. "I hated what he did to my script, but more for what he did to Esther and Chloe. Jeremiah promised her, I promised her, that she'd live in this role. Esther's death was never, ever on the table."

"Let me tell you something about my Chloe. She's tough. A rebounder. Taken her share of disappointments and . . ." He shook his head, releasing a small laugh accented with irony. "Become a better woman. Most actresses would've quit. But not my girl. She's genuine. She believes in her craft as a way to communicate, tell stories, and change lives. She expects no advantage because we're her parents. She earns her jobs and her accolades. She has an amazing eye for details and photography. She'll be a better director than me one day. After Haden, she found faith, which made her all the more . . . beautiful. Strong." Raymond moved to the chair adjacent Jesse. "But you know what you did more than anyone in this town? Stood up for my girl — and I'm grateful."

Jesse felt Raymond's confession, the swirl of an imperfect father wanting to do what's right by his daughter.

"She deserved it."

"Are you in love with her?"

Jesse shot a glance at Raymond. "W-what?" Hackles rose on the back of his neck.

"Are you in love with her?"

"Who?" Did he seriously mean Chloe?

"My daughter?"

"W-we're friends."

"And?"

"There's no *and.* She's incredible. Beautiful, funny, and sort of broken and put together at the same time, but we're not lovers, Raymond."

"But you risked your career for her anyway?"

Jesse had no pithy answer or profound reply. Only truth. "I had a girlfriend. In college. She wanted something I couldn't give, but I toyed with her, mocked her, didn't understand the magnitude of my foolishness and stupidity. She went for a walk on a Florida beach alone and never returned. She drowned. Most likely a riptide."

"You feel responsible."

"Aren't I?"

"*Bound by Love* was as much about you as your ancestor."

"I didn't think so until Chloe pointed it out." The intimate conversation knocked against his defenses and disturbed his raw, bruised self. "But, yeah, I wanted to give her life. Something I stole from her."

"Chloe found faith. Hope." Raymond sat back, his arms resting on the chair, looking more like a therapist than a movie director. "Maybe that's the path for you. Maybe that's why you love her."

Jesse tossed back the last of his soda and placed his empty glass on a stone coaster, remembering his open e-mail, the decision he was about to make. "Thanks for the vote of confidence, Raymond. But I need . . . I'm thinking of . . . I don't know, change. A completely different path for me."

"And Chloe's not on it?"

"No, she's not. Frankly, I don't think she'd want to be."

As he exited, the echo of his words called him a liar. He desperately wanted her on his path, in his life. And for all his MIT smarts, he couldn't figure out how to completely let her in.

# 26

## CHLOE

She glanced toward the guesthouse for the hundredth time that afternoon. He must not be home. In the kitchen with Mom and Glenda, she helped prep Saturday's brunch — it was on the lanai today — as guests collected outside where a Hawaiian-shirt-wearing bartender served sparkling juices.

Home for three days, she'd hoped to see him, but the guesthouse appeared vacant. All too quiet. She'd braved a text or two, but Jesse never responded.

"So good to have you home." Mom gave her a squeeze as she passed by. "It's not the same around here without you."

"You have Kate."

"But I don't have you. Glenda, make sure the kosher food is clearly marked for our Jewish guests this time. I think Lev Kirschbaum ate bacon last week."

Chloe grinned. Mom was such a beauty. In every way. "When's your next movie, Mom?"

"Oh, I don't know. Hollywood is getting tired of me. I'm fifty-seven going on a hundred. I refuse to have plastic surgery and —"

"You're too good not to cast." Dad passed through, kissing her cheek.

"— I refuse to play one of those horny old cougars who makes a fool of herself by falling for some hot thirty-something who only has one thing on his mind. What in the world?"

Mom, for all of her experience and spicy roles, valued dignity and modesty. She was practical and levelheaded.

Chloe glanced toward the guesthouse once again. Maybe Smitty knew where Jesse had gone. She snagged her phone from the kitchen counter and started a text.

"I saw Laura Gonda the other day," Mom said as she came in from the lanai, picking up another breakfast platter. "Glenda, this is gluten-free, right?"

"If it's on the blue plate, yes."

"What did Laura say?" Chloe hit send on her text to Smitty.

"That she missed Jeremiah so much she was packing up all the kids and heading to

New Zealand." Mom started for the door and turned back. "Oh, Chloe, she saw a rough cut of your death scene. Said it was spectacular. Had her weeping." With that, Mom exited the kitchen onto the lanai. "Gluten-free, everyone."

Chloe was still deciphering what happened that day. How her rebel yell, "Death, you cannot have me," broke a chain she'd only recently identified. She wasn't cursed. She was free.

Mom swept inside again, her cheeks rosy, her hair swept up into a bright turban. "Hey, Mom, how come you and Dad never got married?"

Mom stopped short. "What?"

"You and Dad. Never married. Why?"

Mom slipped on oven mitts and bent before the open stove, releasing the intoxicating aroma of brisket. "Careers, kids. Just didn't seem necessary after a while." She set the baking pan on the counter, then removed the brisket onto the carving board. "I know you're all about true love and commitment, darling, but it doesn't have to look the same to everyone."

"Didn't you want a ceremony? A celebration? To look into each other's eyes and declare before the world, 'You are my forever love'?"

Mom plugged in the electric carving knife with a backward glance at Chloe. "Isn't that what we're doing?"

"I guess, but technically, you know, either of you could walk tomorrow. You've made no vow."

"Walk? Babe," Dad said, reaching for a piece of meat, "I'd drive the Tesla."

"Raymond." Mom slapped at his hand. "He cannot walk, Chloe. Not easily. We've been together too long and have too much invested."

"So that's what your love is worth? A passage of time and the acquisition of things?"

"Chloe." Mom fired up the carver and raised her voice over the low motor. "What's this about? Your happy-ending theory? What are you afraid of? It will never happen for you?"

Chloe glanced through the open French doors toward the guesthouse. Yes! A thousand times yes! She feared it would never happen for her. *Then do something about it. Stop waiting.*

"I'm going to see if Jesse wants to come."

"Chloe." Dad met her at the door. "He's not there."

"He's not? W-where is he?"

"I'm not sure." He brushed aside her bangs, like he did when she was little. "But his things are gone. He left a thank-you note saying it was time to move on."

Chloe backed up to the nearest kitchen stool and sat. "He was so kind, Dad. Brave. You should've seen him, sticking up for his script, the movie. For me."

"Do you love him?"

"I don't know."

"I think he's one you could trust, Chloe."

"Really? Dad, he just left without telling me good-bye. He doesn't return my texts." More guests arrived and lively conversations buzzed all around them. "Apparently he doesn't want me." She smiled her bravest smile. "But you know what, I'm okay. I am learning to trust God for these things."

Dad sat next to her, touching his shoulder to hers. "I'm sorry I didn't steer your career better. Step up and guide you."

"It's okay, Dad. I think I've been on the right path all along. It just looked like a wilderness when really it was an oasis."

His eyes glistened as he cleared his throat. "I'm proud of you, sweetie."

Chloe kissed his cheek, then stole a strawberry from the bowl Glenda was carrying out to the lanai. "You should propose to Mom."

"Raymond, Monte Wilson is here." Mom beckoned him from the door.

"What if she says no?" Dad teased, sliding from the stool. "Chloe, if you have any feelings for Jesse, any inkling he could be what you've always wanted, call him."

"I told you, he doesn't answer."

"Then, dear girl, be creative. Write him a letter." Dad's expression was so kind. "Isn't that what started all of this?"

"Write him a letter. I don't even know where he is."

Her phone pinged. It was Smitty.

*He went to Boston.*

"Chloe," Mom said, brushing by again as she stared at the screen. "Claude Durand is here. He wants to see you."

"Me?" Boston? Jesse went home?

"Raymond, Chloe." Claude burst into the kitchen with his arms wide, his voice booming. The French director looped his arm through Chloe's. "How do you feel about traveling into the future? I just got the green light on a space navy film. I want you as the lead. Faith Freeman. I'm launching a superheroine series. And you will be my star."

## HAMILTON

The cart hit every rut in the road. His severed leg throbbed, each jolt inspiring a lightning bolt of pain.

At one point, his body went numb. Colored spots collided before his eyes. He was hot, then cold, wavering on his perch, Tilly's reins loose in his hands. Yet he urged her on, the cart a swift and light load.

On the eastern horizon, black clouds promised another storm, obscuring the midmorning sun and the peaceful blue of a spring sky. A low, distant thunder rumbled.

As he rounded the next bend, he scanned the road for Sir Michael's sleek gold-and-black carriage.

With no sight of it, his thoughts twisted with doubts and questions. What would he say when he came upon her? What words, what offering could he make to lure her from her father's security, comfort, and will?

He was grotesque, with a craggy, sawed-off leg, scars on his face and arms. Thin and pale, unshaven, unwashed.

Yet he hoped in one thing. His heart. Surely it was his greatest treasure, and Esther's for the taking. This was no hour to retreat from his own desires and wants. This battle for Esther was for keeps.

If she'd say yes to him, he would give himself completely to her, without reservation, striving to overcome anger, regret, bitterness, and to cherish her with every part of his being.

"Come on, Tilly! Ya!" He slapped the reins, and the mare quickened her pace. He must seize Esther before she arrived in Charles Town. Once there, she'd be lost in the bowels of Tory commerce.

The cart jostled and bounced as the road rose and fell. The wind whistled, pushing northwest against his journey.

But around the next bend, his hopes quickened. At last! He spotted the gloss of the black-and-gold carriage.

"Good girl, Tilly. Good girl."

The mare, as if sensing her master's pleasure, broke into a run, her mane flapping, her head bobbing, every muscle in synchronism.

Sitting tall, filled with tension and anxiety, aware of every pain, Hamilton prepared to overtake them.

*Esther, I've come for you . . .*

*Esther, I've little to offer you, but here is my whole heart and my love.*

*Esther, if you have any affection for me . . .*

*My love, come with me. See what life we can build together.*

*My letter . . . I wrote you a letter. It simply said, "I love you."*

Closer, closer the cart jostled, careening into and out of a rut. One, then another and another. Then Tilly stumbled, and the

449

cart listed to starboard.

"Steady up, girl."

The cart straightened as another bolt of lightning cracked. Tilly balked, and her right front hoof landed in a hole, sinking nearly up to her knee. The mare cried out and tossed her head, trying to scramble free.

"Easy, girl, whoaaaa."

But she was frightened, jerking to the right, then left, her foot still trapped. With a brilliant flash, white lightning struck the ground and Tilly freed her foot, rearing with a shriek, pawing the air, tipping Hamilton's little two-wheeled cart up, up, up.

"Tilly!" Hamilton leaned forward, holding on to the reins. "Yaw!"

The mare landed on the run, fleeing her fears, hitting every rut, every lump of grass with breakneck speed. Lightning whipped the devilish clouds into a melee of thunder.

"Easy, girl . . . easy."

But she had a mind of her own, racing against the noise. Hamilton gave her the lead. She'd tire in a moment, and then he'd settle her down.

But the cracking and booming of heaven urged her on.

The road dipped and Hamilton nearly bounced from his seat, bracing his quivering right leg against the front of the cart. "Tilly!"

The road disappeared as it curved down a hill, and Tilly took the bend at full speed, sailing over a section of washed-out earth, catapulting Hamilton and the cart.

Unable to hold on, Hamilton hit the ground with a thump, his breath forced from his lungs. He gasped as he rolled down the hill, reaching for anything to stop his trajectory. A blade of grass, a low limb. His wounded leg smashed against a jagged tree stump and he cried out.

At the bottom of the hill, he landed in a watery ditch. Every inch of his body pulsed and ached.

"Tilly!" The skittish mare was his only hope.

With another smack of the clouds, the rain, cold and thick, descended. Hamilton surrendered to his fate. "Esther, I tried. I tried."

In that moment, a warm glow fell across his face. Hamilton squinted to see a man leaning over him. A familiar stranger.

He stretched out his hand to Hamilton. "Come, follow me."

# 27

## ESTHER

*Manhattan, New York*
*June 1790*

The pristine library bore the fragrant odor of new lumber and paint. The windows invited in the morning without a single hindering smudge. And as of last evening, her new furniture had arrived.

With a sigh, Esther moved to the open window by the quiet fireplace, a sweet breeze tangling with the draperies. She glanced over the lawn.

"Alice," she called to the children's nanny. "It's a beautiful day. Take the children outside, let them run and play. Summer is no time to be cooped up inside."

Within a few minutes, the young woman with narrow features, her reddish hair tucked under a cap, entered with the children.

"Mama!" Michael, four, the future Viscount of Berksham, and Lady Catherine, three, named for Wallace's mother, ran across the room and threw themselves against her legs.

"My darlings." Esther bent to kiss them, snuggling her nose against their sweet scent and soft skin. "I could eat you, you're so sweet."

They giggled and Catherine teased, "Go on, Mama. I taste like sugar."

"I could eat *you*, Mama." Michael pretended to bite her nose, and she squeezed him to herself. What joy! She never imagined two little angels would enter her life and make her new.

But why must she be surprised? She'd surrendered. She'd followed her Lord.

"All right, children, come along." Alice took each child by the hand, leading them from the library. "Let's see who can run the fastest to the barn."

"I can." Michael, without any hesitation.

"No, me." Catherine, who insisted she keep up with her brother.

Upon the children's exit, the butler entered the library. "Your newspapers, ma'am."

"Thank you, Wiley." Esther reached for her daily reading. From London. New York. Boston. And Charleston, the new name for Charles Town. "What do you think of the finished library?"

The man glanced around. A scar ran across his cheek, a product of the war. "Peaceful," he said. "Exquisite. Master Wallace spared no expense."

Esther grinned. "True. So now he *must* make our venture here a success."

"Of that I have no doubt."

Their venture was an American farm. On the western side of Manhattan. Along the Hudson. A boyhood dream her husband seemed determined to fulfill.

Settling into her chair by the hearth, Esther embraced contentment. She was home. Happy. Satisfied. Wanting for nothing.

Yet there was on occasion, a lingering . . . a wondering.

She drew herself from those distant thoughts and turned to her reading. There was no need for such musings. Her days in South Carolina were a lifetime ago.

She glanced up when the children's laughter drifted through the open window. They were happy, thus she was happy.

Back to her newspapers, a printed flyer slipped from the stack to the floor. Esther bent to retrieve it. An advertisement. For a religious meeting in midtown.

Wallace entered, a large frame in hand, along with one of the farm workers, Bristol. "Good morning, my dear. I see you have the children out exercising. I dare say they'll run Alice ragged." He bent to kiss her lips. Still with passion after all these years.

"She's young, she can keep up. What have you there?"

"The family crest. Father insisted on sending it over. Especially now that the library is finished. He's terrified the children will become too American and forget their English heritage." He turned the frame around for her to see, his expression seeking her approval.

"Perfect." She nodded, the white-and-black crest with the golden star, a warrior's helmet, and a shield of crosses no longer just Wallace's family crest, but hers also.

The House of Hobart. Warriors. Lovers. Followers of Christ.

"And how could the children forget their heritage? Your father will not let them. Not as long as he breathes," she said, laughing, squeezing Wallace's hand. "Nor I. The Hobarts are a distinguished family one cannot easily dismiss. Our children will know from where we hail."

"Have I told you today how I adore you?" Wallace kissed her cheek, then turned to the room. "Where shall we hang this? Bristol, do as my wife bids." He handed the crest to the devoted worker. "I built this place, she runs it. Darling, I wonder if you only married me for my money."

"As you only married me for my beauty."

Bristol stifled a laugh.

"Blast, you've found me out." Wallace retreated to his desk, sitting with a flip of his coat tail and gazing about the grand room with no fewer than four thousand books. He looked every bit the king admiring his castle.

"Where shall I hang this, ma'am?"

"Over the fireplace." Esther pointed to the vacant spot over the mantel.

Wallace's buoyant laugh burst out. "Michael is trying to be Catherine's pony."

Esther joined him at the window. "Now will you concede to my wish? Buy the children a pony, Wallace. Look at all the land." She pressed her cheek to his arm. She loved him. More than she ever imagined possible.

He encircled her in his arms. "I've already sent word to a breeder."

She raised her gaze to his. "I've at last won you to my side."

He kissed her the same way he did the day they married. Full-lipped and passionate, his love free and evident. "Don't you know?" He brushed his finger along her jaw. "I cannot resist you."

"Nor I you." She returned his kiss, her desire for him awakening. Their love was pure, sincere, kind and reciprocal, generous and open.

Marriage. Such a sacred union. She understood now the reveries of the poets. Of the Song of Solomon. She no longer blushed at the passionate verses but found inspiration to love her husband with her whole heart. Not just Wallace, but her Lord.

With him, she was at peace, happy, living in a cocoon made only for each other. With each kiss, each passionate night abed, with each "I love you," each "My apologies," and every incidental touch and absentminded caress, her love grew.

"So you see," Wallace said, returning to his desk, his fingers running down her hand and lingering. "You have bewitching powers to which I must surrender. Treat me with kindness."

Something in his tone aroused the echo of a past argument.

"Wallace," Esther said low, for him only. Across the room Bristol hammered a nail into the smooth panel over the fireplace. "You know I would never hurt you. I am most devoted to you."

His focus was fixed on his almanac and farming books. "I know, love, and I do not doubt you." He peered up at her. "But there are times when I remember you loved another."

She crouched next to him.

"It was a long time ago. I've not seen or heard from Hamilton Lightfoot in years."

He gently touched her bowed head. "But my human weakness reminds me I am not your first love."

"But you are my last love. My one and only love."

Tall and fit, Wallace was as handsome as the day she married him in 1784. The third son of an earl, he was set to inherit wealth but not land or title. Trained as a barrister, employed by Lord Whatham, he had visions of America, the land of hope, a place to leave land and legacy to his children.

He caressed her, bending to kiss her. "I love you, Esther."

"And I you. Forever, my love."

"How's that, Mr. Hobart?" Bristol stood aside for his handiwork to be inspected.

Taking Esther by the hand, Wallace faced the fireplace and nodded his approval. "Very good. Thank you."

When Bristol had gone, Wallace returned to his work and Esther her newspapers.

"Did I tell you I met a man in town?" he said after a moment. "A rather enterprising young man. Astor's the name. He's invited me to dine with him, talk business."

"Astor? From where do they hail?" Esther returned to the flyer. A church meeting. Her spirit stirred with the urge to attend.

"Germans by way of England and Baltimore. They seem rather settled in Manhattan now. Very industrious and Americanized."

And so the afternoon went. Moments of silence peppered with nuanced conversation.

"Do the Astors have children?"

"I'll inquire."

"No change in fashion this year. Last year's gowns will do."

"The almanac predicts a good year for farming."

"Did I tell you what Catherine said over breakfast?"

"The land agent wants to plant more apple trees. The yield from this year was hearty."

"Mother wrote. She's planning on a visit next spring."

"Really? Tell her to write to my parents. Perhaps they could sail together."

Esther rose up from her newspapers. Speaking of Mother put her in mind of Father. He never returned to London, having breathed his last at Slathersby Hill six months after Esther's departure. Another heart episode. But instead of being among his friends and family, he was alone, asleep in bed.

She knew, by intuition or the Spirit, she'd not see him again after she departed Charles Town on the *Glorious*. After his death, Esther saw a different side of her mother. The one with regrets and remorse. Who wept for the loss of her husband and confessed she never should have left him alone so long. But she believed she had time. Plenty of time.

In that moment, seeing her frailty, Esther forgave her everything. Mother became her rock and champion, comforting as Esther's affection toward Wallace grew and she mourned her dream of ever marrying Hamilton Lightfoot.

*"Live in the moment, Esther,"* she'd said as Wallace began his pursuit. *"Choose what is in front of you. Choose to love."*

"We've selected a cow and pig to butcher in the fall," Wallace said. "What do you

460

think of mutton? Shall we bring a lamb to slaughter as well?"

Esther turned to him. "What? A lamb?" Her eyes landed on the flyer once more. She turned it over to read the details.

### WAR HERO HAMILTON LIGHTFOOT PRESENTING

### "COME, FOLLOW ME."

### August 7th, 7:00 p.m.
### First Presbyterian Church
### 10 Wall Street

### COME ONE, COME ALL

She fired to her feet, her newspapers toppling to the floor, her blood cold, her limbs aquiver. "Pardon me, darling."

Out of the library, she ran up the stairs to the bedroom suite she shared with Wallace.

Shutting the door, she leaned against it, her thoughts racing. In days past, she had dreamed of spying him across a crowded room, her heart pounding at the sight of him, their reunion like something from a Henry Fielding novel.

But she was mature now. A grown woman of thirty-one. A mother. A wife.

"I love my husband," she whispered, stooping to pull back the carpet, knocking a floorboard loose with her knuckle. Reaching into the hidden space, she felt around for Hamilton's letter, questioning once again why she had carried the thing from London.

She was in love with Wallace.

When her fingers closed about the letter, she returned the board to its place and sat in her chair by the window, where the light flooded the room.

Hamilton. Was she to see him again? As the wife of another man? Memories eased across her mind. The first time they met as children. The summer afternoons of fishing and running wild in the upcountry. Playing a game by the winter fire. The depth of his gaze when he leaned in for his first kiss. Her longing to hear him say, "I love you."

With a glance at the door, she opened the letter.

Hannah's Cowpens

January 16, 1781

My dearest Esther,

My recent actions have not Demonstrated my sincerest affections. I seek to Remedy any confusion now, on this

Eve of Battle. Remember me as Before. When my Deeds, if not my Words, proved my Heart.

I love you. 'Tis no other Truth.

Affectionately Yours,
Hamilton Lightfoot

Raising her watery gaze, she saw Wallace at the door.

"My dear," she said, standing, folding the letter as discretely as possible and tucking it against her palm. "I didn't hear you come in."

"Is that his letter? Hamilton Lightfoot's?" He moved toward her, holding up the flyer.

Esther sank back down to her chair. "How did you know?"

"I tripped over a loose floorboard one afternoon." He set the flyer on the lamp table and slipped his hands into his pockets. "I was set to nail it down until I discovered a secret beneath."

"Why didn't you say anything?"

"I considered it. Lost a few nights of sleep over it. But determined if you wanted to tell me, you would."

"Yet deep down you wondered —"

"If you still loved him? Yes." Wallace perched on the edge of the chair opposite Esther.

"Did you read it?"

He nodded. "Have I offended you?"

She shook her head. "You're my husband. I have no secrets from you. But I would have preferred knowing you found the letter."

"I'd have preferred knowing you kept it."

"And what would you have said? As a young bridegroom?"

"I'm not certain. Perhaps I would have advised you to toss it away."

"I'm not sure I would have done so even if I told you I would." Esther set the letter on the table. Everything was in the open now. "I know I should discard it, but, Wallace, he was a dear friend and I could not bear to part with his final words to me. Though I should. Heaven knows Wiley is probably aware of my hiding place. I saw him once near that corner of the rug. When I entered the room, startling him, he nearly crashed into the candle stand."

"He's loyal to me," Wallace said. "But tell me. Do Hamilton's words, after all these years, stir something in you?"

Esther's tears spilled over. "I do not know."

"Do you love him?"

"I love you."

"Yet this man of your distant past, a war

hero, stands beside me, and I do not know to whom I am being compared."

"Wallace." Esther reached for his hand. "He's a memory. A promise not kept. You are the man I married. I share your bed, your children, your home. You have my heart."

"Then why the abrupt departure from the library? I know it was because you read his name. Why have you kept his letter?"

Esther returned to her chair. "When I debuted in London —"

"Where we first met."

"During those two years I was desperately in love with Hamilton. I wanted him to write me love letters worthy of Lord Byron, yet he wrote about a half dozen letters consisting of farm details and the latest number of kittens produced by the barn cat."

Wallace smiled. "He sounds like my kind of man."

"I chided him. If he loved me, then he must express himself. In the meantime, his uncle and my father fell out, an argument over the acquisition of their farm. Turns out Father mishandled money and told Lord Whatham he'd purchased the land the Lightfoots owned when he had not. This feud, along with the Lightfoots being ardent

Whigs, caused Father to ban them from Slathersby. Hamilton and I met in secret at a willow tree by the creek. Then a troop of dragoons killed his uncle and burned the church."

"And you were shot."

Esther pressed her hand over her scar, the one Wallace often caressed and kissed. "War changed him. After the Battle of King's Mountain, where he almost killed surrendering Loyalists, he pushed me away. Said he didn't love me. But I did not believe him. I determined to remain true."

She detailed the Christmas of 1780 and Hamilton's devastating wound at Cowpens, her journey to see him, and Father's demand she return home.

"Nothing was ever the same after. Father sent me to London to be with Mother and well, you know the rest."

"How did you come by his battlefield letter then?"

"His aunt Mary gave it to me. I'd stopped at Quill Farm to bid Hamilton good-bye. I had bothered him about writing me a love letter. When at last he did, I was on my way to England. I was in such misery, I stored it in my valise without reading it. I was home three months before it came to my attention again. He wrote me a love letter when our love had no hope. Besides, I was tired of fighting for a love it seemed only I wanted. Tired of being in contention with Father, with Hamilton, trying to persuade them both of my love's worthiness. Isn't love supposed to be generous and giving, overcoming?"

"What of the man? The one who bid you, 'Follow Me'?"

"He spoke to me twice. The first time when Father came for me at the surgeon's. And again when Father forced me from Slathersby."

"What was Hamilton's wound?"

"A saber cut, which cost him his left leg."

Wallace sobered. He'd been at Oxford during the war. By the time he was ready to enlist, the revolution had ended. "If he is the man you say, I'm sure he did not want to burden you with his affliction. I would not."

"So love must only be given when there is no conflict or hardship?"

"To a proud man, one without attachment, yes." He held up the flyer. "Shall we go? Hear what he has to say? We could lodge with the Dinsmores. Charles has been inviting us for some time. He fought in the war, did he not? He's been dying to reminisce about South Carolina with you."

Charles Dinsmore had served in the South Carolina militia under Andrew Pickens. He often drew Esther away to swap stories about their childhood home.

"You would take me to see him?"

"Do you not want to go?"

"I do, but not if it causes any stress between us."

"I feel you have something to say to him. I pray it is merely to wish him well, but —"

"Yes, Wallace, only to wish him well." Esther brightened as a weight she'd not known existed lifted. "But may I be clear, Wallace? While I loved Hamilton, yes to distraction, I did not choose you as second. I chose you because the One who beckoned me to follow Him also chose you. For me."

Without a word, Wallace gathered her in his arms and kissed her with fervor and passion.

# 28

## CHLOE

She'd wrestled with the letter for weeks.
Why bother? Jesse clearly didn't want to
speak to her. He couldn't be bothered to
return a text.

He was hiding. Even his Instagram and
Twitter accounts were silent.

What did she hope to gain by writing him
an old-fashioned letter? On top of that, she
didn't know exactly where he lived in
Boston. Addressing the envelope to Jesse
Gates, Boston, would do her no good.

This was typical Chloe Daschle. Put her
heart out there, after swearing she would
not, then crashing and burning.

*Please like me. I'm not the chubby freckle-
face girl. Please like me. I'm not the crazy
one in the video. Please like me.*

But unlike she had in the past, she didn't
crumble. She didn't sink into despair. She

determined to reach out one last time.

Chloe gathered the stationery she'd purchased specifically for this letter and read her opening line.

Dear Jesse, How's it going?

Stupid. She wadded up the top page, tossed it toward the lanai wastebasket, and missed.

She rested her head on the sofa cushion and closed her eyes. This angst was not worth it. She'd only known him for a few months, right?

But oh, something in her heart told her Jesse Gates was a mine of gold.

"Jesus, I think I love this boy. What do I do?"

"Chloeeee, my lady, what's up?"

She bolted upright as Smitty dropped down in the chair across from her, stretching his short legs onto the coffee table.

"Smitty." She glanced behind her. The gates were closed and locked, she knew because the gardener had told her. Mom and Dad were out of town, so security was heightened. The French doors were open to the kitchen, but she was facing them, so he couldn't have entered that way.

"How'd you get in?"

470

"Over there. Somewhere." He pointed toward the gate, sort of, then to the north corner and around to the lanai. "So, have you heard from Jesse?"

"No." She sighed. "How'd you get in? The gates are locked."

"I saw the gardener." Smitty set his feet down and angled toward her. "Did you write to him?"

She pointed to the wadded stationery.

Smitty grinned. "Not going so well?"

Chloe set the stationery aside, standing, pacing. "I don't even know why I'm trying. In South Carolina I hinted that I wanted something more with him, but he didn't bite. Then he walked off the set and I can't stop thinking about him. Never mind I don't even have his actual address."

"Try his brother's company, Diamond-Bros." Smitty pulled an apple from his white, linen jacket. The sleeves were rolled up *Miami Vice* style. "What's God saying?"

"He's not speaking."

"Are you sure?"

"No." She sighed, sitting with a harrumph. "I'm not sure I can tell if He's speaking. There's soda, water, beer in the fridge if you want something to drink."

"Don't overthink it." Smitty jerked open the fridge and took out a cold can of sparkling water. "Get out of your head and into your spirit." He slapped his belly. "You're too afraid."

"Can you blame me? You know my past."

"Trust yourself. Your faith. Trust Him." Smitty crunched into his apple. "I've got to go." He pointed at the wadded letter. "Write from your heart. Send it. What's the worst that can happen?"

"Never hearing from him again."

The short, dark man made a face as he stepped off the lanai and started across the lawn. "And how much are you hearing from him now?" He disappeared around the side of the house and was gone.

Chloe wadded up a piece of stationery and tossed it in his direction.

Smitty had a point. And what was the business of "death, you cannot have me" if she let herself be chained to her fears? Where was her *victory*?

Taking up the stationery, Chloe set pen to paper.

Dear Jesse,
　I'm not really sure where to begin. How are you? Where are you? Why did you leave? I miss you and our weird relationship. Can I say that?
　I never had a chance to thank you for

472

defending me to Zarzour. Thank you, from the bottom of my heart.

I've tried to call and text, but you never respond. Dad suggested writing an old-fashioned letter since a letter started our relationship. Ha! Since I don't have your address, Smitty suggested I write to you at DiamondBros.

When we met at Violet and Dylan's wedding, I knew there was something special about you. As if God intended our paths to cross. But I was hesitant, scared. Then you kissed me, and I never wanted you to stop. Yeah, that's right. I never wanted you to stop. I wanted to be able to kiss you any time I wanted. Echoes of *Sweet Home Alabama,* anyone?

Since you walked off the set, I've missed you. I can't stop thinking about you. I want to be more than friends, Jesse. I think I love you.

Dad teases me about my quest for a real happily ever after, but I do not have fairy-tale dreams of a perfect love that never fails or doesn't struggle. I get real life. I love real life. That's what I want with you. Love and life. In all of its awkwardness, selfishness, giving and taking, growing and changing.

The image of marriage I have in my head? For some reason, you've set up house in that dream, and I can't imagine any of it without you.

I have no idea if you'll ever read this. Which is why I'm bearing my raw, naked heart. But if you do read this, please let me know. Even if the answer is, "Chloe, move on." I promise not to go nutso on you.

But think, pray, about what I'm saying. Can you forgive your past and move on with me?

Affectionately yours,
Chloe

## HAMILTON

"Here, let me help you." His wife of five years, now pregnant with their first child, eased the prosthetic from his leg. "Your skin is raw, dear. Let me get my liniment."

"What would I do without you, Lydia?"

"Rub on your own liniment?" She sparkled when she smiled, her brown eyes flecked with gold light. Once again, she stole another piece of his heart.

"I suppose I should learn your technique. Once our child arrives you'll be too busy to bother with me."

"You will always be my first duty. Our children will thank me for it." She rose up on her knees and kissed him without shame. Hamilton breathed in her beauty.

"I will thank you for it." He returned her kiss, gratitude sweeping his heart.

She was God-sent. A rare jewel. And she was his. Though how he'd won her heart when he walked in his darkest days remained a mystery.

The daughter of the preacher who'd come to Ninety Six to take Uncle Laurence's post was made of iron.

Lydia removed a bottle from the leather case she carried with her wherever they went, full of remedies and rubbing oils, as well as her much-read Bible.

"What has God given you for tonight?" she asked.

"My usual. Do I have another string on my instrument besides 'Come, follow Me'?" He'd spend a lifetime studying the depths and riches of those three little words.

"Your leg is swollen and bruised. You've been standing too much." Lydia peered up at him. "It's time to go home."

"This is our last stop."

They'd been bound for Quill Farm and South Carolina when a last-minute invitation came from a First Presbyterian parishioner, Charles Dinsmore, a fellow South Carolinian and war veteran. Hamilton felt bound by love to yield to the man's request and traveled north to New York.

"Mr. Lightfoot." A fresh-faced young man peeked around the door. "There's someone to see you."

"Can you ask them to wait?" Lydia capped the liniment bottle and reached for a balm made of crushed roses and lavender. "Mr. Lightfoot needs his rest before preaching."

"Begging pardon, my dear." Hamilton sat forward. "It might be someone who needs ministering." To the young man: "Is it a soul in need of assistance? Or perhaps the reverend? Ah, of course, it might be Charles Dinsmore."

"They say they are the Hobart family, sir."

He exchanged a glance with Lydia, who squeezed his hand and spoke to the young man. "Tell them we'll be right out."

"Do you know the Hobarts?" Lydia smoothed the warm oil over his half leg.

"I do not. Perhaps they've come for some prayer. Or aid." When his wife finished, Hamilton stood, now an expert at balancing on one leg. Lydia retrieved the crutch from her wonder bag and quickly assembled the pieces.

"Go on," she said. "I must wash my hands."

Hamilton turned to go, then reached back, bringing his wife to him for a kiss. "Thank you."

She pressed her hand to his face. "Any time, my dear."

He exited the small room and made his way down the narrow corridor, his crutch clacking against the stone floor. The clap of his foot in rhythm had become the music of his life.

The young man waited by yet another door. "They're in the sanctuary, sir."

Hamilton nodded his thanks and peered into the large, square room. Sunlight fell through the colorful, stained glass windows and glided across the polished pews.

A family of no small means, judging by their attire, waited on the front row. A gentleman and his wife, along with two young children.

"May I help you?" he said as he crossed the stone floor, wondering how he might minister to them.

The woman stood, gripping the handle of her reticule. Hamilton stopped, his crutch nearly slipping out from under him.

"Esther."

"Hello, Hamilton." Her voice wavered,

and her eyes glistened as she walked toward him, hand outstretched. "It's good to see you."

"Esther, dear Esther." He gripped her hand. "W-whatever are you doing here?"

"Why, we came to see you, of course." Her smile, so much the same but refined with age, captured her beauty. "You look well. Content and happy."

"As do you. More beautiful than ever."

For a moment he was a boy again, carefree and whole, with Esther a permanent part of his days.

"A-hem."

Esther turned. "Wallace, so sorry. Hamilton, may I introduce my husband, Mr. Wallace Hobart, Viscount of Berksham, and our children, Michael and Catherine. Say hello to Mummy's friend, Mr. Lightfoot."

The husband was a fine man with a confident deportment. Good-looking and well formed. The boy bowed while the little girl curtseyed, and with one refined voice they inquired, "How do you do?"

A lump welled in his throat. These were Esther's children. The girl looked like her. "I do very well, thank you. And you? Are you well?"

"Yes, sir."

"What happened to your leg?" Well, not

only did the girl look like her mama, but she was as sweet and bold.

"Catherine." Esther pressed her hand onto her daughter's shoulder. "It's not polite to —"

"I don't mind," Hamilton said. "I lost it during the war."

"How did you lose your leg?" She furrowed her brow.

He laughed, taking a seat on the pew. "In a battle. A sword came down and . . ." He glanced up Esther. "It was an accident."

"Did it hurt?" This from the boy.

"I'm blessed not to remember much."

"You must be very brave," the child said. "Papa says if we're brave and don't cry when we get hurt, we can have a sweet treat."

"That's right. You must always be brave."

"Children." Wallace took each one by the hand. "Come with me. Leave Mama to speak with her friend." His accent was one of an aristocrat. Of one worthy of Esther.

Esther whispered something to him. He nodded, then departed with the children. She joined Hamilton on the pew. "My dear friend, are you well?"

"Very."

"Happy?"

"Most."

She sighed. "I'm very glad."

"What of you? Happy?"

"Most."

"How did you know I was here? Last I heard you were in England."

"I received a circular with the morning papers. 'Come hear war hero Hamilton Lightfoot.' "

He shook his head. "Hyperbole to arouse interest. So, do you live in New York?"

"We moved here four years ago. Wallace always dreamed of owning a farm in America. We bought land on the Hudson. He has cousins here who started a growing venture, so he joined them." Esther removed a flyer from her bag. "I couldn't believe it when I saw your name. Surely it was not my — rather, the same Hamilton Lightfoot. I had no idea you'd become a preacher."

"It was redemption a long time in the making." He examined the pamphlet. "This is the work of Dinsmore, no doubt."

"Dinsmore? Charles Dinsmore? You know him?"

"We were at King's Mountain and Cowpens together."

"But of course," Esther said. "He spoke of the war, but I never concluded —"

"You know him as well?" Hamilton said.

"Yes, he's well acquainted with my . . .

husband. They've formed a gentlemen's club together. You should join them."

"We leave tomorrow," Hamilton said. "My wife is with child and —"

A door opened and closed, footsteps resounded on the stone floor. Lydia. Hamilton rose to greet her.

"Lydia." He offered his arm. "May I introduce my friend, Esther Longfellow —"

" 'Tis Hobart now."

"Mrs. Esther Hobart."

"How do you do?" Lydia's hand rested on her round belly. "I didn't know you knew anyone in Manhattan, love."

"We're old friends. From South Carolina."

Lydia stepped a little closer to him. He'd have some explaining to do later. While she knew of his exploits in the war, he'd never spoken to her of Esther, choosing to leave his failure with her behind.

"We have a farm." Esther motioned to the west. "Well, my husband is trying to have a farm. So far we've found success."

"I wish you all the luck." Lydia slipped her arm through Hamilton's.

"Esther and I grew up together in South Carolina. Before the war."

"He rarely speaks of the war or his life before," Lydia said. "Pardon my ignorance."

"You are with child," Esther said. "When

is your time?"

"In three months. We're going home to prepare."

Hamilton looked at Esther. "Did you know your father returned Quill to us right before he died."

"No, I'd not heard," Esther said. "But I'm very glad. Father's last days were turbulent, but he's at peace now."

From the back, the nave doors eased open and small footsteps echoed up the center aisle. "Mama?" The girl clung to her mother's skirt. "I'm hungry."

"I'm sorry, my dear," Esther's husband said. "We'd gotten no farther than a block down than the children reminded me of their empty bellies." The man tipped his hat toward Lydia.

"Mr. Hobart, may I introduce my wife, Mrs. Lydia Lightfoot."

"How do you do?" he said, bowing to her.

"My, aren't your children adorable?" Lydia saw life in everything and everyone.

"Shall we dine before the meeting?" Wallace turned to Hamilton. "Please, join us. Our treat."

"Thank you, but no. I should be getting ready for the service."

"Indeed, he should." Lydia stepped forward. "Will you return for the meeting? His testimony is so powerful."

"We are eager to hear your sermon, Reverend Lightfoot." Hobart offered his hand.

Esther reached for her daughter's hand. "I must learn what has happened to my old friend and how he came to follow the Lord."

"Until then." Wallace took hold of the boy and started down the center aisle, Esther by his side.

For a moment, Hamilton watched, letting her go, then released himself from Lydia. "Pardon me, my dear." With his crutch cracking against the stone, he called to Esther, "May I have a word?"

"Of course." She released the girl's hand. "Go with Papa. I'll be along."

Her husband paused, then with a nod, took his girl's hand and departed the sanctuary, stepping outside into the late-afternoon sun.

"What is it?" Esther said. "Your wife is lovely. I can tell she adores you." She lightly touched his arm, then withdrew, anchoring her hand by her side. "As she should."

"She is my delight, my gift," Hamilton said. "And . . . Wallace . . . I sense a solid kindness in him."

"Yes, yes, you've described him perfectly. Solid and kind."

"Then we have both done well." Hamilton offered a curt bow.

"We have, yes."

He hesitated, glancing over his shoulder to where Lydia waited, giving her a reassuring smile.

"You should go. Your wife awaits, as does my husband. I'm sure the children have reached the end of their tether." She turned to go.

"Wait, Esther, a final word?" Hamilton moved closer, the echo of his crutch so loud and reverberating in the pitched nave. "Can we sit a moment? I'll be standing long enough later this evening."

Esther moved to the nearest pew, and he slid in beside her. "I've imagined this day so many times," he said. "Now that it's here I don't know what to say."

"Whatever is on your heart. We were always honest with each other."

"Were we?" He angled forward, leaning on his crutch, being for a moment the man he was before he'd lost his leg, before the Lord beckoned, "Come, follow Me."

"Our youth may have deceived us somewhat."

"I heard you the day you came to see me. At Quill Farm. The morning your father sent you away."

"When I stormed into your room, demanding you speak to me?" Esther faced forward, folded her hands on her lap. "I feel rather foolish about it, looking back."

"As do I. My pride, my kinship with self-pity, prevented me from responding. The moment you departed, I was filled with regret. Aunt Mary helped me hitch Tilly to the cart, and I pursued you."

She pressed her hand to her heart. "I had no idea, Hamilton. What happened?"

"Tilly and I rode hard in the little cart, but the treachery of the road bested me."

"I remember. I bounced across the carriage seat as if a rag doll. Though I was too racked with despair to care."

"There was a storm —"

"Lightning slithering across the sky," she said.

"Thunder rumbled louder than any cannon fire."

"Our horses were spooked. Isaac exerted every ounce of strength to keep us on the road."

"At one roaring thunderclap, Tilly reared and tipped the cart." After nine years, he still recalled the events in detail.

"Isaac pushed on to the next town, where we lodged for the night before we drowned in the deluge."

"The cart tossed me to the ground. I lay

in the tall grass being baptized by heaven's tears until Moses found me." He cleared his throat. Did he tell her the rest? Of the Man? No, she would hear his story tonight.

"When Father died, I knew I'd never return to Slathersby Hill or South Carolina."

"You wouldn't have wanted to marry me as I was, Esther."

"I dare say, you'd not have wanted to marry me. I was so —"

"Bitter."

The word traveled from their tongues in unison.

Esther smiled, pressing her hand on his. "The Lord has been good to both of us."

"A truth I cannot deny." He brought her gloved hand to his lips. "We shall always be friends."

Esther's hand broke free of his, and she touched her fingers to his clean jaw and the tip of the ragged scar. "We shall always be friends. Our love, however long ago, was not wasted."

"My dear Esther, when love is given and received, at any level or along any course, it is never wasted. Certainly not any of my affection for you."

She opened her reticule and retrieved a small note. "Your letter," she said. "From the battlefield."

He reached for it, unfolding the thick stock, the pencil markings smudged from touch and time. "I'd thought it lost. Aunt Mary confessed she burned the letter you left for me at the surgeon's. She feared you'd grow tired of me and leave, breaking my heart beyond what I could bear."

"But that was for us to decide."

"Those were empty, frightening days."

"Even when I stood in your room and demanded your attention —"

"I thought it best for you to be free of me. Then Aunt Mary confessed her fears and actions, and that's why I came after you." Time, the beauty of grace, allowed this confession. A time to heal. He had Lydia to thank for teaching him to express his heart well. Hamilton folded the page, offering it back to Esther. "How could we have known the path the Lord had for us?"

She did not reach to take the letter, so he set it on the pew between them. "Why did you not write to me then? Right after I departed?"

"After I landed in the grass and lay there, the rain soaking me to the bone, I realized I could not saddle you with my condition. Not my leg, but my anger and bitterness. I needed to know the love of my Savior before

I could love myself. Before I could love you."

Her eyes were full and glistening when she looked at him. "I didn't open your letter for some months after I returned to London. I couldn't bear to read what you wrote. If of love, then I was thousands of miles from your arms. If of detachment, then I'd be bereft of hope. Then Father died, and I buried my attachments to South Carolina with him."

"Aunt Mary and I attended his funeral. In doing so we bid good-bye to the grudge, to our friend, and in my heart, to you." Hamilton ran his hand over his leg and the blunt end. Lydia was right. He'd overextended.

"Do you have regrets, Hamilton?" Esther said.

"To live in faith is to live without regret." He leveled his gaze at her, the light from the stained glass window haloing her in gold and blue. "Do you?"

"No." She peered away from him. "I do not see the point in worrying over matters beyond my control. The Lord has been gracious to me." She pointed toward Lydia. "She seems most anxious."

"She worries I'll tire myself. Overextend my leg. She tends to me with more diligence than a surgeon." He rose. "I should rest

488

before tonight." The letter remained on the pew. "The letter is yours, Esther. Do with it as you see fit."

She cupped it in her hand, returning it to her reticule.

"Good-bye, Esther," he said.

She exited the pew into the aisle. "Good-bye, Hamilton. Godspeed."

"And to you, Esther. Always to you."

# 29

## JESSE

*May*

One month to settle in, adjust, find an apartment, decorate his office. Another to form a routine, develop disciplines. A third to pretend it felt like home.

He rose at four o'clock five days a week and drove to the gym in predawn darkness. He worked out to podcasts on the latest technology.

At six, he ate breakfast. By six thirty he was seated at his desk, reading, working, rewiring the cords of his existence from sunny LA to dreary Boston. From actor and screenwriter to engineer and software designer.

At eight thirty, he'd pour his first cup of coffee and stop by his brother's office for an informal chat about DiamondBros projects and personnel.

On Wednesdays, Dan, Jesse, and VP Paul golfed together. Sundays, he dined with his parents.

He did not decorate his apartment or office. No art or photos. The creative man who'd written a screenplay made into a movie by the great Jeremiah Gonda was dead. If he'd ever lived at all. And the engineer wearing a starched white button-down with dark-blue summer slacks had yet to figure out if he preferred eclectic modern or contemporary feng shui. Whatever that meant.

Dan sent a decorator to his apartment as a surprise one Saturday. Did not go well.

Jesse shoved back from his computer and the design spec open on his screen. He refilled his coffee cup and stared out the window at the busy Boston street. A splash of May rain battered the glass, and he lost his reflection in the clouds.

Chloe. She crossed his mind a thousand times a week, and he had yet to figure a way to purge her from it. An algorithm? Write some code, apply a few electrodes to his heart, and run a zapping program worthy of a sci-fi film?

But he didn't want to forget. The pain of missing her made him feel alive. Even forced him to finally close all doors leading to Loxley.

Just this week he'd reached out to her parents. To his surprise, they invited him for coffee. Tonight. Anxiety twisted his gut. Whatever they dished out, he'd take it, because he deserved it.

Meanwhile, Jeremiah e-mailed updates on *Bound by Love* editing. He worked long distance with his team to keep the project on schedule. He filmed *Sea Dragon* during the day and reviewed cuts of *Bound* at night.

It's good, Jesse. Really good.

Gonda had also leveraged a release date from Zarzour by threatening to hold back the final scenes of *Dragon*. *Bound by Love* would premier in January.

Great way to kick off the new year!

Had Jesse been rash in leaving Hollywood? In the middle of the mess, leaving felt right. Dan was eager to have him back at DiamondBros, and Jesse's return was seamless. He flicked off the first pass of regret. No use looking back now.

But if being here was right, why did he feel . . . empty? Time. That's all. He just needed more time.

A light rap sounded on his door, and Dan peeked in. "You coming? The TimeQuest meeting is in five. Conference room A."

Right. The meeting. He was still adjusting to the demands of the almighty calendar. "On my way."

Jesse set down his coffee and reached for his iPad. Dan crossed to Jesse's desk, letting the door close behind him.

"Mom said you're having coffee with the Brants tonight?"

"Yeah, I called them last week." Jesse came around his desk, but his brother stopped him, hand to his chest.

"Are you sure you want to see them? Last time they —"

"I have to try."

"What do you hope to accomplish?"

"Nothing." Everything. "Let's go."

Dan refused to let Jesse pass. "They'll mess with you. Get you upset again. I can't have you running off to LA this time, Jess."

"Give me a break, Dan." Jesse pushed past him, past the fact his big brother's concern might be rooted in truth. "Come on, let's get to this."

The long shadows of sunset fell on the row houses of the old Boston neighborhood of

Charlestown. A few minutes before seven, Jesse turned down the street given to him by Mrs. Brant. They'd moved from the suburban residence where they raised Loxley to an up-and-coming historical neighborhood.

Reading the house numbers, he parked his truck along the curb and cut the engine, ignoring every urge to drive on.

He needed to be here. He wanted to face them. LA, for all its pretentiousness, had been the perfect hiding place.

Mrs. Brant, smiling and wearing an apron tied about her waist, opened the door when he was still on the sidewalk. She looked more like a fifties housewife than an executive director for a charity organization.

"It's been too long." She embraced Jesse as he entered. "You look well. How long has it been? David, Jesse is here."

"Eight years." Apples baking in cinnamon perfumed the house.

David Brant came from a back room, hand outstretched. "Jesse, good to see you."

"You too, sir." Jesse's hand clapped into the police captain's broad mitt with a sense of relief.

If they were still angry with him, this was an Oscar-winning performance.

"How do you like this place? Barbara has

been wanting to move to this neighborhood forever. We found this house already renovated and couldn't pass it up."

"It's nice. I remember you talking about moving here one day." Jesse followed Mr. Brant toward the kitchen, trying to be at ease, but feeling more like an interloper.

"Death has a way of putting life in order," Mrs. Brant said, standing in the stainless steel and white-tile kitchen, cutting large slices of apple pie. "Do you like your pie á la mode?"

"S-sure. Thank you." He didn't need to watch his diet now that he was no longer in Hollywood. Not that he ever watched his food intake that much.

"Have a seat, Jesse." Mr. Brant motioned to the table where a fork rested on a cream, linen napkin and a china cup waited for coffee.

"Cream with your coffee?" Mr. Brant asked.

Jesse nodded, a burning beginning in his chest. Why were they being so nice? Kind? Mentioning Loxley's death without a flicker of ire?

Mr. Brant set a matching china creamer on the table and filled Jesse's cup. "We heard you were back from LA," he said. "Don't tell me you missed our winters."

"I needed to take . . . a different . . . My life . . . my path . . . changed."

Mrs. Brant set a pie plate in front of him. "Did you miss engineering? I know Loxley would've never given up —"

Jesse shoved away from the table and fired to his feet. "Death . . . Loxley . . . you talk as if it's all okay. What happened. As if she didn't drown. As if I weren't responsible. I'm sorry, but . . . I have to say this. I expected you to be cold and rude and bawl me out. I sent you ten thousand dollars for your scholarship fund, and you sent it back." His skin prickled hot under his T-shirt despite the cool breeze blowing through the open window. "There aren't even any pictures of her on the wall."

Mr. Brant touched his shoulder. "Follow me."

He led Jesse to a small room off the kitchen, perhaps once a servant's quarters, and clicked on a lamp.

"We call this our Loxley room." The room, furnished as a den, contained one wall of photographs and awards. "When we sold our house to move here, we knew we had to move on, but didn't want to forget our girl. So we set this aside for us, for family and friends. We can come here any time we want. But out there" — he pointed toward the kitchen — "we can live the life we've been given."

"I'm sorry . . . I didn't know." Jesse stepped toward a familiar image. One of him with Loxley and the Brants at Martha's Vineyard when they'd started dating.

"Why did you frame this one? I don't deserve to be on this wall."

Mr. Brant motioned for Jesse to sit in an oversized, leather chair as he took the one adjacent.

"For a long time we blamed you, because grief must have a target. We couldn't blame our girl, so we dumped our anger, frustration, hurt on you."

"As I deserved."

"But did it make us feel better? Relieve any of our pain? No. It only made us hard and bitter. One day I happened by the department's chaplain. A good man. Tony George is his name. I retired from the force, you know."

"I did not."

"Anyway, he said, 'David, how are you doing?' I tell you, I could've punched through a brick wall with everything broiling inside. Barbara and I were not doing well. We both worked too much. Hardly spoke to one another when we were home."

Jesse listened. It's what he came to do.

Mrs. Brant set two plates on the center table. "Let's have our pie in here. I'll be back with the coffee." She exchanged a smile and a knowing glance with her husband.

Jesse hesitated, unsure there was room for pie amid the tension in his gut, no matter how tempting the aroma. But when Mr. Brant took up his, Jesse followed.

"Where was I?" he said.

"Punching a brick wall."

The man grinned, cutting a bite from the tip of his slice. "Tony just asked if he could pray for me. Fat lot of good it would do, but I agreed. Nothing else seemed to work. When he was done, I felt peace for the first time in years. Even since before Loxley died."

Jesse stabbed at his pie and the melting ice cream. "I wanted to tell you how sorry I am for my part in her death." He set down the plate and stood, his nerves buzzing. "I pretended to propose to her. I mocked her. She thought we were in love, but I already knew I didn't feel the same. Instead of being honest, I made fun of what she wanted, of how she felt, of who she thought we were."

Mr. Brant set down his plate and leaned

forward, hands folded. "And she walked off?"

"I tried to follow her, but she told me to leave her alone." Jesse paced along the wall where Loxley smiled at him from a different world.

"Sounds like our girl."

"I guess she got in the water. I don't know. When she didn't come back, we looked for her." The words spilled out of him. A story eight years in the waiting.

Mrs. Brant entered with the coffee and her own pie plate. She sat on the love seat next to her husband. "Did you tell him?"

"Not yet. He's filling me in on the details of that night."

"I see." She sipped her coffee, so calm, so in control of her emotions, while he felt like a runaway train. "You should tell him. He's about to jump out of his skin."

"Tell me what?"

"Loxley called us that night. We knew you two had had a fight and that she was walking the beach alone."

Jesse returned to his chair.

"We tried to get her to calm down," Mr. Brant said with a glance toward his wife. "I told her to take a swim. Cool off."

"W-what? You told her to take a swim? And you never said anything?"

"We were too hurt. Too angry. Why blame ourselves when we could blame you?"

"I am not innocent here by a long stretch, but —"

"Did you know there was a riptide?"

"There wasn't one on our part of the beach," Jesse said. "At least not that I can remember."

That night was a blur of emotions, of a long-angled sunset, of searching through the night and calling the police. Then, at last, the hope of the dawn.

"Jesse," Mrs. Brant said, "we don't blame you. We forgive you of any part you played. We've spent the past eight years learning how to forgive ourselves." She pointed to the pictures. "We couldn't look at these for a long time. Now we love our Loxley room."

"Wow, I don't know what to say." Jesse sat back, and for the first time in eight years, he felt relief. "I went to LA to move on and forget. I had a small studio apartment, and I went on one audition after another. I didn't party or socialize. I had one friend, Smitty, from an acting class. I didn't date. Didn't go to the beach for years. Then my screenplay went into production, and I rented a place on the beach. Finally, the past was behind me, you know." The Brants listened with patient expressions. "And I met someone. Chloe Daschle. An actress. We clicked the moment we met. Like she —"

"Was someone you could love?" Mrs. Brant offered no sarcasm with her observation.

"Yeah, maybe," Jesse said.

"Loxley would've loved this, Jesse. You writing screenplays, acting in movies," Mrs. Brant said.

"Barb, you know she'd tell him to get back to engineering. He's so talented."

Jesse eyed his hosts. "I still don't understand how you can talk about her as if . . . as if . . . it's okay she's dead? As if I played no part in it all?"

Mr. Brant set down his pie plate and reached for a thick book on the table by his chair. "Sit, Jesse. Let me tell you about a man named Jesus."

## CHLOE

Friday night she closed the script for *Faith Freeman, Stargazer*. Unbelievable. Aaron Heinley's screenplay knocked it out of the park.

What an amazing role. Not only to play a character who lived, but one who flew through space conquering some serious evil lords.

Faith Freeman was real, confident, and flawed. This was going to be fun. Chloe could learn a lesson or two from this fictional woman. Like how to step out in *faith* and believe. How to let go of past mistakes and live for today.

She retrieved a Diet Coke from the fridge and peered out the living room window, staring down on the pool, the front of the guesthouse, the backyard still full of the evening sun.

Nothing seemed right without Jesse. Not even her childhood home. Six weeks had passed since she'd written him. Either he didn't get her letter, or he was ignoring it. But a quick response would've been nice.

Chloe returned to her chair, draping her legs over the side, sipping her drink, staring at the ceiling.

She understood his silence. At least she'd tried. His issues with Loxley were unresolved, and he had to figure out how to heal. Maybe he would find closure in Boston.

Yet she hated that he was two thousand miles away. That he'd given up on writing and acting. He was brilliant at both.

Reaching for her phone, she checked the time. Dad called earlier and asked her to meet him in his office at seven.

Twenty-nine going on thirty, and her big Friday night was hanging out in her dad's office. But that was fine with Chloe. Home was a great place to hang. And the timing was perfect. She wanted Dad's honest opinion about Claude and the Stargazer series. About playing Faith Freeman.

An energetic hammering rattled her door. "Chloeeee!"

"Kate?" Chloe set down her drink and answered the door.

"We're engaged!" Kate nearly knocked Chloe down with her embrace, spinning her around, then blinding her with a spectacular diamond. "Can you believe it? Engaged. Rob and I!" She floated around the apartment in a low-cut, little black dress and strappy heels.

"Engaged? Congratulations." Chloe swallowed, surprised more than jealous. Okay, a little jealous. Kate had never dreamed of marriage the way Chloe did. "I'm stunned. H-how did this happen? I-I thought you didn't care about marriage. You were happy just living together."

"I didn't . . . until he asked." Kate swooned against the couch pillows and kicked one slender leg into the air. "All those years of you preaching the glorious virtues of marriage must have sunk in without me realizing." She reached for Chloe's hand and pulled her down to the couch. "Thank you."

"Y-you're welcome." Chloe perched on the edge of the cushion. "At least one of the Daschle girls will have a happily ever after. Have you told Mom and Dad?"

"They already knew. Can you believe it? Rob asked Dad for my hand." She made a face, fanning herself with her hands. "I'm so happy." She crossed fingers. "Let's just hope it's for ever after." Kate squeezed Chloe in a hug. "You, of course, will be my maid of honor."

"Of course . . . you didn't even have to ask."

It seemed at times the luck of love happened to those who didn't even believe.

"We're thinking of October." Kate spied the script and flipped through the pages. "Dad told me about Claude's movie. It sounds perfect, Chloe. I'm so happy for you. This is the break you've been waiting for." Kate dropped the script onto the table. "Does Faith have a true love?"

"Eventually. She meets him in this script."

"Love and *life* in one character. See, you get what you want eventually."

"It's not real, Kate. It's a movie. I may

have played characters who died, but in case you missed it, I'm still alive."

"Yes, I did notice." Kate sobered, sitting up, facing Chloe. "Give this part all you've got. In a year's time, you will have worked with two of the best directors in the business. We both know actors who would kill, literally, to work with Jer and Claude. Show the world who you really are, Chloe." Kate squeezed her hand. "If that's not happily ever after . . ."

"You can't compare my movie gig to love. To your engagement, Kate. I know women who would kill, not literally, to have what you have with Rob."

"I know and I'm grateful."

Chloe reached for her soda can, taking a drink. The beverage had grown warm and lost its appeal. "I've given up on love. Really. It has just never worked for me."

"Then give yourself to your career. Be one of the grandes dames of acting. Everyone will admire you. You'll win Oscars. Get inducted into Halls of Fame."

"I don't want *everyone* to admire me. Just one man." She laughed softly. "Is that too much for a girl to ask?"

"Ooo, speaking of men, I saw your old flame Finley the other day. He looked happy."

"He is. We talk once in a while. We were always more friends than lovers."

"What about Haden? Do you talk to him? You know I never liked him."

"What?" Chloe laughed. "You are such a liar, Kate. You loved him. I believe you sat right there and told me if I didn't want him, you'd take him."

"Please . . . I was kidding."

"You were completely serious."

"I plead temporary insanity." Kate raised her hand to admire her ring. "Rob is amazing. So, did you send your letter to Jesse? Now, he is the type of man a girl mourns losing."

"Over a month ago."

"And?" Kate said.

"Nothing." Chloe walked to the kitchen and dumped out her soda, then tossed the can away.

"What do you mean, nothing?" Kate walked into the kitchen and leaned against the island.

"Nothing. No. Thing. He never responded."

"Really? I'm surprised. He didn't seem like the kind to go silent." Kate brushed Chloe's ponytail away from her shoulders. "You really are a diamond. I don't know why you've had such bad luck with love."

"It's for the best, you know. I'm dodging a bullet here." She kept the story of Loxley to herself. Kate didn't need to know. "He's got a lot of . . . baggage."

Chloe's phone pinged and she exited the kitchen, shutting off the light. "I'm meeting Dad in the library. Want to come?" She grabbed the script.

Kate flashed her ring. "I've got a ring to show off, people to blind." She straightened her skirt and checked her appearance in the mirror by the door. "We're going out to dinner with Violet and Dylan. They have no idea . . ."

The sisters chatted wedding details as they headed down the stairs and across the lawn, parting at the alcove that led to the driveway.

"Kate," Chloe said. "Why did Rob propose? After all this time?"

"You." She smiled. "Something you said about marriage changed his heart."

"What did I say?"

"That marriage is the only place where two lovers can exist in a world all their own. That the deep places come from the commitment, the pledging of hearts and lives until death. You called it a covenant, and that touched him. He wanted that with me." Kate's eyes welled up. "Thank you."

In the amber glow of outdoor lights, the

sisters hugged, sniffing away happy tears. "I'm really happy for you."

"One day I'll be happy for you, Chloe. I just know it."

"Good night, Kate."

As she passed through the kitchen on the way to Dad's office, Chloe checked the fridge for leftovers. Grilled chicken. Perfect. Time to get fit for the Faith Freeman costume and stunts.

Putting a cold chicken breast on a plate, Chloe headed to the library. She found Dad on the sofa talking to an older, dark-haired man.

"Chloe, good, you're here." Dad and the man stood.

Chloe studied the two of them, glanced at her plate, then set it on the table by the door. "What's going on?"

"Chloe, this is Oliver Hanson." Dad was bubbly and animated. He was never bubbly. And rarely animated.

"How do," Oliver said, offering his hand to Chloe. Dressed in jeans and a plaid, snap shirt, he appeared to be about Dad's age but carried the aura of a hardworking, blue-collar, salt-of-the-earth working man. "Pleasure to meet you."

"And you." Chloe liked him instantly.

"Are you one of Dad's high school buddies?"

"Me? Naw. First time I ever seen him."

"Oliver contacted me through Gonda Films. Becky thought his e-mail might interest me. Well, actually, you." Dad moved to the wet bar, then returned with three cold Perriers.

"Me?" Chloe made a face and reached for the cold bottle. "Did I win a million dollars?"

Oliver shook his head. "Not from me."

"I had to check him out before bringing his story to you. Do a bit of research." Dad leaned toward Oliver as if they'd been acquainted for ages. "We've had some crazy claims and accusations before."

"I can imagine. Don't bother me none if you checked me out."

Indeed, the Daschles had endured their share of hoaxes, false claims, and lies. A long-lost "relative" looking for a chance to be "in the pictures." A wannabe starlet claiming to be the mother of Dad's love child. An actor swearing Mom was *his* mother. A line of swindlers, posers, elbow rubbers . . . all wanting a piece of Hollywood royalty.

"Oliver is in possession of a letter," Dad motioned for him to take up the story.

"Sure enough. I've had this here letter in my family for ages. I'm from New York, but I was doing some contract work in Chesnee, South Carolina, this spring when I heard someone was making a film. I'm on a crew what goes around fixing up schools, gymnasiums, historical buildings, stuff like that."

"O-okay." Chloe twisted the cap from her water. Where was this going?

Oliver slid a brittle, yellow envelope across the smooth, glistening surface of the teakwood table.

*Esther Longfellow, Slathersby Hill*

"Esther Longfellow?" Chloe reached for the letter. "Jesse's grandfather wrote to an Esther Longfellow."

"My granny had this for years," Oliver said. "Kept it in her jewelry box. Said her granny gave it to her and well, far as I can tell, it's been in the family for a good long while. We don't rightly know where it came from but . . ." The man paused, twisting the cap from his Perrier, inspecting the bottle with an arched brow. "Granny said, 'I'll tell you what my granny told me. This letter belongs to somebody. We've been entrusted with its care.' Made no sense to me being as it's over two hundred years old. But when I heard about the movie based on a letter, I got to thinking and researching, and well, here I am."

"I'm confused." Chloe peered inside the envelope to find a slip of paper inside, the edges slightly tattered, the paper delicate on the folds. "What does this have to do with me? You should be talking to Jesse Gates. I can give you his number, but good luck with getting him to call you back."

"Read it," Dad said.

Chloe unfolded the note, a sudden expectation weighing on her.

Hannah's Cowpens

January 16, 1781

My dearest Esther,

My recent actions have not Demonstrated my sincerest affections. I seek to Remedy any confusion now, on this Eve of Battle. Remember me as Before. When my Deeds, if not my Words, proved my Heart.

I love you. 'Tis no other Truth.

Affectionately Yours,
Hamilton Lightfoot

She looked up. "Oh my word. Dad, Jesse needs to see this. This is from his ancestor. It's the companion letter to the one he possesses. The one that inspired the movie." She offered the letter back to Dad or Oliver, whichever, ignoring the churning between her ribs. "Why'd you bring it to me?"

"Hold on now, Chloe." Dad did not reach for the letter. "I thought the same thing until Oliver and I continued talking, until I did some research."

"My ancestors are from New York," Oliver said, the expensive, green water bottle so small in his broad, work-hardened hands. "Workers. Maids. Butlers. Family legend is the letter came down from an ancestor who worked for a rich family in Manhattan. I had to call around to my relatives to get more of the details, but a distant relation took the letter from his mistress. Stole it. Said she shouldn't be keeping a love letter from another man when her husband was so good and kind to her. Ever play the telephone game? Can't get the story straight between three or four folks, let alone a half dozen generations, but that's what we know."

"Who was your ancestor's employer?"

Oliver pointed to the letter. "We believe Esther Longfellow."

"Hobart," Dad added. "Esther Longfellow Hobart."

Chloe lifted her gaze to the coat of arms hanging on the wall behind Dad's desk. Hobart. "*Our* Hobarts?"

"Yes, our Hobarts. I'm still researching, but this is what I have so far." Dad retrieved a yellow folder from his desk and handed it to Chloe. "There was an Esther Longfellow who lived in South Carolina in the late 1780s."

"The one from Jesse's grandfather's letter?" That much she knew.

"More than likely. She was the daughter of Sir Michael Longfellow. They lived outside of Ninety Six, South Carolina, at the time of the Revolutionary War."

Chloe set her water aside and inspected the folder's contents, scanning the pages of copied notes and records. "I wonder if Jesse's aunt Pat has any of this?"

Dad tapped the edge of the folder with his finger. "Maybe, but does she know what became of Esther Longfellow?"

Chloe flipped the pages to a ship's passenger record. *Mr. Wallace Hobart, Viscount of Berksham, from Nottingham, with his wife, Mrs. Esther Longfellow Hobart, and their children, Michael, 2, and Catherine, 6 months.*

"Are you saying Hamilton Lightfoot loved my great-great-great-great-great-great-grandmother?" This was too much. Too weird. Too . . . amazing.

"Yes, that's what I'm saying, Chloe. We, you, are descended from Esther Longfellow, the object and desire of Hamilton Lightfoot."

She tossed the folder onto the coffee table. "Wait . . . no . . . impossible. This can't be." She turned to Oliver. "What are you trying to pull? This could be any sort of fabrication. You heard about the movie and made this up." She flipped her hand toward Dad. "How could you let him suck you in? It's been 240 years since Hamilton wrote his letter. We can't accurately depict what happened last year between two people, let alone two centuries ago."

"Hold on now, Chloe. I've done my homework." Dad took the folder and shuffled through the pages, producing a lineage of their family. "Esther married an English aristocrat, Wallace Hobart, in 1784, and they sailed to New York in 1787. According to deed records, they bought a large plot of land on the Hudson." Dad handed Chloe a stapled collection of papers with names and dates. "Wallace died young, in his early forties."

She reviewed the pages, seeing the information compiled from an outside source. "Then Hamilton wrote to her, asking her to marry him." She peered up at her father. "That's the letter Jesse's family found, because he never sent it."

"Chloe." Dad used his director's voice. "*You* and Jesse are the end of their love story."

She sat back with a scoff. "I'm not the end of anyone's love story. Not even in the movies!" She stretched for her water but did not take a drink. Just held the cold glass against her cheek. "No offense, Oliver, but where'd you get that letter? Old Documents R Us? What do you want really? To be in one of Dad's films? Be on the crew? You've written a screenplay?" Her chest rumbled with a low, dubious rattle. "W-what's your angle?"

The men regarded her with a calm, steady demeanor, unmoved by her bravado. A simple letter had rattled her to her very core. Challenged her sense of self and well-being. Her ancestor had been in love with Jesse's? Impossible!

Oliver sat back, mouth shut, and let Dad do the talking.

"Chloe, it's true."

"This is a scenario worthy of the big screen. Just like something Hollywood might concoct. It's not real life, Dad. At least not mine." Couldn't he see? Jesse didn't want her. Just like Esther probably hadn't wanted Hamilton. This wasn't the culmination of the love story, this was retribution. Where does unrequited love go? On the rampage, looking for some unsuspecting descendant. Of course, just her luck, it landed on her. "Why . . . why bring this to me now?

"Because I thought you could let go and . . . well —"

"Well what, Dad?" She sat up, trembling, blinking away tears.

"Oliver thought he finally found the true owner of the letter, and he wants to right a wrong done by his ancestor."

"He shouldn't have stolen the letter," Oliver said.

"Oliver, I appreciate what you've done, but —"

"Chloe," Dad said. "Let go. It's okay to love again. We can fly to Boston and —"

"And do what?" She flicked the dew from the corner of her eyes. "Beg him to love me because his ancestor loved mine?"

"Well, no, but we can show him the letter and —"

"Dad, I've told him I love him. I even wrote him that letter. He's never responded. Oliver, it was nice to meet you, and I'm glad to know more of my family history, but this changes nothing. Hamilton and Esther never made it, and frankly, neither will Jesse and I."

## JESSE

For three days, an earthquake rumbled through his entire being. His insides shook while working out, eating breakfast, and during his morning reading.

The Brants taught him their formula for forgiveness by pointing him to a cross. A cruel, ugly, brutal cross.

"If you want to move on, Jesse, look to the Cross."

"I can't."

"It's where forgiveness begins."

Then Mrs. Brant began a song and broke the fallow ground of Jesse's existence.

They prayed over him. Forgave him. And at last accepted his ten-thousand-dollar donation to the Loxley Brant Scholarship fund.

The following Monday, Dan popped his head in the door of Jesse's DiamondBros office. "You okay?"

"Yeah, why?" Could he see the shaking? Hear his roaring pulse? Jesse was on the verge of making a doctor appointment. Something was wrong. Or perhaps, yes,

517

perhaps for the first time in his life something was truly right.

Dan sat in the chair beside Jesse's desk. "You seem different."

He made a face. "How?" But he was different. He was free. A redeemed man without guilt or shame.

Last night he had his first contact from someone in LA other than Jeremiah. Smitty texted.

Next time you're in town I'll take you to church.

"You just do." Dan leaned forward. "We have a new client this afternoon, remember? They're on their way up. Pam is setting up lunch in the conference room. But before we go in and give them a song and dance about your genius, I have to ask, are you happy here?"

Jesse gave his big brother the little-brother stink eye. "Yes, and stop asking or I won't come to your stupid meeting."

"Now that's the little brother I know and love." Dan headed for the door. "You coming?"

"Right behind you." Jesse collected his data and research, his phone pinging just as he headed out. A text from Jeremiah.

Sent you a link to a rough cut of the ending scene. What do you think?

Jesse glanced at his watch, then rounded his desk and sat in front of his computer. He didn't have enough time to watch the whole thing, but he could fast-forward, get a feel for what Jer had done.

And see Chloe.

He clicked on the link and *South Carolina, 1781* splashed across his screen.

"Jesse." Pam entered, waving an envelope. "You're not going to believe this, but I found a letter addressed to you. I checked the postmark. It came for you when I was on vacation, or I'd have given it to you."

"Vacation?" He hit pause and reached for the envelope. "Wasn't that over two months ago?"

"Guess what temp agency we're never using again? That girl, I'm telling you, she'd walk into the wall if you told her it was a door."

Jesse examined the envelope. "It's from Bel Air." And the Daschle estate was the return address.

"One of your Hollywood friends?" Pam came around the desk to read over his shoulder and kill him with her perfume. She'd been vying for an invitation to *Bound by Love*'s premiere since he arrived.

"Probably." He sat back, pressing the letter facedown on his desk. "Close the door on your way out, Pam. Tell Dan to start lunch without me. I'll be there in a minute."

"Darn it. How am I ever going to meet Clive Boston if you don't let me in on what's going on?"

"Trust me, the only Boston you want to know is this one." He pointed out the window to the sunlight glinting off steel and glass.

When he was alone, he set the letter on his desk. He didn't have time to read it, though his every heartbeat declared *o-pen-it, o-pen-it.* But he wanted to read it when he had time. Not on his way to a meeting. And there was the clip Jeremiah had sent.

On impulse, not letting reason have its way, he clicked play, then tore open the letter.

Chloe had written the letter by hand on cream-colored stationery.

Dear Jesse,

On the screen, the movie played. Jesse aimed the light remote at the sensor and dimmed the overhead lights, letter still in hand, burning his fingertips.

He'd been in half a dozen romcoms, two dozen commercials, but nothing compared to the experience of seeing his story come to life on the screen.

Rough cut or not, Jesse embraced the wonder and beauty of it all.

Chris Painter ran across the battlefield as Hamilton, rifle in one hand, yelling commands to his fellow militiamen.

As the battle raged, the camera panned to Chloe-slash-Esther, running toward the fight, stopping to watch from behind a tree.

Jesse hit pause, his throat thick with emotion. He loved her. Dang it. He loved her. With a glance at the letter, he hit play again. Yeah, he was going to be late to Dan's meeting.

The scene cut to a redcoat firing and Hamilton reeling with the blast, gripping his shoulder as he fell.

Esther dashed onto the battlefield, screaming his name, unaware that Hamilton's rival and enemy, Lieutenant Borland, rode toward her, pistol aimed. Jeremiah cut to a plume of smoke, and though the sound effects had yet to be added, the redcoat fell from his horse.

Esther fell to her knees next to Hamilton, declaring she loved him. Jesse was captivated.

When Esther picked up Hamilton's dagger and charged a red-coat, Jesse stood, shooting his chair backward into the window.

"Death, you cannot have me!" She flew through the air about to ram the dagger into the man's chest before a shot was fired and she collapsed.

The camera hovered over her as she lay so calm and still.

Unbelievable. Jesse paced around his desk, then sat, then stood, running his hand through his gelled hair. Was that in the rewrite or did it just happen? He rewound the scene, putting every ounce of his imagination on the battlefield with Chloe.

She charged the redcoat, screaming, "Death, you cannot have me." She collapsed, "dying" with beauty.

"Chloe Daschle, you are amazing."

In the face of disappointment and adversity, she put her shoulder to the wheel and went to work. What did he do? Walk off. Let his emotions, his past, dictate his future.

Well, that ended today.

The camera panned away from Esther on the ground and faded to black. Jesse exhaled, pulling his chair forward, taking a seat, trying to take it all in.

His office lights flickered on as Dan

barged into the room. "What are you do-ing? We're waiting. They want to meet you. Paul started his sales pitch, but I need you for the technical magic show."

"She's incredible, Dan. Incredible."

"Who?"

"Chloe Daschle." Upon his confession, the internal quaking he'd endured for three days ceased, and his heart filled with won-der. "She's incredible. In the face of adver-sity, she delivered the best dying scene *ever.*"

*Death, you cannot have me?*

"Jesse, what's going on? You're watching a movie? You told me you were all in *here.*"

"I am, I am. But I still have a movie com-ing out." He glanced down at the screen as the black gave way to light.

"Jesse, let's go." Dan reached for the mouse, but Jesse slapped his hand away.

"Hold on."

Hamilton walked into a hazy, cold sunrise, a limp Esther in his arms. The camera shifted, and the viewer was inside a house, zooming in on Esther's books, then peering out a window to see children playing in the yard.

"Dan, Jess, what in the world?" Paul burst into the office with no subtle amount of anger. "Clevon is starting to think you two have abandoned them."

"Shh!" Jesse held up his hand. Clevon could wait.

Esther ran from the barn, arms flailing, laughing, pointing, falling into Hamilton's arms, a big rooster chasing her. The children ran to Hamilton, clinging to his leg.

Wait. This was the first day. He was Hamilton. Not Chris. And this was his *idea.* To use the B-roll as a way for Esther to live. He'd said it to Raymond off the cuff.

The shot panned to the American flag with thirteen stars. It flapped against a blue sky as credits began to roll.

"Yaw!" Jesse shot from his chair with abandon. "She lived. She lived. You son of a gun, Jeremiah Gonda, you're a genius!"

"Who lives? Dan, can we please get to our client?" Paul was not amused.

"She lived. Don't you get it? She lived. Ha-ha! And that's me in the final scene as Hamilton. Not Chris Painter." In an instant, Jesse understood all roads led to his salvation. And the journey began with Chloe Daschle.

He hugged his brother, then a very stiff and formal Paul.

"I'm going back to the meeting before we lose one of our potentially biggest accounts. Dan?" Paul left without looking back.

"On my way." Dan turned to Jesse. "I'm glad she lived. I assume you mean some character. But right now I need you, all of you, in that conference room."

"Yeah, okay." Was he smiling? Because his face hurt. "Let me make a quick call." It was 9:30 a.m. in California. Perfect.

"Call after the meeting." Dan pressed his fingers to his forehead. His telltale sign of frustration.

"Yeah, okay. Sure." Jesse tucked his phone into his pocket and took a glance at Chloe's letter. Raymond must have told Jeremiah his idea. There was no other explanation. "You're right, I need to be present with you." Jesse grabbed the air with his fist. Today he could literally catch the wind.

"Thank you." Dan paused as Jesse met him at the door. "Where are your notes? The white paper?" He pointed to the cream envelope in Jesse's hand. "Don't think this is going to cut it."

"Ah, right." Jesse returned to his desk. "I'll be right there."

Tucking his laptop under his arm, Jesse headed to conference room A, pulling out Chloe's letter on the way. She'd texted him several times after he left LA, but when he got a Boston address, he cut off his LA phone service in exchange for one paid for by DiamondBros. If he was going to make life in Boston work . . .

Dear Jesse,

   . . . I never had a chance to thank you for defending me to Zarzour.

   . . . suggested I write to you at your brother's company.

   . . . an old-fashioned letter. Ironic, since a letter started our relationship. Ha!

   . . . I knew there was something special about you.

   . . . Since you walked off the set . . . can't stop thinking about you.

   . . . I think I love you.

   . . . I have no idea if you'll ever read this.

Affectionately yours,
Chloe

He stopped in the middle of the office's main thoroughfare. To his left, a row of windows overlooked the city. To his right, developers and coders tap-tapped on their devices trying to break technological barriers.

She loved him. She loved him! The June sun shot a ray of light at his feet.

Dan poked his head from the conference

room. "You coming?"

"No. I'm not," Jesse said. "I'm sorry but, Dan, I have to go." He dashed into his office, dropped his laptop on the desk, and snatched up his truck keys. "She loves me." He laughed. "I love her." With each confession, the scales of the past fell off and his heart stretched, awakening from a long, long sleep. "I've got to go . . ."

But Dan blocked his exit. "Is this about Chloe?"

"I love her, Dan. And she loves me." He waved the letter under his brother's nose. "She sent this two months ago. I can't imagine what she's thinking."

"Want to know what I'm thinking?"

"I already know."

"That we went after a huge client because of the technology and design idea you developed. Chloe can love you after this meeting. Two more hours isn't going to make a difference. We need your brain and charisma in there. We lose this deal without you."

"Really?" Jesse pushed past Dan into the hall. "Because you had this client on the hook way before me. You're the man, Dan. You have the skill, the talent, and the reputation. Have you ever talked to Shantel Hannah? She's brilliant. Sixty percent of what I put together came from her. She could easily take my place."

"Jesse, if you leave . . ." Dan shook his head, hands propped on his waist, sorrow in his eyes. "You're not coming back. I mean it. Paul will go crazy over this. And you've signed a noncompete. You cannot work at any other tech company for three years. Think about what you're doing. Think!"

"Think?" Ha-ha. "For once, big brother, I am thinking. This time with my heart and not my head."

# 30

## CHLOE

*June*

You see, love stories never worked for her. She never got the guy. In life or on screen. Instead, she died. She was, as *Variety* claimed, "the queen of the death scene."

If she didn't know before *Bound by Love,* she knew it now. But then Claude brought her the indelible Faith Freeman.

*Stargazer* might change her career. Not her love life.

However, the appearance of Oliver Hanson and the knowledge she was Esther Longfellow Hobart's descendant also changed nothing about her love life. Hamilton and Esther's love story may linger forever without resolve.

Chloe was not the answer to their longing. Nor was Jesse. The notion was too preposterous to entertain.

Unrequited love was just that — unrequited. Perhaps it would find satisfaction and justice in the next life.

Dad tried for a few days to entice her to fly with him to Boston. He had business there. But she refused. How much rejection could a girl endure? Not when she'd just begun to hope a little. Let her dreams breathe.

She woke up this morning determined to do something . . . different? No, the same.

*It's just You and me, Jesus.*

She wasn't morbid or depressed. She just needed to figure out a plan for the next fifty, sixty years that did not include a longing for the intimacy of marriage. Kate was right. She should aim to be some sort of grande dame of film.

Maybe after the Claude Durand film she would move to London, audition for plays. There was something peaceful and anchoring about playing the same role night after night. In the meantime, she'd enjoy her summer. Memorize the entire *Stargazer* script.

She was sunning by the pool, reading, when Jeremiah called.

"Can you come to the house in an hour?"

"Everything okay?"

"Yeah, I want to show you some of the edits."

She showered and dressed, dropped the top of her '64 Mustang convertible, and drove the short mile to the Gondas'.

When she rang the bell, Jeremiah opened with three of his seven children clinging to him, baby Eva no longer a baby but a budding, beautiful little girl.

Judah rode his back like a monkey, and Elianna gripped his ankle. Jer dragged her over the marble tile as he led Chloe to his screening room.

"Welcome to the circus." He laughed.

"Apparently they've missed you." Chloe shook Judah's hand and tousled Elianna's golden curls.

"Not as much as I've missed them. The shoot in New Zealand went over by a month, but we got it done."

"A blockbuster?"

Jer grinned back at her, setting Eva down. "Big blockbuster. It was a pain but a lot of fun. Chris was amazing. Pilar?" He called over an intercom. "Can you get the children?"

The nanny appeared and peeled the children from their father, promising them a trip to the park.

The oldest, Ezra, appeared in the doorway,

ball glove in hand. "I thought we were going to practice."

"We are. Right after I talk with Chloe. Say hi to Miss Daschle."

He muttered a sorrowful greeting, shoulders slumped, and disappeared.

Jer called after him, "Buddy, I'll only be an hour. Get Avner and Daniel to play for now. And find Liel. She'll want to play."

"Jer, if you need to play with you kids —"

"I have the rest of the day and all next month. They're fine." Jeremiah nudged Chloe toward an oversized, leather theater chair. "Laura wanted to be here, but she's meeting her agent. She's up for a part she really wants. Can I get you anything?"

"No, I'm good. So, is this the rough cut of the film? I'm excited to see it."

He sat beside her. "Feels a bit like déjà vu, doesn't it?"

She smiled, rocking back in the chair. "A little. Ten months ago I was begging you for the part of Esther. Here we are with the movie shot and —"

"Almost in the can. Sharon Lee's been working night and day. I owe her." Jer aimed a remote, and the room dimmed as the projector shot a beam against the screen. "I don't have the complete cut yet, but I wanted you to see this."

"Hey, what do you think about me playing Faith Freeman in Claude Durand's *Stargazer*?"

"Do it. It's perfect for you."

"He said without a thought."

Jeremiah cast her a sideways glance. "If you want to change your career, then change it. Playing a superhero? There's no way you're dying. That's a role even Greg Zarzour can't touch."

"Other than killing the project."

"Are you kidding? People are already forming fan clubs for this film. I hope you like Comic Con, because it's going to become a permanent part of your life."

"I'm more curious why Claude picked Chloe Daschle for the lead."

In the bluish light of the projector, Jeremiah frowned. "You know, you can talk yourself out of success if you want, but, Chloe, why not just take the opportunity and run with it?"

Chloe slumped down in her chair. He was right. Of course. Why not call upon her experience to own the role instead of trying on various forms of self-deprecation?

Jer aimed the remote at the projector. "Roll 'em." He laughed. "I always like saying that."

"What? No popcorn and candy?" Chloe

said. "What kind of cheap theater is this?"

"The kind where the wife doesn't believe in carbs and sugar," Jeremiah said, pressing his finger to his lips as the older kids, one by one, snuck in and crawled into the wide theater seats. "But what I ate in New Zealand stays in New Zealand."

"You know your kids are listening."

Jer spun around, offering the boys a high five as film rolled against the screen. "They have their daddy's back."

On the screen, Esther leaned against a tree watching the battle on the field. Chloe cringed, seeing herself on screen, imagining what she'd do differently. But there were no retakes after Zarzour blew through.

"Is this the final?"

"Almost."

Chloe held her breath as Esther ran to the wounded Hamilton. This was her death scene.

Was she believable? Did she wear the part well? Did her appearance put the viewer in mind of an aristocratic woman raised in the backwoods of South Carolina?

As she watched Esther kneel over Hamilton and confess her love, Chloe felt her sincerity, felt her love.

My dearest Esther,
I love you.

> Affectionately Yours,
> Hamilton Lightfoot

Chloe brushed away a tear and swallowed a mixture of emotions. She'd confessed her love to Jesse and signed it, *Affectionately Yours.*

Up on the screen, Esther leaped at the redcoat, dagger in hand. "Death, you cannot have me!"

Behind her, Ezra muttered, "Cool move."

But for Chloe, it was nothing but tears.

"Beautiful moment," Jeremiah whispered. "What were you feeling?"

Chloe smiled softly. "Alive."

The camera zoomed in on her as she lay crumpled on the ground. Chloe winced. She could've posed better, but in truth, she didn't remember anything after her declaration.

The screen faded to black. She sighed. "Think that death scene was good enough for Zarzour?"

She started to stand and stretch, but the screen brightened. Hamilton was carrying Esther into the morning light.

"You captured that?" Chris had scooped her up after a run-through on the battlefield.

Right before Zarzour arrived.

"B-roll."

"I like it." She patted his arm. "It gives the viewer a little bit of hope. She's dead but loved, you know?"

"Agree." Behind him the boys whispered, smacking their baseballs into their gloves. Jeremiah turned, giving them the fatherly eye of "quiet or else."

"Know what Chris is saying here?" Chloe said. " 'Daschle, what'd you have for breakfast? You weigh a ton.' "

The scene changed once again. Chloe followed the camera into the Kingsley home, into the parlor and the stack of Esther's books on the desk.

"An epilogue?"

"Something like that."

The shot moved outside, to an upcountry sunset over the barnyard.

"When was this?" Chloe said, then instantly recognized the first day and the attack of the evil rooster. Esther bumped into Hamilton. "Wait, isn't that Jesse? Chris wasn't there yet."

Jeremiah smirked. "Zarzour said to use B-roll."

"Jesse as Hamilton is the final scene? But this wasn't in the script."

"We came up with the idea later. Well,

someone came up with it. A really smart guy suggested it."

Hamilton walked alongside Esther as the children clung to him, and the lens focused on the American colonies' flag flapping in the breeze. Freedom.

"What do you think?" Jeremiah angled to see her face.

Chloe turned to him. "Are you telling me that's the ending?"

"That's the ending."

"Of *Bound by Love*? The one where I died so beautifully? Just like Greg ordered."

"You did die beautifully, Chloe. But this is a love story. And if love doesn't triumph, we have no movie."

"So I don't die. I mean, Esther doesn't die?"

"She lives. Happily ever after."

"Oh my gosh . . ." Laughter bubbled up. "Are you serious? I can't believe it. Thank you. Truly. Jeremiah, you are the best of the best! And you can tell my father I said so." She fell into the embrace of her friend, her hero. "This is amazing! Esther doesn't die. Hear that, boys? She lives. Your dad is a genius."

"I can't take the credit. The idea wasn't mine."

"Then who? Sharon? Dad? Wouldn't it be

just like him?"

"None of the above. Though I did hear about it through Raymond." Jeremiah stood, motioning to the kids in the light of the projector. "Come on, let's go play ball. Leave these two alone."

Chloe jumped up. "What two? Where are you going?" She snatched her bag up from the floor.

"You're staying, Chloe." Jeremiah raised the canned lights just enough for a romantic hue to fill the room. There in the back row sat Jesse, his dark hair loose and flopped over his brow. "With this guy. He's the genius behind the ending."

"Jesse."

He stood. "Hello, Chloe. I got your letter."

# 31

## JESSE

She ran into his arms, knocking him against the wall. Her soft weeping filled his ears. He loved the feel of her against him.

"Shh, it's okay, it's okay." He sank into the nearest chair, cradling her in his arms. "I didn't get your letter until four days ago."

"But you're here . . . you're here." She roped her arms about his neck as he tightened his embrace, her kiss finding his over and over again.

"I love you, Chloe. I didn't think I could love anyone again, but I do, heaven help me, I do." He kissed her again, hungry, giving, pleasing.

She sniffed away her tears between kisses. "I love you, Jesse. Heaven help me, I do." She tipped her head to the screen. "The ending was your idea?"

"Before I left the guesthouse, your dad

invited me into his office to talk about the consequences of walking off a set. I suggested an easy solution to let Esther live. I was ranting. Didn't think he really heard me. Then I went to Boston. Four months passed. Then four days ago Jeremiah sent me a link. At the same time, the admin at DiamondBros found your letter. A temp had stashed it away —"

She kissed him again, her touch powerful, her breath warm, her hands embracing him.

"I can't believe you're here."

"I can't believe it took me so long to get here. With you."

"I was okay with dying, you know." Her kisses filled his shallow, dry well. "Did you see my dagger move?"

"Yes, and now I'm a little scared."

She laughed, bold and free. Love broke chains. Unlocked doors. Healed wounds.

"I have a lot to tell you," he said. "I-I've met someone."

She reared back, eyes narrowed. "Hmm, this feels like a bait and switch. Who did you meet?"

"Same Man you met at church."

"Smitty?"

"No, Chloe —"

"Jesus." She brushed her hand over his shirt. "How'd you meet Him?"

"The Brants, of all people. Loxley's parents. Now I know I'm forgiven."

She pressed her cheek to his chest. "I can hear Him in there. Tossing out some old furniture. Wait, He's saying something . . ." She held up her finger, pretending to listen. "He's asking if He can hang something on the wall."

Jesse laughed. "What?"

"A picture. Yes, I see a picture. It says, 'Home Sweet Home.' "

"Perfect."

"And He's sitting in your chair. Says He's got the con."

Jesse scooped her closer, his kiss wild and abandoned, possessing her until he lost the edges of his being and existed in a space without borders.

When he pulled away, she settled back against his chest, pretending to listen.

"Wait, He's hanging another picture, Jesse. He's still moving in."

"A picture of me and you?"

"No, it's a letter . . ." She sat up, hands pressed on his chest, her expression full of wonder. "The one Oliver gave to me."

"Oliver?"

She slipped from his lap, hand over her own heart. "It's true."

"What's true, babe?"

She peered at him. "Babe? You called me babe. No one has ever called me babe before."

"I'm happy to be the first. But what truth are you talking about?"

Grabbing his hand, she pulled Jesse to his feet. "Come on, I have something to show you."

## CHLOE

Jesse sat in the passenger seat, relaxed, at home, his head against the head rest, his arm stretched across the console, resting on Chloe's shoulder.

He wound his fingers through her hair, brushing his hand over the back of her neck until she thought she'd jump out of her skin.

She was at home with him. At peace. The moment she saw him it was as if they'd never been apart.

After parking in the shade of the Greek column at the Daschle estate, they walked into the house hand in hand.

"Dad?" She went to his office first, but his desk chair was vacant.

"Good, we're alone." Jesse tugged her to him, sweeping in for another kiss.

"I need a million of those."

"Then let's get started." He dropped to

the couch, bringing her with him. She laughed, scrambling up.

"I really have to show you something. Ah, here it is." Chloe retrieved the yellow folder from the edge of her father's desk and sat next to Jesse. "A man came to see us. Said his family had this letter in their possession for centuries." She handed him an envelope.

"I'm starting to value letters these days." Jesse took the envelope and kissed her cheek. "I love you, babe."

She curled her legs behind her and brushed her hand over his soft hair, watching as Jesse opened the letter with care, scanned the page, then read aloud, " 'My dearest Esther . . . Yours affectionately, Hamilton.' " He peered at Chloe. "It's from Hamilton. Where did you get this?"

Chloe detailed Oliver's story and Dad's journey into family history for the truth. He listened with a furrowed brow, nodding, humming.

"Jesse, your grandpa Hamilton was in love with my grandma Esther. We are their descendants."

"This is crazy." He read the letter again. "It's his handwriting, all right. I recognize it. So, Esther is your ancestor? This is wild. Like something that would —"

"Happen in a movie?"

"Yeah, like something that would happen in a movie." He set the folder aside and scooped Chloe into his arms. "But this isn't a Hollywood ending, Chloe. This is *our* ending. You and me. This is what the movie, the letter, meeting at Dylan and Violet's wedding, the sense of something happening between us when neither of us wanted it."

"So, where to from here, Hamilton Lightfoot's grandson?" She leaned for a kiss, his words freeing her to be who she always wanted to be. "I like that I can kiss you any time I want."

"Then why wait?" He released her and slid down to one knee.

"Jesse?"

"The letter just confirms what I already knew. We are meant to be together. Chloe Daschle, granddaughter of Esther Longfellow, will you marry me?"

"I think love has been waiting 240 years to hear this word: *Yes.* I will marry you, Jesse Gates, grandson of Hamilton Lightfoot."

# 32

"Critics love *Bound by Love.*" — *Los Angeles Times*

"Weekend blockbuster? Period film *Bound by Love* owns the box office." — *Variety*

"Painter and Daschle are pure chemistry." — *Movie News*

"Did anyone know Chloe Daschle was this talented?" — Harvey Beckham, critic

## CHLOE

*January*

You see, love stories worked for her. She got the guy in the end. At least in real life.

This year *Variety* dubbed her "the one to watch." Death could not have her any longer.

So when the Academy Award nominees were announced, she laughed to see her name listed under Best Actress.

But a week before the biggest night in Hollywood, the Gonda, Daschle, and Gates clans, along with their dearest friends, gathered on a Santa Monica beach for a sunset wedding.

Smitty reappeared in their lives after months of silence, clapping his hand on Jesse's shoulder. "It's about time. I never thought I'd get you two together."

Then he vanished again, leaving them to ponder and wonder, *Man or angel?* Either way, they would never forget his divine help.

A stringed quartet played as the celestial lights dimmed and the stars beamed along the horizon.

Dad offered Chloe his arm. "Last chance to change your mind."

"And break Hamilton's and Esther's hearts all over again?"

Chloe walked down the white runner to where Jesse stood under an ivy arch. She carried Hamilton's first love letter tucked into her bouquet.

She never determined what happened to unrequited love, but when it wondrously, mysteriously landed on her, she yielded.

Jesse's sweet aunt Pat worked overtime to confirm Chloe's connection to Esther. Mom paid an artist to paint both family trees. Chloe bound it in a gilded frame and presented it to Jesse as a wedding gift.

He winked at her when she stopped at the top of the runner. "Hello, gorgeous."

"Hello to you."

Their pastor, Shawn Bolz, opened in prayer, then asked Dad, "Who gives this woman to this man?"

"Her mother and I." Sniffing, he placed her hand in Jesse's, and Chloe stepped into the role she was *born* to play. Wife, lover, and friend.

They spent their honeymoon in Bora Bora and watched the Academy Awards from their ocean hut, eating chocolate-covered strawberries and sipping champagne.

"You're going to win, babe," Jesse said during the commercial before the Best Actress category.

"I've already won." She kissed him, then searched his eyes, finding love in his deep blues. "Are you happy?"

"What do you think?" Cupping her face in his hands, he kissed her as a man in love. Chloe sighed and shivered.

"I think I'm never letting you go."

The commercial ended, and the camera zoomed over the Oscar stage. "Hey, there's Mom and Dad."

The great Raymond Daschle and Rachel Hayes smiled for the viewers.

"Jer and Laura are right behind them." Jesse popped another strawberry in his mouth, then waved at the TV, calling hello.

"You're ridiculous." But Chloe savored every moment of her new life with him.

The show announcer introduced Chris Painter, who walked to the podium amid hearty applause.

"The nominees for Best Actress are . . ." He read Chloe's name first. "In *Bound by Love.*"

Chloe ducked behind a pillow as a clip from the movie played, the reality of playing her great-great-great-great-great-great-grandmother sinking deeper and awakening an awe for the beauty of God's orchestration over her life.

She never, *ever* imagined this journey.

"This is my favorite scene," Jesse said, settling his hand around her waist, drawing her against his chest, kissing her head. "You're going to win."

"Babe, God has done a lot this year, miracles even, but taking me from queen of the death scene to Oscar-winning actress in twelve short months is a bit of a stretch."

"You think He can't?"

"Oh, I know He can. But I have you, babe. I have the letter and the *rest* of the story. I have this amazing testimony about love.

What else do I need?"

"You're going to win."

"You're not biased or anything, are you?"

"Maybe a little."

Chris introduced the other nominees, then tore open the envelope. He smiled.

"You won, babe. You won. Look at his expression . . ."

Chris peered into the camera. "My good friend, Chloe Daschle."

With a shout, Jesse jumped up, bouncing on the bed, sending the chocolate strawberries flying. "I told you!" He pumped the air with his fist. "I told you!"

"I-I can't believe it." Chloe exhaled and fell against her pillows, arms wide, and laughed. "I won. I actually won." She sat up with a fist pump and a "Yes!"

On the TV, Chris held her gold statue. "Chloe wanted to be here tonight, but the shock of being nominated killed her." The Oscar audience laughed. "No, seriously, she's on her honeymoon, so she's having a better time than any of us right now. I know she'd want to thank her parents and sister, Jer and Laura Gonda and everyone at Gonda Films and Premier. And of course, her costar. Me."

"He's slaying this," Chloe said.

"Also, her new husband, Jesse Gates, who

wrote the screenplay. And, um . . ." Chris cleared his throat. "God. She'd like to thank her Lord and Savior, for all of His bless-ings."

"Wow," she whispered.

When the show ended, Jesse clicked off the TV and reached for her hand. "Let's go for a walk on the beach."

The night breeze was silky as they strode along the shore, hand in hand, the waves gentle and low.

Chloe leaned against her husband's arm, their footprints leaving a trail in the sand. The waves would wash them away before morning, but their journey toward happily ever after would stand forever.

And perhaps generations from now, their descendants would find clues through their lives to the answers they sought. The notion gave Chloe chills.

"Hey, Jesse, we should write a screenplay about our romance."

"You know, I was just thinking the same thing . . ."

# ACKNOWLEDGMENTS

This book tied me in knots. I'd sit in a beach chair in our garage and stare at the white board hanging on the wall trying to figure how the letter connected six people over 250 years.

I drew a nice, elaborate scheme and at the end of the day, deleted it.

The story became its best when I simplified and focused on the four it impacted the most: Hamilton and Esther, Chloe and Jesse.

Thanks to my editor Erin Healy for listening, sounding out my structure issues, and reading this book at least three or four times! At least. Your insight, kindness, and inspiration gave me courage when I made those big changes. I appreciate your faith in me!

To my in-house editor, Karli Jackson, all love and blessings as you begin this new phase of your life. Being a stay-at-home mom is the best job of all.

To my new editor, Kimberly Carlton, I'm looking forward to the journey.

My writing partner for thirteen plus years, Susan May Warren. Thank you for always being there when I need help. Or to kick me back in play when I surrender to "I'm-the-most-boring-writer-in-the-world" lies.

To Beth Vogt, stellar author and friend, and my FaceTime partner.

Amanda Bostic, Kristen Golden, Allison Carter, Paul Fisher and the entire Harper-Collins Christian Publishing team. It's an honor times a hundred to be working with you all to bring my stories to the world.

My thanks and appreciation to the HCCP sales team, the boots-on-the-ground force, as well as Matt Bray, Jason Short, and the rocking digital team.

Most of my research was done online and reading books. I'm so awed and appreciative for the men and women who recorded our amazing American history. There is so much to read on the Revolutionary War, I was overwhelmed.

However, and there's always a however, lining up all of the historical facts proved to be daunting. As well as deciding how to mold my fictional characters into real history. I did my best.

The Battle of Cowpens was a real and vital battle in winning the war with Great Britain. General Morgan's success there changed the tide of the war.

The movie *The Patriot* is a fictionalized Battle of Cowpens. I picked this historic, southern battle for two reasons. One, we don't talk much about the south when discussing the Revolutionary War. And two because what's not to like about the name "Cowpens"?

As I researched and realized this battle was the boilerplate for *The Patriot,* I endeavored to keep as true to the story as possible.

My husband and I stopped by the battlefield in Chesnee, South Carolina, on our way home from vacation. As we walked the grounds along Green River Road, it was hard to imagine men fighting there 237 years ago. Yet I was awestruck. And grateful.

The letters of John and Abigail Adams provided emotional insight to the mindset of our eighteenth-century ancestors. Reruns of *Poldark* helped me find the cadence of the language.

Any misses in dialog and historical facts are all mine.

John Irwin; John Brown; William Brown; Jacob Broadway; Robert Nelson, surgeon; and Andrew Pickens are real men of the

Revolutionary War. General Morgan's speech to the troops before the battle is also real.

*Off Camera* with Sam Jones gave me some insight into the life of an actor as well as the book *Must See TV.*

I owe many thanks to screenwriter and blogger Lori Twitchell who answered all of my movies questions. Again, any mistakes are mine!

I dedicated this book to my husband because I cannot imagine doing life without him. He is my living "love letter."

To all of you, who give your time and precious dollars to read and/or buy a book: Thank you. You are the reason I do this.

Above all, thanks to Jesus. I wouldn't be here without Him. The Prince of Peace is the Prince of my heart. He makes all things beautiful!

# DISCUSSION QUESTIONS

1. Do you have any historical family artifacts? How have they helped you discover
more of your family or yourself?
2. The book asks the question, "What happens to unrequited love?" Even though I
asked the question as the author, I'm not
sure love is its own entity, drifting through
time, looking for a place to rest. Yet I was
fascinated by the idea of two people falling in love yet finding themselves sepa-
rated by war, life, social status, or circum-
stance beyond their control. What do you
think of unrequited love?
3. Hamilton and Esther were on different
sides of the war. In my research, I came
across stories of entire families split apart
by the fight for independence. What are
other things that can destroy families and
friends? How can we overcome obstacles
like politics or social constructs to love
one another?

4. Chloe hasn't had much luck in the romance department. Don't we often think successful, beautiful people have it all, yet many times they are the most lonely and lost? How can we pray for those who seem to "have it all"?

5. Jesse bears the burden of Loxley's death. How have you dealt with guilt in your life? How can you encourage others?

6. Chloe makes a fascinating statement about marriage. It's the one place where only those two people exist! What do you think about her view of marriage?

7. Jesse tried for a long time to make it in Hollywood. When he finally did, he gives it all up on principle. What would you have done? What would you give to stand by a friend?

8. Esther is very loyal to her father. Did she make the right decision in the end?

9. Hamilton didn't want to fight but found himself drawn into the militia. What did you think about his final battle?

10. Jesus appears to Hamilton and Esther. What did you think of His beckoning, "Come, follow me"? In what way is He beckoning you in your life?

# ABOUT THE AUTHOR

**Rachel Hauck** is the *New York Times, Wall Street Journal,* and *USA TODAY* bestselling author of *The Wedding Dress,* which was also named Inspirational Novel of the Year by *Romantic Times* and was a RITA finalist. Rachel lives in central Florida with her husband and two pets and writes from her ivory tower.

Visit her online at rachelhauck.com
Facebook: rachelhauck
Twitter: @RachelHauck
Instagram: @rachelhauck